D0482881

CAST IN COURTLIGHT

MICHELLE SAGARA

LUNA™

www.LUNA-Books.com

LUNA™

First trade printing: August 2006

CAST IN COURTLIGHT

ISBN-13: 978-0-373-80244-9
ISBN-10:   0-373-80244-7

Copyright © 2006 by Michelle Sagara
Author Photo by: John Chew

This edition published by arrangement with Harlequin Books S.A.

® and TM are trademarks of Harlequin Books S.A., used under license.
Trademarks indicated with ® are registered in the United States Patent
and Trademark Office, the Canadian Trade Marks Office and in other
countries.

www.LUNA-Books.com

Printed in U.S.A.

This is for Tanya and Fe,
with gratitude for long years of friendship
that involved phone calls about all
of life's little anxieties and triumphs,
none begrudged.

The home team, again, came through: First and foremost Thomas, Daniel and Ross, who put up with my imaginative flights and figurative absences; John, Kristen, Jamie (affectionately referred to as His Majesty), Gary and Ayami, who do the same; and my mother and father.

The away team: For this book, my editor, Matrice, patient with my unusual inability to deal with outlines; my agent, Russ Galen; and of course, as always, Terry Pearson, who read it all a chapter at a time.

Thanks, guys.

CHAPTER 1

In the old days, before the Dragon Emperor—sometimes called the Eternal Emperor by those responsible for toadying—had invested the Halls of Law with the laws which governed the Empire, angry Dragons simply ate the idiots who were stupid enough to irritate them. Or, if they were unappetizing, burned them into a very slight pile of ash.

Ash had the advantage of requiring little to no paperwork.

Marcus Kassan, Sergeant for the Hawks—one branch of officers who served in the Halls of Law—stared gloomily at a pile of paperwork that, were it placed end to end, would loom above him. At over six foot, that was difficult. The desire to shred it caused his claws to flick in and out of the fur of his forepaws.

The desire to avoid annoying Caitlin, the woman who was—inasmuch as the Hawks allowed it—den mother to the interior office, which set schedules, logged reports, and prepared duty rosters and pay chits, was just *slightly* stronger. In their personal life, Leontines disavowed all paperwork, usually by the expedient of chewing it, shredding it, or burning it, when it wasn't useful for the kits' litter.

Then again, he'd been at his desk for the better part of an hour. He expected there'd be a shift in the balance before the day—which looked to be long and grueling—was over.

Caitlin smiled at him from the nest she made of the paperwork she endured, day in, day out. It was a slightly sharp smile that looked, on the surface, quiet and sweet. That was Caitlin. Human all over. She'd been with him for years. He was aware of her value; the three people before her had lasted two weeks, three weeks, and four days, respectively. They had all babbled like morons.

Fear does that, Caitlin had said when she'd applied for the job. She was bird-thin and fragile to the eye, and her voice was soft and feminine—no growl or fang there. But definitely some spine. She was one of two people who manned the desks who could stand six inches from his face when he was on the edge of fury. She barely blinked, and attributed that, regretfully, to his breath.

At any other time of the year, paperwork was optional. Pay chits and duty rosters weren't, but he was enough of a Sergeant to at least sign off on them when he wasn't actively composing the lists themselves. No, *this* hideous mess was courtesy of the Festival. Permits, copied laboriously by clerks in some merchant branch of the Imperial palace, had been sent by dim-witted couriers in bags that were half again as large as Caitlin. Bags. Plural.

But not just permits. Festival regulations, which seemed to change year after year. The names of important dignitaries from the farthest damn fringe of the Empire of Ala'an, manifests of cargo transports, and diplomatic grants were also shoved in the same bags. The latter were, however, sealed in a way that screamed "special privilege." Diplomatic immunity.

Marcus hated the Festival season. The city was enough of a problem; throwing foreigners into the streets by the thousands was just asking for trouble.

Not only that, but every get-rich-quick scheme that had occurred to any half-wit moron in the street could be expected to rear its imbecilic head during the next two weeks. Unfortunately, every get-rich-quick scheme that occurred to any cunning, intelligent person would *also* rear its head during the next two weeks. The money that flowed into the Empire's capital during the Festival was staggering, and everyone wanted a piece of it.

The Swordlord, and the men who followed his orders, were probably in worse shape, and this provided a moment's comfort to Marcus. He was Hawk, through and through; the Swords were his natural rivals. Not, of course, his enemies; they all served the Lords of Law, and they all worked in the labyrinthine buildings referred to as the Halls of Law by people who saw them from the outside. But the Hawks and the Swords had their own way of doing things, and when the Festival season was at its height, there were always disagreements.

On the other hand, at least the Swords *were* in the streets; the damn Wolves were at bay. It was hard to hunt in the city during the Festival, even at the behest of the Wolflord. The Wolves were kept in reserve in case of riot, when *all* servants of the Law could be called into action. This was, however, downtime for the Wolves, and Marcus sullenly resented them their freedom.

Paperwork was best left for bureaucrats.

Unfortunately, bureaucrats were damn good at shoveling the work onto the shoulders of men and women who were already too busy, where being too busy meant they didn't have time to kick up enough of a fuss to give it *back*.

He heard a door slam. It was followed by a raised, angry voice—only one—and the sound of a very heavy tread. Deliberately heavy.

Paperwork looked almost good in comparison.

"Oh dear," Caitlin said. "That's three this week."

"Two. One of them left last week." He rearranged the paperwork in the vague hope that this would provide some sort of fortification against the red and dour expression of a very annoyed mage.

Sure enough, down the long hall that led from the West Room, which had been ceded to the Hawklord for educational purposes, the swirling robes of a man who had probably been ancient ten years ago came into view. His fists were bunched just below the drape of long sleeves, and his forehead was engraved with permanent wrinkles. The kind that said foul mood.

The office had grown somewhat quieter as people stopped to listen in. You could count on curiosity to get the better of work at Festival time. Well, to be fair, at *any* time, but during the Festival it was more costly.

The man stormed over to the Sergeant's desk. "You will tell the Lord of Hawks that I am *finished* with this—this ridiculous task!"

Marcus raised a brow. Given that his face was entirely composed of golden fur, this should have been discomfiting at the very least.

"The girl is *untrainable*. She doesn't listen. She barely *reads*. She thinks like a—like a *common soldier.* She is rude beyond bearing, she is stupid, and she is an insult to the Imperial Order of Mages!"

The other brow lifted slightly as the Leontine attempted to look surprised. This was, however, lost on the mage, who was as human as Caitlin—as human, in fact, as most of the other paper pushers who called the office their second home.

Leontines were many things, but actor wasn't one of them. They were sort of the anti-actor.

"Tell your superior that I will have *words* with the Imperial Order about this!"

As he'd now heard a variant of this speech three times, he had it memorized. It generated some paperwork, on the other hand, which soured a mood that was worse than sour to begin with.

Holding his tongue was difficult. Holding his claws was a shade more difficult. He managed to breathe shallowly enough that the growl couldn't be heard over the mage's shouts.

Which went on for another five minutes before he stormed off. It was a wonder he wasn't followed by black clouds and lightning bolts.

"Oh dear," Caitlin said again, rising. "He didn't last two days."

Marcus shrugged, letting the growl into his words. "I told the Hawklord," he said.

"I know. I think we all tried. There must be a suitable mage somewhere in the Order—"

"I doubt it. You know how the Dragon Emperor feels about mages and sanity." Marcus pushed himself out of his chair. His claws clicked against the floorboards.

"I'll tell the Hawklord," he said with a shrug.

"I'll talk to Kaylin," Caitlin added.

Kaylin Neya was sitting in the West Room, her arms folded across her chest. There was a candle on the desk; it had been cut in half.

"Dear," Caitlin said quietly, "I *think* you're supposed to *light* it."

Kaylin muttered something about light and places in which it didn't shine. She was the youngest of Marcus's Hawks, and it showed.

"He really is a nice old man," Caitlin began.

"They're *all* supposed to be 'nice old men.'" Kaylin shoved herself out of her chair as if she were a miniature Marcus. On the other hand, she had boots instead of bare pads, and her very human nature didn't lend itself to extended claws and long fangs. "They're arrogant, they're long-winded, and they think they know everything."

"They do know a lot—"

"They know a lot about useless things! Light a candle?" She rolled her eyes. "I can light a candle in five seconds, the normal way. I can kill a man just as easily as a mage—and probably more efficiently." Her hands fell to her daggers and rested there. "I can run faster, I can see farther, I can—"

"Kaylin," Caitlin said, raising both her hands. "No one is doubting your competence as a *Hawk*. You're an officer of the Halls of Law."

"And how is *this* supposed to help me?"

"You cut the candle in half, dear?"

"It didn't get that way by itself."

"No, I imagine it didn't." Caitlin shrugged. "You've already annoyed a number of the Imperial mages. I do think it would be best for the Hawks if you tried not to annoy any *more*." She paused. Added, "You've got to *expect* a little arrogance, Kaylin. These men are old, they've survived the Emperor's service, and they are considered experts in their field. Given your general reaction to any power that isn't owned by the Hawks, I'll forgo mention of the fact that these men *are* powerful. And you're insulting their life's work."

Kaylin's lips were set in a line that could be called thin. Or invisible. "I don't want to be part of their life's work," she said at last. "I want to be part of *my* life's work. I want—all I've wanted since the first day I was introduced to all of you—is to be a Hawk."

"You *are* a Hawk, Kaylin."

"The Hawks don't employ mages."

Caitlin's smile froze in place. "You do realize that annoying them probably won't stop them from coming?"

"I can try."

The older woman's expression gave trying a different

meaning. "I believe the Hawklord will want to speak with you. Again."

Kaylin's shoulders sagged. She walked past Caitlin and out of the room.

The Hawklord's tower boasted a fine set of stairs, one that curved upward against the inner wall in a continuous stacked spiral. There was good stonework here, girded by brass rails, and the echoes went up forever, bouncing against the walls.

Or against the breastplates of the guards on the various landings Kaylin walked past.

She nodded at them; they nodded back. If they were inclined to smirk, they managed to hide it, which was just as well. A brawl on these steps could cause injury. And, following it, more injury of an entirely Leontine nature. Marcus didn't approve of Hawks fighting each other in the Halls; he'd long since given up on Hawks squabbling after too many drinks in their private time.

The door to the Hawklord's inner sanctum, with its much-hated magical ward, was as usual closed. Kaylin, grimacing, placed her palm squarely against that ward and waited while the familiar prickle of magic ran up her arm and caused her hair to almost stand on end. The first time she'd touched it, she'd sworn her head off. Unfortunately for Kaylin, the most severe of the words occurred as the doors were opening; the domed cavern that the Hawklord ruled had reminded her of the unpleasant existence of acoustics. The Hawklord himself reminded her about the correct use of language in his presence.

It mostly consisted of "don't talk" in exactly the wrong

tones. Kaylin wasn't a firm believer in soft-spoken threats, but if anyone could make her one, it was Lord Grammayre, the Aerian who held the title of Lord of Hawks.

She walked across the threshold.

The Hawklord, pale white wings turned toward her, was waiting in the silence. When he turned, she could see a piece of paper in his hands. It seemed to command most of his attention.

And given what it probably said, that wouldn't last long.

She paid him the obeisance the difference in their ranks demanded: She knelt. This was only partly because she was his junior in every possible way. The other part—the one that wanted to remain a member of his Hawks—was not above a little groveling, especially when there were no other witnesses. It wasn't the worst thing she'd done in his presence by a long shot.

His eyes, narrow gray, traveled along the top of her head as if they could scalp her and keep the scalp as an object lesson for *other* Hawks. Marcus, all bristling fur and exposed fangs, was no match for the Hawklord when it came to intimidation. Kaylin had annoyed them both in her time, and had more than ample experience as proof.

He handed her the piece of paper. She had to rise to take it. "That," he said, "was the third member of the Imperial Order of Mages you've managed to offend in less than ten days."

She recognized Leontine scrawl; it was bold, dark, and put holes in the paper.

"He started it" was not an option, and she bit the words

back, swallowing them. "I've never been a good classroom student," she said at last.

"We're well aware of that," he replied, his words dry enough to catch fire. "We've attempted to keep your academic transcripts from the mages who have condescended to tutor you. Unfortunately, they seem to think it necessary to review them."

She said nothing, as it seemed safest. It usually was, and she frequently failed to remember this until after her mouth had engaged. "I don't understand why you even think it's necessary," she said at last, when his silence grew a little too weighty.

He raised a pale brow. His eyes, Aerian to the core, were shading to blue, which was never a good sign.

"The Hawks don't employ mages," she said woodenly.

"You are not a mage."

"Then why—"

He lifted a hand. "I have always considered patience a virtue when dealing with the Hawks," he told her, "but I find that, as usual, you tax precious resources.

"Therefore, I will be blunt. You are a Hawk, but you are also—as you well know—blessed or cursed with magical ability. You can't control it well enough—you don't understand what it is, or what it can do. It is the opinion of experts that the power itself *can* be wielded in a manner similar to the way that mages channel their power."

Which experts?

"Do not even think of asking, Kaylin." He knew her far too well.

"It's *Festival*," she snapped. "We're up to our armpits in

work—if we're lucky. We've just gotten the tally of so-called diplomats and Important Visitors—" she managed to wedge a powerful sneer into each syllable of the last two words "—and we're undermanned, as usual.

"I *don't* have time for this right now."

"I will agree that the timing is not the most opportune," the Hawklord said in a tone that implied the exact opposite. "But as the timing is not of our choosing, we have little choice.

"I understand what you're attempting to do, Kaylin," he added, his voice smoothing to velvet. "And I will now insist that you cease this. It is unworthy of you. You can insult and infuriate every mage who crosses the threshold on my behalf, if it pleases you. But they will not stop coming. Do you understand?"

She didn't.

He raised a hand to his brow. As gestures went, it was human, and even if it hadn't been, it was transparent. "The Emperor himself has taken an interest in your education."

They were not the words she expected to hear. They were also the last words she *wanted* to hear. Unfortunately, lifting her hands to stop her ears wasn't an option.

"How much does he—"

"He *is* the Emperor. It is to the Emperor that the Lords of Law are beholden. How much do you think he knows?"

The words *too damn much* flitted about, but she tried to ignore them.

"You fought a Dragon," he added quietly. "You fought the only Dragon who has ever survived being outcaste among his kin. The battle was felt all the way to the palace. Some diplomacy was necessary—you can thank Tiamaris for his intercession—and there was, perhaps, a surfeit of actual facts offered. But enough was said. The Emperor knows that you bear the marks."

Her eyes fell to her sleeves automatically; they always did when anyone spoke of the strange writing that ran the length of her arms and her thighs. They had been symbols to be hidden when she had been a child on the edge of adulthood; she knew them now as words. Or names. But whose words and whose names were still mostly mystery—and in Kaylin's universe, it was vital that they *stay* that way. She was used to them, in any case; the new ones bothered her more.

"He is," the Hawklord continued, "also aware that you bear a Barrani mark."

"Everyone is," she said.

"Were it not for Tiamaris, he would not be inclined to…give you the benefit of the doubt. He has shown some forbearance in this. But he has made clear that you present a danger *if you cannot be trained.* And it seems that you intend to demonstrate your intractability in the worst possible way. For you," he added, as if it were necessary. "I will send for another member of the Imperial Order of Mages."

She was stony silence defined.

"If you happen to offend him before the week is out, you will be suspended from active duty. Have I made myself clear?"

"Yes, sir."

"Good."

She was aware that he had just won someone the office betting pool, but could not for the life of her remember who.

Just as well. She waited for a few minutes, but he had turned from her, and was now studying the opaque surface of the room's long mirror. The fact that it *was* opaque made it clear that whatever he was looking at was keyed to his eyes alone.

She started toward the door.

"One other thing, Kaylin."

"Sir?"

"If you are late for any *more* of these lessons, it will come out of your pay."

"Yes, sir."

Kaylin and punctuality lived on separate continents. Another happy source of petty betting in the office. She looked at his profile; he hadn't bothered to look in her direction.

But something about his expression was stiff and wrong. She watched the lines around his mouth deepen until his face looked like engraved stone, but less friendly. Whatever it was he was looking at was something he didn't like—and at Festival time, Kaylin could honestly say she had no interest whatsoever in knowing what it was.

She chose the better part of valor and left. Quickly.

Tain, his black hair flowing in a healthy trail down his back, was at the center of the crowded office when Kaylin made it back down the stairs. As he was the only Barrani in attendance, it answered a question, albeit not a pressing one.

He smiled as she slid silently through the open arch and along the nearest wall. Even without breathing, it was impossible for her to sneak up on a Barrani Hawk; she knew. She'd been trying for seven years.

"Kaylin," he said, looking up. His eyes were that shade of bottomless green that made jewelry superfluous. It meant, on the other hand, that he was happy. Or as happy as any Barrani ever got when they weren't killing someone or winning some invisible-to-human-eyes political struggle.

If Leontines were incapable of acting, Barrani were their opposite; they were incapable of not acting. Immortal, stunningly beautiful, and ultimately cool, they had a quiet love of showmanship. It had taken her years to understand that, as well.

They were, however, plenty capable of being smug, which Tain was now demonstrating to the office staff; he had coins in his hand.

Had *she* won, she probably wouldn't. But there was no such thing as a friendly bet among the Barrani, and no one—not even the men and women who were nominally his equals in rank—wanted to be in the wrong kind of debt to a Barrani.

Still, it didn't stop them from betting. She prided herself on being the person who had introduced the office to this pastime; it was one of the few that she'd enjoyed in her childhood. Then again, anyone who grew up in the wrong part of town—the huge neighborhood known colloquially as the fiefs in the right parts of town—enjoyed gambling. There wasn't much else about the life *to* enjoy.

Certainly not its brevity.

She shrugged and made her way to Tain. "You won?"

"It looks that way." His teeth were chipped; they made his smile look almost natural. They also made him obvious to anyone who hadn't known the Barrani for months. They looked so much alike, it was hard for humans—or mere humans, as the Barrani often called them—to tell them apart. Much malicious humor could be had in mistaken identity—all of it at a cost to the person making the mistake.

His smile cooled slightly as his gaze glanced off her cheek. There, in thin blue lines that could be called spidery, was the mark of Lord Nightshade—the Barrani outcaste Lord who ruled the fief that Kaylin had grown up in. The mark meant something to the Barrani, and none of it was good.

If she were honest, it meant something to her. But she couldn't quite say what, and she was content to let the memory lie. Not that she had much choice; Lord Nightshade was not of a mind to *remove* the mark, and short of that, the only way to effect such a removal also involved the removal of her head. Which, according to Marcus, she'd barely miss anyway, given how much she used it.

In ones and twos the dozen or so Barrani—well, fourteen, if she were paying close attention—that were also privileged to call themselves Hawks had been brought by either Tain or Teela to look at the mark.

In one or two cases, it was a good damn thing Teela was there; they were almost unrestrained once the shock had worn off, and the restraint they did have was all external.

Kaylin had gotten used to this.

And the Barrani, in turn, had grown accustomed to the sight of the offending mark. But they didn't like it.

They didn't like what it meant.

Kaylin understood that the word they muttered under their breaths was something that loosely translated into *consort*. Very loosely. And with a lot more vehemence.

"This Festival," he said quietly, "the castelord has called his Court. It has been a number of years since he has chosen to do so. I don't think you were even alive for the last one."

She had never been good in the classroom. She had never been bad outside of it. "Teela's gone to Court," she said flatly.

"She was summoned, yes."

"But she's—"

"She has not been summoned as a Hawk," he continued quietly. "She will take her place among her peers in the High Caste."

Kaylin almost gaped at him. "Teela? In the High Caste Court?"

His expression made clear that there was nothing humorous about it, although Kaylin wasn't laughing. He nodded. The nod was stiff for a Barrani nod; they kind of epitomized grace.

"Is she in trouble?"

"She may well be."

"Why?"

"She failed," he said softly, "to bring the nature of your…mark…to the castelord's attention."

"But he—" She stopped. "Evarrim."

"Lord Evarrim. You attracted his interest," he added softly. "What have we told you about attracting the interest of a high lord?"

"It's lethal."

"Yes. But not always for you." The disapproval in the words was mild, for Tain. "She will be called upon to defend her oversight," he added.

"You're worried?"

Tain shrugged. "She owes me money."

Kaylin laughed. It was a bitter sound. "Severn's there."

"I note that you haven't tried to kill him since you returned to active duty."

She shrugged. It was easier than words. Everything about Severn had changed. And much about Kaylin, to Kaylin's horror, had changed, as well.

What they had —what had driven them apart—had been the foundations upon which she'd built this life; he'd kicked them out from under her feet, and she still didn't know where to stand. Not where he was concerned.

But she'd been given the opportunity to be rid of him. And she'd rejected it, in the privacy of the Hawklord's tower. There wasn't likely to be a second such opportunity offered.

"Why is he on duty roster there?"

Tain didn't answer.

"Why am *I* not on—oh. Never mind." She lifted a hand and covered the mark on her cheek. To Tain, it made no difference; she could have gouged a chunk of her face off, and he'd still see it. Anyone born Barrani would.

"It will be over in one way or another."

"Over good, or over bad?"

"It depends," he said. His voice was the kind of guarded that implied imminent death. "On the castelord."

"But she's a *Hawk!*"

"Indeed. The Hawks comprise many races, however, and the caste-law of the race has precedence in exceptional circumstances. As you would know, if you'd paid more attention in your classes."

Exceptional circumstances: When either of two situations proved true. One: No other species was involved in the commission of the crime or its outcome. This was about as likely as the sun never rising or setting, at least in *this* city. Two: No member of any other species could be found who would admit that they had been damaged in some way by the commission of the crime in question. This, given the nature of the Barrani's exceptionally long memory and their famous ability to nurse a grudge down a dozen merely mortal generations, was entirely *too* likely.

"He can't make her outcaste. She's already pledged to Imperial service."

"The Lords of Law are pledged to the service of the Emperor. Employing an outcaste Barrani would not be in the best interests of any one of those Lords."

"Marcus won't let—"

"Kaylin. Let it go. As I said, it is a Barrani affair. Teela accepted the invitation. She has gone."

"You let her go." She didn't even bother to try to keep the accusation out of her voice.

"And had you been summoned by your castelord, we would have done the same."

"Humans don't have castelords. Not like that."

"No. Not like that. You couldn't. The span of your years is too short. Were it not for the intolerable speed at which you breed, there would be no humans in Elantra." He turned away, then.

And she realized, as he did, that he'd slipped into High Barrani, and she hadn't even noticed.

Mouth set in a thin line, she worked her way over to Marcus's desk. He was, to no one's surprise, on lunch. On early lunch. She was certain there was some betting going on about the duration of the lunch itself.

But that wasn't her problem.

She began to leaf through the notices and permits on his desk, moving them with care, as if they had been constructed by a finicky architect who'd been drinking too much.

After about ten minutes, she found what she was looking for—the writs or grants of rights given to foreign dignitaries.

CHAPTER 2

When Marcus came back from lunch an hour and a half later, he walked to his desk. The circuitous way. He paused in front of the schedule nailed to the wall, glared at the various marks made by the Hawks that were lucky—or unlucky—in their assigned duties, and added a few of his own. Although the schedule itself was an official document, this particular rendering of it was not; it was meant, or so office parlance said, as a courtesy. What he added was against the spirit of the thing, but he had a Leontine sense of courtesy; it wasn't as if he'd drawn blood.

And if the Hawks didn't like what he appended, they could come crying. Once.

He stopped by Caitlin's desk, and threw the mirror on the wall a thoroughly disgusted glare; like anything that made noise and conveyed messages, it *never* went off at his convenience. It had been dull and silent for the entire morning. If there was anything of import to be reported, the Swords and the Wolves were having all of the luck.

He had paperwork.

Oh, and Kaylin.

She was perched in the center of his chair, looking like a leather-clad waif, her hair pulled up in imitation of Caitlin's, and with vastly less success; she'd stuck a stick through its center, and hair had already escaped it in great chunks.

"What," he growled, "are you doing in my *chair*?"

His chair was large; he was heavier than any of the humans he commanded, and wider by far than the Barrani. It wasn't his favorite piece of furniture; he'd broken three chairs this year because of the shoddy workmanship of the craftsmen employed by the Halls of Law. Armrests were not meant to snap off *that* easily.

She appeared to be taking notes.

And, as was so often the case when she wasn't locked in a classroom, her concentration had shut out most of the office noise. His presence dimmed the rest. He could walk silently; as a hunter, he had to. He was seldom given the opportunity to use the skill.

When he was exactly behind her, he roared in her ear.

Papers went flying like loosed birds.

As she tried to catch some of them, she gave him a reproachful jab. As he was smiling, this was safe. Barely. But this was Kaylin; she hadn't the grace to look flustered or embarrassed. Not for the first time, he thought she'd been born in the wrong skin; she was like a young Leontine kit—a female, at that—and very little unnerved her for long.

Then again, she'd been under his care for seven years, and

she'd come as a youngling. If he hadn't been entirely protective in the normal Elantran sense of the word, he *had* protected her, and she took advantage of the fact without shame. Or notice.

"If you want to do paperwork," he said, sitting on the sparse inches of desk that weren't covered by paper, "you could have volunteered."

"Would it get me out of those damn lessons?"

"No."

"Overtime pay?"

"No."

She shrugged. "Well, then. I guess I'm not stupid."

His roar was mostly laugh. Many humans found differentiating between the two difficult—or at best, unwise, as the cost of a mistake was high—but Kaylin didn't labor under that difficulty.

Which was good, considering how many *other* difficulties she had. He held out a hand, and she dropped the papers she'd picked up across his palm. He glanced at them, and then back at her face. "You're suddenly interested in diplomats?"

She shrugged. "Had to happen sometime."

"Then you guess wrong. You *are* stupid." His dark eyes narrowed slightly. "These appear to be Barrani," he said. He had the satisfaction of hearing her curse. In Aerian. He wasn't entirely conversant with Aerian, but, like any good Hawk, he knew the right words.

"Flight feathers don't fit," he replied calmly. He looked over her head, his eyes snapping into their habitual glare. "What are you looking at? You don't have enough to keep you occupied?"

To a chorus of mumbles, which were a type of applause if you were stuck behind a desk for any length of time, he turned back to Kaylin. "You heard," he said flatly.

"Tain told me."

"If Tain told you, he also informed you that any interference on our part would *not* be appreciated."

She shrugged. "There are a lot of lords and ladies in that bundle."

"There always are." His fangs appeared as he drew his lips over them. "Do not get involved in this, Kaylin."

"But she's a—"

"She has her place. You have yours. At the moment, they're not the same." When she met his glare, and equaled it, he let his shoulders fall; they'd risen, as had his fur. "Given the snit the mage left in, you've probably managed to buy yourself a couple of days."

"You didn't put me on the duty roster."

"Observant girl."

"Is it because of the damn mages?"

"No. I take my orders from the Lord of Hawks."

"Then why—"

"I used the word *orders*, Private. Try to pay attention." He reached out with a claw and drew it across her cheek. The gesture was gentle. "You've been marked. You've already caused enough grief for this lifetime. You can wait ten years until I retire and give the poor fool who takes my stripes hell. Lord Evarrim has written, did Grammayre mention this?"

"No."

"Then he probably thought it best you didn't know."

"I don't."

"Good." He shoved her to one side and sat; the chair creaked. He'd managed to split leather twice. "Do not mess with the Arcanists."

"Sir."

"How many Festivals have you patrolled?"

"Officially?"

"Or unofficially."

"Enough." The fact that she was evasive meant that some of those patrols had occurred while her life was rooted in the fief of Nightshade. She'd been a child, then. And she probably hadn't been there to preserve the peace or prevent a crime.

"Good. You *are* aware that a few unscrupulous men—"

"A *few?*" Very few people did sarcasm as well as Kaylin.

"Very well, if you insist on being picky. A few *competent* and unscrupulous men work under the cover of the Festival crowds for their own ends?"

"Sir."

"Good. In all of your many colorful descriptions of High Caste Barrani Lords, did any of them include stupid?"

"No, sir."

"Good. Lord Evarrim is not a stupid man."

"He's not a man, sir."

"That's enough, Kaylin."

"Sir."

"If he is aware of your presence in the streets, it is likely that he will take the opportunity to interview you. As we've now denied his pleasant request three times, he'll be composing less pleasant requests, which are often misunderstood by little Sergeants like me—" and here his voice did break in a growl "—and mislabeled as threats. It isn't as if he hasn't asked politely, after all.

"Have you ever been to the High Court?"

"No."

"You think of it as a place of refinement and unearthly beauty."

"No, sir! I—"

He lifted a paw. Inspected it for invisible splinters. Let her splutter for a few more minutes. "It is beautiful in exactly the same way the Emperor's sword is beautiful—it is a work of art, and it is usually drawn for only one purpose. You *do not* want to be present when the blade is exposed."

"Sir."

"Good. You will sit this Festival out. And before you start whining, may I just point out how many Hawks would switch places with you in a second?"

"Yes, sir." She sounded deflated.

He wasn't fooled. "Give me the notebook, Kaylin."

She didn't spit; this was an improvement over her thirteen-year-old self. But it took her a minute to find the notebook, which, given it was clutched in her hands, was an accomplishment.

As she began to walk away from the desk, he said, "If you access Records for this information, I'll have your hide."

"Yes, Marcus."

She accidentally met Severn just outside of the Quartermaster's hall. Where accident had much to do with a bit of careful deduction, the information on the duty roster, and a damn boring wait.

The fact that he'd nursed her to health after saving the lives of many orphaned children had made an impression; enough of an impression that Kaylin had chosen to avoid him in every way possible for the past couple of weeks.

If he noticed, he gave no sign. But that was Severn all over. After all, he'd joined the damn Wolves and *waited* for her to find him for seven long years, watching from gods only knew which shadows, a window into the past.

She wasn't fond of windows. For one, it encouraged thieves, and for two, it made heating a small room that much harder.

But she *could* look at him, now. She could stand beside him without feeling guilt about the fact that he hadn't yet died. Or, if she were being truthful, that she hadn't killed him.

He raised a brow as she slid off the long bench that discouraged loitering. "Kaylin." His tone of voice told her pretty much everything she needed to know.

She fell into step beside him; he was practically gleaming. Official armor fell off his shoulders like a curtain of glimmering steel, which is pretty much what it was. The Hawks wore surcoats; he hadn't bothered to put his on. Like Kaylin, he'd grown up in the poorest streets of the city, and like Kaylin, he'd had no parents to rely on. No one to tell him how to dress, and when, and why, for a start.

No one to dress his wounds, to tell him to avoid the streets of the fiefs at night; no one to tell him how to avoid the men who preyed on children, or pressed them into early service.

Like Kaylin, he'd learned those lessons on his own.

"You've seen your assignment?" he asked her. He had to look down, and it irritated her. There should, she thought, be strict height limits on entry.

"Yes."

"I heard a, ah, rumor."

"It's true."

"You don't know what it is yet."

She shrugged. "Doesn't matter. It's *probably* true." She hesitated and added, "Which rumor?"

"You offended another Imperial mage."

"Oh, that." She shrugged. She half expected him to smile. But not even Kaylin was up to the delusion required to see his curt frown as mirth. "Have you heard about Teela?"

He said a lot of nothing, and kept walking. She took that as a yes. "I was thinking," she began.

"Oh? When?"

"Very funny. You've never worked a Festival before—the Wolves don't mingle well."

"I've been called upon for the Festival," he replied, his words carefully neutral. It surprised her, though.

"You have?"

His smile was like a wall. A fortified wall.

"Never mind. Working as a Hawk isn't the same."

"No. It's been more…interesting."

"It won't be. You'll be given permits and the new ordinances, and you'll be sent out to talk to a bunch of whiny, hot, would-be merchants. The unlicensed variety."

"I believe I've met a few." He shrugged. "I won't be near the market."

"The market isn't the problem. Well, okay, breaking up the fights between actual, licensed merchants is—but the Swords do most of that."

He stopped walking. "I am not taking you with me."

"I wasn't going to ask."

"Good."

"But I noticed you haven't been assigned a partner, and I was wondering—"

"Kaylin, do I look like I'm still breathing?"

"It's been five years since Marcus actually killed anyone—"

"I'd like to see six." He shook his head. "If you're concerned about Teela, take my advice. Don't be. She's Barrani. These are her games."

"She's a Hawk!"

"She's been a Hawk for a very, very short time. She's been Barrani for a very, very long time."

"You don't know her as well as I do."

"Clearly."

"Severn—"

He held up a hand. "While tolerance for your interpretation of punctuality seems unnaturally high, it also seems to be granted only to *you*." He started to walk again, and then stopped. "I don't want you out in the streets," he said without looking back. "For the same reason that neither Marcus nor the Hawklord do. But I'm not Marcus, and I'm not the Hawklord."

"What's that supposed to mean?"

"I have more to lose if you disobey your orders."

A reminder. One she didn't want.

"I'll tell you what I can," he continued, without looking back. "But stay here. Not even the Arcanum will attempt to reach you in *these* halls."

"I have to go home sometime."

He hit the wall. The movement was so fast she didn't see it coming; she jumped back in surprise. "I know," he said softly. And left her.

Severn was not there to walk her home, for which she was profoundly grateful. The area in which she lived wasn't noted for its crime, and the only major threat to the streets that bounded her building had been a few ferals that had managed to make it across the Ablayne River.

In the fiefs, ferals were common. So were murderers, and they both had the same effect—but there was something about shiny, long fangs bunched in the front of a half ton of rank fur and large paws that made the ferals seem the greater threat. They weren't exactly intelligent; they certainly didn't care much whether their meal was rich or poor, something that couldn't be said about any of the other occupants of the fiefs.

But they *were* occupants of the fiefs.

They had, apparently, caused mayhem and fear for a night this side of the river; it took all of a second night for the Wolves of the Law to hunt them down and exterminate them. No such Law existed in the fiefs, and the streets at night in the fiefs were deserted for that reason.

No, crime in the fiefs happened during the sunlight.

Here? They happened most frequently when the sun went down.

But oddly enough, there seemed to be a game in this, and you lost if you complained.

Everyone knew, after all, that the Barrani had only been part of the Law for some two decades—the whole of Kaylin's life. And they had memories that lasted a lot longer.

There were no deals going down.

Even the petty criminals seemed to have decided their stash was better sold on the streets that the Festival occupied. And the streets? Once the carters had got in and done their work, they were almost impassable. You couldn't walk a foot without someone trying to sell you something, usually at a three hundred percent markup over what it would cost at any other time of year.

She found herself at the foot of the bridge. It was, by foreign accounts, a perfectly normal, if somewhat unimpressive, bridge; you could take a horse across it, and you could certainly march a contingent of men that way—but a wagon was almost impossible, unless the driver was unnaturally gifted and the horses under perfect control. Perfect.

She didn't much like riding. She stood there, and then leaned over the nearest rail, watching the water pass under her feet. Here, on the boundary of her old life, she let the day unwind. The night was cool, for a Festival night; the air was clear. She wondered, sourly, if the Arcanum was controlling the weather; it was unseasonal. It would also be illegal.

Technically. In this city, even on this side of the banks, power was the order of the day; if you had it, the Law was a petty inconvenience. As long as no one was killed, or more likely, you were very, very good at disposing of the bodies.

Her cheek was throbbing dully; she lifted a hand almost absently to touch the flower placed there by the magic that she most hated. Well, second most. The magic that she *most* hated was engraved on her arms, her legs, the back, now, of her neck.

But it had been quiet. If it weren't for the arrogance of the Imperial mages, she would have had nothing to complain about, and this was unnatural. Complaining, according to Garrity, was the gods-given right of people who were Doing Something Useful; it was a little luxury. When, you know, duty forbade larger luxuries, like drinking.

And she wasn't Doing Something Useful, as Garrity would put it. The Festival season had been expressly forbidden her; she was surprised that they hadn't sent her out of town on the first coach.

Her cheek was actively painful, now. She touched it, wondering if it was swollen; if the lines engraved there were like the lines of a burn, and had taken some sort of stupid infection. Her skin was cool to the touch, her palm a little too dry.

She let her hand fall, casually, to her side. It was the side at which her daggers were neatly arranged.

Straightening slightly, she turned.

A man was standing at the foot of the far end of the bridge, except that he wasn't. A man, that is.

Surprise robbed her of words for a moment, but it added the hilt of a dagger, and the rest of the blade followed as she drew it. A warning, really. Or perhaps a gesture of greeting; it certainly wouldn't do her much good in a fight.

He was Barrani.

She wasn't. The odds favored him.

Even had she *been* Barrani, the odds would still favor him. He was, after all, Lord Nightshade, the crime lord under whose sway the fief of Nightshade prospered.

"It is sunset," Lord Nightshade said as he stepped onto the bridge. The wooden planks didn't even register his weight. Which, given the age of the bridge, said more about his movement than it did about the planks.

"Almost." She managed to shrug.

"You shouldn't be out in the streets, Kaylin. I was, I believe, most explicit about that."

She shrugged again before his words really registered. Sometimes nerves made her quick; sometimes they slowed her down. Quick was preferable. "Explicit to who?"

He raised a perfect, dark brow. It was perfect because he was Barrani. In fact, his eyes, which were a deep, startling green, were also perfect, and framed by—yes—perfect lashes. His face was the long, fine face of Barrani everywhere, his hair, the long perfect raven-wing black. He moved like a dancer. Or a hunting feral.

But he wore clothing—a long, dark cape over a robe that was both fine and edged with gold. Nothing about Barrani dress was ever less than ostentatious, even when it happened to be the same uniform—sized up—that she herself was now wearing.

She hated that. Anyone sane did.

Well, all right, anyone sane who wasn't also immortal and perfect and didn't take unearthly beauty for granted.

"Why are you here?"

"Because you are," he replied. "You've been calling me for the last week."

She frowned. "I haven't."

His shrug was elegant; it made hers look grubby. And unlike Teela or Tain, he didn't even make an effort; he spoke Barrani, and at that, the High Caste Barrani she most despised. Teela spoke Elantran when she was with the Hawks. Even when they were Barrani. When Teela broke into Barrani of *any* flavor, it meant trouble.

"As you like," he said quietly.

He drew closer, but stopped about two feet away. He did not, however, lean against the railing.

"You're almost on my turf," she said quietly.

"*Almost* is a mortal word." He gazed at the river, and gestured; it seemed to freeze in its bed, like sleek glass. She could see herself clearly in the momentary reflection; she could see him more clearly, and in the end, it was the fieflord she looked at. Who wouldn't?

"You have not come to visit," he said quietly.

She started to reply, and caught the words before they left her mouth, for perhaps the first time today. The fieflord was not known for his sense of humor. Or perhaps he was: He regularly killed people who offended by implying it existed at all.

Bravery was costly in the fiefs. Defiance was more painful, but not ultimately more costly.

"No," she said when she could talk. "I haven't."

Before she could move, he reached out to touch her cheek, his fingers caressing the skin that bore his mark. He did not touch any other part of her face, but he didn't have to—his meaning, in the gesture, was plain.

"You could remove it," she told him softly.

"Yes, I could. But not without cost." His smile was unsettling. "You speak my name when you sleep," he said softly. "My true name. And there is no way to avoid hearing it—not for me."

"I can't speak it," she said, something like fear informing the words.

"I know. I believe you did try when Tiamaris asked."

"I tried. Once."

"What did he hear?"

"Nothing."

"But I heard it," he said softly.

"You were in Castle Nightshade."

His brow rose. "Yes," he said, and it seemed there was caution in the affirmation. "I was."

"Why did you—why are you here?"

His eyes shifted in color. It was sudden, but it was entirely unexpected; nothing Barrani did could be expected, almost by definition. You just couldn't trust them, and predictability implied a certain belief in routine. "The castelord has called the High Court," he said quietly. The wrong type of quiet.

"I…know."

"Anteela will be there."

"An—oh. Teela." She remembered that Lord Evarrim had called Teela that, what seemed like another lifetime ago. "She's gone. But none of the other Barrani are."

"They wouldn't be. None of the other Barrani, as you so casually put it, withdrew from the Lord's Court to pursue the idle life of a…Hawk."

"She's a—"

"In Elantran, you would call her Lady Anteela," he said, using the word *Lady* with some distaste. "If she desired it. She does not."

"So she left."

His smile was cold. "The Hawks are trained to observe, are they not?"

"They are."

"Then the training given is poor indeed."

"We like to observe fact."

"Fact, as you so quaintly put it, is something that is rarely understood if it is observed with no understanding of context. She withdrew from Court. Her absence was noted. It was not, however, appreciated."

She didn't ask him how he knew.

"Wise," he told her. "Understand, Kaylin Neya, that you will be at the heart of many discussions when the Court convenes."

"And that will be?"

"When the moon is full," he replied. "And silver."

"Which moon?"

"There is only one that counts."

She didn't ask. As far as she was concerned, there were two. "Why are you here?" she said again.

"I am unwilling to risk you in the games that will no doubt unfold. You are too ignorant of our customs."

"You're outcaste," she said without thinking. "They're not your customs anymore." She caught up with her flapping mouth and shut it hard enough to hear—and feel—her teeth snap.

His eyes were now a blue that was sapphire. Midnight

sapphire. "Come," he said, and he began to walk away, down the gentle slope of the bridge.

On the wrong side.

"You can't—you can't go there!"

"While it is true that I seldom venture outside of my domain, I am seldom stopped when I do so."

He continued to walk, and after a moment, she pushed herself back from the comfort of bridge rails and leaped after him. His stride was a good deal longer than hers, and she had to work just that little bit harder to keep up; it was hard to look cool and composed when one was breathing too hard.

She followed him, looking back and to her side in growing unease. No one seemed to notice that the damn *fieflord* of Nightshade was walking the streets of Elantra. Then again, she wouldn't have believed it either; she would have seen just another Barrani, in the company of a junior Hawk.

But as she followed him, the streets grew familiar. Not even the gaudy ribbons and wreaths, the symbols of a dozen different gods, the statues—layers of new paint over layers of old paint, like some miniature ode to geological formations—could make *these* streets so new or strange that she wouldn't recognize them; if she closed her eyes and slowed down, her feet would know the path.

He was walking her *home*.

She stopped walking, in the vague hope that he would. Instead, the distance between them grew until she'd have to really sprint to close it. She did.

She couldn't bring herself to touch him; had he been Severn, she'd have had two handfuls of elbow as she swung him around. Instead, she tried hard to avoid looking at any of the details of her daily life that *made* her life bearable. As if, by ignoring them, she could protect them. She walked.

He stopped in front of her building, at the locked door. She fumbled for her keys, but because it was deliberate, a way of buying time, he taught her a small lesson; he passed his hand over the lock, and she felt her cheek flush. Just the one.

The door opened, gliding with a creak on its hinges.

He didn't speak a word; he simply met her gaze and waited. This much, that gaze seemed to say, he was willing to grant her for the sake of her dignity. But it was his to grant, and his to deny.

"I should arrest you," she muttered as she hurried in the door. It closed behind them.

His smile never reached his eyes. "I think that not even your Sergeant would demand that you carry out that duty. You are, of course, free to try."

She walked past him and up the narrow flight of stairs, stopping at the bend. He followed, and again, he followed in such a way that the stairs didn't acknowledge his weight.

Not even Teela could do that.

"She can," he said.

"Will you *stop?*"

"No. If you wish to shield your thoughts, it is something you will have to learn. And I fear that your ability to learn this simple act is hampered by your inability to *learn* what is not taught by fists, knives, and the streets."

She knew he was referring to the mages. She almost accused him of spying—but what would be the point?

"Very little."

And she wanted to hit him. She unlocked her door instead.

Her room, as usual, was a mess. It had been a bright and tidy place while she'd been recovering from her fight with a gods-cursed Dragon, but that had been Caitlin's doing, and once Caitlin had no longer judged herself necessary, it had reverted over the course of a few busy—and, yes, late—days into the place that she called home. Piles of laundry were the only works of art along the floor; her shutters were closed, and tied with a small length of chain, and her mirror was covered.

Her bed was unmade, of course. Everything seemed to be. Even the chair looked untidy, which was odd, as chairs didn't normally require much making once they'd left the carpenter.

She headed toward the kitchen, and Lord Nightshade raised a hand. She felt it; her back was turned, so she couldn't see it.

"You are here," he told her quietly, "to gather the belongings you feel are necessary for your comfort."

"What?"

"I have no intention of leaving you in this part of the city for this particular Festival."

"What?" She felt like a parrot.

"Rooms have been prepared for your use in Castle Nightshade. You will remain there until the Court has adjourned."

"But I—I have to—work—"

His response was a silence that was all blue. "Understand, Kaylin, that this was not a request."

"And if I don't want to go?"

"You don't," he replied with a Barrani shrug. "What of it?"

The dagger that she'd forgotten to sheathe looked pathetic in the scant light. She stared at it for a moment, and then looked at the fieflord. Here.

She was cold.

After a moment, she started to gather her clothing, her weapons, the sticks she shoved into her hair. She shoved these into a sack.

"You will be free to return—if you desire it—when things are less…difficult."

CHAPTER 3

Inasmuch as Kaylin understood class—the adult form of bullying and condescension—she felt like a class traitor. Lord Nightshade was rumored to be a mage of great power, and in spite of the fact that she'd evidence of that with her own eyes—and Hawks had their own arrogance when it came to trusting opinions formed by gathering information—she was almost disappointed when they *walked* down the same set of narrow, shoddy stairs and into the wide streets. She had expected something less mundane.

Hell, she'd once seen him walk through a mirror and vanish. Then again, her mirror would bisect him, so it was probably just as well.

Her bag hung over her shoulder, and her uniform gathered in uncomfortable, trapped wrinkles; she felt like a street urchin again. Especially when compared with her companion. She took care not to make the comparison more than once.

He led the way, and she followed; she would have led, but his stride was the longer of the two, and his dignity—Barrani dignity—did not allow him to trail behind something as lowly as Kaylin. It did, however, allow him to stand behind his chosen guard when he chose to venture into the streets of the fief he ruled.

He'd brought no such guard with him.

When they reached the bridge, she paused. He had walked ahead, and he, too, paused at the gentle height of the bridge's curve. He turned to watch her. Met her eyes.

"I assure you," he said in a tone of voice that had the opposite effect, "you are not a prisoner. This is not a kidnapping. I do not intend to…interfere…with your duties in the Halls. I merely wish to insure that no one else has the opportunity to interfere with them."

"I'll have to tell—"

He grimaced. "If it comforts you, I have altered your mirror. If someone chooses to invoke it, it will carry your message to your room within the Castle."

"Where you'll hear everything that's said."

He raised a brow.

"The Hawklord isn't going to be happy about this."

"The Hawklord is not your lord. He rules your life when you labor under his command. What you do in your…free time is not his concern. Come, Kaylin. It will be dark soon, and while I am not afraid of ferals, I do not think facing them will be in your best interest."

Enough of a warning. She made her way across the bridge, marking the point at which her new life was discarded and her old life opened up before her in the roads and causeways of Nightshade.

It was not the only fief she knew; not even the only fief she had called home. But it was the fief in which she had lived almost all of her life. The other, she didn't name and didn't think about.

"Why is the Barrani castelord—"

He held up a hand. "Now is not the time for that discussion." His smile was slender and cool. "If we are lucky, there will be no time for it. If we are not, you will have answers. The castelord of the Barrani is a subtle lord, and he has governed for centuries. He has not, of course, been uncontested."

She didn't ask what happened to the challengers; she assumed they were dead. And if they were, no complaint had been made to the Emperor or the Halls of Law, and no investigations—that she was aware of—had been started. Then again, if there had been, she probably wouldn't be aware of them; Barrani weren't as interesting, in terms of criminal activity, as the rest of the mortal races, and if she'd been forced to learn their language, she'd never much cared to learn their history, even as it pertained to the Halls of Law.

Barrani were unpleasantly cold, but they kept to themselves, and while they valued *power,* they were one of the few races she could think of that didn't equate said power with *money.*

Money made people stupid.

Or starvation did. She'd never heard of a starving Barrani before.

"Severn won't like it," she said without thinking.

"No. But I assure you, Kaylin, that he will like even less the possible outcome of an entanglement with the Barrani lords. He did not," he added without a shift in expression, "appreciate the fact that you would be living alone in an indefensible hovel while the Court convened."

"Is there *anything* about my life you don't know?"

"Very little," he replied smoothly. "You bear my mark, little one. You hold my name. Did you think that these were merely decorations or human familiarities?"

"No. But I *was* trying."

"Expend your efforts, then, on something worthwhile. We have fought the outcaste Dragon," he added, "and we have killed the dead. There is always a cost."

Yes, she thought bitterly. Always. And we're not the ones to pay it.

"A lesson, for those who want power."

She wondered why anyone did.

"Because if you *have* power, you make the decisions, Kaylin."

"You have," she said, the words an accusation. "And what *decisions* do you make that make power attractive?"

"Ah. I am not one of the dead."

Which wasn't very helpful. The streets narrowed as they walked them; they were almost empty. The tavern owners and the butchers and the grocers who were chained to this side of the river were busy pulling in the boards and wheeled carts they used for display. If they noticed the Barrani lord, they gave no sign; at night, the ferals were more of a threat.

And night was coming.

She followed Nightshade, her cheek tingling. She wanted

to brush it clear of the odd sensation, but she'd tried that many times, and all it did was make her hand numb. But she hesitated as the Castle came into view.

"There are no bodies in the cages," he said quietly.

She looked up to examine his profile; he hadn't turned to speak. "I guess people are busy preparing for the Festival." It sounded lame, even to her.

"Too busy to offer offense?" His smile was sharp, but again, she saw it in perfect profile. "No, Kaylin Neya, it is a gift. For you."

"You knew I would be coming here."

"Yes. And I do not intend—at this time—to make your stay more difficult than it must be."

There were two guards at the black facade of the gate. They offered Nightshade a deep obeisance, a formal and graceful bend that did not deprive them of weapons or footing. He did not appear to notice.

But they offered no less respect to Kaylin. It made her uncomfortable; it put her off her stride.

"They are here for protection," he told her as he made his way to the portcullis. "And I am seldom in need of protection here."

She hesitated, hating the portcullis. It never actually *rose*; it was a decorative set of heavy, black iron bars that should have been functional. She'd seen them before a dozen times in other buildings, and had learned to listen to the grinding of the gears that raised them.

But these? They weren't. Raised.

You didn't enter Castle Nightshade without an invitation, and when you did—you walked *through* the lowered portcullis; it was a very mundane depiction of a magic portal. And it took you somewhere else. She wondered if the court-yard that could easily be seen through the spaces in the bars was real, or if it was a backdrop, some sort of tiresome illusion.

She really, really hated magic.

"Kaylin?" Lord Nightshade said. It sounded like a question. It was, of course, a command. He held out a hand to punctuate the fact, and she forced herself to move slowly enough that it didn't *seem* like an obvious hesitation. Given that she wasn't her audience, she couldn't tell whether or not the watching Barrani guards could tell the difference. She doubted they cared.

But they were…different.

"Of course," Lord Nightshade said in a voice that barely traveled to her ears. "They know what you fought, Kaylin. They know you survived. They could not, with certainty, say the same of themselves in a like situation."

And the Barrani respected power.

She took a deep breath and followed Lord Nightshade into the castle.

Her stomach almost lost lunch. She hadn't had time for dinner, which was good; dinner wouldn't have been an almost.

But she wasn't in the vestibule, which had the advantage of looking like the very rich and opulent end of "normal," she was in a room. A room that had no windows but shed an enormous amount of light anyway.

The floor was cold and hard, but it was beautiful; a smoky

marble shot through with veins of blue and green, and the hint of something gold. It was laid out in tiles that suggested the pattern of concentric circles, and at the center of those, she stood, her bag on her shoulders, her uniform hanging unevenly at the hem. In other words, out of place in every possible way.

Not so, Lord Nightshade.

He gestured; she looked up as he did, because his hand started at waist level and stopped just above his head, drawing the eye. She couldn't help it. Years of working the beat at the side of Teela and Tain hadn't in any way made her ready for Lord Nightshade; he was Barrani in the almost mythic sense, and they—they were *real*.

He was beautiful, in the cold way the floors were.

The ceiling above her head was rounded, like a gentle dome; it was rimmed by something that looked like marble, and its surface was engraved with runes. She didn't recognize them.

She didn't want to.

"The words—those runes—were…already here…when you took possession of the castle?"

"They were," he said, sparing her a brief glance. His eyes traced the runes, and the light that rippled across them, as if it were reflected by the surface of a small pond in sunlight. "But they are not, I think, a danger to you. Can you read them?"

This was polite, as it was often polite to ask questions for which you technically weren't supposed to have the answers. She distrusted polite in men of power. "No."

"Ah. A pity. I believe that among the runes above us there

are words you can invoke, should it come to that. They will afford you some protection."

She said nothing.

"I have taken the liberty of giving you one of the outer rooms," he continued. "You will not be required to enter the Long Hall. If I remember correctly, it causes you some discomfort."

"It's not the hall," she said, before she could stop herself. "It's the Barrani. The ones that don't move and seem to be interested in blood."

"Even so." He pointed. Against the far curve—there was no direction in this room, given lack of anything that offered a directional anchor—was a large, round bed. With pillows, even. It was pristine, and covered in silks she thought were worth more than two years of her pay. It was annoying. On the other hand, it lacked a canopy, which seemed to be the thing to attach to the beds of people with too much money.

"I don't suppose you have a map of the Castle?"

"One that wouldn't change?"

"I'll take that as a no."

He smiled. "There is a wardrobe for your…belongings. You will also find—"

"I don't need anything else." She remembered, clearly, her first visit; she'd lost her uniform and had woken up in a really impractical dress. A really beautiful, attractive, impractical dress.

"If you dine with me—as I hope you will—you will need less…political garb. I have seen to that," he added, his voice cooling by several degrees.

She remembered that annoying him was not a good

idea. Not that she wasn't willing, but she wanted to choose the fights.

He walked over to the wall and gestured. Stone separated, and a section of the wall reflected light evenly. Perfectly. "This," he told her quietly, "is the mirror. You may use it, if you wish."

"But you'll hear everything."

"Indeed."

"And anyone who wants to reach me?"

"They'll be…directed…to this one. You are free to explore the Castle. I suggest, if you do, that you take a guard with you."

"Which one?"

"One of the two," he replied, "who stand outside this door." And he walked toward it. "I have much to attend to this eve. We will talk on the morrow."

"I have to work—"

"You are not a prisoner here, Kaylin. You are no longer a child. You know the way to the upper city."

The mirror didn't wait.

She was almost asleep—she had trouble sleeping in strange, obscenely comfortable beds—when it went off. For a moment, she was disoriented; she was already out of the bed, and padding on cold stone toward the wrong wall when she remembered that she wasn't home; she corrected herself as wakefulness caught up with her instincts.

She touched the mirror, keying it; an image began to form in its depths. Familiar face, and a dreadful, familiar expression.

"Marya?"

"Kaylin, thank the gods!"

Marya was a midwife. Which pretty much said it all.

Kaylin reached for her pack. "Where?" she said.

"Stevenson Street. It's Worley's old house."

"How long do I have?"

There was a small, stressful silence. Silent answers were always the worst. Had she been home, it would be a five-minute sprint, a fifteen-minute jog. She wasn't anywhere that close.

"Marya—I'm not at my place."

"I gathered. The mirror had trouble."

Kaylin cursed mirrors. And Barrani. And time.

"I'll be there," she said quietly, yanking her boots on under her nightdress. "I'll be there as soon as I can. Tell her to—to stop pushing. To stop doing anything. Do you have worryroot?"

Marya's nod was brisk. "Everything we can do, we've done. The baby's not—"

Kaylin lifted a hand and shattered the image. Her way of saying she was on the move.

She dressed quickly and sloppily; she looked like a walking human crease. Her hair, she shoved back and staked. It wouldn't hold through a real run; it would have to do for now. She stopped for a moment as a glint of light at her wrist was caught in a downward spark by the mirror's reflective surface.

Caging her power, opulent and ancient, the bracer that had been both gift and bane, its jeweled surface cool and distant. She could hear Marcus now. She had her orders: it was not to come off.

And she had her imperatives. She couldn't wear it and do what—what probably needed to *be* done. With a grimace, she touched the stones in a sequence that was so familiar she couldn't consciously say it out loud. A loud click, and it opened. She dropped it on the floor.

It would find its way back to its keeper, sooner or later— and at the moment, that keeper wasn't Kaylin. That much thought she spared before she ran to the door. The next thought was for the guards that stood outside of it.

She almost tripped over the men who now barred her way.

They were both beautiful, both perfect, and both utterly impassive. She snarled something in very rude Leontine.

They failed to understand. This could even be because they *couldn't*, although she wouldn't have bet money on it. "I don't have *time* for this!"

But she did. The baby didn't. The mother didn't.

They exchanged a glance. She lifted a hand to her cheek, and drew back in surprise; the mark was *hot*. She hadn't even seen it in the mirror, in the brief glance she had given herself before she'd tried to flee the room.

"We are not empowered to let you wander alone," one of the two Barrani said. She looked at him carefully.

"I have to leave. Now. You have your duties," she added, "and I have mine. But I will *never* forgive you if you keep me here, and I will *never* forgive you if any delay you cause costs me."

The man's gaze never wavered. But he drew his sword and nodded at the other guard. "I will accompany you," he said. "Where will you go?"

"To the upper city," she replied, pushing past him.

"The ferals—"

She knew. It just wasn't allowed to matter. Not for the first time—and not for the last—she wished she was an Aerian; she could fly above the reach of ferals with ease, had she but wings.

She started to run, stopped, and turned to look at the guard. "What is your name—no, what should I call you?"

A dark, perfect brow rose. "Andellen," he said at last, as if she'd asked him something that had never been asked by another living creature. Or not one who wanted to stay that way.

"Good. Andellen. I don't know the Castle. I need to get out. Can you lead me?"

He nodded. Whatever hesitation he had shown had vanished the moment he had agreed to accompany her. He was stiff; he wasn't at all like the Barrani Hawks she knew. He spoke High Barrani, and he chose a sword as his weapon; the Hawks usually used a very large stick.

He also wore armor.

But the armor didn't seem to slow him down, or if it did, it didn't matter; he was moving at a speed that Kaylin could barely match.

They made the vestibule, and Kaylin gritted her teeth as she passed through the portal and into the world.

There was no time for conversation. They made a lot of noise as they ran, and that was bad. It was dark, although the skies were clear enough that the moon provided light. For them, certainly. For the ferals, as well.

Fighting ferals usually involved a lot of running, but that

took time. She made her way straight toward the Ablayne, and the single bridge that crossed it, praying silently. It's funny how someone who couldn't follow the names of half the gods in Elantra could pray with such conviction.

At her side, the Barrani guard ran. He glanced at her only when she stumbled, but did not offer her any assistance; she found her footing and continued, thinking of Worley's house. Thinking of how best to reach it. Thinking of only that.

It helped.

When they reached the bridge, she exhaled, a long, slow movement of chest. The bright and dark moons across the water were a benediction. The guard, on the other hand, didn't have the grace to look winded. Had she the energy, she would have whiled away time in idle hatred for all things Barrani; as it was, she looked up at him once. His expression, being Barrani, gave nothing but ice away.

Which was good; had he intended to stop her, it would have looked worse.

She started to adjust her pack, and Andellen surprised her; he grabbed it instead. His hair flew in the stillness as he shouldered its weight, but he said nothing.

And she let him do it. As if he were Teela or Tain.

She led now, and he followed; he probably knew the entire city by heart, but the only roads he usually traveled were those ruled by Nightshade. She wanted to ask him how often he left the fief, but she couldn't spare breath.

Wasn't certain he would answer if she could.

The streets were now lined with stalls; there were men and women beneath the low glow of torches and the high lamps that decorated the skyscape; they would work all night, and well into morning, decorating, carving, nailing or sewing as the Festival season required. This was their best chance to make money for the year, and if sleep suffered, it suffered.

They noticed her as she ran past, but that was probably because of Andellen. He didn't wear a uniform. He wasn't a Hawk. And a smart person didn't get in the way of a running Barrani.

She made it past her apartment, turned the corner, skidded and fell; she rolled to her feet, cursing like a Leontine—and in Leontine—and kept going. Five minutes passed like a lifetime. And it wasn't *her* life.

And then, two rights, one short left, and three small buildings, and she was there. A lamp was hanging by the side of the door, the dark, glowing blue of the midwives' beacon. She leaped up the three warped steps and pushed the door open; it wasn't locked.

Marya was waiting for her. Her eyes were dark, and her face was that kind of pale that speaks of whole days without sleep. "Kaylin! She's in the—" Her dark eyes rounded when she saw what followed Kaylin in.

"Marya," Kaylin said, half shouting as she grabbed the midwife's hands before they picked up the nearest candlestick, "he's with me. I don't have time to explain. He *won't touch anything*. He means no harm." She could not force herself to add, *trust him.*

Before Marya could answer, a thin, attenuated cry carried the distance of still room and closed door. A younger woman, fingers clutching the frame of the door for support, appeared as the door swung open and slapped the wall. "Marya—she's started to bleed—"

"Kaylin's here," Marya said, her voice pitched low, but pitched to carry. "Kaylin's here now."

And Kaylin pushed past the poor girl and into the bedroom. "Get water!" she shouted as she ran to the bed. "Drinking water!"

But Marya was already in motion, a comfortable, busy blur. Marya had worked with Kaylin before; she would know what was needed, and when.

Kaylin took the hand of the woman whose eyes were beginning their slow slide into shock. She pressed her free hand up and against the stretched, hard curve of belly and winced as the body told its story.

Late. She was late. She could feel the rupture.

She looked up and met the eyes of a young man that she didn't recognize; he was so white he was almost green. "Get out," she told him. He shook his head, mute, his defiance the product of fear.

"Marya—"

"Gerrold, come away," the midwife said, her voice above Kaylin's back. "Now. Your wife needs her privacy."

"But she—"

"*Now.*" A mother's tone. With just the edge of anger in it— and at that, the right kind of anger. Pity, compassion, or fear would have watered the command down so badly it wouldn't have worked—but Marya had confidence in Kaylin.

And the poor man? He had nothing. He tried to stand. Stumbled. Kaylin wondered if he was going to pass out. Better if he did.

Without another word, she drew her knife. It wasn't clean, but it would have to do. She heard a stifled scream from a long, long distance away; heard Marya's angry words attempt to drown it out.

And then she gave herself over to the sound of two beating hearts; one labored and slow, the other so fast and soft it could barely be heard at all.

Two hours later, she was finished.

Marya caught her hands, and forcibly broke all contact with the young woman who sat in the bed. Kaylin could hear the sounds of infant cries; could see the bundled—and cleaned—baby resting in its mother's arms. The wound—what there was left of it—was new and raw, but it wasn't bleeding.

"The—the father?"

"He's there, in the chair," Marya said in the soothing voice reserved for the injured. "He was a bit upset about the knife, dear," she added. "We had to restrain him." She paused, and then added, "Your man was most helpful, there."

"My man?" Kaylin shook her head. "Who—". She turned her head sideways, which was much more effort than she would have liked, and saw Andellen. "He's not my—he didn't hurt him, did he?"

Marya shook her head. "Not much, at any rate. I think he'll have a bruised jaw, but dear, he simply *wasn't* listening."

Kaylin could imagine. Blood had that effect on most people. She tried to say as much, and Marya took the opportunity to trickle water into her mouth. "It's not for me—"

"You should see your mouth." There was no point in arguing with Marya. "I've made sure she drinks," Marya added.

"Tell her—"

"Later, dear. There *will* be a later, thanks to you." She paused, and added, "It's a girl."

"Oh. Good." There wasn't much else one could say to something like that.

Kaylin tried to rise, and her knees locked.

"There's a chair for you, if you need it. I sent Darlene home. She was…a little upset herself."

"Did she see the baby?"

Marya nodded, the smile never leaving her face. It was a slight smile, and framed by etched lines, but it was like bedrock. You could stand on a smile like that.

"She'll know better next time," Marya added quietly. "This is only her third birthing. She's never been at a birthing when we've had to call you before, but she's a smart girl, a solid apprentice. She'll learn."

Kaylin forced herself to stand. "Gods willing," she said, keeping her tone polite and professional, "she'll never have to see it again."

"Aye, gods," Marya said with a shrug. She turned her attention to the mother, and then frowned at the poor young man in the distant chair, his dark hair splayed flat against his forehead, his skin still winter-white, except where it was purple. "I forget what it's like, with the first babe. Gerrold, come help with your wife. She needs to drink a lot of water, and she's likely to be a bit weak. You've saved any money, make sure she gets meat, and not that terrible stuff the merchants are pawning off on foreigners either, understand?"

He nodded. Kaylin highly doubted that he'd heard anything more than his name. She made her way toward the chair that Marya had produced, but before she could sit, Andellen was there, all six feet of him.

His armor looked damn odd in the very small room.

"Kaylin Neya," he said quietly, "it is time that we returned."

She nodded. But she couldn't quite stand.

"Leave her be," Marya said, her voice a slap.

"You serve your master," the Barrani replied, "and I, mine." But his words were shorn of contempt, and if they weren't respectful, the lack of contempt said something. What, exactly, Kaylin was a bit too tired to figure out. Later.

"She doesn't have a master," Kaylin told him.

"What did he say, dear?"

Kaylin shook her head. "It's Barrani."

"I recognize the language." Marya was too tired to keep disdain from her words. "And them that's polite use language other people can understand when they've got company."

"The Barrani aren't famed for their manners for a reason, Marya."

"Well, they could start learning. It's never too late, and it's not like courtesy ever killed anyone."

Kaylin almost laughed. What could she say to Marya that would make sense of this armored stranger? That he was one of the fieflord's personal guard?

Andellen, however, chose to take no offense at the old woman's words.

"We could stay at my place," Kaylin told him. "It's night

in the fiefs. We were lucky enough to miss the ferals the first time."

But Andellen did not reply; he was watching—of all things—the babe.

"Andellen?"

The Barrani shrugged. "You are too weak to walk," he said at last. It was the first sign of hesitance that she had yet seen him show. "I will take you to your home."

Five minutes passed like three hours. Kaylin wanted to sleep off the healing on the nearest stretch of cobbled stone that didn't have merchanting crap all over it; the problem was finding one. Well, that and the big Barrani who herded her forward every time she looked like she might fall. He took care not to touch her; it seemed odd. Had she been with Teela or Tain, they would have given up on her half a block past, and carried her the rest of the way. Oh, she would have cursed them in at least three languages, but they were used to that.

Andellen gave her space.

He made certain that anyone whose curiosity was stronger than their self-preservation instinct also gave her space, and she finally reached the door of her apartment. She fumbled with the key and dropped it twice, while he watched, impassive. Waiting.

She tossed out a few recreational Aerian curses, just to keep in practice, and made a third attempt at the lock. This time, it worked.

The stairs looked very, very steep from where she stood. She made her way up them, hanging on to the rails until she ran out of railing. Her door was there. She was surprised that it was open.

And more surprised when she saw who was waiting in the room. Severn, in the moonlight. He'd even opened the shutters, the bastard.

Andellen was behind her. She knew this because the stone of Severn's expression shifted into something a lot less friendly.

"When did I give you a key?" she muttered.

"You didn't."

"What the hell are you doing here?"

"Waiting."

Sarcasm took too much energy. She stumbled over the threshold. Andellen followed.

Great, she thought, *they're going to fight. I'll lose the apartment.*

But…they didn't. Nothing made sense. Severn was stiff, and obviously angry, as he made his way toward her.

"Waiting?"

"Someone sent word," he said as he caught her. His hands were cold. And stiff.

"The fieflord entrusts her to your care," Andellen's voice said. She didn't actually see him. Couldn't. She could see the hollows of Severn's collarbone, and they were the whole of her vision.

"You're bleeding," he said in her ear.

"Not my blood," she replied dimly. "But the baby was a girl."

It was the last thing she said, and she thought she smiled.

Sunlight was the bane of her existence.

Mirrors were also the bane of her existence. And the inside of her mouth? That was bad, too. Her eyes were crusted together, her arms felt as if she'd been doing chin-ups in the drill yard, and her legs—well, never mind; they were worse.

The mirror was snarling. Covered, and snarling.

The glare of the damn sun made her glad that opening her eyes was difficult.

"Kaylin Neya!"

No one, she thought bitterly, should have to wake up to *that* voice. Marcus Kassan was in a mood.

"Kaylin, take the bloody cloth off the damn mirror and answer me!"

"Coming," she managed, and rolled over.

Either her bed had changed shape significantly over the course of the night, or someone else was in it. She jumped up, hit the open shutters with the back of her head, and cursed in loud and angry Leontine.

Which, of course, Marcus heard. It certainly added color to *his* reply.

Severn lay on his side, propped up on one elbow. His hair fell over one eye, and the scar along his cheek was white in the sunlight. He didn't look sleepy.

"How long have you been *here?*" she hissed as she crawled off the bottom edge of her mattress.

He shrugged. "Long enough."

"Why didn't you answer the damn mirror?"

"The Sergeant is in a mood," he replied. He sounded almost amused. But he didn't look it, so she didn't hit him.

There were rules that she tried to follow when she undertook a healing of any difficulty—and chief among those was Don't Crouch; crouching for hours at a stretch almost destroyed her knees. Unfortunately, emergencies tended to drive common sense out of her head, as if it were something sheeplike.

Oh, it was bad. The sun was well past high, and the shadows it cast were a very strong reminder that she was—yet again—late for something.

Marcus was practically *eating* the mirror by the time she got to her end and pulled the cloth down from its less than pristine surface. When she saw his face, she thought briefly of putting the cloth *back*. Unfortunately, he'd seen her.

"Where the hell were you?"

"Out."

He snorted, but there was a little less edge in the sound. He knew what she did when she was off duty, even though it was technically both illegal and impossible.

"You've got a meeting," he growled.

"When?"

"A half an hour ago."

Some days it just didn't pay to be alive.

"How important is this meeting?"

"It depends."

"On?"

"On how much you like wearing the Hawk."

She groaned. "Stall for me?"

"I have been," he snapped, exposing the full line of Leontine teeth. They were really impressive teeth, too. "And Kaylin?"

"Yes, Marcus?"

"I'm not enjoying it."

"Yes, sir."

"Get your ass into the office."

"Yes, sir."

"NOW."

She broke contact. "Don't laugh," she said to Severn, who was, in fact, chuckling. "You've got beat duty, and if you're here, you're not there."

The smile didn't fade. "I'm not you, Kaylin."

"Meaning what?"

"I cover my ass." He reached into the folds of his uniform—he hadn't even bothered to remove it—and pulled out a curled piece of paper. She really hated paper. "The Hawklord's orders."

"He *told you* to babysit me?"

"I don't believe that was the term used, no. But my duties this Festival are somewhat elastic, owing, no doubt, to my inexperience."

"Meaning?"

"You don't have time for the explanation."

She tossed him out into the hall and dressed.

CHAPTER 4

"What are you not going to do?"

"Severn, I *don't have time* for this!" Although Kaylin's apartment was close to the midwives guild, close to the Ablayne, and reasonably close to the poorer market, it was not all that close to the Halls of Law. Close to the Halls was about three times farther than her lousy pay could stretch; she'd settled for what she could.

"Let me try that again. What are you *not* going to do?"

"Breathe anymore, if I don't get there quickly!"

"Third time lucky," Severn said in a tone of voice best reserved for truculent children. Kaylin bristled.

"I'm *not* going to offend the Imperial mage. If that's what's waiting. I was *supposed* to have a few days free." She kicked a rock. It hurt her toe. The hopping around on one foot after the fact didn't do much for her dignity, either.

But she was off her stride; Severn in the morning, Severn

in her small bed, Severn by her side—it was too much to take in with good grace. And as Kaylin and good grace were often on opposite sides of the city, she struggled not to be exceptionally cranky.

But not too hard—cranky was better, in Kaylin's books, than confused. She was damn tired. If Marcus had half a heart, she'd still be sleeping off the night's work.

She was dressed in a wrinkled surcoat; she looked like Hawks might if they'd been involved in breaking up a bar brawl. She'd left her best pants in the damn Castle, and her second best, at the moment, had holes in the leg. Which wasn't her fault; someone trying to cut her knee off could be considered damage taken in the line of duty.

The exceedingly stingy man often referred to as the Quartermaster had other ideas.

Severn frowned.

He had a way of moving that suggested violence without descending to it, but the sudden glint of steel in his hands was not a comforting sign. Rocks and temper forgotten, Kaylin stilled instantly, her hand dropping to a dagger hilt.

"What?"

"Barrani," he said quietly.

She squinted. The sun was just too damn bright, and her mouth didn't feel much less like she'd eaten a dead mouse. But as she eased into a fighting stance, she saw the man Severn referred to. Wondered how damn tired she must be to have missed him in the first place: he wore red.

And not a little red; it covered him from shoulder to foot in a long, expensive drape that caught sun and deepened color at the same time. Kaylin had a word for people who could spend *money* on magical *clothing,* but it wasn't one she wanted to use where said person might actually hear it, given how synonymous money and power actually were in this city.

Red. "Arcanum," she said in a tone that was usually reserved for the more colorful words she knew.

"Lord Evarrim," Severn added. "He's persistent."

"He's not alone."

"I'd noticed."

There were four guards with him, but they were dressed in a less obvious fashion. Where less obvious was armor that glinted beneath translucent surcoats. They wore their hair beneath wide bands, but they wore it Barrani style; capes that fell well past their shoulders. They were, of course, of a height, and they walked in perfect unison.

"You feel like jogging?" Severn asked, without moving.

"Not much."

He shrugged. "You've got thirty seconds."

His words sunk in. "I'm not leaving you here."

"They're not interested in me."

Her turn to shrug. "They're not interested in the Dragon Emperor either, and these are pretty damn crowded streets. I'll take my chances."

"Then let's keep walking, shall we? The Halls are only four blocks away."

Four long blocks. Kaylin nodded. Whatever animosity there was between them had turned sideways and vanished. They had time to squabble later. For now, they both wore the Hawk, and if Kaylin's had seen better days, she was still proud of it. It was one of the very few things in her life that she'd worked to earn, and consequently one of the very few things she accorded real respect.

At block two, Lord Evarrim seemed to notice that Kaylin was walking toward him. Kaylin was underimpressed with the quality of his acting; it was good, of course, but it was cheap. Lord Nightshade would never have stooped to pretense.

Then again, he owned any street he walked in, so pretense was kind of superfluous.

"Private," he said, nodding to Kaylin as if she were just barely worthy of notice. "Corporal." The rank still rankled. Kaylin came from the Leontine school of acting, but struggled not to let it show anyway.

"Lord Evarrim," Severn said, bowing. He hadn't bothered to sheathe his dagger, and Lord Evarrim hadn't bothered to notice the weapon. His guards were slightly more critical, but as swords were considered more of a public menace than daggers—and gods alone knew why—they didn't draw weapons in the open streets.

They didn't have to.

Severn did *not* come from the Leontine school of acting; he appeared to be both polite and deferential. It was a Barrani trick—the more polite and deferential you looked, the less of either you actually felt.

This, Lord Evarrim did notice.

"I hope the Festival season is uneventful," Lord Evarrim continued after a minute pause. "And I hope it finds you in good health."

"And you, Lord Evarrim."

"You are, I believe, new to the ranks of the Hawks," the

Barrani Lord said. He looked bored, but his eyes were a clear green—a dark green that held hints of blue.

Severn nodded.

"But the private is not. Private Neya." Blue now, definitely blue. What the Barrani could keep from their faces, they couldn't keep from their eyes; like Dragons, like Aerians, like Leontines, the color of their eyes told a story. In this case, it was a chilly one.

"Lord Evarrim," she said, striving to match Severn's tone.

"I believe you keep company with a member of the High Court."

"I keep the company of Hawks," Kaylin said carefully. *Not that it's any of your business.*

"Good. See that you continue to do so." Blue was not Kaylin's favorite color. He lifted a hand and Severn took a step forward. Four Barrani guards did likewise; the street, where they were standing, became a lot more crowded.

"I wouldn't, if I were you," Kaylin said softly.

Severn stepped on her foot.

Lord Evarrim's smile did not reach his eyes, but his eyes darkened. "The mark is no protection here, little one. Remember that. No Barrani Lord is required to heed the mark of an outcaste."

"And no outcaste," Severn replied before she could speak, "is required to heed the law of the Dragon Emperor."

There was a silence; it followed and engulfed the Hawk's words.

"We will speak later," Lord Evarrim said at last. "After the Festival." He turned and walked away, and red swirled around his feet like blood.

They picked up the pace. "What was that about?" Severn asked her when he was certain the Barrani Lord had passed beyond hearing.

Kaylin, less certain, took her time answering. "I think it was a…threat."

"Got that," Severn said. "Why?"

She shrugged. Any answer that made sense wasn't one she liked. She wondered what Teela was doing. It was better than wondering what was being done *to* her.

But at least she no longer felt tired.

The guards at the front doors were Swords. She recognized them, but she didn't stop to talk; they were slightly officious men and she was clearly underdressed.

She passed beneath the vaulted ceilings of the Aerie; it was almost empty. One lone Aerian flew across the cavernous space, his gray wings unfolding beneath colored glass. Severn tapped her shoulder gently, and she remembered that she was late.

She made it to the doors, and through them, at her usual speed—a dead run, with a small pause between two Hawks that she *did* know. They were almost smirking.

"Tanner," she said to the taller of the two, both humans, "how much trouble am I in?"

He laughed. "It depends."

"On what?"

"On how much Iron Jaw fancies entertaining an Imperial mage. For an hour."

She cringed.

* * *

Iron Jaw, as Marcus was affectionately called—depending on your definition of affectionate—was indeed speaking with a man who wore the robes of the Imperial Magi. They were gray with blue edges, a hood, and an unseemly amount of gold embroidery that faded under dim light.

The fact that the mage wasn't shouting was a hopeful sign; the fact that Marcus wasn't puffed out like an angry cat was better. His arms were folded in front of his chest, and he'd chosen to abandon his chair, but that might have been because the paperwork would have hidden him otherwise.

She could hope.

Severn peeled off just before she reached the office, and she didn't have time to either thank or curse him, which was just as well. She had enough time to try to straighten her tunic as the office staff turned to look at her. Well, most of the office staff. Some of them were too busy to notice anything that didn't involve a lot of screaming, fire, or blood.

Marcus was, of course, aware of her; he'd probably been aware of her presence before she'd laid eyes on him. Leontines had good hearing and an exceptional sense of smell. But he was being Polite Leontine today.

Which was scary.

She made her way to his desk, and stood there, to one side of the back of an Imperial mage.

"Private," Marcus said in a rolling growl.

Okay, so it wasn't all good.

"Sergeant Kassan," she replied. She didn't snap a salute, but she did straighten up. It added an inch or two to her unimpressive height.

"Good of you to join us. In your absence, I've been explaining some of your unfortunate nocturnal habits to our *guest*."

The emphasis on the last word was like a warning, but with fangs and fur.

The Imperial mage turned; he was slightly bent, as if age was a burden, and his hair was a fringe of pale white. But his eyes—his eyes were a golden hue, and his smile was a quirk of lips over pale teeth.

She recognized the man. "You—but you're a—you aren't a—you—"

"Kaylin is not usually lauded for her ability to give impromptu speeches," Marcus said dryly. "I believe you've met Lord Sanabalis?"

They were sequestered in the West Room. Marcus led them there, opened the door, and held it while Sanabalis walked past him. Kaylin hesitated for just a moment, and then she made her way toward the room's round table.

"Do *not* annoy this man," Marcus said in her ear.

She nodded automatically. Of course, had he told her to stand on her head with her fingers in her ears in that same tone of voice, she would have nodded, as well.

But in this case, the desire to cause annoyance was vanishingly small; Sanabalis was a member of the Dragon Court. She'd seen him only once, and once had been enough.

He waited for her to take a seat.

She waited for him to do likewise.

After a moment, the older man—if that was even the

right word—shook his head; his eyes were still gold, which was a good sign. In Dragons.

"Please," he said, "sit."

She obeyed, and almost missed the chair.

He chose, tactfully, not to notice this error, and once she'd managed to stay seated, he took a seat. The table between them felt brittle and thin, although a man with an ax would have had some difficulty splitting it. A large man with a large ax; the table in the West Room had been built to last.

"Yes," he said before she could think of something to say, "I *am* a member of the Imperial Order of Mages. I am, as you are also aware, a member of the Dragon Court, and I confess I am seldom called away from that court." His smile was genial, even avuncular. She didn't trust it.

But she wanted to.

He reached into the folds of his robes; you could have hidden whole bodies in it. And bodies might have been preferable to paper, which was what he pulled out. It hit the table with an authoritative thud.

"You will, of course, be familiar with much of what these documents contain. These," he added, lifting a half inch's worth, "are your academic transcripts. With annotations."

"You're not supposed to have those—even I don't have access to—"

"As a man who is considering accepting you as a pupil, I have, of course, obtained permission to access these."

"Oh." She hesitated and then added, "What do they say?"

"You tell me."

This wasn't going the way the previous lessons had. So

far, he'd failed to make mention of her "unfortunate begin-nings." Which meant he'd also failed to offend her.

"I'm waiting, Kaylin."

"Probably…that I'm not very good at classroom work. Academic work, I think they call it."

He raised a brow. "That was a very short sentence for this much writing."

"They're clever, they can say the same thing over and over without using the same word twice."

At that, he did smile.

Oh, what the hell. "I'm not fond of authority."

"Good."

"I'm not fond of sitting still."

"True, as well."

"I get bored easily."

"I believe the phrase was 'dangerous levels of boredom.'"

"I'm not great with numbers."

"You manage an argument over your pay chit at least once a month."

"Oh, well, money's different." She frowned. "They said *that*?"

"No. That was private investigation on my part."

"I'm a bit brusque."

"'Actively rude.'"

"I'm blunt."

"'Arrogant and misinformed.'"

"I'm a bit on the, um, assertive side."

"I think the previous statement covered that, as well." He put the papers down. "The rest?"

"Variations?"

"Not precisely." He leaned forward on elbows he placed, with care, to either side of the documents in question. "You are, according to the teachers who failed you, frustratingly bright. One even used the word *precocious*. But you have no focus, no ability to pay attention to anything that doesn't suit you. Would you say that's fair?"

"No."

"What would you say, Kaylin?"

"I want to be *out there*. I want to be *on the beat*. I want to be *doing something*. I didn't sign up with the Hawks to sit still while other people risk their lives—"

He lifted a hand. "I believe that this was also covered. And quoted. At length. Don't feel a need to revisit it on my behalf. You did manage to learn to read. And to write. In two languages."

"I had to," she said woodenly. "The Hawklord—"

He raised a white brow.

"Lord Grammayre," she said, correcting herself, "said I was *out* if I couldn't manage that. Because the Laws are written in Barrani—High Barrani—and if I didn't know them, I couldn't enforce them."

"'Represent them' were the words he used, I believe. You learned to use weapons."

She nodded.

"And you were skilled at unarmed combat."

She nodded again. "Those were useful."

"History does have its uses."

"To dead people," she said sullenly.

"Living people define themselves by their dead."

She said nothing.

"You almost passed comparative religion. You paid very little attention to Racial classes."

More nothing.

"Very well. Your teachers—Hawks, all—were of a mind to allow you to stretch your wings on the streets. I believe they thought it would knock sense into you."

"You didn't come here to discuss my academic record."

"Actually, Kaylin, I did. I assure you I seldom discuss things that are not of interest to me. That would be called politics," he added. "And I see that you—"

"Failed that, yes."

"Why?"

"Because I'm not going anywhere *political*. If you've read the records you *know* I'm a fiefling. I grew up there. I lived there. I probably broke a hundred laws without knowing I was doing anything illegal." She had folded her arms across her chest, and she now tightened them. "I was born to the streets. I *know* them."

"The streets of Elantra are *not* the streets of Nightshade. I'm certain your other teachers were willing to accept this rant at face value. Do better with me, Kaylin. I'm old enough to value my time."

She stood up and started to pace.

"Don't cling to your ignorance."

"I'm not."

"Don't hide behind it, either."

"I'm *not* hiding. Yes, the *rest* of Elantra is different. But people with power are the same everywhere—here they just have to be more clever about breaking the law. I'm not good with people who are above the law."

"Or beneath it?"

"No, I understand *them*."

"You've been willing to learn many things," he continued, failing to notice that she'd left her seat. "You spent four weeks—without pay—at the midwives guild."

She stopped moving.

"I told you, I do my homework. You also, I believe, spend time at the foundling halls—"

"Leave the foundling halls out of this."

"—teaching the orphans. To *read*. To *write*. You could barely stand to do this yourself, and I cannot think that this is an overt display of aggression. How, then, do you explain it?"

"I don't."

He nodded, as if the answer wasn't surprising. "Very well. Let us change the course of this discussion somewhat."

"Let's not."

He raised a brow over golden eyes. So far, she'd failed to annoy him; there wasn't even a *hint* of orange in them.

"I am aware that teaching or learning are not the only things you do, at either the midwives guild or the foundling halls." He raised a hand. "I *am* advisor to the Emperor, Kaylin. I am aware of the power you do possess. Sadly, so are the rest of the Hawks. Secrecy is not a skill you've learned."

"Emergencies don't lend themselves to secrecy."

"True. Power does. Do you understand that you *have* power?"

She hesitated; the ground beneath her feet was shifting, and in ways that she didn't like. She thought better of her need to leave the confinement of the damn chair, and sat again, hard.

"Yes," he said softly, the tone of his voice changing. "I know what you bear on your arms and legs. I've seen the records. I've even examined them. I know that you've healed the dying, on many occasions. But I also know—"

She held up a hand, palm out, and turned away.

He was a Dragon, through and through. "I also know that you've used that power to kill. To kill quickly, yes, but also to kill slowly and painfully. I understand that the Imperial Order of Mages can at times be insular. I understand that their insularity feels like condescension. I will not even argue that it is anything else, in your case.

"But you are playing games with something that you don't understand."

"You don't understand it either."

"No," he said without pause. "And it is because it is not understood that it is feared. You've treated this as a game, Kaylin Neya. The time for games has passed." His eyes were still gold, but his lower lids rose, lending opacity to the clarity of color.

"The Dragon Emperor is well aware of what you faced in the fief of Nightshade. We do not name the outcaste, and because we do not, I do not believe it has occurred to the Emperor—or his Court—that you *can*."

She frowned.

"Names have power, Kaylin."

"I…know."

"Good. It is not to light candles that I have come—and yes, I am aware of what you did with the last one—although candles are a focal exercise that even the most junior of mages must master."

"Why?"

"Because it shows us that they are in control of their power, and not the inverse. And for most, it *is* a struggle. You would be an object of envy for many of the students that pass through our doors."

"I don't want to pass through your doors."

"No. And I think it best for the Order that you never do. I will be honest with you, because it is something you understand. We—none of us who know—are certain you *can* be taught. Do you understand this? We do not know what you are capable of yet. It is to test your capabilities that we have been sent."

"Why didn't they just——"

"Say so? It may have escaped your notice, but the Imperial Order of Mages is not accustomed to explaining themselves to a young, undereducated girl."

"You are."

"I have less to lose," he replied quietly. "And I am aware, as perhaps they were not, of how much *you* have to lose, should we fail. Or rather, should *you* fail."

This caught her attention and dragged it round in a death grip.

"Yes," he continued in that serene voice. "Should you fail, you will be called up before the Dragon Emperor. The fact that you are, without question, loyal to the Hawks has caused the Emperor—twice—to stay his hand. I cannot think of a person for whom he has stayed his hand three times. If you cannot be trained, if you *cannot* learn to abide these classroom chores, these boring hours spent staring at an unlit candle wick, you will be removed from the ranks of the Hawks."

"Will I still be alive?"

Sanabalis did not answer the question.

"Can I ask a different question?"

"You are free to ask anything."

"Who else has he stayed his hand with twice?"

Sanabalis's frosted brows drew closer together. "Pardon?"

"You said you couldn't think of a person to whom he'd granted clemency three times. That implies that you *can* think of a person to whom he's granted it twice. I mean, besides me."

At that, the Dragon laughed. The sound almost deafened her, and she was glad she was in the West Room; nothing escaped its doors. "You are an odd woman, Kaylin Neya. But I think I will answer your question, since it is close to my heart." She didn't ask him which heart; she understood it was metaphor.

"Lord Tiamaris of the Dragon Court."

Her jaw almost dropped; it probably would have if it hadn't been attached to the rest of her face. Tiamaris, honorary Hawk, was so…prim and proper it was hard to imagine he could ever do anything to offend his Lord.

"Lord Tiamaris was the last student I chose to accept," he added. "At my age, students are seldom sent to me."

"Why?"

"I am the Court of last resort, Kaylin. If I judge a mage to be unteachable, or unstable, no one else will take him."

"Because he's dead?"

Again, the Dragon was silent.

"In your case," Sanabalis continued smoothly, after the momentary silence, "you could have offended a full quarter of the Magi before you reached me. But because of the unusual nature of your talents, that was not considered a viable option." He reached into his robes and pulled out a candle.

She wilted visibly.

"This is like, very like, Barrani," he told her as he set the candle on a thin base and placed it exactly between them. "If you fail to learn it, you lose the Hawks."

"And my life."

"I am not convinced that they are not one and the same. I will take you," he added quietly. "If you are wearing your bracer, you may remove it."

Kaylin froze. Well, everything about her did but her eyes; they flicked nervously down to her wrist. Which was just wrist. The artifact, golden and jeweled, that could somehow dampen all of her magical abilities? Not there. She had a good idea where it actually was, too. "I'm not wearing it."

A pale brow rose. "I believe the Emperor's orders in that regard were quite clear."

She swallowed. Being in trouble was something that she lived with; she always was. Getting the Hawklord into *Imperial* trouble was something she would almost die to avoid.

And Sanabalis was *good*; he didn't even make the threat. She would have to watch herself around him, inasmuch as that was possible.

"I had to take it off," she told him, swallowing. "Last night." It wasn't technically true, but it would have to do.

"Ah. The midwives?" His eyes were gold; one brow was slightly above the other, but he chose to accept her words at face value.

"They called me in. I can't do *anything* when I'm wearing that bracer. I certainly can't deliver a baby that's—"

He lifted his hands. "I am squeamish by nature, I would prefer you leave the feminine nature of your nocturnal activities unspoken."

She wanted to ask him to define squeamish, but thought better of it.

"Where is it now?"

"At home."

"Whose home?"

She cursed. "Is there anything about me you didn't 'investigate'?"

"No."

And sighed, a deep, short sound that resembled a grunt. "Severn's. Corporal."

He nodded. "Very good. Get it back. I will overlook its absence, since you wouldn't be wearing it during these lessons anyway." He paused. His eyes were still liquid gold, and his expression had never wavered; there was some deep sympathy lurking in the folds of his face that she didn't understand.

And she wanted it.

"Lord Grammayre has been very cooperative, he has aided me in every conceivable way in my investigations. I believe he would like you to survive these trials. Inasmuch as the Lord of Hawks can afford to be, he is fond of you. And inasmuch as it is wise, he does trust you."

And you, old man? she thought, staring at the candle that

was unremarkable in every way. Dull, white, mostly straight, with a small waxed wick, it stood in the center of the table.

"Not yet," he replied. "And if you wish to keep your thoughts to yourself, you will learn to school your expression. I'm old, and given to neither sentiment nor tact. If I trust you, in the end, it will because you've earned it.

"And I understand you, Kaylin Neya. You value nothing that you have not earned. You want it, covet it, hold it in some regard—but you don't value it." His face lost its perpetual smile, and his lower lids fell, exposing his eyes again. "Begin with the shape of fire," he told her quietly.

What the hell shape did fire have, after all?

It was going to be a *long* lesson.

Or it should have been.

But the West Room had a door, and when the door swung wide, Kaylin jumped out of her chair. Literally. She had a dagger out of its sheath, and she was moving to put the table between herself and whatever it was that had *slammed* that door into the wall.

Her brain caught up with her body, and she forced herself to relax, or to mimic it. It was hard when the door was full of bristling Leontine.

Sanabalis, however, had not moved an inch. As Kaylin stilled, as she took in Marcus in full fury, he lifted his chin an inch or two. "Sergeant Kassan?" The inquiry was about as friendly as a rabid feral, but a whole lot politer.

"You're wanted," Marcus said to Kaylin, ignoring the mage he'd told *her* not to offend. "Tower. Now."

"The Hawklord?"

"No, the tooth fairy. *Go*."

"I believe the lesson will have to wait," Sanabalis said, rising.

On any other day, that would have been a good thing. But Kaylin had to walk past Marcus, and Marcus seemed disinclined to actually move his bulk out of the door. His fangs were prominent.

"Marcus?" she dared as she approached him.

He turned red eyes on her, and she flinched—which was always a bad thing to do around a Leontine. But his eyes lost their deep flare of red as he saw her expression. "No," he said curtly, the single word a raw growl. "It's not about you. Yet." He stepped aside then, and she ran past him. The office seemed quiet, which was usually a bad sign—but not when Marcus was in a mood. When that happened, the word that best described the room was *empty*. This wasn't, quite.

She caught Caitlin's expression; it was frozen on her face. The rest of her had retreated to a safe distance. It was an art that Kaylin could appreciate and couldn't master; she didn't try.

"How bad is it?" she asked.

Caitlin only pointed to the far door, the tower door, and shook her head.

Kaylin practically flew up the stairs. Fear did that; it shoved exhaustion into a small corner for later use. Given the previous night, it was going to see a lot of use.

The door, thank whatever gods the Hawklord worshipped— if he did—was already open; he was waiting for her.

Standing beside him was a tall, elegant stranger in a fine, dark dress the color of mythic forest. She wore a small tiara, with an emerald that would beggar small houses to own, and her slender arms were gloved in a pale green that echoed the dress.

Her hair, Barrani black, was loose; it fell past Kaylin's immediate vision. Barrani hair wasn't worth noticing; eyes were. Hers were blue. But they were an odd shade of blue, not the dark, deep sapphire that marked so many of the Barrani; these were almost teal.

Kaylin couldn't recall seeing that shade before, and it made her nervous.

The Hawklord, however, was grim, and that was perversely calming. Kaylin started to bow, and he cut her off with a gesture. Formality was out.

"Kaylin," he said, his voice a shade grimmer than his expression, "your services are required."

She stared at him blankly. Something about the woman was familiar. Something— "Teela?"

"She hasn't gotten any faster on the uptake, has she?" Teela said to the Hawklord.

"Nor has she become more punctual. Teela will take you where you need to go." He paused. "Do *exactly* as she says. No more. No less."

"Where are we going?"

"Definitely not faster," Teela said, her Elantran jarringly at odds with her appearance. "We go," she added, sliding into High Barrani, "to the Court of the castelord."

"But you said—"

"I know what I said. But we don't have time."

"What—you don't need me as a Hawk."

"Smart girl. Slow, but smart."

"Teela—what's happened?"

"There has been a minor difficulty at Court," Teela replied, reaching out for Kaylin's arm. Kaylin was too stunned to move out of the way. "If we do not repair to the Court in time, it will become a major difficulty."

"How major?"

"War."

That was major. Kaylin looked down at her pants, hating Nightshade.

"Severn is waiting below," the Hawklord told her quietly. "I've summoned a carriage. It's an Imperial carriage."

Teela began to drag her out of the tower room, but the Hawklord had not yet finished. "Go quickly, and return quickly. Do *not* leave Severn's side."

CHAPTER 5

Severn was waiting. He was tucked into a corner of the carriage, and appeared to be sleeping. Or he would have, had she known him a little less well. She watched him for a moment; his closed lids were like fine-veined membranes, round and edged in a black fringe. His hair was actually pushed up over his forehead by a knotted band; she didn't recognize the knotwork, but it was expensive enough to be official. He looked nothing at all like the boy she'd grown up with.

And yet, at the same time, exactly like him.

She shook her head; too much time spent looking and not enough *moving*. When she scrabbled up on the bench beside him, he opened an eye.

"Did you offend the mage?"

She snorted. "The mage is probably impossible to offend." Then, slightly more quietly, "No. I didn't."

"Good."

Bastard. He was smartly attired; he wore dress uniform, and it even looked good on him. His scars made him look like a Ground Hawk in any case; there was probably no clothing so ostentatious that it could deprive him of that.

The door slammed shut.

"Where's Teela?" she asked.

"She's driving."

"She's *what?*"

"You have a problem with that?"

Gods, Kaylin thought. This was an *Imperial* carriage.

It lurched to a start. "Yes!"

Severn managed to grip the window; it was the only reason he was still seated. He glared up through the coach wall. "Never mind."

"What happened to the driver?"

Severn's head disappeared out the window, and reappeared just as quickly; the window was *not* a safe place to hang a necessary appendage if you wanted it attached at the end of the journey. Not when Teela was driving. "He's the large man in livery with the purple face?"

"I'm not looking," Kaylin told him.

"Just as well."

The carriage didn't stop. Not once. It teetered several times on the large base of its wheels, and Kaylin and Severn tried to balance the weight by throwing themselves in the opposite direction. But Imperial carriages were heavy enough to carry four Dragons; they didn't tip easily. If she had thought Teela was aware of this fact, it would have eased her somewhat—but she'd been in a carriage that Teela had driven before. Once.

She'd promised herself—and everyone else who could hear—that she'd never do it again. So much for promises.

Then, Tain had been her companion, and he had found the entire journey amusing, especially the part where Kaylin turned green. You had to love that Barrani sense of humor; if you didn't, you'd try to kill them. Which was, of course, suicide.

Severn was not turning green. As if acrobatics on the interior of a very unstable vehicle were part of his training, he moved in time with the bumps, raised stones, and ruts that comprised the roads that Teela had chosen.

But these passed quickly by, as did the large, narrow buildings that fronted the streets, casting their shadows and shielding the people who were smart enough to get the hell out of the way.

The roads widened, and smoothed, as the carriage picked up speed. Beyond the windows, the buildings grew grander, wood making way for stone, and stone for storeys of fenced-off splendor that spoke of both power and money. The towers of the Imperial palace could be seen, for a moment, in the distance; the red-and-gold of the Imperial standard flew across the height of sky. Only the Halls of Law had towers that rivaled it, and that, by Imperial fiat; no other building erected since the founding of the Empire of Ala'an was allowed, by law, to reach higher.

There *were* other buildings with towers as high, but they were in the heart of the fiefs, where even Kaylin had not ventured. Not often. They were old, and had about them not splendor but menace; they spoke of death, and the wind that whistled near those heights spoke not of flight but of falling.

She shook herself. Severn was watching—inasmuch as he could, given the rough ride.

"The fiefs," he said. Not a question.

She swallowed and nodded. The years stretched out between them. Death was there, as well. In the end, Severn looked away—but he had to; the carriage had tipped again.

There was *so much* she wanted to know. And so much she was afraid to ask. She'd never been good with words at times like these; they were awkward instead of profound, and they were almost always barbed.

Instead, she tried not to lose the food she hadn't had.

"Remind me," he said when the carriage began to slow, "never to let Teela drive again."

She tried to smile. "As if," she told him, "you'll need a reminder." Her legs felt like liquid.

He had the grace not to ask her how she was; he had the sense not to ask her if she would be all right. But as the carriage came to a halt in front of tall, stone pillars carved in the likeness of a Barrani Lord and Lady, he opened the door that was nearest him. He slid out, dragging his feet a few steps, and then righted himself.

She closed her eyes.

His hand touched her arm. "Kaylin," he said quietly. "Come."

She nodded, biting her lip as she opened her eyes and met his gaze. The pillars were perfect in every aspect; Barrani writ large, like monumental gods, the falling folds of their robes embroidered with veins of gold and precious stones.

They dwarfed her. They made her feel ungainly, short, squat—and very, very underdressed.

But Severn wasn't Barrani. He didn't notice.

He offered her the stability of his arm and his shoulder, and she let him. The sun cast his shadow across her like a bower.

Teela jumped down from the driver's seat, and re-arranged the fall of her emerald skirts until the gold there caught light and reflected it, suggesting forest floor; the skirts were wide and long, far too long for someone Kaylin's height.

Teela spoke a few words to the horses, low words that had some of the sound of Barrani in them, but none of the actual words. The horses, foaming, quieted. Their nostrils were wide enough to fit fists in.

"Don't speak," Teela told Kaylin quietly as she left the horses and approached. She didn't seem to feel the need to offer the same warning to Severn.

Kaylin nodded. Speech, given the state of her stomach, was not something to which she aspired. She took a few hesitant steps, and mindful of the facade of the building that was recessed behind those columns, stopped. She had once seen a cathedral that was smaller than this. It had been rounder; the Barrani building favored flat surfaces, rather than obvious domes. But it was, to her eye, a single piece of stone, and trellises with startling purple flowers trailed down its face. A fountain stood between two open archways, and water trickled from the stone curve of an artfully held vase. The statue that carried the vase seemed a perfect alabaster woman, half-naked, her feet immersed.

She looked almost lifelike.

And Kaylin had seen statues come to life before, in the halls of Castle Nightshade.

"Kaylin," Teela said, the syllables like little stilettos, "*what are you doing?*"

"Staring," she murmured. Half-afraid, now that she was here. It was almost like being in a foreign country. She had never ventured to this part of Elantra before. Would not, in fact, have been given permission to come had she begged on hands and knees.

Standing here, she knew why; she *did not* belong on this path. Unnoticed until that thought, she looked at what lay beneath her feet. She had thought it stone, but could see now that it was softer than that. Like moss, like something too perfect to be grass, it did not take the impression of her heavy—and scuffed—boots.

Teela jabbed her ribs. "We don't have time," she whispered. It was the most Teela-like thing she'd done since Kaylin entered the Hawklord's tower, and the familiarity of the annoyed gesture was comforting. And painful; the Barrani had bony hands.

She swallowed and nodded, and Teela, grabbing her by the hand, began to stride toward the left arch.

It was work just to keep up. Kaylin stumbled. Her legs still hadn't recovered from the ride. But she had just enough dignity that she managed to trot alongside the taller Barrani noble. Severn walked by her side with ease and a quiet caution that spoke of danger.

She noticed, then, that he wore a length of chain wrapped round his waist, the blade at one end tucked out of sight.

He had not unwound it, of course; he wasn't a fool. There were no obvious guards at either arch, no obvious observers, but Kaylin had a suspicion that Teela would have taken it upon herself to break his arms if he tried.

Kaylin wanted to marvel at the architecture, and buildings rarely had that effect on her. She wanted to see Aerians sweeping the heights above, and Leontines prowling around the pillars that were placed beneath those heights, as if they held up not only ceiling but sky. She wanted to stop a moment to look at—to touch—the plants that grew up from the stone, as if stone were mooring.

But she did none of these things. Beauty was a luxury. Time was a luxury. She was used to living without.

A large hall—everything was large, as if this were designed for giants—opened up to the right. Teela, cursing in Elantran, walked faster. Kaylin's feet skipped above the ground as she dangled.

She saw her reflection in marble, and again in glass; she saw her reflection in gold and silver, all of them distorted ghosts. She couldn't help herself; Teela kept her moving, regardless.

There were candles above which flames danced; nothing melted. There were pools of still water, and the brilliant hue of small fish added startling life to their clarity. Too much to see.

And then there were doors, not arches, and the doors were tall. There were two, and each bore a symbol.

Her natural dislike of magic asserted itself as Teela let her go. But Teela stepped forward, and Teela placed her palms flat against the symbols. The doors swung wide, and without looking, Teela grabbed Kaylin and dragged her across the threshold.

She didn't even see the doors swing shut. She saw Severn skirt them as they moved, that was all. She had scant time to notice the room they'd entered.

It was an antechamber of some sort. There were chairs in it, if that was even the right word. They seemed more like trees, to Kaylin's untutored eyes, and branches rose up from their base, twisting and bearing bright fruit.

These, Teela passed.

They had walked a city block, or two, in Kaylin's estimation; everything was sparse and empty.

The chamber passed by, and they entered one long hall. This was older stone, and harsher. It was rough. There were no plants here, and no flowers, no gilded mirrors and no pools. Weapons adorned the walls instead; weapons and torch sconces of gleaming brass.

But the weapons were fine, and their hilts were jeweled. If the gems were cold, they added the fire of color to the hall itself. "Don't touch anything," Teela said in curt Elantran.

At the end of this hall was a single door.

Kaylin stopped walking then.

Teela didn't.

"Kaylin?" Severn asked. It was hard for him not to notice that her feet were now firmly planted to the floor.

"The door—" She looked up at him, trying not to struggle against Teela's grip. She hated to lose, even now. Animal instinct made it hard; she *did not* want to pass through that door.

"Teela," Severn said, curt and loud.

Kaylin's ineffectual struggle hadn't actually garnered the Barrani's attention; Severn's bark did. She stopped walking and looked back at him.

Kaylin's gaze bounced between them a couple of times, like a die in a random game of chance. "The door," she said at last, when she came up sapphires. Teela's eyes.

Teela frowned, and those eyes narrowed. But she asked no further question. Instead, she turned to *look* at the door. It was a Hawk's gaze, and it transformed her face.

Her cursing transformed her voice. It was short, but it lingered. "Step back," she said. She turned back down the hall and dragged a polearm from the wall. It was a halberd.

"Farther back," she added as she readied the haft. Severn caught Kaylin by the shoulders, frowned, and then lifted her off her feet. He ran back the way they'd come, leaving Teela behind. Kaylin could hear his heart. Could almost feel it, even though he wore armor. Funny thing, that.

"What are you—"

Teela *threw* the halberd. It wasn't a damn spear; it shouldn't have traveled like one. But it did.

The door *exploded*. It shattered, wooden shards the size of stakes blowing out in a circle. The halberd's blade shattered as well, and a blue flame burned in its wake.

Without a pause, Teela grabbed another weapon from the wall. It was a pike. She set its end against the floor and stood there, hand on hip, as if she were in the drill circle in the courtyard of the Halls of Law.

"What's it look like now?" she asked Kaylin.

Severn set her down gently, but he did not let go of her.

"It looks like a bloody big hole," Kaylin replied.

"A scary hole?"

"Could you be more patronizing?"

"With effort."

"Don't bother."

The fleeting smile transformed Teela's expression. It was grim, and it didn't last long. "Good spotting," she said, as if this were an everyday occurrence.

"Don't you think someone's going to be a bit upset?"

"Oh, probably." She didn't put the pike down. "Look at what it did to the frame." Her whistle was pure Hawk.

The stone frame that had held the door and its hinges looked like a standing crater. The roof was pocked.

"What *was* that?"

Teela shrugged. "A warning."

"A *warning?*"

"Of a sort. I imagine it was meant to be a permanent warning." She seemed to relax then. "Which means we still have some time." Then, thinking the better of it, she added, "But not much. Don't gawk."

That was Teela all over. Any *other* Hawk would have had the sense to ask Kaylin why she'd hesitated to go near the door. To Teela, the answer wasn't important. Which was good. Kaylin herself had no idea why, and extemporizing about anything that wasn't illegal betting was beyond her meager skills.

"Welcome," Teela added, her voice so thick with sarcasm it was a wonder words could wedge themselves through, "to the High Court." And taking the pike off the ground, holding it like she would the staff that was her favored weapon, she walked through the wreckage of the door.

Kaylin noted that Severn did not draw a weapon. And did not let go of her shoulder. They followed in Teela's wake.

There were no other traps. Or rather, no magical ones. Teela led them through another series of rooms and past two halls, and finally stopped in front of a curtained arch.

"Here," she said quietly. "There will be guards." She paused, and then added, "They're mine."

Which made no sense.

"In service to my line," Teela told her, as if this would somehow explain everything.

"Loyal?"

The muttered *humans* was answer enough. Teela pushed the curtains aside and entered the room. It was much larger than it looked through fabric.

There were chairs here, kin to the great chairs she'd seen in the large room, but smaller and paler in color. There was a still pond to the side of the room, adorned by rocks that glistened with falling water. Except that there wasn't any.

There was a table, but it was small; a mirror, but it, too, was modest.

Beyond all of these things was a large bed, a circular bed that was—yes—canopied. Golden gauze had been drawn, but it was translucent. She could see that someone lay there.

By the bed were four guards. They were dressed in something that should have been armor, but it was too ornate, too oddly shaped. Master artisans would have either wept or disdained such ostentation. Teela tapped the ground with the haft of the pike.

As one, the four men looked to her.

"This," Teela said, nodding to Kaylin, "is my *kyuthe*. She honors us by her presence."

Kaylin frowned. The word was obviously Barrani; it was stilted enough in delivery that it had to be High Barrani. But she didn't recognize it.

The guards looked at her. Two pairs of eyes widened slightly, and without thinking, Kaylin lifted a hand to cover her cheek. It was the first time she had remembered it since Severn had helped her out of the death trap that was otherwise known as a carriage.

"Yes," Teela said, her grip on her weapon tightening. "She bears the mark of the outcaste. Even so, you will not challenge me."

There was silence. A lot of it. And stillness. But it was the stillness of the hunter in the long grass of the plains.

Kaylin started to move, and Severn caught her arm in a bruising grip. He had not moved anything but his hand. But she met his eyes, and if human eyes didn't change color, if they didn't darken or brighten at the whim of mood, they still told the whole of a story if you knew the language.

Seven years of absence had never deprived her of what was almost her mother tongue. She froze, now part of him, and then turned only her face to observe Teela.

The Barrani Hawk was waiting.

Kaylin couldn't see her feet, and wanted to. She'd learned, over the years, that Teela adopted different stances for different situations, and you could tell by how she placed her feet what she expected the outcome to be.

But you couldn't hear it; she was Barrani, and almost silent in her movements. She looked oddly like Severn—

waiting, watchful. She did not tense, and the only hint of threat was in the color of her eyes.

But it was mirrored in the eyes of these four.

Hers, she'd called them. Kaylin had to wonder if Teela's grasp on the subtleties of Elantran had slipped.

The room was a tableau. Even breathing seemed to be held in abeyance. Minutes passed.

And then Teela turned her head to nod at Kaylin.

One of the four men moved. His sword was a flash of blue light that made no sound. He was fast.

Teela was faster. She lowered the pike as he lunged, and raised it, clipping the underside of his ribs. Left ribs, center. The pike punctured armor, and blood replied, streaming down the haft of the weapon—and down the lips of the guard.

Almost casually, the wide skirts no restriction, Teela kicked the man in the chest, tugging the pike free. Her gaze was bright as it touched the faces of the three guards who had not moved, neither to attack nor defend.

The Barrani who had dared to attack fell to his knees, and then, overbalanced, backward to the ground. Teela stepped over him and brought the wooden butt of the pike down before Kaylin could think of moving.

"*Kyuthe,*" Teela said. "Attend your patient."

Kaylin was frozen. Severn was not. He guided her, his arm around her shoulders; even had she wanted to remain where she was, she wouldn't have been able to. There was something about the warmth of his shoulder, the brief tightening of his hand, the scent of him, that reminded her of motion. And life.

She had seen Barrani in the drill halls before. She had seen them in the Courtyards. She had seen them on the beat, and she had even seen them close with thugs intent on misconstruing the intent of the Law. But she had never truly *seen* them fight.

Teela wasn't sweating. She didn't smile. She did not, in fact, look down. She had spoken in the only way that mattered here. And the three that were standing at a proud sort of attention had heard her clearly. They showed no fear; they showed no concern. The blood on the floor might as well have been marble. Or carpet.

Kaylin tried not to step in it.

She tried not to look at the Barrani whose throat had so neatly been staved in.

"Do not waste pity," Teela told her in a regal, High Caste voice. "There is little enough of it in the High Court, and it is not accorded respect."

Severn whispered her name. Her old name.

She looked up at him, and he seemed—for just an instant—so much taller, so much more certain, than she could ever hope to be. But his expression was grave. He reached out, when she couldn't, and he pulled the curtains aside.

There was a Barrani man in the bed.

His eyes were closed, and his arms were folded across his chest in the kind of repose you saw in a coffin. He was pale— but the Barrani always were—and still. His hair, like his arms, had been artfully and pleasantly arranged. There were flowers around his head, and in the cup of his slack hands.

"Who is he?" she asked, forgetting herself. Speaking Elantran.

"He is," Teela replied, her voice remote, her words Barrani, "the youngest son of the Lord of the High Court."

Kaylin reached out to touch him; her hands fell short of his face. It seemed…wrong, somehow. To disturb him. "What is he called?" she asked, stalling for time.

Teela did not reply.

Warning, in that. She reached out again, and again her hands fell short. But this time, the sense of wrongness was sharper. Harsher. Kaylin frowned. Her fingers were tingling in a way that reminded her of…the Hawklord's door.

Magic.

She gritted teeth. Tensed. All of her movements were clumsy and exaggerated in her own sight.

But they *were* hers. "There's magic here," she said quietly.

Teela, again, said nothing.

Kaylin opened her palms, forced them to rest above the only exposed skin she could touch: his face, his perfect face. Now magic crawled through her skin, ran up her arms, burning sharply.

If I explode, she thought sourly, *I hope I kill someone.* She wasn't feeling particular.

She forced her hands down, and down again, as if she were reaching from a height. She would have fallen, but Severn was there, steadying her. She whispered his name, or thought she did. She could feel her lips move, but could hear no sound.

No sound at all save the crackle of magic, the fire of it. She kept pushing; it was an effort. Like bench-pressing weight, but backward. Holding on to that because she was stubborn, she continued.

Severn's arm was around her; she could feel it. She could no longer feel her feet, and even her legs, which were almost shaking with exhaustion, seemed numb. She whispered his name again. It was as close to prayer as she came.

Hawk, she thought. And Hawk she was.

She plummeted as her hands, at last, made contact.

Kaylin had never tended Barrani before. Oh, she'd helped with the occasional scratch they managed to take—where help meant Moran's unguents and barbed commentary—but she had never *healed* them. The Barrani did not go to Elantran midwives. Leontines did; Aerians did; even the Tha'alani had been known to call upon their services.

They were all mortal.

The Barrani were not, and they really liked to rub people's noses in the fact.

Nor had Kaylin tended their young, their orphans. The only orphans in the foundling hall were human.

She had once offered to help a Dragon, and she had been curtly—and completely—refused. She understood why, now.

"He's alive," she managed to say. More than that would have been a struggle. Because *alive* in this case meant something different than it had every other time she offered this assurance to onlookers, many often insensate with fear and the burden of slender hope.

His skin felt like skin. And it felt like bark. It felt like moss, and fur, and the soft silk of Barrani hair; it felt like petals, like chiton, like nothing—and everything—that she had ever touched before. And there was more, but she hadn't the words for it.

She almost pulled back, but Severn was there, and he steadied her. She could feel his hair brush the back of her neck, and realized her head was bent. Her eyes were closed.

The room was invaded by scent: rose and lilac, honey, water new with spring green; sweat, the aroma of tea—tea?—and sweet wine, the smell of *green*. The green. Behind her eyes she could sense the bowers of ancient forest, could almost hear the rustle of great leaves.

But here, too, she found silence. The silence of the smug, the arrogant, the pretentious; the silence of concern, of compassion; the silence of grief too great for simple words; the silence that follows a child's first cry. She found so many silences, she wondered what the use of language was; words seemed impoverished and lessened.

But she did not find the silence of the dead.

Her hands were warm now. The fires had cooled, banked. What they could burn, they had burned, and embers remained. She moved her fingers slowly, and felt—skin. Just skin.

When she had healed Catti, the redhead with the atrocious singing voice, she had almost had to become Catti. Here, she was alone. There was no wound she could sense, and no loss of blood, no severed nerves along the spine. There was nothing at all that seemed wrong, and even in humans, that was unnatural.

So. This was perfection.

Unblemished skin. Beating heart. Lungs that rose and fell. An absence—a complete absence—of bruise, scar, the odd shape of bone once broken and mended.

She wanted to let go then. To tell Teela that this Barrani Lord—this son of the castelord—was alive and well.

But she didn't. Because her hands still tingled. Because there was something beneath her that she could not see, or touch, or smell, that eluded her. Like dim star at the corner of the eye, it disappeared when she turned to look.

She opened her mouth, and something slid between her lips, like the echo of taste.

Without thinking, she said, "Poison?"

Which was good, because the only person who could answer was Kaylin. Yet poison…what had Red said? Poison caused *damage*. And there was nothing wrong with this man.

Except that he lay in bed, arranged like a corpse.

Had she not seen Teela dispose of a Barrani, she would have wondered if *this* was how immortals met their end. But the dead man had bled, and gurgled; his injuries had been profoundly mundane.

War.

The word hung in the air before her, as if it were being written in slow, large letters. As if she were, in fact, in school, and the teacher found belaboring the obvious a suitable punishment. Humiliation often worked.

It just didn't work well on fieflings.

The Barrani Lord slept beneath her palms. Time did not age him; it did not touch him at all. But Kaylin, pressed against his skin, didn't either.

This is beyond me, she thought, and panic started its slow spiral from the center of her gut, tendrils reaching into her limbs.

Severn's arm tightened.

She heard his voice from a great remove. "Anteela," he

said, pronouncing each syllable as if Barrani were foreign to him, "your *kyuthe* must know what the Lord is called." Not named; he knew better than that. And how? Oh, right. He'd passed his classes. She'd had to learn it the hard way.

"He is called the Lord of the West March," Teela replied.

"By his friends?"

"He is the son of the High Lord," was the even response. It was quieter but sharper; she could hear it more distinctly. And she could read between the lines—he didn't have any friends.

"Anteela, do better. Your *kyuthe* cannot succeed at her chosen task, otherwise."

But Teela did not speak again.

Lord of the West March. Kaylin tried it. As a name, she found it lacking. He must have found it lacking, as well. There was no response at all. There was nothing there.

Swallowing air, Kaylin opened her eyes. And shut them again in a hurry.

But she was a Hawk, and the first thing that had been drilled into her head—in Marcus's Leontine growl—was the Hawk's first duty: observe. What you could observe behind closed eyes was exactly nothing. Well, nothing useful. There were situations in which this was a blessing. Like, say, any time of the day that started before noon.

But not now, and not here. Here, Kaylin was a Hawk, and here, she unfurled figurative wings, and opened clear eyes.

She was standing on the flat of a grassy slope that ended abruptly, green trailing out of sight. Above her, the sky was a blue that Barrani eyes could never achieve; it was bright, and if the sun was not in plain view, it made its presence felt.

There were, below this grass-strewn cliff, fields that stretched out forever. The sun had dried the bending stalks, but whether they were wild grass or harvest, she couldn't tell. She'd never been much of a farmer.

The fields were devoid of anything that did not have roots.

She turned as the breeze blew the stalks toward her, and following their gentle direction, saw the forest. It was the type of forest that should have capital letters: The Forest, not *a* forest. The trees that stretched from ground to sky would have given her a kink had she tried to see the tops; it didn't.

But she wasn't really here.

Remind me, she told herself, *never to heal a Barrani again.*

She wondered, then, what she might have seen had Tiamaris not had the sense to forbid her the opportunity to heal a Dragon. She never wanted to find out.

There were no birds in this forest. There were no insects that she could see, no squirrels, nothing that jumped from tree to tree. This was a pristine place, a hallowed place, and life did not go where it was not wanted.

This should have been a hint.

But there were only two ways to go: down the cliff or into the trees. The cliff didn't look all that promising.

She chose the forest instead. It wasn't the kind of forest that had a footpath; it wasn't the kind of forest that had any path at all.

It was just a lot of very ancient trees. And the shadows they cast. *All right, Lord of the West March, you'd better bloody well be in there.*

She started to walk. In that heavy, stamping way of children everywhere.

* * *

Shadows gave way to light in places, dappled edges of leaves giving shape to what lay across the ground. She got used to them because they were everywhere, and she'd walked everywhere, touching the occasional tree just to feel bark.

If time passed, it passed slowly.

Her feet—her boots still scuffed and clumsy—didn't break any branches. They didn't, in fact, leave any impression in what seemed to be damp soil. Rich soil, and old, the scent mixed with bark and undergrowth. She could plant something here and watch it grow.

Her brow furrowed. Or at least she thought it did. Aside from the forest itself, everything—even Kaylin—seemed slightly unreal.

She reached into her pockets, and stopped.

Her arms were bare, and in the odd light of the forest, she could see the markings that had defined all of her life, all action, all inaction, all cost.

She held them out; the marks were dark and perfect. It had been a while since she'd looked at them in anything that wasn't the mirror of records. She touched them and froze; they were raised against her skin. They had never had any texture before.

Lifting a hand, she touched the back of her neck; it, too, was textured. She thought she might peel something off, and even began to try.

"Kaylin."

She stopped. The voice was familiar. It was distant, but not in the way that Severn's words had been distant.

"Hello?"

"Do not touch those marks in this place."

It was Nightshade. Lord Nightshade. She turned, looked, saw an endless series of living columns. There was no movement, no sign of him.

"They're—I think they might come off."

"Do not," he said again, his voice fading. "I am far from you, and you are far from yourself. Leave, if you can."

She shrugged. "There doesn't seem to be a convenient door."

"Unfortunate."

"Where are you?"

"I am both close and far, as you are close and far. You have my name," he added softly. "Remember it."

"I…do." Even in sleep. "But I…don't think it's a good idea to speak it here."

CHAPTER 6

His laughter was a surprise to her; it was almost youthful. "You are a strange child," he said when it had trailed into silence. "What do you do, Kaylin Neya?"

"I—" She frowned.

"Where are you?"

"In a big damn forest."

The silence that followed her words was heavy, a different silence. She could not interpret it, who'd been offered the space of so many other silences simply by touching a stranger's skin. "Kaylin," he said in the tone of voice she *least* liked, "what have you done?"

It was, of course, a tone she was familiar with. Severn used it. Not many of the Hawks did, though; they had to drill with her sooner or later, and she sometimes forgot the rules.

"Teela dragged me to Court," she said curtly.

"To Court, Kaylin?"

"To the—to the Barrani High Court. Because the Lord of the West March was—wasn't—" Frustrated, she tossed the sentence out and started again. "I think he's been poisoned. I think he's dying. But not dying. *I don't understand it.*"

"I cannot come to you," he replied, as if she'd asked.

"No. You can't." The minute she said the words, they were true. As if words had that power in this place.

"Words have power in all places," he replied. She hated it when he did that. He couldn't even see her face, so the convenient "you're an open book" excuse was beyond them both.

"I can't leave if he doesn't wake up."

"You are not as foolish as you often appear. You are, unfortunately, far more reckless. I would have bet against it, were I offered odds."

She almost laughed.

"I *do* live in the fiefs," was his wry reply. And it hid nothing from her; she could sense his worry.

"I don't know how to make him wake up. But I thought—"

"Careful, Kaylin."

"I don't know his name," she said, flat now. "I don't have any way of finding him here. He's lost. I'm lost. I thought if I could plant something—"

"Plant something?"

The rich loam of the soil was beneath her hands as she bent. She knelt, and felt it, damp, against her knees. Which meant she wasn't wearing her old pants.

Looking down, she saw that she was, however, wearing

her tunic, and it was a good deal cleaner—and longer—than it had been minutes or hours ago. The Hawk was a thing of gold and flight. Death or freedom.

His silence was not a comfort.

She wanted to cling to his voice because she didn't want to be alone here. And she hated herself for the weakness because it meant she was buying into the illusion.

"It is not illusion," he said.

So much for morale.

She looked at her arms, above the wrists. "Nightshade," she whispered, "you'll just have to trust me."

"Oddly enough, I do. I trust you to be Kaylin Neya."

She chose to make the effort not to be insulted, and said, "For you, I could do this."

"Yes. For me. But you have my name, and it binds us. Were you to heal me, you would be a part of what you see."

"Would I see forest?"

Silence.

She responded in kind, but she didn't stop. Her fingers made impressions in the dirt, and the dirt turned her nails a rich, dark black. Digging was easy. It gave her something to do with her hands, and that was better than wandering around like an idiot pilgrim.

When she'd made a furrow a hand's depth in the dirt, she looked again at her arms. At the symbols that graced skin, that seemed more solid in this place than they had ever seemed. They didn't burn or glow; they just *were*.

They had been written by the Old Ones in ways that no "new ones"—that being anyone living, or having lived, in the last millennia—could understand. Certainly not Kaylin, whose grasp of the historical was accurate to the day. The one she was living in.

They had been changed by death and sacrifice, the sigil shapes shifting and altering almost imperceptibly with time. And they had been altered again, when she had returned to the heart of Castle Nightshade.

What they meant now, no one knew.

She studied them all, her eyes tracing thick curves and thin, as if they were a mandala that moved with her, lived in her. They looked the *same* at first glance. They looked the same at a tenth glance, and a few solid glares.

But there were differences. Very subtle differences.

Probably imaginary ones, given how long she'd been staring.

She chose one at random. Her fingers brushed its surface, and she felt it again, like a raised welt with sharper edges. Her nails were short enough to be useless and long enough to be dirty. She struggled to use them for some time, but they were blunt instruments.

So she reached for her daggers.

They weren't there. At least not the ones she was familiar with. She'd bought them with her own money, and she'd paid a small fortune in trade with a mendacious man who had actually been capable of some magic.

What was left in their place was dagger shaped. It even had a hilt. But it was translucent and fine, like a sliver of worked glass. It shone blue.

Blue was bad. This kind of blue, like a sliver of sky, reminded her of magic, and she *did not* want to lay it against her skin. Although curiosity had its uses, she had a bad feeling that shedding blood here would be costly.

"It will."

"Thanks." She sat in front of a trough of dirt, feeling like a pig. She was tired, and her stomach was rumbling.

Not the words, then. Not the marks.

They were hers, but they *weren't* hers.

And there was only one thing that she now wore that she valued. The Hawk shone gold.

Removing it was harder than she expected.

Laying it in the furrow, folding the tunic so that it could rest an inch below the space she'd managed to dig was worse.

Worse still, burying it. She had to close her eyes.

"Well done, little Kaylin." The voice was so soft now she could barely catch the words.

It's not real, she told herself as she stood and took a step back. But it *was* real. It was the only thing that was.

And because it was real, the ground closed over it. The scratches she'd made in its soft surface vanished; the rough, loose texture of new-turned earth smoothed out, as if the forest floor had flexed its hand and made a flat fist.

She watched a tree grow.

It was unlike any other tree in the forest. It was a pale color, and its bark was soft, almost golden in hue. There was no almost about its leaves; they shot out as branches unfurled, as roots spread beneath her feet, pushing her back. Even stumbling, she still sought sight of the sky through the bower of the other trees. Seeking sky, she caught gold instead. The leaves were like feathers, flight feathers, and they hung in the air as the branches that bore them rose, bursting toward the sky.

She watched; astonishment was too meager a word for what she felt.

It should have gone on forever.

Instead, the leaves began to fall. The breeze carried them. The wind swept them into the other trees, and where gold touched green, color happened. Red, yellow, burgundy, a riot that spoke of autumn, and the change of seasons.

When she looked down—when she could bear to look down—she saw that she still wore her boots. And that she wore an undershirt and loose-fitting pants.

It was better than being naked. But not by much.

She walked over to the trunk of what was now an immense tree, and wondered at the nature of age. It was of a height with the forest although it resembled no other tree that grew there, as if, although it was bound by the forest's rules, it was also bound by hers.

She leaned against the smooth, smooth trunk and picked up a leaf. It turned to dust in her hands, but it was a golden dust that made her skin shimmer.

A shadow crossed her hand as she stared at it, and she looked up. A Barrani man stood before her, his eyes the green of the leaves before they turned.

"You're the Lord of the West March?" she asked quietly.

He nodded; he barely spared her a glance. She would have mumbled something about gratitude, but his gaze had gone up to the leaves above, and he was staring in wonder. She almost hated to break the trance. She understood what he saw.

But she understood, as well, that they could not remain here forever. So she cleared her throat.

He looked down at her then. He was tall, even for a Barrani. "You are Kaylin Neya," he said.

"That's what I'm called."

"Ah. It is a title?"

"A name."

His brow rose. His eyes narrowed. "It is not a name," he said quietly. "There is only one name here."

"Yours, I take it."

But he stared at the tree. "And yet…I read it, there, in the leaves. You are a bird of prey. Whose jesses do you wear?"

"The Hawklord's," she replied, rising.

He bent and lifted a golden leaf. In his hands, it didn't crumble. Then again, ice probably wouldn't melt in his mouth, either.

He looked at her face. Frowned. Reaching out, he touched her cheek.

Her right cheek. "Nightshade," he said.

"It's a plant."

His smile was odd. "It is, as you say, a plant. I do not believe it grows here."

"No."

"And yet he sent you."

"No!"

"No?"

"I came."

"Bearing that mark, you dared the Court?"

She frowned. "How do you know where you are? You aren't—"

"I am aware." For just three words his voice held the ice of impassable distance; he was a man accustomed to power, or at least the respect best called fear. Then again, he *was* a Barrani High Lord. Not all of them could be as uncharming as Lord Evarrim.

"It was Teela."

"Teela?"

"Anteela."

"Ah. My cousin. The rebel."

"That's not what we call her."

"We?" His frown was more subtle this time, but then again, this time she wasn't calling his knowledge into question. "You—you're a Hawk?" He spoke the words slowly, as if only aware that she'd spoken them.

"A Ground Hawk."

He looked at the leaves that had scattered, touching the heights of other trees. "That is not all you are," he said at last. "But you are not lying."

She shrugged. "It's not one of my skills."

"Even were it, you would not be able to use it here."

"Look," she said, her hands sliding up to her hips and perching there, "if I understand the situation correctly, you're dying. You're going to stop me?"

His smile was more perturbing than his frown. "I was lost," he said. "You *are* human."

"More or less."

"This is not the place for you."

No kidding.

"What did you do here?"

"I...planted something. It grew."

His eyes were a shade of green. Just green. "Anteela must trust you. She has grown addled, and in so short a time." But he held out a hand. "It must be part of the nature of mortality."

"What must?"

"To be worthy of trust. You only have to manage it for a brief span of years. If you live forever, the task is more difficult." He held out a hand.

She stared at it.

"Do you know her name?"

"Do you?"

He laughed. "The Barrani do not trust each other."

"Well, then, she hasn't grown as stupid as you think. She doesn't trust me that much, either."

He shrugged. "I would not. You bear the mark of—"

"Yes, yes, I know. I don't mean to rush you, but I think we have to leave."

"Yes," he said, gazing above her head. "Here, when night falls, there will be no dawn."

"Good. How do we leave?"

He looked down again, one brow rising. "You came here without knowing how to return?"

She shrugged. "It seemed like a good idea at the time."

"I do not want to know what you consider a *bad* idea."

She looked away. "Asking you your name."

He touched her hand and she looked up.

"There are those among my kin who would die before they surrendered their name."

"That…seems to be the choice."

His eyes were still bright, and still green. He hadn't grown any shorter, either. He released her hand and walked to the trunk of the tree that had grown from the tunic. Wordless, he touched it, and his lashes fell. "There is perhaps another way," he said, his eyes closed. "But it would be poor gratitude for your daring." His hands crept up the surface of smooth bark, and he tilted his face as they moved; gold leaves fell about him in a shower of warmth and color.

Hawk's feathers.

When his eyes opened, they reflected gold. She had *never* seen a like color in the Barrani before. It was as if he were hollow, and the leaves themselves the only thing that filled him.

"You have given more than you know," he said quietly, "and you may yet regret it. I will not say—or have it said—that an ignorant human is capable of going where a Barrani High Lord will not.

"What will you do with my name?"

"Wake you," she whispered. And knew it for truth.

Had known it before she touched his still face in a room a world away.

He whispered a single word. *Lirienne.* His eyes did not leave her face, although the gold in them faded.

She hesitated.

"You are afraid."

She nodded.

"Why?"

"Names have power."

He laughed again. Leaves fell; breeze moved the branches high above them, changing the shape and texture of the shadows that dappled her feet. "You do not understand what a name *is,* Kaylin."

"I know," she whispered. And then, before she let hesitance rob her of all voice, she whispered another word.

The sky shattered.

She sat on a bed, her hands cupping the cheeks of a pale, beautiful face. Her own face was warm and wet. The room was dark beyond the fall of curtains; dark and lifeless. Where trees had stood, there were walls, and stone; there was marble along the floor, and the trickle of water beyond her shoulder.

And behind her, breath, stillness: Severn. His arm still locked around her waist, he whispered her name. Over and again, as if he had done nothing else since she had approached the Lord of the West March.

"I'm here," she told him, her voice cracking.

Her name died into stillness.

She lifted her hands, or started to.

The Lord of the West March caught them in his own, moving so suddenly, so unexpectedly, she almost cried out.

His eyes snapped open, and unblinking, he stared at her face. *Her* face, which was so square and dark and imperfect.

Before she could move, he let go of one hand, reached out, and pushed her sleeve up, past her wrist. There, exposed for just a moment, were the marks of the Old Ones, black against white.

He let the sleeve fall. "You do not know who you are," he told her quietly, and pushed her hands aside. The flowers that had been placed in his hands were now bruised, but their fragrance filled the room as he rose.

"Anteela," he said.

Teela offered him a *perfect* bow. "Lord," she replied.

"Where are my men?"

"They have been much occupied."

His eyes passed over the room. If he noticed the body that lay across the floor, it didn't seem to be worthy of comment.

"My father?"

"He holds his Council," she replied. Her voice was like smooth steel. Her eyes were blue. "But I believe that he waits upon you."

"Does he?"

She said nothing. Nothing at all.

"I will require my men," he told her at last. His voice was colder, as well.

Kaylin withdrew; felt Severn's chest against her back. She didn't move away. Didn't even want to. He was the only warmth in the room, and she felt like a moth must when drawn to the fire.

"You brought the mortal?"

"She is my *kyuthe*. She offered her aid, and I accepted it on your behalf. If I have displeased you, I will bear the burden of that displeasure." She set the pike against the wall.

"I have not existed for so long that living is unpleasant to me," he replied gravely. "But she is marked by the outcaste, and I do not feel that the Court is safe for her at this time. See her out."

Teela bowed again.

"Kaylin Neya," he said as Severn moved her toward Teela and the possibility of freedom, "do you *know* what the word *kyuthe* means?"

"It's High Barrani," Kaylin said. Which wasn't exactly a lie.

He raised a brow, and looked at Teela. "How much have you explained?"

Teela did not reply.

He turned to Kaylin, and the hint of a smile touched his lips. It did not, however, touch his eyes. They had darkened. "You cannot lie to me," he said softly. "Not there, and not here. My cousin has called you *kyuthe.*"

"Kaylin—" Teela began.

But the Lord of the West March raised an imperious hand, and Teela, raising her chin slightly, fell silent. The type of silence that precedes thunder.

"What you saw, you will not speak of, and live."

Kaylin nodded; Severn tensed.

"But what you saw, you changed. I will not ask you how. It is not relevant. *Kyuthe* means, in Elantran, 'blood of my blood.'" He waited, and when Kaylin's confusion became obvious, he frowned. "I have spent much time in the West," he said at last, "and little of it in the company of mortals. You cannot be kin, you are not Barrani. But Kaylin, what you planted was an offering, and nothing will unmake it.

"What Teela called you in haste, you are in truth—but you are mine. *Kyuthe.*" He was silent for a moment.

It was Teela who spoke, and heavily. "It means," she said, speaking in Elantran, "that you are, by choice—by all that choice implies—my clan. Blood of my blood is not accurate, although it is close. You are the blood of my choice, the family I would choose, if choice was given."

"It is more than that," the Lord of the West March said. And he, too, spoke in Elantran. "It is a choice that *you* have made, Kaylin."

"But I—"

"And among the Barrani, ignorance excuses *nothing*." He stood then. Turning to the men that Teela had called hers, he said, "You will summon the Warden. Now."

They nodded. And left.

"Ask your Lord," he told Kaylin quietly. "He will not be pleased, but he may be able to explain it in a fashion that you will understand."

Kaylin nodded.

Teela said, "He means Nightshade, not the Hawklord." She turned to her cousin and added, "That was unwise."

"They are yours. If you cannot control them, kill them."

"It is not of them that I speak. There is magic in the air, the like of which I have not seen since—" She looked at Kaylin and fell silent.

The Lord of the West March nodded. "It will not help," he added. "We will meet again, Kaylin Neya. But I have much to do now. Leave this building, and leave it in haste. Anteela will summon a—"

"We'll walk," Kaylin said quickly.

And the Barrani High Lord laughed. It was a sound that reminded her of the forest that lay at his heart.

"You *do* know my cousin," he said.

"You drive like a maniac. What else was I supposed to say?"

Teela, her hand upon Kaylin's arm, hurried her through halls that looked familiar. "Precisely nothing."

"Severn, back me up here."

"I prefer wisdom, myself."

"What's that supposed to mean?"

"It means I'll hurt *him*," Teela snapped. "What did I tell you?"

"To—"

"To say *nothing*. What do you think nothing means?"

"I only said we'd walk—"

"He called you *kyuthe*. He called you *kyuthe* in front of witnesses."

"Does it show?" She lifted a hand to her cheek in sudden panic.

"What do you mean, does it—oh. No, he did not mark you in any way. To do so would probably kill you."

"So then it's just a damn *word*, right? Who cares if he called me *kyuthe*? So did you."

"I could not bring you here and call you anything less."

"But he—"

"He's the Lord of the West March, Kaylin!"

Kaylin frowned. "You don't like him?"

"He's a *Barrani High Lord*. What does 'like' have to do with anything?"

"But—but you brought me to save his life, didn't you?"

Teela turned to Severn. "I'm having trouble remembering why I haven't strangled her yet."

Severn shrugged. "I have that problem myself some days. At the moment, though, the only betting pool in the office seems to be on the Sergeant."

"Ha-ha." Kaylin said with a distinct lack of cheer. And then, because she was a fiefling, "What odds?" He cuffed the top of her head.

The halls of stone and weapons were gone; the heights and the vast open spaces of the rest of the building opened up before them. Kaylin could breathe here. Very, very carefully.

She was *so* damn tired.

"Teela," Severn said quietly.

Teela paused. Which meant that she slowed enough that Kaylin wasn't tripping over her own feet in a futile attempt to keep up. The Barrani Hawk snorted, and grimacing, she swept Kaylin off her feet and picked up the pace again.

"I have your back," Severn said quietly.

"You'd better." Teela's voice was almost a perfect imitation of a Leontine's. "I don't want to see either of you at Court again. I don't want to see you in the High Halls. I *do not* want to see you in the company of *any* Barrani who doesn't wear the Hawk. Kaylin, are you listening to me?"

"Severn is," Kaylin murmured. She closed her eyes, but not on purpose; her lids were really heavy.

"Teela," Severn said in the comfortable darkness, "why did you summon Kaylin? The Barrani are famed for their magic. Was there not a healer among them—"

"No," Kaylin said without opening her eyes. "Not a single one."

Teela's arms stiffened. "How do you know this?"

Kaylin's shrug was almost Barrani; it said nothing, and meant that there would be an awful lot of nothing.

"The Emperor—"

"Not there either. Let it go, Severn."

"He has *three* healers."

"They are seconded to the service of the Emperor," Teela said coldly. "And in the interest of not starting a third Barrani-Dragon war, the less said about that the better."

"They're all human, though" Kaylin began. And then a thought occurred to her. "Third?"

"Kaylin, take history again, and this time, *try* to pay attention."

She felt breeze and sunlight on her face, and made an effort to open her eyes. It was an utter failure.

"Who tried to kill him, Teela?" She asked.

"He's a Barrani High Lord," Teela replied coldly.

"That means," Severn added, "anyone. Or everyone."

"I think he'd make a decent Hawk."

"Keep that opinion to yourself." Teela's voice softened. "You did well," she told Kaylin. Her fingers brushed strands of hair from Kaylin's face. "I will not ask you what you did, or how. I will not ask you what you saw. Because if you speak of it, he *will* kill you. I believe he would regret it, if that's any consolation."

"Not much."

"Here. Corporal. You take her. You can even drive her back to the Halls of Law. But I warn you now—"

Severn said something that made Kaylin's eyes snap open. "Lord Evarrim, incoming."

The red Arcanist's robes were like fire—moving, living fire. Kaylin thought it a wonder that a scorched path didn't trail in his wake, and thought further that she understood—for just a second—what the *shape* of flame was. Sanabalis would be pleased.

Of course, picking up Evarrim and lighting a candle with him would probably get her killed.

His guards numbered four. She thought they were the

same guards that had gathered around him earlier in the day, but she was tired enough that she could no longer differentiate; the Barrani looked, to her eyes, the same.

Except for Evarrim. He had donned a tiara, with a ruby the size of a child's fist in its center. His hair lay beneath the fine circlet, and his lips were the color of his skin. It was very seldom that this much expression marred Barrani features.

And Kaylin would have been happier not to have witnessed it. The Barrani were famed for their intense dislike of weakness, and they often did away with the witnesses on general principle.

Teela took up position in front of Severn and Kaylin, and Severn—with reluctance—set Kaylin down. "Can you stand?" he whispered.

"Yes." It was mostly true. She kind of listed, and had to hope no strong breeze would happen along to topple her.

"Anteela," Lord Evarrim said as he approached. His expression had lost some of its stretched thinness. His eyes, however, were a very dark blue. Almost, but not quite black.

"Lord Evarrim," Teela replied, her voice like a cold snap. One that killed plants overnight. "I have resumed my position at Court. Formality is requested."

"Very well, Lord Anteela. I am fond of you. You must forgive my familiarity. I assure you, no insult was meant by it."

"And I assure you, Lord Evarrim, that none has been taken. You are early for the Council session."

He stilled. "The Council was suspended for three days."

"Ah, my apologies. The Lord of the West March has been most insistent."

"The Lord of the West March, Lord Anteela?"

"Even so."

"I had heard rumors—"

"The High Court is always home to rumor, Lord Evarrim. Some even concern the Arcanum, and I am certain that you would be the first to decry them. In this case, rumor is unfounded, but it was spread quickly, and its ramifications have yet to be felt.

"I am pleased to see you," she added, her eyes blue-green. She was amused. And angry. "I have no doubt the Lord of the High Court will look favorably upon your presence."

Lord Evarrim was silent for a few minutes.

He was even silent when his gaze engaged Kaylin's. The look reminded Kaylin that engagement had more to do with military actions, in Lord Evarrim's presence, than any sort of romantic fulfillment.

"Why is this mortal standing before the High Halls?" He spoke in a tone of voice that would have been more suited to asking about the composition of the slime clinging to the undersides of his boots. Except, of course, being Barrani, there never was any. At least not on the boots.

"She is an officer of the Law," Teela replied with a shrug. "And, as you are no doubt aware, I have pledged my service to the Lord she also serves. She is not conversant with the ways of the High Court."

"She could not be, she is mortal."

"Indeed. And because she is of inconsequential rank in the service of Lord Grammayre, she was unaware that I had taken a leave of absence for the High Festival. She merely sought to deliver a message."

"It is death to walk these halls," Lord Evarrim said to Kaylin.

"She will not walk them," Teela replied. Kaylin had re-membered Teela's command, and kept her mouth shut. It was difficult. Although Lord Evarrim did not, in fact, wear a smug or superior smile, the effect of his words implied such, and she wanted to wipe it clean.

But she was also attached to living.

"You may go," Lord Evarrim told Kaylin.

Severn's hand was suddenly attached to the small of her back. She forced herself to smile, and nodded. He led the way to the stables in which the carriage had been housed.

"He knows," Severn said quietly.

"Yes. I'd like to think he's stupid. But even I don't have that much imagination."

Severn opened the door; it was blue-and-gold, and the paint was new. Not even Teela at the driver's seat had dam-aged it. Kaylin had never been in an Imperial carriage be-fore, but she was damn impressed with the workmanship. The wheels were still attached, after all.

"I'll take you back to the Halls," he told her as he helped her inside. "And I'll drive the main roads."

"You've driven a carriage before?"

He nodded.

"When?"

"Three years ago. And no, I'm not going to say why, so don't ask. You shouldn't even be awake." He paused. And then, his eyes the dark they always were, he lingered in the door. "How did you wake him, Kaylin?"

She shook her head. "I'm not sure I understand it myself."

"You're a terrible liar."

"I'm not lying," she said quietly. She was staring at her arms.

"I didn't say you were lying to me."

"Thanks."

He closed the door very quietly, and she felt the slight spring of the wheels as he mounted the driver's bench.

CHAPTER 7

When Kaylin woke up, she was in the infirmary, staring at the back of Moran's speckled wings. They were moving up and down. Moran was seated on a backless stool, grinding something with a pestle. Kaylin felt instantly well. The very thought of any of Moran's potions or unguents usually had that effect on the Hawks—or Swords or Wolves—who were unfortunate enough to be offered them.

Where offered was kind of like "ordered to take," but with more force.

Moran wasn't a Leontine, but she did have ears. She turned, the seat of the stool swiveling neatly. "You're awake," she said.

Kaylin nodded. "How long have I been out?"

"An hour and a half. Corporal—"

"Could you just call him Severn?"

Moran lifted a brow. "Severn, then. He brought you in. I examined you, you look like shit."

"Thanks."

"But not the type that sleep won't cure. More," she added darkly, "than an hour and half's worth, although I'd be obliged if you gave me back the bed."

Kaylin sat up slowly, and swung her legs toward the floor. In all, she did feel better. If running a marathon and being near to collapse was better.

"The Hawklord wants to see you when you're awake. The Sergeant wants to see you first. They had a few choice Leontine words about precedence, but I believe the Sergeant won." She shook her head. "It's been less than a month, Kaylin. If I told you to take a leave of absence, would you listen?"

"See these fingers? See these ears?"

"Ha-ha. You're a Hawk," Moran said with a shrug. "Try not to visit so often, hmm?" She slid off the stool as Kaylin managed to gain her feet. Moran's usual frosty expression thawed. "I won't tell you not to go to the midwives," she said quietly. "I won't ask you to live with that. But there's a damn Dragon Lord in the office, and his butt seems fastened to a chair. Marcus's chair," she added with a grim smile. "In case you failed to pay attention in Race class—"

"Moran, please?"

"Dragons are trouble. Arguments between Grammayre and Marcus are trouble. Barrani are trouble, and the Arcanum is trouble. Mixing them *has* to be worse. I might have failed to mention that Lord Evarrim was here until about forty-five minutes before you arrived.

"I *do not* want to see you on Red's slab. I especially don't want to have to deliver you there myself, all right? Humor a selfish woman, Kaylin."

Kaylin swallowed and nodded.

Lord Sanabalis was, in fact, in Marcus's chair. Moran had the gift of bardic embellishment, but then again, there wasn't much need for it. Sometimes truth really was stranger than fiction. The Dragon's eyes, however, were a shade too orange for comfort. He saw her well before she reached the desk, and he raised his lower membranes over those eyes.

"Private Neya," he said, rising.

"Where is Marcus—Sergeant Kassan?"

"He is currently speaking with Lord Grammayre. I took the opportunity to rest old legs."

She almost snorted. Dragons lived forever; age was a matter of cosmetics. She wondered why Sanabalis chose to appear aged, but was too smart to ask. "If you can breathe fire," she said instead, "Marcus would be much obliged if you happened to hit some of that paperwork."

Sanabalis raised a white brow.

"You have already missed our first lesson," he replied. "And I am a busy man."

"Which is why you're still here."

"I can see why the Imperial Order of Mages found you difficult." He stood. "But I am at least as stubborn as you think you are. Perhaps more—I have the advantage of experience.

"You will be wanted, but I will wait. I believe Sergeant Kassan is almost here."

"I don't hear—"

Marcus strode through the arch that led to the tower. The fur around his face was standing on end in a way that exposed the softer, whiter skinfur, and his eyes were all the wrong color. But she noticed the fangs first.

She lifted her chin almost automatically, exposing her throat.

"Neya!" He growled, and leaped the distance that separated them. The fact that a Dragon happened to be in the way didn't seem to occur to him, but he must have known, because there was no collision. Which was almost too bad; Kaylin's natural instincts had taken over and she was calculating the odds of a scuffle and the attendant empty office. Luckily, she could in fact bet and stand still at the same time.

Claws touched her exposed throat. She felt each one press against the skin, as if testing its give. She wasn't afraid; there was no point. Marcus had drawn blood a time or two —some of it hers—but although office legend spoke of the bodies he'd left on the floor, she'd never actually seen them.

His claws receded into pads, and she felt the soft side of his paws against her throat before he at last withdrew them. His eyes were yellow and bright, but his lips once again curled protectively over his fangs. Where protectively referred to her, and not to his teeth.

"You're alive," he said gruffly.

"More or less. If it helps, I feel like crap."

His gaze skirted her cheek with a question. She shook her head. "No trouble."

"Teela kept an eye on you?"

"You could say that."

"No violence."

"You could say that, too, but it would be a hell of a lot less accurate."

"Did *you* start hostilities?"

"No, sir."

"Then there was no violence."

"Yes, sir."

"The Hawklord is waiting."

"Yes, sir." She started toward the tower.

"Private?" Oh, he was in a *mood*.

"Yes, sir?"

"Did you happen to meet Lord Evarrim of the Arcanum while you were at the High Hall?" *High* was said in exactly the wrong tone.

"Yes, sir."

"Did you speak to him?"

"Not a word, sir."

"Good." He paused. "Lord Sanabalis thought it wise to engage the Arcanist in conversation. It was…interesting."

She turned to look at Sanabalis, whose eyes were now thoroughly gold. The Dragon winked.

The Hawklord was standing beside the mirror, his hand spread against its surface. The surface showed no reflection. This wasn't an act of vanity; he was accessing records. But when Kaylin entered the room through the open door— open, twice, in one week—he let his hand drop instantly, and the surface broke in a wave that ended with silver, bright and flat.

"Kaylin," he said, meeting her gaze in that reflective surface before turning to face her. "I see you've returned."

She nodded. Lord Grammayre disliked the word *sir* on general principle, understanding its value as a distancing tool. When he was inspecting his men, he expected to hear it; when he was not, he expected actual information.

"The difficulty?"

"It was…resolved."

"How?"

She winced.

"Let me tell you the rumors that came to the tower."

She nodded.

"The younger son of the castelord was, by all accounts, dead. Is this accurate?"

She shook her head.

"Was he dying?"

She hesitated. "I…I don't know."

"Teela seemed to think so."

"He looked—to me—like he was sleeping. But not so much with the breathing."

The Hawklord winced slightly at her use of language. And switched into Barrani, the bastard. "Was he wounded in any way?"

She was silent. At another time, he would have been angry. That he wasn't said much about his understanding of the Barrani High Court. Which, given how little he was present there, was impressive.

"And now?"

"He's an arrogant son of a bitch. When I left, he was giving orders."

"Good. Have you been informed that—"

"Lord Evarrim was here?"

"I see that news travels."

"If it's bad."

At that, the Hawklord smiled. Winter touched his eyes and lips, leaving the former gray. Ash-gray. "He has set a petition in motion," the Hawklord told her quietly.

"With *who*?"

"The Emperor."

"And this would be about me?"

"Indeed it would. He was not pleased when you were not here."

"He's never pleased."

"I doubt that, Kaylin. But I hope you will never have cause to be disabused of your notion."

"What's the nature of the petition?"

"It involves the dead Barrani."

"The ones who served the—"

"Outcaste, yes." The word was sharp; a warning.

"Well, what about them? I think they're all dead."

"They were already dead."

"Well, not moving as much, at any rate." She shrugged.

"It will be of interest to the High Court Council," Lord Grammayre said quietly. "The Emperor is aware of the facts. Very few others are."

She nodded.

"I expect—eventually—to be summoned to Court by the Barrani castelord."

"But he's not *your* castelord. You don't have to—" She stopped. "Do you?"

"I am not compelled to present myself, no."

"You will."

"This is a difficult city to govern, Kaylin."

"You're not the governor. The Emperor is."

"The Emperor has not been summoned. He has not been invited, either."

She frowned.

"I wish you to make yourself absent, if possible."

"Because you think they'll ask for me."

He reached over to the mirror, and it moved beneath his hand.

A Barrani in very fine robes began to speak. And speak. And speak. Kaylin's attention started to wander, but the words *Kaylin Neya* drew it back.

"They want me to go with you."

"I would say they want you, period. I don't matter."

"Lord Sanabalis is waiting for you. Continue your lesson for the day. No one will disturb you while you are in his company."

"And after that?"

"Go back to your temporary domicile."

Kaylin frowned. The frown turned on edge. "You knew."

He said nothing. It was very Barrani of him.

"This is a delicate situation," he told her quietly. "And you are not there as an officer of the Law…you are there as a guest. Although I do not expect you to understand this, there are worse places to be."

"You *asked* him, didn't you?"

"Kaylin, understand that you are accusing me of not only communication, but also cooperation, with one of the more notorious crime lords in Elantra. I will assume that you are exhausted, and your lack of critical faculty stems from that exhaustion. Is that understood?"

"But you—"

He lifted a hand. "I am happy to hear that rumors about the ill health of the castelord's son were unfounded. Go."

Lord Sanabalis was waiting.

He didn't speak when she met him; he merely gestured to the West Room, and she took her lead from that gesture.

The lump of waxen candle sat on the table. Kaylin glared at it, and if, as the saying went, looks could kill, it would have been molten. If, however, the rest of the world was being turned inside out, the candle as a fact remained standing. Too bad.

"Kaylin," Sanabalis said quietly.

She frowned and looked up.

"You appear…fatigued."

"Welcome to my life," she muttered.

He lifted a pale brow. And she sighed, and gave in with as much grace as she could muster. "I'm dead tired."

"Better," he told her. "Let us set the candle aside for the day. You appear to harbor it some animosity, and if my reports are to be believed, you have even been known to attack one. With a long knife." He swept the candle to one side.

She shrugged. "I'm not allowed to carry a sword in the West Room."

The answer fizzled somewhere between Kaylin's mouth and the Dragon Lord's ears. "The Lord of the West March," he said quietly.

She shook her head.

"I am senior advisor to the Dragon Emperor. You are aware of this. You should also be aware of the fact that while I undertake other duties, none of those duties supersedes my responsibility to the Emperor."

She nodded.

"I am fully capable of demanding your cooperation. I have only to speak with Sergeant Kassan or Lord Grammayre, and you will be obliged to speak freely."

She was thinking about the Hawklord as he spoke. And cursing him silently in every language she knew.

"If I am forced to that," Sanabalis continued calmly, "it will be a matter of official record." The last two words hung in the air, as if written there for the benefit of the dim. As she was the only other person in the room, it was hard to find a good way to take it.

She thought about the Hawklord again, and modulated the cursing into something less harsh. Slightly. She wondered if he *ever* stopped thinking.

"I wasn't at the High Court as a Hawk," she said quietly. "And according to—"

"Elantran Law was designed at the whim of the Emperor. It was, it can even be said, designed for his benefit. With some effort, the Law can be changed. I would not, however, suggest that it would be without difficult ramifications in future."

She shrugged and tipped the chair back on its hind legs, depositing her feet on the table. She also folded her arms across her chest, tucking her chin down as she did. "I get it."

"Good. Demonstrate what your understanding is worth."

"I was invited to the High Court as a guest."

"Indeed. An honor seldom granted the mortal. You accompanied the Hawk called Teela."

She nodded.

"Teela has an interesting background. I would not have thought to find her among the Hawks."

"She suits the Hawks. She seems out of place at the High Court."

"Does she?"

Kaylin thought back. But not very far. She shrugged.

"The Lord of the West March was…sleeping. I woke him at Teela's request."

"Sleeping?"

She shrugged again. The old Dragon's eyes did not shade into orange; they were gold. And gold was both power and comfort here. "I thought—I don't know why, but I thought he'd been poisoned."

"And you think otherwise now?"

"Poison leaves damage," she said carefully. "I've seen it before. Red—"

He lifted a hand. "That would be the chief Coroner for the Halls?"

She nodded.

"He is a competent man. Continue."

"There was no damage. Look—I've never had to heal Barrani before. Do you have *any* idea how hard it is to injure a Barrani?"

"Some," the old Dragon said, with the hint of a smile that was distinctly unpleasant.

"I've never had to heal a Dragon before, either. Tiamaris wouldn't let me near him."

"He is wise," Sanabalis said with a nod. "And he obviously values you."

"Everyone I've healed has been mortal. I understand mortality. I understand death."

Sanabalis's lower lids rose. "And yet you thought the Barrani High Lord had been poisoned."

"I must have been wrong," she replied.

"Oh?"

She really hated Dragons. "He was sleeping," she said firmly. "He woke up."

"Yet none of his kin were capable of this waking."

She shrugged. "Not apparently. Or maybe they didn't want to try. The Barrani are very political that way."

"I would definitely say his unnatural sleep was a product of their politics, yes. The Lord of the West March has many enemies."

She snorted. "Who doesn't?"

"A good question. No man with power is free from enemies. And you, Kaylin, have shown yourself to *be* a power."

"Someone didn't want him to wake, that's for sure."

"Why do you say that?"

"A door."

His brow rose.

"It was magically trapped. It kind of exploded."

"Who touched it?"

"No one."

"Why?"

"I guess no one wanted to *die.*"

"Kaylin, I am famed for my patience. But even my patience has limits. Who made it clear that the door was enchanted?"

She shrugged; it was uncomfortable. The eyes she faced were slightly orange, and without the benefit of lower membranes, the orange was striking. She promised herself she would never hate candles again.

"I did."

He nodded, and the color in his eyes dimmed. "How?"

"I don't like magic," she told him, loosening her arms, letting the chair thud back against the floor, and resting her elbows on the tabletop. "Every door that any official hides behind is magical. Even the West Room door is magical."

"And this door?"

"Magical, as well. But—different magic."

"Different how?"

"You read my transcripts, right?"

"Yes. You failed Magical Manifestation. Do you want to offer an explanation for that?"

"Too many damn ridiculous words, all of which were more than two syllables long, and all of which meant 'bad.'"

"Very well. Allow me to accept the inevitable. Put your impressions into your own words, and let me try to make sense of them."

She shrugged. "No one else could."

"They were not Dragons."

"You didn't meet Mrs. Maise."

His smile was both thin and genuine. "In fact, I tutored Mrs. Maise."

"If you tell me you taught her everything she knows—"

"I will leave that to your imagination. The door, Kaylin."

"It just felt—wrong. Bad wrong. It had the hand symbol, and it was a normal door. A single door. It was framed by solid damn rock, and there were sconces to either side of the door. They were empty," she added. Seeing as a Hawk saw. "But the hair on my neck stood on end when we approached it. Teela was dragging me. We didn't have a lot of time."

"You stopped her."

"Severn heard me… Teela wasn't paying attention. She often doesn't."

"She heeded the Corporal's warning?"

Kaylin nodded. "She threw a halberd at the door. A really fancy, really expensive halberd. The walls down the length of that hall were adorned with weapons—crossed swords, crossed spears, crossed polearms. They had a lot of gemstones encrusted in stupid places," she added.

"It was one of the old halls, then."

"It wasn't as pretty as the outer ones, no."

"What happened to the halberd?"

"It shattered. The blade did. The door shattered when it made contact. The frame was—" She hesitated. "It looked like a standing crater."

"Not a small amount of power was expended there."

Kaylin shrugged. "I don't know."

"And had Teela opened the door?"

"Barrani would have spent weeks picking us off the floor and walls."

"But Teela didn't sense it."

"She's not a mage."

"No. She's not. But neither are you." He closed his eyes slowly. "You have a strong sensitivity to magic. This is not uncommon. Some people are born with a strong sensitivity to smell. But your sensitivity is different. You knew the spell was inimical."

"I knew it would kill us."

"That is what I said."

Kaylin, however, was frowning. "Teela came straight here," she said. The frown was joined by narrowed eyes; she straightened slowly. "Her men knew that she was leaving, I think. They were left to guard the Lord of the West March.

"Just how damn long would it take to cast a spell like that?"

"Without risk? Hours."

"They didn't have hours."

"No," he replied, his eyes going opaque. "There are two ways in which this could be done, two ways in which I would do it. The first, and probably the less costly, would be to simply trap the door. But if the door was used at all, the victim intended would not be guaranteed to be the one to set it off.

"The second, and more efficient? Set it up hours before. Possibly before the Lord of the West March went to…sleep. Key it to Teela. Or to a human. In the second case, time would be less critical."

She nodded. "I'd go for the second."

"As would I. Continue."

"Could an Imperial mage have done it?"

"Not legally."

"And the Arcanum?"

"Not legally."

"Evarrim was *here*," she said mostly to herself.

"Indeed. He was, I think, surprised to see me."

"I can't think why."

Irony was lost on the mage. Probably at his choice. "No one in the Halls of Law will file a report," he said quietly, "because there will be no complaint."

"I could."

"Yes. You could. Think carefully before you make that decision."

She nodded. "Sanabalis?"

"Yes?"

"Who exactly *is* the Lord of the West March?"

"If you mean the person, I fear you now know the answer far better than I. But I assume you mean the position."

"Is it?"

The look he gave her was just shy of incredulity. "It appears," he said after a long pause, "that I will be responsible for far more of your education than I first expected."

"Did we even cover that?"

"Apparently not." His voice was so dry the words should have caught fire by sheer proximity to one another. "He is the younger son of the castelord. The West March covers the stretch of almost uninhabited land that goes toward the mountains beyond the Empire itself. It is one of the ancient Barrani demesnes, and it is seldom open to outsiders."

She nodded.

"The position is usually granted to one of the cousins, but the castelord and his consort have been blessed. The consort bore three children—two sons and one daughter." He paused, and then added, "Given the span of Barrani years, this will no doubt not impress you…it does not impress me.

What does? The fact that all three of their children still live. Usually, by this time, there is only one."

"By this time?"

His eyes shaded slightly orange; wrong question. Kaylin tried a different one. "This isn't a bad thing, then."

"It depends. The surviving son of the castelord has, historically, become the castelord."

"And he has two."

"Very good, Kaylin. At least you think like a Hawk."

"How much difference does that make if the castelord is going to live forever anyway?"

The Dragon's upper lids closed completely. "Remind me that you failed history."

"Completely failed it."

"Then you no doubt slept through the official history of the pre-empire Kingdoms."

She shrugged. It was a yes shrug.

"Then let me continue to torment myself with your ignorance. The Barrani can in theory live forever. There is, however, a difference between immortal and invulnerable. In the history of the Barrani High Court, I cannot think of a single castelord who has died of old age. I *can* think of three for whom that claim was made."

"But you don't believe it."

"If the definition of death by old age involved a severed head, I would be more inclined that way, yes." He paused for a moment. "In two cases, it is less clear. And perhaps we will see a third."

"Isn't that murder?"

"Not among the Barrani."

"But we have *laws* now, don't we?"

"We have laws if the Barrani castelord chooses to invoke their use. This would imply two things. The first, that the castelord survived the attempt...the second, that his successor would somehow draw attention to the crime that promoted him.

"And Kaylin, before you show the depth of your alarming ignorance again, let me add that *any* castelord who was fool enough to do that would not be castelord by the time the Law actually *arrived*. I understand that you are attached to the Laws—they seem to be one of the few things you *did* learn—but you must also understand, given your experience, that there are always two sets of laws, beyond those which govern the castes.

"And the caste-law is a separate entity. Were it not for that codicil to the laws which govern Elantra, there would be no Elantra."

"A third Dragon-Barrani war?"

"A continuation of the second one."

She nodded.

"But there is something in the codicil," she added thoughtfully.

"That being?"

"That any being of any race who wishes to be excommunicate can avail themselves of the Laws of the Dragon Emperor."

"How often has that happened, Kaylin? No, wait, I forget to whom I speak. Let me answer briefly."

"Never?"

He smiled.

"So…if the second son died, why would it mean war?"

At this, Sanabalis frowned. Everything about his posture changed; it was as if he had suddenly snapped into place and become fully real. "It would not mean war."

She hated hated hated her big mouth. "Teela told me that if we didn't—wake him, it would mean war."

"That is the first bit of interesting information you've divulged." His frown was a bit too wide; it was definitely too deep. "I will leave you now, Kaylin. We will resume our lessons on the morrow." But his eyes were narrow now, and his expression thoughtful.

On him, it wasn't an improvement.

When she arrived, the office was emptying; it was the end of the day. Marcus, however, was besieged by paper, and sat at his desk, his familiar growl more of a sensation than a sound. She walked up to his impromptu fortress.

"You're finished?" he asked, glaring at the dead mirror.

"For today. Apparently."

"Good. Go home."

"Marcus—"

"Home is not here."

"I just want to ask—"

"I could swear my mouth moved."

"This year, this Festival—those diplomatic seals—what do they mean?"

"And when my mouth moved, I believe it gave an order."

"Do the words *West March* feature prominently on any of those papers?"

His growl was very loud. "You are not to involve yourself in the affairs of the Court. That's an order, Private."

"Bit late for that, sir."

"Kaylin, unless you want to sleep in the brig, go away."

"Yes, sir."

She expected to see Severn when she left the Halls of Law.

She saw Barrani guards instead, and they were a vastly less welcome sight. But their armor was armor she recognized, and if some child-part of her mind was telling her to turn around and run back to Marcus, the Hawk-part was easing her hand off her daggers and her whistle.

"Andellen?" she asked as one of the six men broke away from the group and approached her on the steps.

He nodded curtly. "We are your escort for the evening," he told her. "We are to return with you to Castle Night-shade." He paused and then added, "We are not to linger here."

She hesitated. "Has there been difficulty?"

"This close to the Halls of Law, no. But there may well be difficulty before we reach the bridge."

"How much difficulty?"

"It is not your concern."

She closed her eyes. "Yes," she said to no one in particular. "I'll go."

But the route Andellen chose did not lead to the bridge. It led to the Ablayne's banks. Kaylin started to ask a question, and let it go; there was a boat moored on those banks. She marveled at the fact that it hadn't been stolen, until two more Barrani guards appeared. The nature of the incline had provided them cover from prying eyes.

"The bridge is watched," Andellen told her quietly.

His voice was the stilted voice of the High Courts, but there was music in it, and she loved the sound. She certainly liked it better than the inside of a boat weighed down by eight armored Barrani.

"Who's watching?"

Andellen did not reply. When he failed, Kaylin realized what had been so strange about the walk: He had answered most of her other questions. He'd *talked* to her.

"I wanted to thank you," she said quietly, when the oars began to struggle with the moving current.

His look was as smooth and expressionless as glass. Dark glass. Clearly, gratitude was going to offer offense. Which was his problem.

"You helped me last night."

He said nothing, which was about what she expected. But after a moment, he looked at her; he and one other Barrani were not involved in the oaring. They were, however, carrying unsheathed swords.

"Why do you do it?" He had dropped formal Barrani, which was probably as close to Elantran as he was *ever* going to get.

She understood that Barrani and humans had very little in common, but not even Tain had asked her why.

"Why do I help the midwives?"

He nodded. His glance met hers on the odd occasion it wasn't absorbed by the approaching bank.

"If I don't, people die."

"People die all the time. Do you feel responsible for their deaths?"

"No." Pause. "Sometimes. It depends."

"On what?"

"On whether or not there was anything I could have done to prevent them."

"This matters to you."

She shrugged.

"You have power. If you desired more, you would become *Erenne.*"

"I don't want that kind of power."

"Power is the only guarantee you have that your will is made manifest. There is no other 'kind.'"

She frowned. "Is there much betting going on? About my being the *Erenne?*"

His look was odd; it changed the shape of his face. It took Kaylin a moment to realize that the man was almost *smiling.* Betting was universal. At least in the fiefs.

She kept that to herself. "If I became *Erenne,* if I became Lord Nightshade's consort—"

"They are not the same, Kaylin Neya."

"Let's pretend they are. If I did, how would *I* have power? The power in Nightshade is *his.* It begins and ends with him. And he lets nothing go."

"No. But he is Barrani."

"There's no advantage in it." She spoke like a fiefling.

"There is safety."

"If I wanted safety, I wouldn't wear the Hawk."

"If you desire it, he might extend his protection to those of your choosing."

She shook her head. "He's Barrani," she said quietly.

"Yes. What we wonder, Kaylin Neya, is what *you* are."

"Just Kaylin."

The boat bumped against the shore. The sky was not yet dark; danger, if it came, would not come from ferals.

"I believe," Andellen said quietly, "that you have angered the Arcanists. I would consider that unwise."

"I didn't do it on purpose."

"Of course not…humans never do. What humans rarely survive long enough to understand is this—lack of offense is also a choice."

CHAPTER 8

Lord Nightshade was waiting for her when she arrived—nauseated and dizzy—in the front vestibule. Kaylin promised herself that one damn day she'd be able to either step through the portcullis and arrive where *she* wanted to, or she'd just have the damn thing melted down.

Saying so, however, fled her mind when she met Lord Nightshade's eyes. Although she'd lived among the Barrani Hawks for the entire time she'd been one—and every day before that, when she'd wanted to wear the Hawk so badly—no eyes were as clear, or as cold, as Nightshade's. She could see them clearly behind her lids when she closed them.

Not that she wanted to; there was always something about Nightshade that put her on edge. But on edge was a balancing act that she'd become good at over the years.

"Lord Nightshade," she said, using the wall as a brace.

"Kaylin. You seem…tired."

"*Green* is the word you want," she replied in Elantran.

"Dinner has been prepared. I would normally require you to be more presentable, but I believe that you have failed to eat today."

Damn it. She had. "It was a busy day."

"It must have been, if you're so lacking in imagination you offer that as an excuse." He waited beneath a chandelier, absorbing all the light it cast. Which, given he was wearing black, should have been more difficult.

His expression was set in a graceful frown.

Kaylin's was a moving grimace, just shy of actual pain. She pushed herself free from the wall and wobbled a bit on knees that really weren't meant to support her weight. Or anyone's, at the moment.

But he did not approach her, did not offer a hand or an arm. He simply waited.

And that was all she wanted, at the moment. That he wait. That he allow her the illusion of strength, or failing that, the illusion of an absence of weakness.

"How fares the Lord of the West March?"

"He's well," she said, approaching him in something that approximated a straight line.

"I gather he must be. There has been some difficulty in the Arcanum."

"Difficulty?" She didn't ask him how he knew.

"Lord Evarrim has been unusually active."

"It's the Festival season," she offered. She'd reached his side, and as she did, he turned toward the hall.

"It is a rare season that sees fire in the Arcanum."

"*Fire?*"

"I believe that is the word for the thing that consumes wood and causes smoke, yes."

She glared at the side of his face. "What caused the fire?"

"To the casual observer? An experiment gone wrong. I believe that will be the official report tendered the Imperium. The Imperial Order of Mages," he added, as if he expected her not to know the word. Given that she didn't, she settled for grinding her teeth.

"To the less than casual observer?"

"Ah." He had led her down a hall that she had not seen before. Then again, geography in the Castle itself defied both understanding and description. Kaylin had a Hawk's training; she *remembered* what she saw.

But there was nothing remotely familiar about the hall she now traversed. She wondered if it would always be like this.

"While the Castle is mine, yes," he replied.

"A precaution?"

"It would be. But no, it is simply an artifact of the Castle itself. I understand it, I can follow it. But my servants see a different path when they approach the same room we now repair to, and they walk different halls. Were you to wander without my guidance, you might eventually find yourself in the dining hall—but the passage there would be less...convenient."

He reached out to touch her cheek. Or she thought he had; she could feel the cool tips of his fingers against her skin, tracing the pattern of deadly nightshade almost gently. But his hands remained by his sides.

She was *really* tired.

"You did not suffer in the High Hall."

She shook her head. "Not more than I usually suffer when I'm with Teela." In fact, given that they hadn't actually been drinking, a lot less.

"And none made comment?"

Again, the ghost of his hands touched her face, lingering at the base of her jaw.

"The Lord of the West March noticed," she said at last. Her voice was higher than she would have liked.

"And he did not attempt to have you killed?"

She shook her head. "I—I liked him, I think. Not that he wouldn't kill me tomorrow if it was useful to him—he's Barrani, after all. But he didn't seem to really care one way or the other."

"Perhaps he was content to be alive."

"He wasn't precisely dying," she said softly.

"How can you recognize dying in the Barrani?"

She thought about the guard Teela had so efficiently dispatched. "I can recognize death," she said at last.

"They are not the same, I think."

"Obviously not."

A set of doors opened in the hall ahead. She could see, glimmering in the center of the nearest of the two, a golden flower. Palm-magic.

"You may open any door in the Castle without worry," he told her, his voice as gentle as his hands—or his non-hands—had been. "I understand that you are not comfortable with the magic that graces my doors. They are there for privacy, and for minimal protection…you require none of the former and a great deal of the latter. It renders the doors superfluous. Come."

He entered the hall ahead of her. She followed in his wake, almost stepping on the edge of his robe as she stumbled. She'd forgotten just how dirty she was. And the scent of food drove pretty much anything but hunger out of her mind entirely.

When she was seated, when her plate appeared, as if by magic, in front of her, and when she had actually started to eat, he sat across from her. The table that had seemed narrow was actually very wide—it was also too damn long. Mess Hall in the Halls was probably smaller than this single room.

"You asked an intelligent question," he said quietly. "About the Arcanum. I will answer it now. To the less casual observer, the explosion that resulted in fire might appear to be a backlash."

Chew. She had to remember to chew. The swallowing was a little too intensely reflexive. "Backlash?" More words meant less food.

"If a spell is set," he told her quietly, "and if it is complicated, it requires an anchor. Very often the anchorage is provided by a person. In some cases, that is considered too much of a risk."

"So you think this was anchored by something."

"Indeed."

"And it broke."

"As you say."

She frowned. "You *also* think I should know this already, don't you?"

"I believe these explanations would be considered condescending by the rest of your compatriots, yes."

"We did set off a spell," she said as she drained the glass

by the side of her plate. Or tried; most of it came back out with a distinct lack of dignity. "What *is* this?"

"Not water," he said with a pleasant smile. As if he ate with ill-mannered humans every day. Messy, ill-mannered humans. "The nature of the spell?"

She tried to speak around the fire in her throat. After a coughing fit that would have had the Hawks snickering for days, she managed to get control of her tongue; she knew her face was red. "It was meant to kill whoever tried to open a certain door."

"How?"

"Mostly? By ripping them into tiny bits, if I had to guess."

Lord Nightshade frowned; it was the frown of thought, not disapproval. "I do not think that such a spell would be anchored in the Arcanum," he told her after a pause. "Would you care to tell me why?"

"Because they'd expect it *to* be set off."

"Correct. Perhaps you managed to pay attention in your classrooms in the upper city."

"I had to pay some. Hamish used to throw erasers at the back of my head."

His expression made clear that he found the anecdote less amusing than she did. Which wasn't hard.

She ate more slowly as hunger receded. "You think it had something to do with the Lord of the West March."

"I can tell you the minute it happened, if it is of interest."

She shrugged. "Not really. I can't tell you when he woke up to the minute, so there's not much to compare." She set her fork down. "Tell me about the High Court."

"Can you not access your vaunted Records?"

"Not without being suspended."

"Ah. Then it seems that those who have your interests at heart prefer you to be without the information."

She nodded. "They expect that I'll be able to avoid the High Court."

"Then they are optimistic in a fashion that I am not. You are aware that he is the younger son of the castelord."

She nodded

"You are also aware that the castelord has a surviving older son."

She nodded again.

"He also has a daughter."

"I knew that, too. Do you think it was the older son?"

"The Lord of the Green?"

"Is that what he's called?"

"By those who are conversant with the High Courts, yes."

"Him, then."

"Historically, it would be a good guess."

She smiled. "And this would be one of the times when lack of historical knowledge isn't a liability?"

"It is said that the brothers are fond of one another."

"And you believe it."

"I have seen them. I believe it."

"The sister?"

"She has nothing to gain by the death of either brother. The Barrani Court has its place for her, and that place will not change."

"Then who would want to kill him? And please don't tell me that he's a Barrani High Lord as if that were enough of an answer."

"No." He had not eaten at all. "I am not yet certain, Kaylin."

"People seem to think that the death of the Lord of the West March might cause a war."

"The Lord of the West March is not an empty title. Humans use empty titles, but it is seldom that a Barrani Lord finds one. He is popular, in the fashion of our kind. And he is, as you have guessed, unusual."

"I guessed that, did I?"

"You must have. If I am correct, there was only one way to wake him." His eyes were a mix of emerald and blue. He stared at her intently.

She swallowed air. Food went down with it, and she dropped her fork; emptiness had been replaced by something a little too crowded for comfort. She chose her next words with care. "I can't speak of it."

"He understands what the mark you bear means."

"He didn't make exceptions."

"No." He lifted the stem of an empty glass and gestured, his fingers running along the rim. She wasn't particularly surprised when the glass filled. "He gave you his name."

She kept her face carefully blank.

"I could almost hear it, Kaylin."

"But he—"

"When *you* spoke it. I know what you saw," he added softly. "And I will not speak of it. You planted the Hawk," he added, "in the heart of the Lord of the West March."

She nodded.

"Do you understand what that portends?"

"No."

"He must understand it. I would not have been surprised had he killed you. He did not, however, and that saves me much difficulty."

"Because?"

"You bear my mark," he replied, as if that was answer enough.

"The mark of an outcaste."

"Of a surviving outcaste Lord."

She was smart enough to understand the difference. "He told me to ask you something," she said, lifting her own glass. The candlelight bent as she stared through the clear liquid. She wasn't quite brave enough to drink any more of it.

"And that?"

"*Kyuthe.*"

"Ah. I assume that Anteela used the word."

"She did. And he implied that she—that she didn't have the right to use it."

Lord Nightshade was silent a moment. His gaze did not leave her. He was utterly still. He might have been a statue of black marble, burnished to catch light.

"He called you *kyuthe.*"

"Yes," she said softly.

"And you don't understand why."

"No. But he said that ignorance excused nothing. Am I in trouble? I mean, in more trouble?"

"It depends, Kaylin. You have the eyes of the Arcanum upon you. I would not have said more trouble could be possible." He rose; she watched him as if she were no longer an active participant in her own life. Watched him move,

listened to the rustle of dark cloth, the almost absent fall of
feet. He came around the table slowly, and she felt his presence as shadow, a thing cast by light, a thing that said light
was absent.

She felt the lack of movement just as keenly; her cheek
was warm. He stood beside her, and above, as if he were
bower. Or waiting cage.

"The Hawk is more than a symbol," he whispered, his
words too deep to tickle, too quiet to resonate. "And you
offered him all that it means. To you. He was on the edge of
our twilight, although you could not see it clearly, and he
accepted what you offered."

"How do you—"

"It grew, Kaylin. It grew, there. The Lord of the West
March is like—very like—the Barrani of old. What you saw
was real, in its fashion. You left it there. He accepted it."

"It was the only way I could call him," she whispered.

"Yes. And your instincts are far sharper than you know.
You called, he heard. He came. What you offered, he could
have destroyed. Did he?"

She shook her head.

"I did not see the shadow of that loss upon you, and it
tells me much. As he knew it would. You had no words for
what you did, although if you struggled, you would find
them. Words have power, but the power of words are not
yours...you found a different way.

"But you gave, in some measure, what he returned. He
knows *you*. If he speaks your name, Kaylin, you will hear
it, and you will be bound in some fashion to him."

"But we don't *have* names. Not those ones."

"No. You are mortal, the learning of your name is simply the sum of what *can* be known. It is not always the sum of what you claim to know. They are not the same. But you left him something of value, and he retains it. You offered, and he accepted. The Lord of the West March does not use the word *kyuthe* lightly—he is not Anteela. He has not been exposed to the frailty of mortality." His hands touched her shoulders.

"Kaylin," he added, "the castelord has called High Court. From the West, and the East, from the mountains and the seas, from the forests that man has not yet encountered, the Barrani have come at his call. They are not numerous yet, but their presence will be felt in Elantra. It *is* felt now, by the Emperor."

"Why now?"

"That is the only question that needs be answered. If you understand it, you will understand the whole of this game. The Lord of the West March was seen as a threat. Had you not interfered, he would have died.

"But he is not—he has never been—a fool. He must have been prepared for a hundred different attacks. This one was subtle, and it succeeded—but it should not have succeeded. What does this tell you?"

She shook her head. "I don't even know what was *done*."

"What is not as important as how. Think on that." She felt the chair slide; she moved with it. She even started to rise, but her legs were like jelly. And her eyes were too heavy.

"Can I think tomorrow?"

She felt, rather than saw, his smile. "Tomorrow, then. Do you not have an appointment with Lord Sanabalis?"

She was lifted, and cradled; she could see candles flare and fall silent, their voices stilled. "Is there anything about my life you *don't* know?"

"Lord Sanabalis is one of the world's ancient powers," Lord Nightshade told her as he carried her out of the room. "And when the ancient powers move, they are felt. He is not without guile, and not without cunning, but he has been content these many years to serve the Dragon Emperor. If he has consented to teach you, you are honored, whether or not you know it.

"Sleep. I will watch you."

It was night, she thought. In the fiefs. And at night, only one other had ever watched her sleep. She wanted to tell him this, but she couldn't hold on to the words, just the fear.

"You love too easily," he told her. "Perhaps, in our youth, we once did the same. It was a different season, and it will not return to us, no matter how much we might wait. But what we learned in that youth, we hold as truth now. I would not have made the mistakes you made, Kaylin.

"But I would not have hated Severn for his choice, either. I would count myself in his debt."

And what of the dead? What of Steffi and Jade? How would you repay the debt you owed them? How would you forgive Severn for their deaths?

He brushed hair from her face. "By learning, little one. By learning never to let the innocent be weapons that could be used against me."

His words were like the lull a ship knows in harbor. "Did it take a long time? To learn that?"

"I never said it was a lesson I had to learn, but I have often learned from the mistakes of others. And yes, Kaylin Neya, for others it was costly, and it took many, many years."

"More than I have?"

"Many more."

She was silent for a moment, surrendering wakefulness. "Good."

When she woke, she woke to light. But it wasn't sunlight; it didn't cast the shadows by which she told time. She wore her clothing, she did not wear her boots. Those had been tucked neatly against the wall, and looked so out of place they were almost embarrassing. Then again, the same could be said of everything she owned.

The room itself was empty; a single flower blossomed in red-and-blue above the lip of a silver vase on a table beside the bed. She stretched experimentally. Her arms and legs were stiff, but the pain of the previous day had left them.

The mirror stood at the opposite end of the room; she could see herself—and only herself—in its surface. No angry growls had broken her sleep. She got up, changed one uniform for another, and put on pants that didn't have slashes or holes. She pulled her hair down, removed the stray bits of wood that had managed to lodge there, and then tried to brush it. She really resented the Barrani their hair.

As she buttoned her sleeves, she paused, and rolled them up; she inspected the marks on her arms with care. One day, she would read them.

She wondered what would happen then, if they would kill her, or if they would slip away, their story finally told.

A knock interrupted her rare introspection. She hurriedly

buttoned her sleeves and then shouted at the door. It opened.

Lord Nightshade stood in the frame. If he was unaccustomed to being shouted at through a closed door, it didn't change the general friendliness of his demeanor. Then again, knives probably wouldn't. "You will be late," he told her quietly, "if you do not leave soon. I have had food. You may take it with you."

She nodded, fetched her offending shoes, and shoved her feet into them, knotting the laces.

"Kaylin."

She looked up.

"You were dreaming."

And looked back down again. If she dreamed much, she generally didn't remember them, and given her life, she counted that on the plus side of the ledger.

But he didn't move, and after she'd finished putting her shoes on, she walked over to where he stood. "Was I talking?"

He nodded.

"In Elantran?"

"No. And that was odd."

"Aerian?"

"No."

"Barrani."

"Yes. High Barrani. Do you know what *leoswuld* means?"

She frowned. Shook her head.

"Were it not for the expectations of Lord Sanabalis, I would not allow you to leave the castle," Lord Nightshade said quietly.

"It's a bad word?"

"It is not a word that I have heard spoken by my kin since—" He smiled. It was a sharp smile. "It is, as you suggest, a *bad* word. Do not repeat it." His frown deepened, and the shade of his eyes were a blend of blue and green, both too deep for comfort. "But it would explain much." He lifted a hand. "Do not speak of it. It is death for outsiders."

She wasn't certain she could.

But she knew he was worried, and anything that actually worried a fieflord was probably something that could eat her alive and spit out the chewy bits without pausing for breath. Or, even worse, political.

"Tender my regards to Lord Sanabalis," Lord Nightshade said as he moved to one side. "I will see you out."

Seeing her out, as it happened, meant walking her to the banks of the Ablayne. The skiff was waiting for her there, and Andellen was once again its makeshift captain. "You will retain the services of Andellen and Samaran."

"I can't take them *into* the Halls of Law—they're—"

"If it is necessary, they will wait outside. Without breaking any of the laws you hold so precious."

"They've already broken at least sixty that I can think of, just by serving you!"

"They will not be an inconvenience."

She looked at his face. "I take them or I don't go?"

He shrugged. "There is always a choice."

She swallowed the words that automatically suggested themselves. They were all Leontine. And she suspected that he would understand every one of them.

"Andellen."

"Lord."

"Do not lose her."

"Lord."

Nightshade turned from the banks. "I have much to see to," he told her quietly. "And people of my own to gather." The day did not diminish him, but it made him seem far more distant. Which was a good thing.

Which should have been a good thing.

He approached her slowly, and in front of his waiting men, he lifted a hand to her cheek, to her unmarked cheek. His lips brushed her forehead before she could move—if she even wanted to; the touch was surprisingly soft. And warm. "I do not know when I will next see you," he told her quietly. "But I do not doubt that I will. And while you are away, I will be preparing."

"For what?"

He said nothing in exactly the wrong way, and let his hand fall.

Kaylin stepped into the boat, hating the way it wobbled. The river wasn't wide, and she'd half a mind to just ford the damn thing—but dripping on the carpets in the Halls was heavily frowned on, unless it was blood, and it would take her boots days to dry out. She disliked squelching on principle.

Six Barrani guards waited by the banks when the skiff reached the opposite side. They did not seem to notice the shift of boundaries. Like all Barrani, they owned whatever piece of ground they happened to be standing on. Or in.

Andellen and another guard, who she assumed was Samaran, followed her up the incline. They wore swords. All of the fieflord's Barrani guards did. She wondered why the Barrani Hawks chose staves instead. Even at their gods-cursed High Court, the weapon of choice seemed to be a long sword.

But she didn't ask. Instead, she turned toward the high city, shading her eyes from sunlight. It was warm on the back of her hand, and she gained warmth of a different kind from the sight of the three flags that flew above the distant Halls. "Let's go," she said without thinking.

But they followed without comment or annoyance.

And to her surprise, she was allowed entrance to the Halls with this strange escort. They elicited no surprise, no weapons checks, and no loud cries for help.

The first person she met in the office, once she'd cleared two sets of guards, was Teela. She almost failed to notice, but mornings did that to her; her brain didn't seem to acknowledge that the rest of her was awake until near lunch.

Andellen and Samaran noticed *for* her, however. They formed a metal wall between Kaylin and her fellow Hawk. She could have kicked them. Even considered it. But pockets of the office were now watching her, and she hated to make money for anyone who hadn't invited her to join in the betting.

Teela was dressed down. As in, almost like a Hawk. Except without the actual Hawk to grant her authority. Her hair was a flat fall from head to waist, and she wore a wide sash in place of a belt. She carried no obvious weapon. This, however, wasn't a problem; she didn't need them. Even the staff she favored was hardly necessary to her in a fight.

She eyed the Barrani with disdain. That was Teela all over. "Kaylin." She shortened both syllables into something that defined curt.

"Where's Marcus?"

"He's with the Hawklord."

"Why are you here?"

"I'm off duty. Does it matter?"

"You tell me. Where's Tain?"

"He's in his office."

Which was usually a bad sign; Tain liked his cubicle about as much as Kaylin liked palm-magic. Or less.

"This is High Court business?"

Teela's smile was all teeth. It should have had fangs. "I'm just making a casual report," she told Kaylin. "Someone's imported Lethe flowers."

Kaylin's jaw slowly unhinged. "Here?"

Teela reached into her pouch and pulled out the crushed and obvious white blossom. Lethe was deadly, in large enough doses. Then again, so were Leontines. What Leontines couldn't do, however, was destroy memory and identity slowly. Or quickly.

"I'll get—"

"No. You won't."

"But Moran should see—"

"I've been to Moran. It's potent."

"This doesn't have anything to do with the Festival, right?"

"You're off duty anyway. I did ask," Teela added with something that sounded suspiciously like pity.

"Teela—"

The Barrani's eyes were a shade of blue that looked a lot

like black. Kaylin took a step back. Lethe didn't work as well on humans as it did on Barrani, and from the Barrani point of view, destroying a few decades of memory wasn't a great crime anyway.

Hawk's eyes narrowed. "Was this used on the Lord of the West March?"

Teela said a very significant nothing. "You've got a meeting," she added quietly.

Kaylin wilted. In all, she looked a lot like the crushed flower. She turned smack into armor, and cursed in healthy Leontine as she rubbed her nose. "You two," she said, when she could talk again, "leave me a *little* space, okay?"

She left the guards on either side of the door to the West Room. They looked as if they would argue, but she smiled, held up a hand, and said, "Dragon Lord, okay?" in her most cheerful voice. If this didn't have the desired effect, it did encourage obedience.

Lord Sanabalis was waiting, the candle on the desk between his hands. His hands were pale, and finely veined, but they didn't look old. They looked, to Kaylin's eyes, like common hands that had seen their share of honest labor. Then again, Kaylin had met a lot of soldiers in her time among the Hawks, and they had similar hands. Honest labor was a matter of perspective.

The Dragon Lord bowed his head as she entered and took a seat. "Private," he said quietly.

"Lord Sanabalis." She offered formality for formality, and only when she met his eyes—his dull orange eyes—did she realize how wrong it sounded.

"What," he asked her, his eyes a shade darker, "is the shape of fire?"

And she thought of Lord Evarrim's robes in the sunlight. Of the color of Dragon eyes. "I don't know."

"Light the candle, Kaylin."

She sighed, and forced herself to look at what was there. Wax. Wick. Brass beneath both, and tarnished brass at that. But the candle was a different color; it was a russet red. The wick was long, and pale, but it seemed, to her eyes, to be yellow.

Because she was incapable of schooling her expression, her brow furrowed. "This candle—"

"Yes."

"It's not the same—"

"Is it not? How clumsy of me."

She stared at it now, the Hawk in her gaining ground. What had seemed flat and unremarkable brass resolved itself in subtle ways into something less ordinary. The plate was covered in thin runes that circled the candle base. Some were faded; the lines were too fine to be read. Others were darker and clearer, but even these defied her ability to read. They weren't Elantran, Barrani, or Aerian. They certainly weren't Leontine.

They weren't, however, old magic as she understood it. If she couldn't read what had been written on her body, she could recognize the shape and thickness of the curves. These were not the same.

"Dragon," she murmured to herself.

Sanabalis said nothing. His expression was about as giving as stone.

Without thinking, she said, "Do you know the word *leoswuld*?" And added another shade of orange to those watching eyes. They were *almost* red. And Kaylin was *almost* out of her seat. She was certainly finding it difficult not to grip a dagger in either hand.

"Where did you hear that word?"

"I apparently said it in my sleep."

His raised brow turned her cheeks the same shade of red as his eyes.

"What," the Dragon Lord said, in a voice that would have carried across a Festival street without losing anything, "is the shape of fire?"

As if this were rote. As if he had said it a hundred times, and had come, at last, to the end of his patience.

"I *don't* know."

"Kaylin," Sanabalis said, his eyes still red, his lower membranes inching into invisibility, "you *do* know. You must know."

"Why? Why now?" She paused, and then added, "Why are you so angry?"

His expression shifted slightly. It didn't get any friendlier, but it lost some of its menace as he gathered the folds of his lips into something resembling a frown. A smile, and she would have run screaming.

"I am not angry with or at you, Kaylin Neya. But circumstances have changed, and the situation has become more difficult. For both of us."

"You've been my teacher for what—two days? Three? How long did you say it took an apprentice to light a damn candle anyway?"

"I didn't."

"Oh."

"But had I, I would have said half a year. For those with the focus and skill to do so. Some will labor for three years before they manage it, some will never manage."

"And I'm supposed to do this in *three damn days?*"

"You have claimed that you have no love for the classroom. This is the classroom, and there is only one way for you to leave it at the moment. You will light the candle." He reached into his robes and pulled out a large crystal. It was clear, and from the center of its cut facets, light played against the walls.

She'd seen crystals like it before; had held them, had even been burned by them. "What happens if I don't light the candle?"

"You will not leave the classroom," he replied. "But the classroom will move."

Move. That was bad. "To where?"

"Where do you think, Kaylin? You said—to any of your teachers, even to me—that you want to be *out there*. 'Out there' is a phrase that has many meanings. You wish to place your life at risk in the service of Elantra. You have even been given the opportunity, several times.

"You are a fool, but you are not a coward, and time will cure the former, if you survive. To survive," he added, "you *will* light the candle." He leaned across the table as he spoke, and his hands—the hands that had seemed so common when she'd studied them—elongated.

She fell over. Or rather, her chair did; she was already rolling along the ground. She came to her feet neatly, without thought or intent. Every movement was instinctive.

But the hands, longer, nails more pronounced, did not alter further. Lord Sanabalis was still...Lord Sanabalis. She had twice seen a dragon unfold, shedding even the pretense of humanity, and she wasn't in a hurry to do it again.

She rose on unsteady feet, and found that she *had* drawn a dagger. Against a Dragon Lord. But the Dragon Lord's red, red gaze did not falter, and her eyes were drawn into its center. To heat, to anger, to a flame that defied death and pain, and offered consumption as its only benediction.

And at the core of those eyes, she thought she saw, flickering and shifting, the outline of letters. As if a word were writ there, and it had finally been exposed.

Not shape, she thought desperately.

The Dragon had not moved.

Not the shape of flame. Not the form of flame.

The *name* of it. She held on to those moving runes, trying to pin them down, trying to fit them into a shape she could utter. But they were as foreign to her as the runes on the brass candleholder; they weren't in a language she knew.

And yet...she knew them as language, as part of language. As something old. Old...

Without thinking, she reached for her wrist; it was free. She hadn't been given the bracer; it didn't contain her, couldn't hold her back.

She pushed her sleeves up, as Lord Sanabalis watched, and she thought she saw him...wince. But the eyes stayed the same, and that was all the guidance she needed.

Her lips stopped moving.

They never moved when she used a *name*.

Think, Kaylin. Think. No. *Don't* think.

She placed her hands upon the desk, lifting herself from the ground. She forced herself to bend, to pick up the chair. Hands shaking, she put it down, opposite Sanabalis, the man she would never forget was a Dragon again for as long as she lived.

And she spoke the word.

Fire erupted in the air above the candle. Fire danced along the wick. It should have melted wax and flesh. It should have turned table and chairs—and Kaylin—into liquid or ash.

But it *didn't*. It hovered above russet wax, yellow wick, and as the wax took heat, as it took flame onto itself, it began to gleam, as if gold were its heart.

And the candle itself grew red and bright as it absorbed the whole of the fire's mass. She was blind for a moment. All she could see was that small dancing leap of flame, of burning candle. She didn't immediately notice that the crystal to one side of the candle now held red light at its heart. But she did notice; she was a Hawk, after all.

The Dragon's eyes were shading toward orange, but it was a deep orange, and a hot one. He raised his lower membranes, to shield her from their color.

"Done," he said softly. Wearily. "Congratulations, Kaylin."

"Does this mean I pass?"

"This means," he said softly, so softly she had to strain to catch the words, "that you have some chance of surviving." He gestured, and the fire guttered.

"And I don't need a tutor?"

His laugh was a roar. "You need far more than that, Kaylin Neya. You will not be free of my guidance for some time yet."

"Then—"

"But you will," he continued, rising, "bear the symbol of the Imperial Order of Mages."

CHAPTER 9

The words made no sense. And because they made no sense, they could be slotted into a category that made Kaylin uneasy at the best of times.

"This is political, isn't it?"

"In a broad sense," Sanabalis replied coldly, "everything is political."

"This is political the way wars are political."

"Ah, yes. That shade. Or close." He reached out for the candle. She saw it, for a moment, as something that bore only the facade of wax, and didn't ask him anything more, aware of the crystal by his side. Aware that she'd already said too much. His nod, still curt, was a small benediction.

Which she needed. She was trembling. Curling her hands into fists to prevent it from being obvious was an old habit, and like all old habits, it died hard. She watched him.

He watched her. And then, with a weary smile that did

not, in any way, alter the color of his eyes, he loosened the collar of his robe slightly and lifted a chain from around his neck. It was gold, and heavy, and far too long, its links forming not so much a chain as rope. "It is mine," he told her gravely, "and I value it. It was given me by a mage long dead. He taught me much. Wear it until I give you a replacement." He stood there, chain in his hands, waiting.

She stared at him.

His expression soured. "Come here," he told her. "The young everywhere lack any sense of ceremony."

She did as bid, partly because the command itself was Dragon in tone and depth, and partly because the comment that followed it hinted at the type of lecture she ran a four-minute mile to avoid hearing. He set the chain over her head and around her neck; the medallion hung at her waist, and after a moment, he frowned, pulled the chain up, and knotted it. As knots went, it stunk. "It will do," he told her.

"Ummm."

"Yes?"

"It's got a Dragon on it."

"Ah. An oversight on my part," he replied in a tone that implied the opposite. "As I said, it is my personal medallion."

"But I'm not—"

"No. You are not. But it is older by far than you, and it will be recognized where you travel."

It was warm. The knot he'd added to the chain had raised the medallion so that it rested just below her breasts; she felt it as if it were another heart. She reached out, lifted it, looked at it.

"It is not a coin, and I advise you not to bite it to ascertain its metallic composition. You will not like the taste."

"Will I still have my teeth?"

"Doubtful." He frowned. Orange was still the high color of his eyes, but gold was beginning to make itself felt. "Do not let others handle it," he told her quietly. "Even if you trust them. Trust is not an issue with this medallion."

"What is?"

"Fire," he whispered. An echo of red.

"What if I hadn't—"

He lifted a hand. "Yours is an odd magic," he told her softly. "And a wild one. But it comes when you call it."

"It didn't any of the other times."

"You didn't need it then. There was no urgency to your call, no life in the balance."

"So you—the hands—the eyes—"

"No, Kaylin. Those were—and are—genuine. I did not, however, have to terrify my previous students into their power."

"But you—"

He lifted a hand. "Nor," he added in a more severe voice, "did I allow them to harry me with questions. Ill-thought questions, at that. I will answer perhaps one more."

"Why did you bring the crystal?"

"You are a Hawk, child." She bridled. Even coming from an ancient Dragon, the word still rankled. "You see well. The crystal is a memory crystal. It will retain the truth of this meeting, and this lesson."

"You're a mage. You could tamper with it."

He frowned. "That was not a question."

"I could rephrase it—"

"Don't. This is Imperial crystal." He frowned. "Kaylin, you *will* pay attention if you are ever returned to a classroom. I waste time here, and it is your time, although you do not understand this fact yet. Imperial crystal cannot be tampered with by lesser magic. By greater, such tampering identifies itself. Its mark will be seen and felt by any who hold the crystal.

"And now, I must leave you. I will see you shortly."

She shook her head. Had to. It was almost spinning. "Did I mention that there *are no Imperial mages in the Hawks?*"

"I believe you did."

"Then I don't want to wear this—"

"But there are no laws against recruitment of such mages. Not within the ranks of the Hawks. Lord Tiamaris was trained by the Imperium. I believe that there are no mages because the Lord of Hawks does not trust them. He did, however, cede the Hawk to Lord Tiamaris, and he was, I assure you, aware of the particulars of Tiamaris's long past."

"But he didn't—"

"Kaylin. Be quiet."

The door opened. Lord Grammayre stood in its frame, and just beyond him, the Barrani guards Nightshade had sent. Behind them stood Teela. And she was wearing a damn dress. Again.

"Kaylin," Lord Grammayre said quietly. He entered the room, and Teela followed. The guards remained where they were standing as the door was shut. The Hawklord's gaze went to the Dragon Lord; they stood thus for an awkward moment.

"She passed," Sanabalis said quietly.

This did not ease the Hawklord's tension. Given his expression, very little would. He looked at Kaylin, and his eyes were slate-gray. He frowned. "The medallion—"

"Yes. It is a symbol of the Imperium."

"It is a symbol of—"

Lord Sanabalis lifted a hand. "Of the Imperial Order of Mages," he said more slowly. At any other time, Kaylin would have snickered, having been on the receiving end of slow explanations more often than she could easily recall. Somehow, it wasn't funny at the moment.

"Lord Grammayre."

"Lord Sanabalis." The Hawklord turned to Kaylin and frowned. "The Quartermaster, it must be noted, is ill pleased with you."

She groaned. "I haven't lost anything—"

"No. But he is unaccustomed to dealing with seamstresses, and they are unaccustomed to dealing with him. I believe they have not yet escalated their negotiations to a point which would make all dealings impossible, but the guildmaster has been summoned to mediate."

Guilds, bad. Guilds pissed off at the Hawks, worse. The rest of his words took time to sink in. "The *seamstress* guild? Why?"

"They do work for us, as you know," he replied. "Or would if you paid attention. Your surcoat is not forged."

"They're not arguing about a surcoat."

"No."

She looked at Teela. Teela met her gaze, blue-eyed, and then turned away. No one was in what could even optimistically be called a good mood.

"You are a Hawk," Lord Grammayre told her quietly, "but you will not be wearing the Hawk. The Quartermaster feels that his budget does not extend far enough to cover what you *will* be wearing, and he is a practical man, not given to ostentation."

"I'm not going to like where this is going."

"I believe you will be foolish enough to like it more than any other person standing in this room."

"The High Halls." She turned to stare at Lord Sanabalis. "You—" She held her tongue; his hand passed over the crystal, and the light dwindled slowly, leaving the suggestion of fire in its wake.

"You knew."

"The suggestion made its way to the Imperial Court," the mage replied. "I came in haste. I was not, therefore, privy to the rest of the discussion. And no, before you waste more time, I am not about to share the content of the discussion I did partake in."

Dragons.

"Teela?"

Teela was wearing a dark, dark green. It was not quite the same dress she'd worn the other day—yesterday? Gods, it seemed so long ago—but it was just as fine. "The Lord of the West March has issued an invitation, Kaylin." And she reached into the pockets of her skirt—pockets that were hidden by seams and yards of drape, and pulled out a—something. It wasn't paper.

"The Lord of the Green has agreed to allow your presence. Acceding to the requests of his sons, the castelord will overlook the insult done him by the mark you bear." Teela might have been speaking of the gallows, her voice was so flat.

"What—what is that?"

Teela stepped forward and held out the flat of her palm. Resting against it was a heavy, gold ring. It was large, and it bore a crest of some sort, one that hinted of ivory and emerald. Kaylin squinted; the crest seemed to move, as if to defy identification. She cursed. "This is magic."

"So, too, is the amulet you now bear." The Barrani hand didn't waver. After a moment, Kaylin took the ring. "I'm supposed to wear this?"

"Only if you don't want to be cut down by the first Barrani Lord that sees you in the High Halls."

"That sounds like a yes." She hesitated, and looked at her hands. They were bare. "Which finger?"

"Whichever finger it will fit."

"But it's big."

"Put the damn ring *on,* Kaylin. Believe me, it won't fall off." Teela's Elantran was heated, but it was a welcome change.

Kaylin was right-handed. She put the ring on the forefinger of her left hand, and felt it *bite.* Magic, all right. And it coursed up her arm, as if it were a damn door-ward. She bit her lip, and tasted blood, before the pain stopped.

And it occurred to her, standing in the West Room, that she now had enough gold on her person to run to Elani Street, hock it all, and leave town by the fastest coach money could buy. Given the gold, that was a pretty damn fast coach.

She met the Hawklord's gaze, and almost blushed. He raised a brow but said nothing. "Why am I going to the High Court?"

"You saved the life of the Lord of the West March," he

replied carefully. "And in some fashion, he is repaying his debt."

"He doesn't like living?"

"Judging by events at Court, one could assume that, yes." The smile that curved the Hawklord's lips was a cold one. But cold was better than nothing. "You are familiar with the word *kyuthe*?"

"Some."

"Good. If you are killed at Court, he will be obliged to find and exterminate the Barrani responsible."

"Which won't help me much."

"No. You'll be dead. It is *supposed* to act as a deterrent, however. The Lord of the West March is not without his resources."

"He was almost dead himself. So much for resources."

Teela pinched Kaylin's arm, hard. "You will speak High Barrani at Court," she said curtly, switching into that tongue herself. "It is harder—far harder—to show such obvious disrespect in this tongue."

She paused, and then added, "You also bear the symbol of the Imperial Order of Mages. Although you are *not* a representative of the Imperial Court, and you *will* not act in that fashion, you will be known." She looked at Sanabalis.

"Yes," he said genially, if fire could be genial. "We do not have the term *kyuthe,* in our tongue."

"Could you teach me some?"

"Of?"

"Your tongue."

"Pardon?"

"I asked Tiamaris, and apparently, it's impossible to swear in Dragon."

Gold flickered in the center of Dragon eyes. His chuckle was loud. "I believe that Tiamaris has benefited from his exposure to your Hawks, Lord Grammayre. And Kaylin, the answer is no."

Teela nudged her. "Try to pay attention," she said when Kaylin looked up.

"I was."

"In her own way," Lord Sanabalis said. He was calmer now. Which was decidedly better than not calm, because for one, a transformed Dragon wouldn't actually *fit* in the West Room. "The Barrani have always been more concerned with kin and the prominence of clan. They are more mortal in that regard."

"Dragons," Teela added coldly, "have been known to devour their kin at birth."

Sanabalis shrugged. "It is true," he added before Kaylin could ask. "And because we do not prize kin above almost all else—publicly—we have developed no words for the relationship of almost-kin. And no traditions for it, either."

"Then this medallion?"

"Ah. If you remember your old stories—which were not taught in a classroom, and therefore have some chance of lingering—you will perhaps have retained some image of a Dragon upon a hoard of gold?"

Kaylin frowned.

"She grew up in Nightshade, remember," Teela told the Dragon.

"Ah, yes. One human enclave is so often like another, I forget myself."

Bullshit. Kaylin, however, was at least wise enough not to say it out loud. Not that she had to.

"The Dragons do have a word that will, however, suffice in the present circumstance. In Elantran, it is simple enough that I am certain you are familiar with it."

"What is it?"

"*Mine.*"

Kaylin laughed. And then stopped, when it became clear she was the only person in the room who found it funny.

Lord Grammayre hovered between amusement and irritation for a moment. "Dragons do not have a hoard of the particular type denoted in human stories," he said at last, settling for irritation. "And the Dragon wars of old—no, Kaylin, I don't actually expect you to remember anything about them. They're almost prehistory at this point—were fought in large part to define the word *mine* in a way that could *allow* the Dragons to coexist."

Sanabalis nodded.

"Even now, they do not congregate in any number, they are rare. But what they gather or claim, they protect. The rules that govern this are difficult. I am not about to explain them."

"I doubt, Lord Grammayre, that you could," Lord Sanabalis said quietly. "The Dragon Emperor is very particular about the laws of hoarding," he added. "And theft, among Dragons, is unheard of for that reason. We do not *claim* friends, in Barrani fashion. We do not claim lives. We do not claim kin. Do you understand?"

She stared at him. And then looked down at the medallion.

He said nothing.

"This is yours," she said slowly. "And I'm wearing it."

"Yes."

"But by law, it doesn't mean—"

"No."

Teela snorted. "It is his. He has granted it to you. In the Court of the castelord—either Dragon or Barrani—it has the weight of a vow. In the Court of Elantran Law, it is simply gold bound with magic. But neither the Dragon Court nor the Barrani will defer to modern law while either still *has* a castelord. What he is forbidden to do by the Dragon Emperor's dictate, he will not do. What he can do, he has done.

"And Kaylin, the only thing Barrani warriors feared in their youth were the Dragon Lords."

"He's not allowed to go Dragon."

"There are repercussions, yes. But, as you so often point out, that doesn't help the dead, or change their status." She took Kaylin's hand almost gently. "You have been called *kyuthe* by a Barrani High Lord. You have been...acknowledged by a Dragon Lord."

She turned to Sanabalis. "This is why I had to pass." Flat words.

He nodded. "In no other way could you bear my mark. It would consume you utterly could you not speak the name of fire. But where you go, Kaylin, all of these marks add up to almost nothing. They are not armor. There is, however, a difference between almost nothing, and nothing." He glanced at her cheek. "And neither the ring nor the medallion will carry the weight of the fieflord's mark. It will bring you enemies in the Barrani Court. They will circle, and if you are not wary, you will be outflanked."

She didn't care much for the analogy.

"The invitation—it's not optional, is it?"

"There is Lethe in the Court," Teela replied evenly. "And worse. You could refuse. It was discussed," she added, meeting the Hawklord's gaze briefly. "But in the end, you may be needed, and I do not believe that I will be allowed to return to the High Court with you a second time, if you do not accept what has been offered. You may enter the High Halls openly, as an acknowledged guest."

She frowned. "Marcus isn't going to—"

The Hawklord grimaced. "The Sergeant has made his opinion widely known." He glanced at Teela. "And he had his supporters among the rank and file."

Kaylin winced. "So I'll just keep mine to myself, shall I?"

"That would be for the best, if it is at all possible."

She looked at the closed door. "So…the Quartermaster is buying a dress?" And snickered.

"*All* of your opinions, Private."

"Yes, sir."

The seamstress guild was definitely working overtime. The Quartermaster, in theory, wasn't. But if any man could be said to possess certain Draconian qualities, it was the Quartermaster. He was accustomed to *respect*. Unfortunately, that respect did not always extend outside of the Halls of Law, his private bastion.

Kaylin made herself as scarce as possible; given office gossip, she eventually found herself in the drill circle in the inner courtyard. It was a way to work off nervous energy, and to her surprise, given the events of the previous day, she still had some.

She became aware, as she worked—backflips, and without a net—that she also had company.

Severn was leaning against the far wall, his arms loosely folded across his chest. This lent him the appearance of a casual observer. Which, in a Wolf, was a bad sign. In a Hawk, it meant a possible jail term, but Wolves had different legal authority.

He'd spent a long time with the Wolves.

She finished and walked over to him. His nod was terse.

"You've heard," she said, grabbing the towel he offered and sponging her face dry.

"The entire office has, as you so quaintly put it, 'heard.'" Apparently, the Wolves didn't gossip; Severn found it alternately amusing and contemptible.

She shrugged.

"You're going."

And nodded.

"Why?"

"I want to go."

"I know."

She stretched, bending at the waist and placing the flat of her palms against dry grass. There hadn't been much rain so far this season. She hoped it poured buckets, but that was just reflexive spite. It would cause the merchants some inconvenience, and given how much trouble *they* caused the Hawks at this time of year, it seemed only fair.

"Kaylin—"

"I'm not an idiot," she said softly between deep and even breaths. "What they won't say, I know anyway. It's the damn timing," she added quietly.

She looked up then. Human eyes didn't change shade, but Severn's didn't have to. He knew what she was thinking. And she knew he knew. It had always been that way. Except for once.

And then the world had ended.

She turned away and rose. He caught her shoulder. They stood there, connected by his hand and their past.

"It's the timing. Of the deaths. Of the sacrifices. Of the Dragon," she said almost helplessly.

"I know. You fought the outcaste Dragon."

She nodded. "I won. I think." She looked at her arms; they were exposed. They seldom were, but she hadn't expected much company, and this particular company probably knew the shape of those sigils better than she did herself.

"But, Severn, the *timing*. He—the Dragon—expected to win. He expected those children to die. He expected their sacrifice to…rewrite what was written. On me. *In* me. What he expected *I* would become, I don't know. A weapon, certainly. His weapon. We thought he would use me then, that he would somehow destroy the streets of Elantra. But what if he held his hand? What if he was waiting for a different event?" She looked up, at the flags; she could barely see them. Too close to the towers. "But it seems too coincidental that he tried so *close* to this High Festival. The Barrani have gathered in Elantra in greater numbers than they ever have. Well, since I've been a Hawk. Some of them have been traveling for most of the year. Many of them don't live within the boundaries of the Empire."

"You think the outcaste Dragon knew."

She shrugged almost helplessly. "I think he must have. I thought—I thought it was over."

His face was pale, and for once, it was Severn that looked away. "Inasmuch as it will ever be over," he said. She could not describe, could *never* try to describe, the tone of his voice at that moment.

She looked away, and rubbed her palms across her eyes. As if she had something in them. Not even Kaylin was a bad enough liar to attempt to say as much; the gesture had to serve as everything.

They were silent for a while. Even pain did not separate them.

"But now—" She shrugged when it was safe to lower her hands. "I'm not his weapon. Whatever I was supposed to be, I'm not. But whatever I was supposed to be used *for*—"

"The Festival."

"You think so, too."

He nodded quietly. "I'm going with you."

"You can't."

His smile was slight. Like the edge of a dagger was slight. "There was Lethe in the Court," he told her. "And Lethe is a matter of the Law."

"It's not—" She stopped. Laughed. "Teela."

He nodded.

"She must either like you, or have lost an awful lot of money to you in betting pools."

"Or both."

"Severn?"

"I'm going," he said again, but quietly. "Have you ever seen Lethe used?"

She shook her head.

"Then I'm surprised you know it at all."

"It's a legal thing. It's useful." She shrugged. "If it helps, I've seen Tain and Teela half kill a dealer by the Ablayne. They take it pretty seriously."

"I've seen it," he said softly. "If they only half killed him, they don't take it seriously enough."

"We're not Wolves," she replied quietly.

He shrugged, Shadow Wolf. "You should take a bath, or something close. I believe you'll be kitted out soon."

In her heart of hearts—as if humans actually had more than one, or as if they were like those funny dolls that nested inside each other—Kaylin had always loved finery. Loved to look at it, loved to dream about it. Usually, she'd dreamed about stealing and selling it, but that was the fiefs; it had a way of breaking the dreams it let you keep.

On the other side of the Ablayne, as a Hawk, she had learned what finery *really* meant, and she had learned, as a consequence, to loathe it. If envy played some small part in making the loathing easier, she wasn't big enough to ignore it.

It was therefore with very mixed feelings that she approached the very livid Quartermaster. She wondered idly if she could get assigned a desk job for a few months, because she was damn certain she would pay for every minute scratch in any of her regulation wear for *at least* that long.

Longer, judging by the white cast of his tight little lips. He handed her a...bag. With a hanger on it. As if it contained poison of a type which had to be imported by people with more money than sense.

"This," he said, "is yours."

"It will need fitting," Severn began.

"The Hawklord gave the seamstresses full access to current medical records. If there are any problems with the accuracy of the measurements, they are to be taken up directly with the seamstress guild." His eyes were a pale blue that verged on gray. Usually, Kaylin liked this color. She had to admit it didn't go well with mottled skin.

She thanked him profusely. She thanked him with as much groveling as a person could decently fit into Elantran. It probably wouldn't do any good, but with the Quartermaster, it was always best to go for overkill.

The worst he could do was laugh.

She took the bag and retreated, and Severn accompanied her. He was dressed as a Hawk. With a chain. And a sword. And several less obvious daggers. She wondered if he ever cut himself just moving.

They turned toward the change room, such as it was—it was mostly storage with a bit of empty space in the middle—and Severn nudged her forward. "I'll watch the door," he told her.

She nodded.

And thought better of it once she'd opened the bag.

It wasn't that she'd never worn a dress before. She had, in the fiefs. But those had been simple, like long shirts with ties. This? It was…impossible. It took her five minutes to unfold enough cloth to figure out which parts were the sleeves.

And her hands? They looked dirty. Mostly because they were; it was her nails. They also looked a bit on the square side, and her knuckles were too damn big. She'd never liked her hands much.

She struggled with string. She figured out which end was up, and figured out that the buttons on the back—all fifty of them, at rough estimate—were actually *not* there for decoration. She dropped something that she thought was a handkerchief, but when she picked it up, she realized she was wrong—unless it was designed for giants. Which weren't real. Mostly.

In the end, she kicked the door, and when Severn opened it a crack, she said, "Get Teela."

"You need help?"

"I don't just need help—I need a full term of classes."

"Which you'd probably fail."

"Ha-ha. Get Teela, will you?"

Teela pushed the door open with all the caution she usually showed when approaching an angry Sergeant. Her expression wasn't all that much different, either. But her brows rose up past her damn impeccable hairline as she looked at Kaylin. She stepped in quickly and shut the door behind her.

"Kaylin, the buttons go on the *back*."

"I figured that out," Kaylin said forlornly. Her arms were sort of loosely inserted into the sleeves. Just not the right way. And the dress was fitted enough that she was afraid of removing it because *if* it tore, she was a dead woman. High Courts had nothing on Quartermasters. At least not while the latter was closer.

"Hang on. Let me pull it—ugh—up."

She managed to pull the dress off, and Kaylin was briefly free. The younger Hawk eyed the deep, deep green with active suspicion. "How the Hells did you manage yours?"

"Mine is less complicated," Teela said smoothly.

Kaylin, who hated to be patronized, snorted. "My ass."

"That's probably less complicated, as well. And if you must know, I generally have help. It's useful, when dressing."

"Rich people can't even dress themselves?"

"It's not—for reasons you've discovered on your own—considered wise. Not if you don't have hours and aren't possessed of double-jointed elbows. Not to mention another dress, when you destroy the one you can't get into or out of on your own."

"I bet the men don't have this much problem."

Teela laughed. "They have different problems. But yes, among the High Court, they also have servants who see to these things."

"You have a servant?"

"Yes."

"Here?"

Teela's smile was all Hawk. "Here, I make do with Tain." Her smile was also all cat.

"It's good to know he can be useful for something." The dress was now on, and properly oriented. It didn't weigh as much as armor, but it was a damn sight less convenient. "These skirts are going to get covered in—"

"Lift them. That's what the loops are for."

"You've got to be joking."

Teela frowned.

"Right. Loops. These?"

"Those. And this," the Barrani added, lifting and retrieving the giant handkerchief, "is worn around your shoulders."

"My shoulders aren't bare."

"No. Be *careful*, Kaylin. Those sleeves cost a fortune."

"I can see that. It's all the gold. Why the Hells do the sleeves have to hang to the floor?"

Teela paused, and a look of pure horror stole up her face. "What are you wearing *on your feet?*"

"Boots."

"Those boots? Not if the Hells were threatening to open up and swallow you whole!" Teela turned and slammed the door. Which, given it opened in, was a feat. "Corporal," she snapped at Severn, "go back to the Quartermaster and tell him to give you the shoes. Now!"

"It's not like you can see the damn boots anyway," Kaylin said. "The skirts are so damn long you can't—"

"Yes, you can. If you can't see them, someone else will. Or they'll hear them. Those are for walking the beat."

"What are you wearing?"

"Shoes."

"Why?"

"Never mind, Kaylin. Just—try to look Courtly. And stand still. I'm not finished with the last of the buttons."

Kaylin wanted a word—or hundred—with the seamstresses. But she also wanted a mirror. When Lord Nightshade had given her a dress, it had at least been wearable. Not in any way practical, and there was admittedly a lot less of it—but it was nowhere near as nightmarish as this one.

Nowhere near as ornate.

She tried to spin, lifting her arms awkwardly.

The door opened, and shoes appeared on the end of one of Severn's hands. "Tell Kaylin she owes me."

"I'm sure she's aware of it. She saw the Quartermaster herself."

"Not the second time."

Teela came in, and in a voice that was pure Sergeant, she told Kaylin how to stand, when to lift a foot, and how to walk. The shoes were…shoes. They weren't exactly hard to walk in, but they felt like little ledges beneath the soles of her feet, and she didn't much like it.

"I couldn't run half a mile in these," she muttered, looking at her ankles.

"If you have to run at all," Teela replied with a sweetness that could have dissolved teeth for miles, "you're already dead." The Barrani Hawk took a step back. "Your hair," she said with a grimace.

"What's wrong with my hair?"

"If I went into detail, we'd be here for two hours. Take the stick out."

"But it'll just get in the way—"

"Kaylin. The stick."

Kaylin pulled. Her hair fell down her shoulders. It was frayed at the ends in places, and it certainly wasn't sleek or straight. Which, given Teela's pained expression, was obvious.

"I don't suppose you own a brush?"

"There's probably one in the stables. Joking! Just joking."

"You don't."

"Well, not really. They're bulky. And I usually just wear my hair—"

"As if it were a bad hat. Yes. We'd noticed."

"You own a brush?"

Teela snorted. No, of course not. That would imply imperfection. "You'll have to do." She took a critical step back.

Kaylin was familiar with the look—but she wasn't used to seeing it outside of a drill circle or an exam hall. She kicked an empty bucket, and really hurt her toes.

"Come on," Teela said. "There's a carriage waiting."

"You're driving, I'm walking," Kaylin replied.

They entered the hall.

Severn was lounging against the opposite wall, and when he saw Kaylin, he kind of got stuck there. His eyes rounded, but nothing else changed; he just didn't move. Or breathe much for a minute.

"Do I look like an idiot?" she asked self-consciously.

"You look very...different."

"Different good?"

He shrugged. "Different. Like a noble."

"If I swear a lot, will that help?"

"You've never spent much time around real nobles, have you?"

"They don't let me."

"I can't imagine why."

She kicked him. That hurt her toes as well; he was wearing shin splints beneath his pants.

But when she'd stopped hopping, he offered her an arm. She stared at it.

"Take it," Teela said curtly. "Or you'll trip and fall flat on your face, which we *don't* need. Showing up at Court with a bleeding lip is likely to make you popular in ways you don't even want to think about."

Kaylin took the arm, and Severn paused to adjust her fingers. "Don't grip," he told her with an odd smile. "It'll make you look like an invalid or a child."

"Then what good is it?"

"It's for show," he told her. "It's all for show."

She hesitated.

Teela's brows were shifting in an awkward way. "What now?"

"My daggers."

"Put them in—oh, never mind. Humans always make clothing as impractical as possible."

"Meaning?"

"You don't take them."

CHAPTER 10

Teela on the inside of a carriage was a good deal better than Teela on the outside, although Kaylin noticed that the Barrani Hawk had stopped to whisper something to the horses. Not, of course, the driver; that was beneath her. Kaylin never quite understood the Barrani when it came to animals.

Then again, if she were honest, she never completely understood them when it came to anything else, either.

Andellen and Samaran chose to sit on the back bench on the outside of the carriage, far enough away from the driver not to cause alarm. Kaylin could see them through the windows; they were stiff and watchful. If they spoke at all, they didn't look at each other to do it.

She turned to Teela.

"Are you going to be in trouble?"

Teela raised a dark brow. "We're going to the High Halls, how could I not?"

"I meant for the Lethe."

The pale, perfect features grew paler, which was never a good thing. In well-enunciated Elantran, Teela said, "I don't give a rat's ass."

Which made her Kaylin's kind of Barrani.

She cleared her throat; even in a carriage, dust came up through the windows. "Did you hear about any difficulty at the Arcanum?"

"No."

"There was a fire—"

"I said no, Kaylin."

"Right. That kind of no. You didn't want me at Court, did you?"

"Good guess."

"And the Hawklord did?"

"Bad guess."

"But I'm going, aren't I?"

"He didn't want you there. He wanted to annoy the Emperor less. Just slightly less, if that's a consolation."

"The Emperor wants me at Court?"

Teela looked at Severn, who shrugged in a "not my problem" way. She stepped on his foot. Which, curse the thin and spindly shoes, had no effect whatsoever.

"Kaylin, the Emperor is in *no way involved*."

"Politics?"

"Got it."

Politics were outside of Kaylin's natural realm because so *much* that was political involved the capacity to lie with a straight face.

Severn said, "You'll learn."

"I'm not sure I want to."

"When has that ever mattered to either of us?" Hints of life on the wrong side of the river. But she nodded. "It's not that different from gangs," he added, staring out of the carriage window. "The person in charge is always looking over his shoulder and waiting to see who wields the knife that'll mark a change in leadership. If he's smart and canny, there won't be anyone, if he's too soft or too brutal, there will be. It's a game."

She understood that game.

"It's the same game," Severn added. "But with more money and a lot more history and education."

"Don't forget to mention subtlety," Teela added, looking vaguely bored.

"Severn, did you pass *everything*?"

He raised a brow. "I was a Wolf," he said with a shrug. "We have different duties."

"You hunt."

"At the Emperor's command, yes. But Kaylin, sometimes what we're hunting isn't running. Usually because they don't have to." It was more than he'd ever said about the Wolves.

"No," he added before she could ask—and damn him, she was thinking about it—"You wouldn't make a good Wolf. The Hawks are different. Remember what we used to say?"

"There are two laws."

He nodded. "One for the powerful, and one for everyone else." He shrugged. "There will always be two laws." But the way he said it turned everything on its head. "You serve the latter. It's better work."

"It's slower," Teela said, looking out the window. "But it

has very little relevance where we're going." She looked at Kaylin's face, and her eyes narrowed when they fell on the mark of Nightshade. They almost always did.

The carriage continued in silence for some time—if by silence one meant the bumping and squeaking of wheels pulled by a set of thundering hooves.

"Remember that you are here as *kyuthe* to the Lord of the West March, that your actions will reflect on his choice."

"And his actions?"

"He is the Lord, you are merely mortal."

The carriage rolled to a halt. "Will I be staying?"

Teela smiled. It was not a kind smile. "You will," she said quietly. "But your clothing may need some work."

"Work?"

"Never mind. You'll see." She looked pointedly at Severn, who rose and opened the carriage door. He offered his hand to Teela, and she accepted it gracefully. Kaylin accepted in her turn far less gracefully, because she was staring at Teela's back.

"Teela?"

"Yes?"

"What exactly does one *do* in the High Court?"

"If you're very, very lucky? Nothing." She paused. "The High Halls were created to be an open space in the confines of a smelly, dark city. They are, even by our standards, graced with beauty. You, however, are graced with lack of education. I am not certain how much you are capable of appreciating."

"Thanks," Kaylin said sourly.

She stood by the carriage, Severn's hand in hers.

"How bad can it be?" she asked of no one in particular. The fact that she was about to find out was no comfort.

The fact that she was about to find out flanked by Barrani who served an outcaste was even less of one. Andellen allowed Severn to escort her, but it was clear from the shade of his eyes that he barely tolerated the intrusion. Samaran, however, was more sanguine. Or perhaps he was simply more aware of where they stood: the High Halls.

She wondered, then, if he had lived here before he had chosen to follow Lord Nightshade into exile.

But Tain hadn't, and perhaps he was like Tain. She could hope.

The High Halls, when seen in a state of emergency that didn't involve imminent death—well, not someone else's at any rate—were impressive. Kaylin entered them on Severn's arm. She tried to mimic Teela's graceful, stately walk, and gave up after about five steps; she didn't have the carriage or bearing, and trying to develop it without a few years of training probably made her look even more out of place.

The statues that had impressed at a run were more impressive at a walk. She looked up to see carved and impassive faces. Perfect faces; she would have recognized them as Barrani no matter where they stood. But the color that graced the Barrani was absent, and in its place, a sharp, hard line of detail left nothing wanting.

She didn't ask who they were, or who they had been. She had the distinct impression she was supposed to know. She passed them, lingering in their shadow, and entered through the right arch. She wondered, given that they both led to the

same long hall, what the difference was—but Teela had chosen the right this time over the left, and Kaylin followed suit.
The door was wide enough to allow four people passage
while they walked abreast.

The Hall was almost empty. One or two Barrani Lords and
Ladies traversed it, involved in their own conversations.
They looked up, but they did not look long. Kaylin won-
dered if they could actually see her.

Teela led them quietly. She paused as Kaylin paused, and
moved when Kaylin's attention was once again in the present. She did not ask what had caught Kaylin's eye. Sometimes it was the floor; the stones there had been laid out like
a mosaic, or a series of mosaics. She almost hated to walk
across them. She saw trees, birds, deer; she saw swords,
armor, and crown; she saw caves and mountains. The rivers
that passed down the mountains were real; fountains were
set at intervals throughout the Hall, blending with the floor.
So, too, were flowers, and these were at least as remarkable
as the floor itself.

"It has been long since mortals walked these halls," Teela
told her not unkindly. "And they often tarry. It will be expected," she added, "and lack of attention to detail might
be seen as a slight."

Given permission, Kaylin did tarry. The sunlight seemed
endless, and the permutations of light through glass—for
the walls were half glass, and all of it colored and composed
like hard tapestry—blended with the stonework of the floor.

She tried to remember that death was waiting. But it was
hard to see death in these things.

The hall came to an end, and the doors were not familiar;

they had wandered in a different direction. Kaylin was certain she could find her way out—but not quickly; she was used to navigating by landmarks that were far more mundane.

Teela was kind again. She opened the doors. Then again, she was the only Barrani Lord present; Kaylin wasn't certain what happened to someone who wasn't if they tried the same thing. She didn't much want to find out.

"Now," Teela said softly as the doors began to open, "be wary."

"'Say nothing' wary, or just wary?"

The brief frown was answer enough.

The doors opened into a garden. Or a forest. Or something that was so dense with living plants, it had no name. Kaylin tried not to gape. "Are we still inside?"

Teela's smile was slightly brittle.

Right. Say nothing.

But Andellen said, "Yes." And after a pause, he added, "The Barrani do not revere life. Do not think it. Do not make that mistake. They cultivate, and they claim, and they change what grows. They are masters. That is all."

Kaylin looked at Andellen's face. It was as impassive as it had been when he'd left the skiff. His eyes were the same shade of blue—given High Court, no surprise there—but his voice had been, for the space of those words, a different voice. "Did they ever love living things?"

He did not answer. But the weight of his silence acknowledged her question. She wondered briefly if this had been covered in Racial Relations classes, and for the space of a few seconds, actually managed to regret not paying attention.

Teela watched Andellen carefully, as if he had only just become worthy of notice. But she did not speak. Instead, she led them onto a small path. Like the stones in the outer hall, this path was composed of small works of art that often lay beneath leaves or blossoms.

Human minds, Kaylin thought with a grimace, could only hold so much beauty; it was like sugar, really. After a while, it was so overwhelming, you almost wanted its absence. Well, her mind, at any rate. She risked a glance at Severn. He looked almost Barrani in the artifice of sunlight and shade.

But no one drew weapons; everyone offered a polite and respectful silence, broken here and there by the clink of armor and the rustle of silk—or whatever it was the skirt was made of, damned if she knew—and the slight turning of leaf. They walked the path, hemmed in on all sides, as if the plants were, rooted, responsible for herding them.

Above, birds flew from branch to branch; they were colored so brightly, they caught her eye. Their voices were not the tiny, fluting voices of sparrows. They were raucous and squawking. She hoped they didn't crap on her dress.

Severn's lips compressed in a line that almost resembled a smile. She wondered if he'd had the same thought.

But the forest—or the trees—cleared, pulling away like a planted curtain, and the stones beneath their feet broadened in a large circle. Flowers were interspersed among those stones, and small fountains were laid along the circle's edge.

If she had wondered where all the Barrani were, she now had an answer: they were congregated here, in this odd chamber, trees rising like columns, and hemming them in like walls. They sat upon the edges of fountains, and stood, as if on display, among the careful artistry of flowering plants. They spoke in groups of three and four, moving slowly and gracefully when they moved at all.

In the center of the huge circle—and it was huge, once it was entered—was a chair that was, like the others she had seen, a living symbol; it had branches that flowered with white blossoms and golden hearts. They rode above the seat like tines, and cast similar shadows, smaller than the ones that rose above, higher and higher, until it broke the line of trees that hemmed them in.

A Barrani Lord sat upon this throne, and it *was* a throne, even if it hadn't yet been cut from the wood that formed it. He spoke with a woman who stood by the side of the chair, dressed in pale green and gold, her arms and shoulders bare, her pale hair bound in a braid that seemed to be composed of equal parts hair and blossom. She looked young, delicate, ethereal. Kaylin had to tighten her mouth to stop herself from gaping. She was the only Barrani Kaylin had seen whose hair was not black.

This was the castelord and his consort. Not even Kaylin could have mistaken them for anyone else. She hesitated, feeling so profoundly awkward she was suddenly certain a step in the wrong direction would crush flowers and crack stone. But Teela moved with a quiet confidence *toward* the throne, and if that was the last place Kaylin wanted to go, it was also the only place she would be allowed.

She knew it. And because she'd been in places far worse—although she had to force herself to remember them, they seemed so far away—she followed Teela, trying not to cling too hard to Severn's arm. She was grateful for the presence of the two Barrani guards, simply because they *were* Barrani. They had their orders; they followed her like shadows cast by unseen light.

The castelord looked up from the gentle dalliance of conversation, and his lips creased in a smile. That the smile didn't touch his eyes was no surprise. How could it? She wanted to cover her cheek. She wanted to fall to her knees. She wanted to be anywhere else.

"Anteela," the castelord said, rising from his throne. "You grace us again with your presence."

Teela's bow was as low a bow as Kaylin had ever seen her offer; it was shorn of her usual insouciance and sarcasm. "Lord," she said, rising at some invisible signal, "I bring you guests, at your command."

His eyes passed beyond Teela, and settled upon Kaylin. She felt as if she were the only person in the circle. As if, in fact, she were the only living thing; the only thing that mattered. His gaze was equal parts green and blue; he was master here, and he weighed her worth in that glance.

It was hard to be found wanting. But she'd had a lot of experience with that.

"You are *kyuthe* to the Lord of the West March," he said. "My son."

She nodded awkwardly. Unfortunately, she had tried to nod elegantly. Teela's command to say nothing was superfluous; she couldn't have spoken a word had she wanted to.

"And you bear the mark of Nightshade."

Her hand slipped up to cover her cheek. But it paused an inch from her face, and she forced herself to lower it; it was harder than bench-pressing her own weight would have been. What had the Lord of the West March said? Ignorance excuses nothing.

"I bear the mark of Lord Nightshade," she said quietly.

"Come into the light, child."

For the first time in recent memory, the word *child* didn't bother her. She stepped awkwardly around Teela, who had not moved. Severn came with her, but stopped just beside Teela. She walked past them both, and stopped three feet from the castelord of the Barrani.

He lifted a hand and touched her chin, raising it. This close, his eyes were flecked with gold and a hint of something that might be brown. He didn't look at her eyes; he looked at the mark, as if by looking, he could will it away.

He did not release her chin, but raised his free hand. It hovered beside her cheek, and she thought—for a moment—he might slap her. She tensed; she couldn't help that. But she didn't move.

"Brave child, to come into this den," he said softly. "And foolish, but that is the way of your kind. You are perpetual in your youth. Even age does not relieve you of its burden.

"The Lord of the Green has spoken on your behalf. Is that not strange?"

She said nothing. There was nothing at all she could say to this man.

"You have not met him. Had you, I would know. But you bear the symbol of my younger son." His eyes narrowed slightly. "And you bear, as well, the sign of the Imperial Order of Mages." His hand fell away from her chin.

Her eyes widened in sudden horror as he reached for the medallion. "Don't touch it—"

His smile was cool but genuine; he did not hesitate, but he did stop for a minute. "I know the name of fire," he whispered. "And I see it, writ there. It will not burn my hand." And he lifted the medallion Lord Sanabalis had placed around her neck.

His gaze did not change; no shift of color, no change of perfect expression, marred him. But he set it down slowly. "Sanabalis," he said softly, as if to himself. He looked at Kaylin. "We met, he and I, when we were both young, and the world was a vast place. Now it has grown small, I fear, for both of us.

"But come, you are mortal, and if I am any judge of mortality, you are considered young by your kind."

"I'm an adult," she said firmly.

His smile was indulgent. "Indeed, so you must be, if you are here. No child is called *kyuthe*. Not even among the Barrani, rare though children are. They have less inclination to interrupt their elders, however." It was a warning. Gently given, but implacable. "You have been marked by one who was once my kin. You have been called *kyuthe,* and have in turn called a Barrani High Lord *kyuthe* in the manner of your kind. You bear the medallion of an ancient Dragon Lord. And—although you do not wear it now—you bear the Hawk of the Lords of Law. You serve the Dragon Emperor in the streets of his city.

"There is more," he added softly. Too softly. "I would hear your tale, child. It will while away the time, and I think that even I will find much strange about it, who seldom find anything surprising."

Kaylin looked at Teela. Teela did not meet her eyes.

This was the trap she'd been afraid of, except she'd been expecting, oh, exploding doors and daggers and poison and magic. She was aware that the silence of the Court had deepened while she endured the inspection of its Lord, and she wasn't surprised to see that many of the Barrani had drawn closer.

Kaylin was an equal-opportunity worshipper; she failed, regularly, to pay her respects to any of the Elantran gods, although she did nod at passing priests. She had the very human custom, however, of praying in the vague hope that one of the deities she hadn't managed to offend might be listening.

She prayed now.

And to her surprise, Andellen approached, without permission. He did not pass her. Indeed, he did not stand by her side; he stood behind her. And he *knelt*.

The castelord's face did not change, but he grew remote as his gaze shifted, and the lingering facade of friendliness faded. "Exile," he said in a cool voice.

Andellen did not rise.

"You are here on sufferance, who should not have passed the arches. Had I not extended my hospitality to your Lord's *Erenne*, you would be dead. Have you chosen to repudiate the outcaste? Have you come to pledge your allegiance anew to the Lord of the High Court?"

"No, Lord," he said. He did not look up; his hair framed and hid his face.

"The freedom of my Halls is not yours. You will be servant to the mortal while she remains. Leave her side, and you will be mine in a different way."

Andellen lowered his head. Without thinking, Kaylin touched his shoulder; it was at the level of her hand, if she raised it slightly. His armor was cold and hard. But he did not shake her hand free. She wanted to send him home then. To spare him this humiliation.

Had anyone told her—even Severn—that she would *ever* feel pity or compassion for one of the fieflord's guards, she would have spit. And then probably run away, really, really quickly.

He bought her time. He had discarded dignity *to* buy her time. She couldn't even thank him because it would be too costly—for him. So she said nothing.

And rescue came from an unexpected quarter, a reminder that praying wasn't always the wisest of recourses; the Elantran gods had a wicked sense of humor.

"Lord," said a voice she recognized. She tried not to grimace. But she did look. Through the ranks of the gathered High Barrani, a familiar set of red robes sucked the color out of the circle. Lord Evarrim of the Arcanum made his entrance.

"Lord Evarrim," the castelord said, inclining his head. He stepped back and resumed his seat, and the woman by his side straightened; she looked like a young and slender sapling. Until you saw her eyes, and Kaylin saw them as briefly as possible.

"The mortal is not *Erenne*."

"She bears the mark."

"She bears the mark," Lord Evarrim said, his voice smooth and neutral, "but it is decorative facade. The outcaste has not claimed what he has marked."

Andellen stood then. His hand was upon the hilt of his sword in the silence, but he did not otherwise move.

Teela, however, did. She came to stand beside Kaylin. Her fingers brushed Kaylin's wrist; they were graceful and they did not linger. But the bruise damn well did. If Kaylin had never appreciated people who talked too damn much, she was beginning to resent people who didn't talk at all.

"It is not as *Erenne* that she is an honored guest of the Court," Teela said quietly. "But as *kyuthe* to the Lord of the West March. Will you question his claim as well?"

"I would," he said.

The hush was profound.

"She is here at the behest of the Lords of Law," Lord Evarrim added. "And stands beside her compatriot, even now."

Kaylin was confused, and looked up at Teela, her eyes at throat level. Teela whispered Severn's name and touched Kaylin's wrist again. The urge to kick Teela passed, but it took effort.

Severn separated himself from them somehow, moving almost as carefully, and as quietly, as the Barrani. He approached the throne of the castelord, and he held out a piece of paper. Paper, in a court this fine, seemed a currency of beggars, and this was plain in the way it was taken from Severn's hand.

But it was read. The castelord's eyes were now bluer, although green still remained at their depths. Kaylin wondered if anything actually annoyed him. "I see," he said quietly.

"During the Festival season," Severn said in smooth, flawless High Barrani, "the Lords of Law are involved in many investigations of a delicate nature. I am sent alone, in order that any investigation deemed necessary be both quiet and diplomatic. If it pleases the castelord, I will be both guest and observer in his Court."

"And if it does not please the castelord?"

"It pleases the Emperor," Severn replied. He did not flinch, or bend.

"And the *kyuthe* of my younger son?"

"She has been given a leave of absence, castelord. She is not required to aid me in any way. She does not fly under the Hawk, nor is she beholden to Lord Grammayre while she resides here. Her actions are her own."

"Lord Evarrim?"

The Arcanist was silent. His gaze could have melted metal, which Severn was wearing in abundance. "Perhaps I have been hasty," he said at last, "in my care for the sanctity of the High Court. It is unpleasant to me to see the mark of Nightshade upon any countenance that approaches yours, Lord."

"No more than I find it myself, but I *have* countenanced her presence, and I will not have it said that the High Court is lacking in hospitality it has extended." His eyes narrowed. "And the Lord of the West March, Lord Evarrim?"

The Arcanist stood taller. The ruby he bore across his brow was not the color of fire; it was the color of blood, and it seemed to be moving.

Even this the castelord accepted without any sign of irritation. "It has not been said that my younger son bears any great love for mortals."

"No, Lord."

"And the acknowledgment of a *kyuthe* is likewise rare."

Lord Evarrim nodded.

"Would you gainsay his claim?"

Blue eyes met Kaylin's. They were very dark. "She is a danger," he said at last. "To the Lord of the West March. And to the High Court."

Kaylin didn't close her eyes. It would have been a sign of weakness.

But Teela's laugh was like the ripple of small, musical bells. "Lord Evarrim," she said, hints of amusement playing the syllables as if they were instruments, and she was a master, "has the Arcanum been so weakened that it sees a threat in one mortal who is barely adult in the eyes of the Emperor?"

Lord Evarrim frowned. This spoke volumes; had he been Leontine, he would have been a mass of standing fur and exposed fangs and claws. "Anteela, how pleasant to see you, cousin. No doubt your time in the Hawks has exposed you to mortals of all stripe and race.

"In fact, given your exposure, I find it odd that you stand before your Lord and mine, beside a mortal who has garnered the interest of the outcaste, the Lord of the West March and Lord Sanabalis. Do you claim that this level of interest in one merely mortal is a common occurrence?"

"In the history of the High Court, mortals have often been of interest," Teela replied, a delicate shrug punctuating her words. "At this time, and in this place, it does not strike me as odd…it strikes me as somehow fitting."

Kaylin had followed the verbal sparring up to that point; she lost its meaning entirely as she wrestled with Teela's words.

"And I would say, Lord Evarrim, that she has also gained the interest of the Arcanum, if you speak so forcefully."

"I do not speak for her presence."

"No, indeed, but you speak as if her presence could possibly be a threat to our Lord. And if you speak from a position of knowledge, I am sure it would please the Court to hear what you have to say."

Kaylin caught the strands again. But she had missed something important, and knew it.

The Lord of the High Court waited.

And the gods turned again. The Lord of the West March appeared at the periphery of a circle that also contained Lord Evarrim. The look that passed between the two was not—could not remotely be construed as—friendly. It was, however, gilded with all outward show of deference and respect.

"My apologies," the Lord of the West March said. "I was occupied, High Lord, and was unaware that my *kyuthe* had arrived."

"Lord Evarrim has cast some doubt upon your claim," the castelord said evenly. It was a challenge. Even Kaylin recognized that. But there was no anger in it.

"It is to be expected," the Lord of the West March replied gravely. "I have never been fond of mortals. Nor, however, have I made my personal business a matter for the High Court. I considered the matter of negligible consequence." He approached. Although the Barrani did not rush to get out of his way, they cleared a path for him. Kaylin couldn't see how, and she'd spent a lot of time on crowd patrols, especially during the Festival season.

"Kaylin Neya," the Lord of the West March said as he approached her, "you honor us with your presence." He bowed. The bow was not as low as Teela's bow to his father had been, but it was *not* perfunctory. "Forgive me my lack of hospitality."

She hesitated. To speak after him would be like croaking, but worse. He didn't seem to notice. Then again, he hadn't noticed the very dead body of a guard left to watch over him, either, so that didn't offer as much comfort as it might have.

"She is *kyuthe*," the Lord of the West March said, speaking to the castelord, and only the castelord. "And I would not have it said that I have offered lie to you, Lord, in pursuit of any agenda that is not yours."

The castelord nodded.

Teela stepped back.

And the Lord of the West March approached her. He smiled. She hated her knees.

"Come, *kyuthe*." He held out a hand, and she stared at it. And then she held out hers; left hand. It bore his ring. But he shook his head. "The right hand," he told her quietly. "It is unadorned."

Andellen stepped forward, and the Lord of the West March met his eyes; the stare lasted a minute. Or an hour. It was kind of hard to tell. But Andellen did not move when the Lord of the West March again raised his hand.

Lifting her right hand, she placed it across his palm.

Light flared between their hands, spreading up their arms. It was golden, and it moved and danced, taking a shape and form that she had seen only once: in the forest, beneath the bower of an impossible tree. Feathers. Flight feathers.

And around these, dancing the autumnal drift of fall, other colors, red and yellow, green and brown, silver and white.

She did not want to let go of his hand.

But when he withdrew, she had no choice. "Is the High Court satisfied?" the Lord of the West March asked. But he spoke to the castelord, and only the castelord.

The castelord's smile was the equal of his son's. "It is satisfied," he replied. "Welcome, Kaylin Neya, to the Court of the Barrani."

She bowed.

"If you will it, High Lord, I will show my *kyuthe* the High Halls. She is mortal, her memory will last decades, no more, but stories will arise from what she has seen that will bewitch those who will never approach it."

"Let it be done," the castelord said quietly. "But return with your *kyuthe* for the twilight gathering. We will sup then, and perhaps we will talk."

The Lord of the West March bowed. He offered Kaylin his arm, and she forced herself to take it as readily as she would Severn's. It was hard.

"Anteela," the High Lord said when Teela moved to follow, "remain with me. Your time with these mortals might be of interest. Entertain us."

Teela bowed again, and turned to face him. She did not look at Kaylin again.

"And with your leave," the castelord said to Severn, "I would also have your company. There is a shadow upon you that interests me."

Severn's bow was almost as good as Teela's. And he, too, failed to watch her leave.

* * *

"The Corporal is competent," the Lord of the West March said when they were well clear of the forest and the doors that enclosed it. Kaylin saw that they were not in the entrance hall. She had no idea where they'd come out. But she wasn't about to question him; she was almost giddy with relief.

She bit her tongue. Pain had a habit of driving giddiness someplace less inconvenient.

"Oh, he's competent," Kaylin said. "I don't think he's ever failed at anything he's tried."

"And how much has he tried?"

She frowned.

"Ambition is the measure of many a man."

"Oh."

"And woman. What is yours, Kaylin Neya?"

"I'd like to survive this," she replied in Elantran, without thinking. Andellen's frown was like a mirror. But it was brief.

To her surprise, the Lord of the West March laughed. "So, too, would I—and there are many who would say that my ambitions outstrip my ability." If he did not speak in Elantran, it did not seem to offend him. "It is why," he added more gravely, "I summoned you."

"You couldn't be certain I'd accept."

"No. Not certain. You bear the mark of Nightshade." He met her eyes and held them. "But you are not his *Erenne*. In that, Lord Evarrim spoke truth."

She hesitated. "I'm not his consort," she said.

"There are very few consorts who would consent to be

so marked," was the grave reply. "Not even the castelord's consort. I am curious. Why do you bear his mark and not his touch?"

"I don't know."

His eyes were green. Just green.

"I didn't know that he would mark me," she added quietly. "And I didn't know what it would mean." She straightened her shoulders. "But I understand that ignorance isn't an excuse."

At that, he did smile. She loved his smile. She loved it the way she had instantly loved Clint's Aerian laughter, its low tones resonant with a deep affection, no matter how it was offered. But Clint was mortal, and a Hawk. The Lord of the West March was neither.

"He did not explain?"

"He said it was for my protection."

"It is poor protection indeed in this Court."

"I'd noticed that."

"Lord Nightshade was not a man known for his patience. Nor was he known for his tolerance."

"You remember him?"

"I remember him. And Kaylin, I speak his name. Lord Andellen will understand the significance, even if you do not."

She turned to Andellen. "Lord?" She whispered.

"One of three who left the Court in the service of Nightshade," the Lord of the West March replied. "It is why he is here as your guardian."

"How do you know that?"

"If I valued you enough to risk the wrath of the Emperor by placing my mark upon you, it is what I would have done." He turned. "I waste your time," he said softly, "and you have little of it. It has long made communication between our kind difficult.

"I had not expected you to bear the medallion of Sanabalis. He is almost legend to us. You have friends," he added quietly. "But they are beyond you here.

"Come, Kaylin. There is a man I wish you to meet."

"Another High Lord?"

He nodded. "He is called the Lord of the Green."

"Your brother."

"My brother." His eyes had shaded into blue, but it was a pale blue. A color that she couldn't yet read.

And yet, unable to read it, she felt it. Regret.

"Yes," he said quietly. "You are strong. Strong enough to wear the medallion of the Dragon Sanabalis without being consigned to the fire." He paused, and then added, "I do not know if that is the strength that is required. But I know that the strength required is beyond *me*."

He led, and she followed, and for just that moment, caught in melancholy and regret that was not her own, she would have followed him anywhere.

CHAPTER 11

There was a subtle change in Andellen. Kaylin noticed it but couldn't say how; nothing about him was different. Not his stance, not his silence, not his expression or the color of his eyes. He walked just behind her, and by his side, Samaran. Their steps fell in perfect unison.

He did not defer to the Lord of the West March; the Lord of the West March did not seem to require or even expect it of him. But something had changed.

She would have asked, had he been mortal. Hell, she probably would have asked had he been a Dragon. But his demeanor, as always, discouraged questions. So instead, she turned her attention to the Lord of the West March. It was a mouthful, that title. Teela was called Anteela at Court; Lord Evarrim had something that could pass for a Barrani name— where name meant something that other people could use without sounding officious or pretentious. So far, no one had used anything but the long title.

And Kaylin, who could have, didn't dare. She couldn't even think of the syllables.

"The High Halls," the Lord of the West March said, "are the oldest standing structure known to the Barrani. There are ruins across the blasted plain to the south that are older still, but no one will cross the plains to reclaim them. Shadows grow there, and little else." He looked at her.

She looked at her feet. Finally, she said, "I don't know what the blasted plains are." She put a different emphasis on the geographical name.

"They are a reminder," he said quietly. "And more, they are our history. The history of the Dragons and the Barrani." He slowed his step to match hers. "You are not a student of history?"

"I'm not much of a student of anything," she confessed.

"Ah. Let us turn, then, to personal history."

Let's not. But she didn't say it. There was nothing intrusive in his tone.

"There are always incidents in our past which we would rather avoid speaking of. Those, much like the history of the plains to the immortals, are common in the broader scope of time. But there are junctures in a life. A single life. Events which can shatter it completely." His eyes were still an odd shade of blue. She thought he must know about the fiefs, about the deaths of Steffi and Jade.

He did not speak their names. How could he?

"In some individuals," he continued after the pause of her thoughts, "those events serve as catalysts. They define the direction and shape of the future, but the future is *not* bound to them, not beholden to them."

She nodded.

"We speak, at times, of the Dragons and their ancient war," he told her. The hall was long, and mirrors caught and reflected those who passed by, bouncing images back and forth until there was no end to what they captured.

"But we seldom speak of what followed. Dragons are primal, Kaylin. They know the names of elements. Like fire," he added softly, staring a moment at the medallion across her chest. "They know much. Their wars destroyed whole forests, killing everything that gained sustenance there. They were without mercy, and without kin.

"But a Dragon Emperor rules Ala'an. He sits upon a throne of gold, and from it he issues the laws upon which the mortals depend. He has, among his councilors, Dragons older by far than he, and he does not waver in the course he set for them when he killed half their number.

"It was the last war," he added softly, "that the Dragons fought. Perhaps it will not be the last war they fight. History speaks of the past, but it does not prevent the future."

She wondered where this was going; she was a Hawk, and saw for a moment as Hawks see. It *was* going somewhere.

"There are those among the Barrani who have witnessed the winds of that slow change. Some are not pleased by it. There has been a long rivalry between our kind that is unequaled among mortals.

"But there those who, seeing what has been built, understand that change is possible." He came to a door. "The understanding is imperfect," he added, lifting a hand to touch the door-ward in its center. "And it is costly. Where the Dragons have warred, the Barrani have warred, and if the war is different, the end is not—there are fewer Barrani. Were it not for the power the Dragon Emperor wields, the Barrani would not have acceded to his rule. Understand," he added, his palm hovering above the ward, "that his rule is tenuous at best, among our kind."

"You aren't killing each other in our streets," she said, mustering some defiance.

"But we are," he replied. "And in the marches, there has been war. In the mountains, there is rumbling."

"I don't understand."

"No. You don't. Change for the changeless is costly, Kaylin. Change—in your life—was no less costly. But what were your choices?"

He *did* know. She was certain of it. "I didn't have a choice," she said bitterly.

"Did you not? Do you not now bear the Hawk in the service of the Emperor?"

"No. I bear it in the service of the people." She said it baldly, because it was the truth, and because she knew she couldn't lie to him. Nor, to her surprise, did she want to.

"You could have chosen death," he told her. His hand still hovered.

"I almost did," she said flatly.

"Almost is not the same," was his soft reply. "It starts now." And he placed his palm on the ward.

The door swung open.

Kaylin wasn't certain what she had expected. Certainly not forest, and forest was nowhere in evidence. What had the brother been called? The Lord of the Green? But the room, the huge room, was *not* green. It was stone, and the smooth, carved walls, rose up in a rounded peak, like an artistic interpretation of great caverns.

One still pond lay in the center of the room; no statues stood in its center; the water was motionless, and seemed almost dull. Pocked stones surrounded and circled it, and tall standing torches rested around the circumference in eight, evenly spaced places.

Her breath echoed. Only hers. No one else seemed to need to breathe.

"Where is he?" she said, and again, the words echoed.

"He is here," the Lord of the West March said.

He walked toward the still water.

Kaylin followed, and as she did, her feet—in shoes with soles so thin she could feel the rough texture of stone push against leather—passed above engraved words. She paused.

"Be a Hawk, Kaylin," the Lord of the West March told her softly. "Be what you are, *kyuthe.*"

She knelt, freed by his command. Unfortunately, his command didn't change the shape of her dress or the folds of the skirts or the tightness of the sleeves that must have been designed to hide the whole of her arms no matter how she moved. The trailing bits were a pain, and she thought about cutting them off.

Reached for her daggers, and remembered that she didn't have them. Gods, she hated politics.

But she let the hate go; the words were waiting. "These are…High Barrani?"

He said nothing. They were, she thought, recognizing

some of the old forms. But not all of them. Some of the writing was wrong, its shape too full, and too round. Her eyes widened, sliding to the green sleeves of concealment she wore. "How old did you say the High Halls were?"

"Old," he replied.

"And this…room?"

"It is, as you guess, the oldest room in the Halls."

"This…this word—" she trailed the shape with her fingers " —this is High Barrani. It's…it means blood."

"Very good."

"And this, this one— -it means life."

His face was utterly still. He offered her nothing.

She crept across the floor on her knees. Tracing. Touching. "This is death," she said. "And this is growth."

"The latter, I know. And you are correct."

She looked up. Met his eyes. "This is containment," she told him. Her fingers read the word; her eyes were his.

"It is."

She stood, and made her way to the torches. What had seemed like water upon first sight seemed thicker and darker on second. "This is why you summoned me," she said, her voice flat.

"I am sorry," he replied. "I could not speak of it without the castelord's leave."

"But you brought me here."

"With his leave."

"Am I going to be able to walk out?"

He said nothing. It was too much nothing.

She walked along the stones that formed the edge of the pool. There were words there. She began to speak them, almost unconsciously. Halfway around, she realized her lips hadn't moved. She looked up, almost in a panic, and met Andellen's eyes.

Saw knowledge in them. And a glimmer of approval, a brown at the edge of blue; he was either angry or worried. For most Barrani, the difference wasn't obvious.

She resumed her walk. And when her foot touched the last stone and passed over it, when she spoke the last word, all of the symbols began to glow green.

The Lord of the West March said, "So."

"You could have done this."

"Yes. I and perhaps one other."

"Why did you—"

"It is a test, Kaylin Neya. And it is not a kind one. But if you have served with Barrani, you will understand that kindness is not in our nature. Stand there," he added softly.

"Another test?"

"No. If you move, you might fall in."

Which was suddenly a very, very bad idea. She could swim; all of the Hawks could. But she swam in *water.*

The thick liquid that wasn't liquid parted slowly, as if four lines had crossed the circle and divided it. As if it were pie made of slugs.

The liquid peeled back in sections. It didn't flow, and it didn't drip. It didn't really surge. It just…peeled away, as if it were viscous skin.

And rising from its widening center was a man. He was as tall as the Lord of the West March, and as perfect; he was as regal as the castelord. She couldn't say afterward what he wore; it seemed to be moving light, something that mimicked clothing without descending to it. He surveyed them all, this man beneath the liquid, ringed by torches that seemed frail enough to gutter.

She almost forgot to stand still.

Andellen was by her side in an instant, his hands upon her arms, his chest at her back. There was no warmth in him, but there was strength. He held her up, when her knees suddenly started to fold.

When she whispered something that wasn't even a word.

"Lord of the Green," the Lord of the West March said, and then, in a voice that was resonant with fury and pain, "brother."

But the Lord of the Green was staring at Kaylin, and Kaylin could *not* look away. His eyes were almost green, but where Barrani eyes were clear, his were murky; there was blue in them, but it, too, was murky. Yet he wasn't blind.

He was also the only Barrani High Lord to look at her who did not first notice the mark that adorned her cheek.

Something about him felt familiar. Not his face, and certainly not his clothing; not his stance, not his movements—because he hadn't. Moved. Something hovered on the edge of her awareness, and had she not been a Hawk, it might have eluded her.

She wished, when she caught it, that she was a Sword or a Wolf instead.

She turned to the Lord of the West March in something that could be called panic, if she were prone to understatement. It had never been one of her failings. "He's—"

"Yes?"

She swallowed. The single word was sharp, as much of a

threat as he had yet offered. She would have looked at Andellen, but he was behind her.

Caution. Caution was crucial here. Because she wanted
to survive. That had been her ambition, and by many standards, it wasn't a remarkable one. But in this Court, it might
just have been rendered impossible.

"He's…dying," she said at last.

"I was dying when you were brought to my side."

She shook her head. "Not—not like this."

"Go on, Kaylin."

Shut up, Kaylin. She swallowed. "Lord of the West March.
Kyuthe," she added, "answer a question."

"Perhaps. Ask it."

"What is *leoswuld?*"

The silence was, as they often said, deafening.

But the Barrani with milky, colored eyes, heard the
word, as well.

"It is the life of the Barrani," the Lord of the West March
replied.

"But it means something else here."

"Yes. The High Lord convened Court in a manner that has
been done only a handful of times in our history. He means
to pass on."

She frowned.

"It is not death as you understand it," he added quietly. "But
the giving of life. What he passes on, he passes to the next Lord
of the High Court." He paused, and then added, "My brother."

She shook her head. The wrongness of the words—even
if she didn't fully understand their significance—made
breathing an art. "He's…dying."

And the Barrani known as the Lord of the Green said, *"Yes."*

The Lord of the West March came to stand beside Kaylin at the edge of the circle. He took no trouble to hide pain or longing, although the word had not been intended for his ears.

"You know of the undead," he said to Kaylin. It might have been talk about the weather, for all its intensity. That was reserved for his brother, and it could not be moved.

But she nodded. Because that's what she could *almost* see in the Lord of the Green. Almost.

"And you know, then, of the folly behind the choice of the undying." Not immortal, but undying.

She swallowed. "The names," she whispered.

"Yes. Names have power. And those who hold our names have power over us." He looked at her then. She said nothing. "If," he added as a concession, "their will is the greater will, and their power, the greater power."

"He's trying to give over his name—" She stopped.

Straightened up again, her knees finding strength. She shook herself free of Andellen, and he let her go. "It's not to be free of the name," she said quietly. "That's not why he's doing it."

"Is it not?"

She wanted to hit the Lord of the West March. Hard. She bit her lip instead, because she had no doubt that he would return the blow, and she wouldn't be the winner in that exchange.

The Lord of the Green watched her.

And then he lifted his hands, palms up. His brother looked away. It didn't help; she could sense the hunger there. But there was something beyond hunger.

She lifted her own hand; the Lord of the Green did not move. Shaking, she reached out, and her sleeves trailed above the liquid that had been his prison. Or his safety.

Their fingers met.

She had touched Barrani before. Hell, she'd had to shove Teela off her bed half a dozen times when the drinking had ended and memory blurred. She'd touched Tain, mostly to annoy him. She'd touched Nightshade. She'd touched the Lord of the West March.

None of them prepared her for this.

Because in touching him, she saw not his life, not his injuries, not anything of *him*. She saw herself instead. Felt her life, felt memories fade in and out of existence, as if she were Records, and he was dredging them. She saw the marks on her arms with horror and fear, as new things, she saw the marks on the dead as intimations of her own mortality. She saw her mother's slack face, pallid skin, re-coiled at the smell of her death. Saw Severn, as she had seen him then, waiting in silence, his eyes mirroring her loss, his words promising that he would protect her from any other loss.

Saw blood—heard

Screaming.

Hers. All hers.

The Lord of the West March caught her hand and pulled it back, breaking the contact; her throat was raw.

But not so raw that she would not speak here.

"He wants my name," she whispered.

"Yes. And mortals have no name. They have life. They are the sum of what they experience."

The Lord of the Green said, "Elianne."

She closed her eyes. "That's not who I am," she whispered. But she was lying. Her fingers burned. Where she had touched the Lord of the Green, they burned.

"It was him, wasn't it?" she asked the Lord of the West March. "It was because of him that you lay—"

"He is my kin," the Lord of the West March replied. "I thought to save him from his choice. I failed."

"It's not—" She struggled with words. She always did when it was important. Her fingers were tingling; they told a story. Her hands were like eyes when they touched the living. She hadn't known it—not clearly—until this moment. When she healed, they watched. They observed. They spoke.

"His name."

The Lord of the West March touched her face gently. "What of his name, Kaylin?"

"Someone else holds it. Something else."

"Why do you say that?"

"Because he *doesn't*. Not...not the way you do. Not the way Teela does. Not—" and she turned to touch Andellen's face before he could move "—the way Andellen does. It's there, but it's *not* there."

"That is the definition of the undying," the Lord of the West March said with just a trace of condescension. It didn't even bother her.

"That's why he's trying to die. That's why he's trying to shed his name. It's not for *power*," she added. "It's not for the freedom from the tyranny of the name. It's for freedom from the man who *holds* it. Don't you understand? He's lost his name. He's trying to divest himself of it in the only way he can because of the *leoswuld*. He's doing it because he knows he *can't* be a vessel for anything if he's…undying. Whatever gift the Lord of the High Court gives, he won't give to the Lord of the Green."

The Lord of the Green looked at her. Only at her.

But he did not deny the truth of her words.

"He can't kill himself," she said quietly. "He doesn't have that much control anymore. I think he tried to make you kill him." She added, "I hold your name." Speaking to the younger brother, holding the gaze of the older.

The Lord of the West March stiffened; she'd almost forgotten Andellen was present. But this was important enough that it almost didn't matter.

"If you wanted to be free of that, how would you do it?"

"I would kill you."

"And that would work?"

"Yes."

"You're sure?"

"Yes."

"Then find the person who holds his name and kill him."

"That, *kyuthe,* is why you are here."

"*What?*"

"In truth I cannot think of the man who could hold my brother's name with any certainty. But there is one who must be able to," he added grimly. "And if I cannot free my brother, it will end here."

The words made no sense. On so many levels. She did her best to alleviate that by starting with the basics. "Your brother almost killed you."

"Yes."

"And not by his choice."

"No. We have argued much, but we have never descended to kinslaying. I did not suspect—I would not have known—but he must have retained just *enough* control of himself that I could escape."

She said, "But you have to *give* your names."

He said nothing.

Kaylin looked at his face. He hid nothing, either. For just a moment. She turned to the Lord of the Green. "I will do this," she said quietly. "I'll...free you."

And he looked at her...and nodded. His face twisted in spasm.

"It is time," the Lord of the West March said, "to leave." He spoke loud words that had the tone and texture of High Barrani. They were not Barrani in any form that Kaylin understood.

The liquid began to move in. The Lord of the Green was swept, slowly, into the depths that had hidden him from all sight.

"If he dies," she said, "you'll be the castelord."

"Yes. And perhaps, in time, I will be the castelord regardless. But not like this, Kaylin. Never like this." He bowed his head for a moment. When he lifted it, his eyes were blue. "I will take you to your rooms," he said softly.

"My—oh, right."

"I have made provision for you there. The rooms are adjacent to my personal quarters, as befits a *kyuthe*." He turned and began to walk out of the chamber.

She called him silently.

He stopped.

"How am I supposed to do what you can't?"

"I do not know," he replied. "But you woke me, you found me when I was lost."

"I can't do that for him. I don't think I could survive touching him—"

"No. You cannot. I do not think he could prevent himself from devouring you whole."

"Then how—"

His eyes were darker now. "Find a way, *kyuthe*. If you, who bear the marks of the Old Ones, cannot, no one can."

She was silent; she followed him out the door. But it occurred to her that the marks he spoke of were marks she had never mentioned to him. And she wondered what else she had left behind in his forest.

Her rooms were sparse and fine, and when she entered them, she paused to look at the west wall; it was glass, colored and divided by something too shiny to be lead. Some panes were clear enough that they looked like openings until they met her palm; the others were dark, like precious gems. If there was a pattern in them, she couldn't see it—but she wasn't concerned about her accommodations.

She was thinking; although she had been forbidden the Hawk, it still defined her. Her fingers had gone the numb that cold causes; it beat burning. But they were clumsy and awkward.

The dress made her feel clumsy and awkward, as well. It was just too pretty, too expensive, too—highborn. If she had dreamed of wearing a dress like this, if she had once dreamed of rescue, in the way children do, she'd grown beyond the dream. Or it had grown too small to contain her. It didn't matter.

If the Lord of the West March had not been standing by her side, she'd have stripped it off. Or tried. She hadn't forgotten about the damn buttons.

"You told me," she said quietly, as she pretended to notice the wall of windows, "that no one else knew about the Lord of the Green."

"It is known that he is at Court," the Lord of the West March replied. "And he has appeared in the company of the High Lords."

"Not as himself."

"He was fey," was the quiet reply.

"The castelord knows."

"The castelord *is* Lord of the High Halls. What passes here, he knows."

She frowned.

"Hawk," he whispered.

She turned to see his subtle smile. His eyes, however, were blue and dark. "Did you tell Teela?"

"Teela? Ah, Anteela. My cousin."

"Yes."

He said nothing for a moment. Then he walked past the windows, to a cabinet that rested in the curve of the wall. He opened it, and brought out a decanter that was probably as heavy as most babies she delivered; it was certainly more solid. "Will you drink?"

"Not on duty."

"You are not on duty."

She hesitated. "I don't generally drink in the company of strangers."

"But I am not a stranger, *kyuthe*. You have my name."

And what did that mean? She could call him; he would hear her. But the syllables that had shattered foreign sky didn't tell her anything at all about the *man*. The Barrani weren't human. They weren't mortal. She had always been aware of it, but she'd never truly *known* it. Not like this. "I'll…drink."

He poured. She watched his hands move, aware that he honored her. She turned. "Andellen," she said quietly.

Andellen nodded.

"I wish to speak privately with the Lord of the West March."

"I do not counsel it," Andellen replied, surprising her.

Surprising the Lord of the West March, as well. "He is yours," the High Lord said. "And he knows what you know. I see no harm in his presence."

"Samaran, however, will wait outside," Andellen added.

Samaran bowed. It was like a little ritual that was beyond her understanding.

The door closed on Samaran's back. They stood in the room, Andellen, the Lord of the West March, and Kaylin Neya.

She said, "As far as the Court knows, the Lord of the Green is well."

"He is meditating, in preparation for the gifting."

She nodded. "So…his attempt…to divest himself of his name—that must have been recent. As far as the Lords know, he's fine. In that case, what effect would your death have?"

"It would grieve the High Lord."

"But it would change nothing, in their eyes."

"You have some understanding of the Barrani, Kaylin. It would change little. Perhaps, at a different time, it would mute the Festival, would quiet the song and the story of the High Court. But this is the time of the *leoswuld,* and even the death of kin does not compare in import."

"I was summoned, in haste, to heal you," she said bluntly. Although Teela was right; it was hard to be blunt in High Barrani.

"Ah?"

"And I was told—as was my Lord—that were I to fail, there would be war."

He nodded, his fingers around the stem of a glass that seemed too delicate to hold air, never mind gold liquid.

"But if I understand correctly, Lord of the West March, war would only occur *if* both of the sons of the castelord were beyond him."

The Lord of the West March was silent.

"You have a sister."

"We have."

"But she can't carry the life of the castelord."

"No. It would doom both she and our people in ways that I will not explain."

"Therefore, it must be either you or your brother who accepts the gift of the High Lord."

He nodded.

Frustrated, Kaylin slid into Elantran; it was like a second skin, and a damn sight more comfortable than the awkward one she'd been wearing. "Look, I'm not stupid. If you're both dead, there's no one to take the gift. Either the castelord does not pass on—or he passes his life to someone else. Deciding who that 'someone else' would be would cause a lot of bloodshed. I'm guessing that it would be whoever was left standing. Tell me when I'm wrong, okay?"

The Lord of the West March looked to Andellen. "Is she always this difficult?" he asked, in High Barrani.

"I have only recently been assigned to guard her, but I would say, given the brief experience, that she is usually *more* difficult."

Kaylin, not a big fan of arrogance, found it hard not to bristle. She did try. She'd come that far. "What I'm trying to say is that Teela *knew*. About the Lord of the Green."

"He understood the implication," Andellen told her gently.

"And the castelord knew."

The Lord of the West March handed her a glass. She half expected it to snap in her hands. It didn't.

"Do you think that Anteela could have left the High Court without his knowledge? Do you think that you—with your outcaste Lord—could have passed between the statues without his knowledge?"

"Well, yes, if you must know."

"Then you fail to understand the castelord. And you fail to understand your compatriot. She *serves* the castelord, Kaylin."

"She serves the Hawklord."

"Even that service is at the whim of the Lord of the High Court. I am not aware of all that passed while I was lost," he added quietly, his eyes never leaving hers. "But I am aware that she must have approached him. I am aware that she must have told him far more of your history than you were willing to surrender at his command. You are not kin," he added. "And any claim she might make on your behalf—and she made a very deep one, for our kind—was tenuous at best. But she went, and in haste. She returned, in haste. She will not speak to me of what occurred, and this is wise.

"She will not answer my questions, however, and this is not." His frown was delicate. It was also lovely. "But Antcela could not have been aware of what transpired between the Lord of the Green and I when we last spoke."

"Who found you?"

He said nothing.

"It must have been Teela. You were with her men." She set the glass down, untouched. "Who would stand to gain by your deaths?"

"Many, if power is the object."

"You're *Barrani*," she said.

His smile was slightly bitter. "I am aware of what I am," he told her quietly.

"How many of the High Lords are old enough, and powerful enough, to hold a name like this?"

"None."

"It can't be none. It demonstrably can't be."

"As you say." He too set his glass down. "We will take dinner in the Lord's Circle this eve."

"*Dinner?*"

"I believe that is the word. An evening meal."

"Now?"

"No. In perhaps three hours."

"You know what I mean."

"Yes, Kaylin. I am surprised that the walls do not evince their comprehension." He bowed. It was curt, but even so, graceful. "I will return for you at that time. Should you desire it, you have the freedom of the Halls—but you will take your guards with you if you choose to avail yourself of that freedom."

She did not understand the Barrani.

But she hurled the glass at the door he closed as he left.

Andellen waited for the space of a few minutes, staring at the golden liquid that seeped into the flat carpets. The carpets were a dark burgundy, but they were, as she watched the liquid, composed of strands of different material that made a textured surface. That hinted at writing.

"Kaylin Neya," the Barrani guard said when the room was silent, "that was poorly done."

She was mutinous. And apologies were superfluous anyway; the Lord of the West March had left her. "He can't be serious. The Festival begins in two damn days!"

"He knows."

"And his brother—"

"He *knows*, Kaylin. But he is the Lord of the West March, he has his duties."

"And one of them is *eating*? At a gathering of useless—"

"Of the powerful," Andellen said quietly. "Of the Lords of the High Court." He looked to the doors. "You are his *kyuthe*. Upon you falls the burden of understanding his responsibilities. You are an outsider here. You cannot—ever—understand them fully.

"That is your strength, if it is also your weakness. All of

your misadventures will accrue to the Lord of the West March, but because of your nature, they will be lesser crimes. You are merely mortal."

"You're saying I can—"

"You can go where he cannot." Andellen closed his eyes. "You will be watched because you are Lord Nightshade's. But after the display in the Lord's Circle, none will vouchsafe Nightshade's as the greater claim. He was not, while a Lord of this Court, equal in rank to the Lord of the West March."

Kaylin barely heard him. She was thinking.

She didn't understand magic. She accepted the ignorance as the flaw that it was—hers, entirely. She had thought its study impractical and stultifying; she had thought the tomes and treatises presented in bored— and boring—Barrani, beneath her. Separate from her chosen duties.

But if she was ignorant, she wasn't without resources.

"Where's Severn?"

CHAPTER 12

Severn was captivated by the damn windows. She wanted to throw something at his head, but with her luck, it would miss, and shattered glass in *these* rooms wasn't something she could afford. She had to hoard offenses, in case of need. A bit of a temper wasn't, even by Kaylin's loose definition, "need."

Andellen was part of the wall. Severn noticed him, but ignored him, inasmuch as you could ever ignore the armed Barrani at your back. She waited while Severn moved across the display of cut-and-colored glass, touching its surface in something like wonder. The color that filtered light offered changed the features of his face, the color of his uniform, the visual nature of gold; it did not touch his silence.

She counted to ten. And then did it again. After the third time, it had lost what little staying power it had. "Enough of the glass," she snapped.

He turned instantly.

And she regretted the words. His face was pale, and his mouth was tight with suppressed pain. She walked quickly to him, annoyance evaporating. "Are you hurt?"

He lifted a hand, mirror to her movement, and caught her wrist. The bruised wrist. "I'm not injured," he told her. "Let it be."

"What did the castelord do?"

"Nothing, Kaylin."

"But—"

"Nothing. You wanted to talk. Talk."

"Actually, I wanted you to talk."

He raised a brow.

She swallowed. "About Barrani magic."

"You might have asked your guard."

"Or the wall. it would have been more helpful."

The glimmer of a familiar smile touched his eyes, driving some of the tightness from his face. But the hollows were still there, like geography, a landmark that she could almost recognize but could not touch. "The Barrani are particular about proper form. If you want to get around the forms, you have to learn them. Gods know," he added, "they make a life of it. They'd be considered honest, otherwise." He paused. "They are never entirely truthful. Try to remember that."

"There's too much I don't understand," she told Severn, as if he hadn't spoken.

He nodded. He knew her well enough to know that she wasn't speaking about the Barrani, even if the statement was also applicable.

"And there's too much I can't explain. As in, not and live."

"That would be the Barrani code."

"Code?"

"They like secrets. In general, they preserve them by killing those who know them. I would guess that you're considered of value." His voice was light. Nothing about that tone reached his face. "What can you tell me?"

"There's something about the Arcanum."

Severn shrugged. "Where magic of a particular type is involved, there usually is."

"Why hasn't the Emperor just destroyed it?"

"The Wolflord has often wondered that."

"You've—you've hunted Arcanists?"

He shrugged. "I've hunted many things."

"How did you survive?"

"Luck."

"Does it rub off?"

He shook his head, the smile creeping up the corners of his mouth. She'd always been able to force a smile out of him.

Her arms were aching. She lowered them, wondering what she'd lifted. His frown was more felt than seen. His question was utterly silent. She shook her head.

"Do you suspect the Arcanum, in whatever investigation you aren't involved in?"

She snorted. "I'd suspect Lord Evarrim of anything illegal that I could remember offhand—and anything I had to look up, too."

"He is not the Arcanum."

"No. He's a damn Barrani High Lord, and he's here. And," she added softly, "he doesn't want *me* here."

"There are many Barrani who find your presence offensive."

"He's vocal."

"He was…brave."

"Which usually means certain of his power."

Severn nodded. But something about his expression didn't mesh with hers.

"You don't think the Arcanum is involved."

"Oh, I didn't say that. But I think Lord Evarrim more canny and less obvious. He is interested in *you*, but his interest is more mundane."

"Mundane?"

"You have power. He knows it. He just doesn't know how much, or how it can be used."

She took a breath and began to speak slowly. For Kaylin. "There was an accident at the Arcanum. I think it happened around the time that the Lord of the West March woke up."

"Backlash?"

"Maybe." He really had paid attention in his classes. As it was now useful, she tried not to resent the fact.

"What time did the incident occur, exactly?"

"I don't know."

He ran his hands through his hair. "Kaylin—"

"I assumed they were connected. I wasn't exactly paying attention to the timing *at* the time. And after—well, there wasn't a lot of after."

"I can probably access records," he said at last. "But not from here. Oh, I *can*, but anything I access will be read."

She nodded. "There's something here I don't see clearly."

"Probably most of it."

She shrugged. "Most of it's not important. I can afford not to see those bits."

Severn nodded. "Have you explored the High Halls?"

"Not…very much."

"You should. They're old."

The last syllable stayed there, playing itself out by vowel and consonant. "All right," she said quietly. "Let's go for a walk."

Andellen peeled himself off the far wall. "The High Halls are not like the Halls of Law. They are not like the Imperial Palace."

She frowned.

"He means it's easy to get lost. And very hard to get found."

"Try living in Castle Nightshade," she replied.

Andellen's eyes were ringed with a pale brown. Brown. She grimaced. The Barrani guard held her gaze, and after a moment, he said, "You do not understand the mark you bear."

"I think we've covered that." She stopped herself from snapping the words.

"Learn, Kaylin. Learn to understand it. Lord Nightshade cannot—will not—stand in the High Court circle again, but he has invested some part of his power in you. It is why you are considered both offense and danger. Were you Barrani, and bore that mark willingly, you would have been dead before you passed the pillars."

"But because I'm human, and of little consequence—"

"It is because you are human that you are considered of little consequence. Even if Lord Nightshade worked through you, even if he used the mark against you, you have little power—in the eyes of the High Court—that could threaten the High Halls."

She looked at her arms.

"Yes," Andellen said quietly. "They little understand the power you do have. I little understood it, until the night you helped to birth the child." He paused, and added, "And I was there when you faced the black one."

"Healing isn't a threat."

"Power is a threat. How it is used is almost inconsequential. There is some power that—in theory—can be used for anything. It is considered a weaker power—the will of the person who wields it is of greater consequence than the magic itself. The stronger powers are said to have a will of their own. If you can use them at all, if you can channel them, you use them as primal force. You must know this. You wear the medallion of Lord Sanabalis.

"It is very seldom that anyone is given the ability to channel more than one type of the latter."

"Which," Severn said quietly, "she would know, if she could actually pay attention in a classroom."

"What you did in the fief against the outcaste Dragon, I believe we might have been able to accomplish, working in concert. Lord Nightshade is not without power, and he was not unarmed."

She remembered his sword. Remember Tiamaris's reaction to it.

"But what you did in the birthing of the babe was as

strong in its fashion. In at least the latter case, you were not even aware of the cost." He paused, and then turned to Severn. "The backlash at the Arcanum occurred perhaps five minutes after the second noon hour."

"When did the Lord of the West March awake?"

"Four hours after the backlash."

Kaylin could feel the ground shift beneath her feet. "But that makes no sense."

"Not yet. But both of these are true. They are the 'facts' of which the Hawks are so fond. It is to make sense of the facts that you've come. Is it not what the Hawks do?"

She nodded grimly. "Severn?"

"I'm here to investigate the presence of Lethe," he replied with a shrug.

It occurred to Kaylin at that precise moment to wonder if there *was* any.

"Good. Let's go, um, find some."

If the skirts were less voluminous, she could have ignored them. If her shoes were boots, she would have. She almost tripped twice, tilting on her ankles as they rolled over the unfamiliar, small heels. Severn caught her both times. "I didn't design them," he told her when she glared.

But he was wearing his dress uniform. If she looked at him, rather than at the ground or her feet, she could almost pretend she was strolling through a really, really rich neighborhood, on a useless patrol that would cause no work. And no paperwork.

Usually, during the Festival season, that was considered part of your job: don't add to the paper piles. The office Hawks were pretty particular about it. And since Marcus was consigned to office hell during the Festival season—in a supervisory role—they had a lot of backup.

So this was…doing her job. Beside Severn, who was doing his. She wondered how much he missed the Wolves; she'd never had the courage to ask. He would be there now if she hadn't been given the choice.

She wondered if he knew.

Thought about telling him. Thought more about how bad the timing was, and let it go. Because although she could pretend ferociously that this was just another neighborhood, she couldn't allow herself to believe it.

He led her down the hall and stopped several times; the walls were composed of gaps that opened into small gardens. Small, perfect gardens. If there was wilderness in the growth of leaves or flowers, it was an artful wilderness. She half expected to see a signature.

"Try to remember these Halls," he told her as they opened up. "They are the domain of the Lord of the West March, and if anything happens, you want to be in them."

"What kind of anything?"

He shrugged.

Andellen said softly, "I can lead you back to these Halls."

It surprised them both.

"You lived here," Kaylin said quietly.

"For many years." He was utterly impervious to compassion, and she didn't insult him by offering it. But she met his gaze, and saw the green in it. He wasn't annoyed.

"Has it changed much?"

"The nature of the High Halls has not changed." Which was sort of an answer.

She smiled brightly. It was a pathetic attempt, but the expression clung to her face anyway, like a poorly fitted mask. "I have an idea!"

Severn winced. "Kaylin—"

Speaking in that forced, cheerful burble, she said to Andellen, "You can show us around!" She spoke in Elantran.

His eyes did not change shade at all. "If you wish," he said, "I will lead you. I am not certain you will find it as interesting as Castle Nightshade, however."

"Good."

His smile was genuine. He stepped past her, leaving Samaran at her back and Severn at her side. And he walked slowly, as if he were revisiting, by simple steps, the whole of the life he had lost.

They followed him, seeing what he saw, and failing to see it at the same time. Occasionally he would pause, lift a hand to touch the smooth wall, and nod. If there was magic in the wall, Kaylin couldn't sense it. But memory wasn't her gift—and Barrani memory was, by all accounts, long indeed. And deep.

Severn caught her hand; she had lifted it to touch Andellen's shoulder, without thinking. As if he were Tain, or Teela, he had stopped her. But as she lowered her hand, he continued to hold it, and their fingers entwined, and other memories intruded as they walked.

The streets of the fief in winter. The chill of the air. The lack of warm clothing. The certainty of death, without shelter. She closed her eyes. They had often walked like this when it was cold, pressed together, as if by simply standing side by side they could form a wall that would keep the winter out.

She opened her eyes.

Andellen stood in an arch, his hands on either side of the smooth, round walls that formed it, his head exactly beneath the keystone that held the rest in place. Beyond him, she saw wall, old stone.

And a symbol.

She drew Severn forward. When she reached the Barrani's back, she saw that the arch opened up into a tower; stairs spiraled up and down as far as the eye could see. Farther, she thought, spinning slightly as she tilted her head too far back.

She frowned. "Andellen—"

He was looking down.

"Severn, the tower—"

He nodded. He'd seen. The stairs went up forever—and forever, even at their vantage, was too high. She had seen the Halls from the outside; she was aware—as every citizen who dwelled within Elantra was—that there were no buildings taller than the Imperial Palace, none that presumed to be of a height, save for the Halls of Law.

And yet…

The symbol on the wall behind those stairs must be High Barrani. She couldn't read it, but it was clear by the stiffness of Andellen's back that he could.

"I fear I have led you astray," he told her quietly. "This is not a place for the idle guest."

"I have been given the freedom of the High Halls," Kaylin countered with care. "And I've run up and down a lot of stairs in my time." The last was Elantran; it couldn't be said in High Barrani.

"What does it say?" She pointed at the rune.

He looked at her slender arm, green trailing from the wrists in a useless drape of shiny cloth. "You see it?" he asked her softly.

She raised a brow.

"Before you descend into sarcasm," Severn told her, tightening his grip on her hand, "I have no idea what you're pointing at."

"It's a symbol. I'm pretty sure it's High Barrani. It's *right there*, Severn."

The look Severn gave Andellen would have caused a lesser man to take a step back. Or several, at a run. Andellen did not move. Kaylin was too busy to try to figure out why Severn was glaring.

"Andellen? What does it mean?"

"It means 'choice,'" he replied, his voice completely neutral.

"You've been here before."

He nodded. "Every Barrani who wishes to be granted the title Lord has come here once. They usually come alone," he added softly. "But whether they come to the tower alone, or no, they enter it alone."

"This is important," Kaylin told Severn.

"How many leave?" Severn asked, ignoring her.

"Those who have gained the right to the title," was the quiet reply.

Severn turned to Samaran. But Samaran was silent in a way that said "disturb and die."

"Choice," Kaylin said softly. "Is that all?"

"In Elantran, it has a different shade of meaning, and more words."

"And those?"

"'By your choice, you shall be known.'"

"What choice?"

He smiled. "That is the question the tower poses, Kaylin. Among others." He lowered his hands and turned away. "This is not for you," he told her.

But the word on the wall seemed to glow faintly, and the light in the runnels was blue. "I think—it is. Because I can see the rune." She turned to look at Samaran, and even his dour expression wasn't enough to silence her. "Can you see it?"

He shook his head curtly.

"Kaylin." She turned back to the exiled Lord who had once called the High Halls home. She thought Andellen would be annoyed; he wasn't. His eyes were green, and speckled with brown. "If you choose to wander here, you will almost assuredly miss the evening circle."

That was about all the incentive she needed.

Severn said, "You can't leave her. By the castelord's command, you cannot leave her."

Andellen met Severn's gaze, and nodded. "That is his law, as given."

"He can't come with me," Kaylin added.

"I'm aware of that," Severn snapped. "And I think it would be politically inadvisable to miss the evening circle."

"Severn, if I open my mouth while I'm there, 'inadvisable' will seem like an act of genius."

He ran his hands through his hair and looked away.

"I know you're making a face," she told him. She hesitated in the arch.

"I'm not Andellen," Severn told her. "Where you go, I go." He looked back at the Barrani.

The Barrani Lord frowned. But it was the frown of someone who has found something both alarming and interesting; there was no anger in it. "We will wait for you here," he told them. He glanced at Samaran. Samaran was distinctly blue-eyed and almost rigid.

But Andellen's was clearly the greater authority, and the hand that fell to his weapon was Andellen's. No other threat was offered; none was necessary.

"The Lord of the West March was not entirely accurate," Andellen added as Kaylin took a step forward.

"About what?"

"About which parts of the High Halls are the most ancient."

She walked through the arch slowly, but her hesitation was that of an observer; she didn't want to miss anything. Especially not anything deadly. Severn did not follow her; he walked at her side.

The rune on the wall was now glowing with a light that seemed at once blue and gold. She turned to Severn. Severn, frowning, executed a full circle, and cursed quietly.

The arch was gone. At their back was now a smooth and slightly rounded wall. They stood on a small flat that merged with stairs, one set spiraling up as far as the eye could see, and the other, down. There were torches. Sort of. Down was darker.

Severn looked at her. He lifted a hand once, to touch the new wall in a way that clearly indicated he wanted the arch back. He pushed against the wall with his full weight. It didn't give. "Occasionally," he told her, looking up to where the keystone had been, "I understand why you dislike magic."

She almost laughed. "Usually it's just the door-wards," she offered.

But he shook his head. "It's everything," he said quietly, and turned to face her. The landing seemed to shrink to an uncomfortably narrow width. "I don't understand you," he added.

"You understand me better than anyone else does." She said it without thought, without hesitation; it just fell out of her mouth, probably because her mouth was open. She shut it.

"I understand part of you better, but even that part often makes no sense."

She frowned.

"It started with magic," he told her. "In the fiefs."

She said, in a flat voice, "It started with death."

He shrugged. "If your mother hadn't died, we wouldn't have been together. Everyone faces death." His eyes were dark; the torchlight hid their color, but not their shape. "But if not for the marks on your arms and legs, we would have made our way in the fiefs. Or even out of them. If not for the magic," he added.

She couldn't pull the sleeves up; they were tight and fitted. Which is to say, she could, but she risked tearing them. Or wrinkling them, which in Teela's eyes would probably be the greater crime.

"When I went to the Wolves, I learned. I learned everything I could. About you. About what might have caused the marks." He shrugged. "I learned the acknowledged rules about the laws that govern the different schools of magic. I learned to understand some of the differences between the Arcanum and the Imperial Order of Mages. I *listened*. Because magic destroyed our lives." He was still staring at her.

She shrugged and looked away. "I didn't."

"I'm well aware of that. But I don't understand why. In the fiefs, we learned everything anyone would tell us about the ferals. Because they were a threat."

"That was you," she said woodenly.

"No, Kaylin. That was *us*."

"Maybe I didn't want to know." She shrugged again. It was not comfortable.

He shook his head. This time, his gaze let her go. "Knowing or not knowing won't change the nature of the threat. It will only change how well we deal with it."

"And if we can't deal with it?"

His smile was slight, but it flickered there, a kind of fire composed of lips. "It looks like we don't have much choice. I don't see another way out."

You didn't have to come hovered on her lips, but it would have sounded childish, even to Kaylin. She managed not to say it. "Choice," she said. She looked at the steps. And at the opposite wall.

"Up or down?" Severn asked.

She almost said down. In fact, she started toward the stairs that led into darkness below.

"Down?"

She nodded, thinking. The shape of the rune drew her eye.

The color of it was almost hypnotic. Thinking, seeing again like a Hawk, she made a decision. Acting like Kaylin, she didn't voice it. Instead, she walked forward, stepping with care not because she was afraid, but because she didn't want to fall over. Severn could walk beside her, and did.

She grimaced. Lifting her hand, she placed a flat palm against the rune. It covered half of it. Before she could change her mind, she lifted her other hand and placed them side by side.

Nothing happened.

The familiar tingle of magic failed to make her palms or arms burn. "Oh well, I guess it's not a door," she said, and let her hands drop.

She swore. In Leontine.

"What is it? What's wrong?"

"The rune," she told him.

"What about it?"

"It's gone."

Severn shrugged, but then again he would—it's not as if he'd actually seen it. Or touched it. "Up or down?" he asked again.

She swore, for good measure. "Down," she told him, and began to walk those stairs.

He fell in beside her. "Not the heights?"

She shook her head. "No." And before he could ask, she added, "We're looking for history. How much history can be above?"

He frowned for a moment, and then nodded.

They both knew that the dead were buried, and the sky wasn't much of a graveyard. If they could even reach it at all.

* * *

The tower possessed no windows for the first half an hour. And half an hour of walking in the shoes the Quartermaster had so grudgingly given over to Severn was about twenty-nine minutes too damn long. With a lot of colorful language as a backdrop, Kaylin sat down on the steps and removed the shoes. She almost pitched them over the railing—which was a delicate twist of brass, molded like the trailing growth of a vine—but Severn caught her hand and removed the shoes from them.

"We don't need them," she said flatly.

"You can't know that," he replied. "Whereas I *do* know what the Quartermaster will say if you come back without them. He was most explicit, and given that he handed them to me, I'd prefer not to antagonize him."

She grimaced. "You win."

"Were we betting?"

"No. Not unless you had money riding on them." She cursed stairs in general, but with her feet flat on the cold stone steps, she was inclined to be less hostile. That inclination lasted another half an hour. When she sat again, Severn sat beside her.

"We don't actually seem to be getting anywhere," she told him.

"No."

"I don't suppose any of that magical study you did involved illusions?"

"Some. If that's what this is, we're in trouble."

"Figures." She held out a hand. He gave her the shoes. "My feet are cold," she offered by way of explanation. She put them back on and stood up. "We're doing something wrong."

He raised a dark brow. Standing, he leaned over the rail and dropped something; it might have been a coin.

There was no sound at all in the tower.

"That's a good drop," he told her, staring over the rail for some sight of whatever it had been.

She nodded, but she was frowning. "We shouldn't be here. Andellen said that himself. If this is a test, it's not a test that was designed for us. I should have asked him how long it took him to get out."

"He wouldn't have answered."

"He led us here, didn't he?"

Severn frowned. "You noticed." There was vastly more sarcasm in the two words than words that feeble should have been able to contain.

"I sort of told him to."

"You told him—and Kaylin, *don't* take up acting as a second job if you think you need money—to show us around the High Halls."

"Yes. But his eyes—"

"Were green."

"And brown."

Severn thought about that for a moment. "And brown is approval. Or respect."

"I think they're usually the same, with the Barrani."

Severn shrugged. It was his punctuation. "All right. Assume that he meant you to be here. Assume that this is, as he said, a test all Barrani must undergo if they want to be Lords of the High Court."

She frowned. "Keep talking."

"About anything in particular?"

"About the High Court."

He sat on a step three above the one she was standing on; he was still taller, but she tried not to resent it. "The High Court is composed of Barrani Lords."

"They all live here?"

At that, he hesitated. "The Lord of the West March lives in the West March."

"Where is that, anyway?"

"No one knows for certain."

"Right. But not here."

"No…"

"And the Lord of the Green? And what the hell *is* the Green, anyway? At least the West March sounds like a damn *place*."

"The Barrani have their own symbols."

"Green usually means they're happy."

"For a given value of happy. They're happy killing each other half the time."

"No, if they're killing, they're blue."

"Does it matter?"

"Here? How the hell should I know?"

"Ah. I think I understand why you want me to do the talking. You're babbling."

"Ha-ha." She frowned. "Teela is a Lord."

"Well, she's not going to be much help to us if we can't get out."

"But if *we* get out, what are we?"

"Alive."

"Try to work with me, okay? Teela used to live *here*. But the closest friend she has is Tain, and I'd bet my own money he never did."

"I wouldn't touch that bet."

"Samaran never did either. But Samaran followed Nightshade."

"They have a complicated clan system."

"They have a bloody complicated *everything*. If *we* get out, we're not Lords of the High Court."

Severn's expression sharpened; for just a moment, he looked dangerous, and his scars were white and ivory in the gloom. It was, to be fair, mostly Kaylin's gloom, as they were standing directly *under* a torch, but still.

"I may be forced to kill Andellen," Severn said slowly.

"Don't. Oh, and why?"

"The Barrani have owned the High Halls since before the founding of the Empire. This Empire. And the previous one. And, if history is correct, the one before that. They've always claimed it, there's never been another race that has."

"They built it."

"Did they?"

"Most of it."

"I'm not so certain." The way he said it, Kaylin suddenly wasn't so certain either.

"Think like a Barrani," he told her, leaning back and placing both of his arms flat behind him. She wouldn't have tried; her feet were still smarting from the constant cold of their contact with the stone. That and the edge of the step wasn't worn enough that she wanted it biting into her shoulder blades.

"Trying." She paused. Looked at him.

"*Not* like Teela," he snapped. And added, "Try to work with me," in very precise mimicry of Kaylin. "Castle Nightshade is *old*. It predates the Empire. All of them. What rules bind it?"

She shrugged. For a variety of reasons—most of them ones she was unwilling to think about at all, never mind with any depth, she didn't spend a lot of time thinking about the Castle. Or the Barrani that served as door-wards in the Long damn Hall. Or the portcullis. Or the forest. Or the room with the seal. "Nightshade," she said quietly.

"Nightshade binds it?"

She nodded, hesitantly grasping the strands of Severn's thoughts. "He rules it," she said. "He didn't build it. I think— I haven't asked how, and no, I'm never going to—that taking the Castle was costly. But it's his. He can go anywhere in it."

"And you?"

"He…said that I could eventually find my way anywhere in the Castle, but I wouldn't get there the same way he did."

"Is that because you bear his mark?"

"I've never asked."

"Well, ask *that* one, will you?"

She nodded, humor absent. The attempt was tiring. "You're saying…that the Lord of the High Halls rules the Halls in the same way the fieflord rules the Castle?"

"I wouldn't bet my money on it. I would bet yours, if that's any help." It was; fief-talk for almost certain, but not quite.

"It still doesn't explain the test." But she looked at the walls. "Or maybe it does," she added. Thinking again. It was comfortable, to think. Compared to, say, panicking.

"No, it doesn't. But Teela lived here. Andellen lived here. Nightshade lived here."

She nodded three times. "So the taking of the test probably meant—before the Dragon Emperor, before the Empires that I don't remember the names of, so don't bloody ask—"

"Wouldn't dream of it."

"—that at some point, only Barrani who *could* live here without getting lost, the way the Castle loses people, did live here."

"The Barrani like to weed out the weak. They're fond of hierarchies and titles. If this was a proving ground of some sort, it probably wouldn't have mattered to them who built it originally. It served a purpose. You came here, and you either made it out or you didn't. It's pretty clear that Samaran never tried. Tain?"

She said, "He didn't try."

Severn nodded grimly. "You think he wouldn't be here at all if he had."

"I think he *would* be here if he had. Or at least as much as Teela is. I don't think pass or fail here is a grade." She bit her lip. "If we can pass this test somehow, we *can* live here. I mean, we can live in the same damn place as the High Lord."

Severn nodded.

"You think Andellen wants that?"

"I could not tell you what Andellen intended."

"By current law—by current *form*—we'd have to be accepted as Lords of the High Court. If we made it out."

"And could prove it, yes."

But she was still frowning. "If it happened that way, though, it's not the Barrani that are doing the testing."

"No."

"It's the High Halls."

"Yes."

She said something in Leontine. And then added something in Aerian. "What I'd like to know," she finally said, stretching her legs and massaging her calves without— quite—sitting on the steps, "is who the hell thought it would be a good idea to design *sentient* bloody buildings." The cold was bad enough that she hesitated for a moment and then slid her feet back into her shoes.

"The problem with that," Severn replied, his voice that shade of too quiet, "is that we're probably likely to find out."

That's the point, she thought. She put her hands on the rails and examined them carefully. "Barrani," she told him.

"You said the mark on the wall was a High Barrani rune."

"No, Andellen said that. I said it looked like High Barrani to me." She frowned, and then added, "The bastard."

"Does that mean I can try to kill him?"

"No. It means you can stand in line. He *didn't* say it was High Barrani. I said it. He just told me what it meant."

Severn said, "I don't like what you're thinking."

"You don't know what I'm thinking. I don't even know what I'm thinking!"

"I know what you will be thinking in about ten seconds…you've got that look on your face."

"I'm thinking," she said pointedly, "that thinking like a Barrani will get us exactly nowhere. I'm thinking that this is like the Long Hall in Castle Nightshade, but it's stretched in the wrong damn direction."

Severn shook his head. "I told you. I don't like it."

"Come on," she added, gripping the rail tightly in whitening hands. "Do you trust me?" She regretted the question the minute it fell out of her mouth.

"That's not the right question," he said, coming to stand beside her. His hand was around her waist for just a moment as he looked down. "Do you trust me?"

"With my life," she said, but bitterly.

She leaped up lightly onto the railing, and Severn did the same; she caught the hand at her waist and held it tightly.

Then she jumped, and her weight bore them both into the darkness.

CHAPTER 13

The world folded, twisting around them as they fell.

Or as they should have been falling. Except that they weren't. They hung suspended over nothing, as torchlight and stairs and brass shattered and blended, re-forming around them as if they were the center of the universe.

The center of a different universe.

Kaylin looked up at Severn's chin. She would remember the underside of his face clearly, because it was the first thing she tried to see. "Can you see this?" she asked him softly. And then, when he didn't answer immediately, "Are you all right?"

His hand was still around her waist; her hand was clutching it. He moved slightly, changing his grip. It was sort of an answer. It wasn't a *good* answer. He said, each word distinct, "For a person who hates magic, it doesn't bother you much."

"Meaning?"

"You're not hysterical."

She shrugged, or tried to. "Would it help?"

He laughed; it was a low sound. "It might help me," he told her. "It might not." He let her go. She did not, however, reciprocate.

Looking at her hand for a moment, he said nothing. And then he straightened his shoulders, and he was Severn again. Because he had become aware that she needed him to be Severn. She let him go, then. Thinking, as she did, that need was a funny thing; you were never sure if you had it by the tail or the jaw. Being needed forced her to find strength; being needed too much forced her to confront failure. Not being needed at all?

She shook her head.

They stood in a long hall. There were no stairs here, and the brass work that had been the railing was now a green set of lines that clung to walls, shadowing them with the green of summer leaves. The hall itself was perhaps ten feet tall, but the ceilings were rough, and suggested dirt rather than rock. The walls, however, were smooth beneath the creepers, and hard.

She looked at Severn, and then beyond him. In either direction, the hall seemed featureless; it was an improvement over the stairs, but only theoretically. "Flip a coin?" she finally said.

Severn dutifully pulled out a silver talon. Kaylin called, and he caught; the coin rested on the back of his hand, beneath the flat of his palm.

"Well?"

He removed his hand. The coin was completely blank.

"Really hating magic," Kaylin told him.

"Not as much as I will if the coin stays this way. I should've used copper."

Kaylin shrugged and began to walk, and Severn fell in beside her. There were no torches here, but a diffuse light peered out from the sparse gaps between leaves; it was enough to see by. They walked in silence for some time.

"What are we looking for?" Severn finally asked her.

"The way out."

"What does that mean here?"

She started to answer, but flippancy evaded her grasp. "I'm not sure," she told him slowly. "I'm not sure where *here* is."

"What does it mean in the Castle?"

She shook her head, and her hand brushed her cheek. "Nothing," she told him. She looked up at the ceiling. "Can you give me a boost up?"

"You can probably reach if you sit on my shoulders."

They'd done this before, but she'd been younger and lighter; muscle counted for something. He knelt, and she straddled his shoulders, discovering that skirts were, in fact, bad for *everything*. But if she'd gained muscle and height in seven years, so had Severn; he gained his feet without apparent effort.

She reached up and touched the ceiling. What appeared as dirt was not—quite—dirt. It was, however, covered in a mottled layer of earth. She ran her hands across it, frowning. "Severn? I think the ceiling is made of…roots."

"Roots?"

"Plant roots. Some are smaller than others. Some are bigger than my thigh."

"Roots usually grow down," he said after a pause. "You think we're underground?"

"As much as you do," she replied. "How far can you walk like this?"

"Not far."

She nodded, although he couldn't be expected to see it. Her hands continued to play against the surface, her nails gathering dirt the way short nails everywhere did. "Let's follow this one," she told him. "Take a couple of steps forward and stop."

He did this, and she once again touched the ceiling. Found the largest of the roots, and, trying to keep her hand beneath it, nudged him forward again. They walked this way for about twenty minutes before Kaylin told him to stop. There was enough urgency in the single syllable that he almost unbalanced, and she realized he'd gone for his knives.

"It's not that kind of stop," she told him as he regained his balance—and his hold. "I can—something's different. I can feel—something engraved here."

"John was here?"

"Ha-ha." Her fingers had found marks or grooves that turned in a curve. In a series of curves, some large and thick, some small and fine. "I think it's writing," she said. "But I can't read it."

"It doesn't matter," Severn told her, and her hand fell a few inches as he knelt. "We're on the right track. Or," he added in a softer voice, "the wrong one."

"How do you—" She slid off his shoulders in silence, looking ahead.

"Just a hunch."

A Barrani man stood in the hall before them. He looked vaguely familiar, which is something that could be said of *any* Barrani of any gender. He wore armor, however, and a sword, although the weapon remained in its sheath.

Kaylin didn't like the look of him.

Severn didn't like it any better, and he didn't like it faster. The hall was narrow enough that it was pointless to unwind the chain of his favored weapon, but the blade in his hand was attached to said chain, and the chain hung low enough to give it play. Or to stop Severn from losing the weapon.

Kaylin reached for the daggers she wasn't carrying.

She could have written a treatise on the danger of dresses in about thirty seconds, but it wouldn't have been printable.

The man, however, did not attack; he didn't move.

He did see them. It was too dark to gauge the color of his eyes. But he lifted a mailed arm and pointed between them.

Go back.

"Uh, no," Kaylin told him.

"Is he alive?" Severn asked quietly.

She hesitated. "He's not dead. I mean, not like the other ones."

"Too bad."

She raised a brow.

"They were a lot slower."

"They kept fighting without their heads."

"True." Severn had bent his knees, spread his feet, assumed a fighting position. But the Barrani didn't move.

Kaylin's arms began to tingle. She cursed.

"Bad?"

And nodded. "Very."

"He's still not moving."

"No. He's not. Something else *is*."

Severn reached for a dagger and handed it to Kaylin, never taking his eyes off the Barrani. He repeated the motion a second time as Kaylin kicked off her shoes. The ground was a shock to the soles of her feet; it was like standing on ice.

She'd done that once or twice in the winter, when old shoes had given way; she'd never done it voluntarily.

The light that hid behind creepers flickered slightly. Kaylin, without thinking, slammed her hand into the wall, crushing leaves in her rush to touch stone. She whispered a harsh word that left her throat raw, and the light strengthened, forward and back.

"Impressive," Severn said. "Do you even know what you said?"

She shook her head. Because she didn't. At the moment, she didn't care.

Behind the Barrani, shadows were moving.

They were familiar shadows; one could even call them childhood shadows. "How many?" she asked Severn.

"I count four."

"They can't attack four abreast."

"No. Not unless they're stupid." His tone mirrored her thoughts: not much hope of that. In the steady light, the creatures padded forward, eyes and teeth gleaming, voices beginning their slow growl.

Four ferals. Four hunting ferals in the High Halls.

* * *

Kaylin stood beside Severn, her daggers ready. She could throw one; she wasn't willing to throw two. But they weren't weighted for throwing, and even if she was damn lucky, a lethal hit wasn't guaranteed. The Barrani Lord stood like a statue; he did not draw sword or otherwise move. The ferals glided past him as if he weren't there. But he was. Had he been a simple illusion, they would have passed *through* him, and probably the hard, stupid way.

Ferals hunted anything that moved or breathed. They hunted in packs, but they weren't picky about their prey. Occasionally, Barrani guards had been caught by the ferals, to the great relief of the human denizens of the fief of Nightshade.

It meant less ferals, after all. And possibly—just possibly—a few less Barrani.

The ferals were about three yards away before they began to howl. It was a trick, and seven years ago, Kaylin would have been transfixed by the sound; now it was simply a warning. Two legs or four, she'd been hunted before. Ferals didn't have crossbows. They didn't have longbows. They didn't have magic.

They didn't, she thought, as she brought the right dagger up and the left back, have scales or jaws the size of horses. They couldn't fly.

But they could *leap.*

As one, the front two did. Kaylin didn't look to Severn, didn't look behind him; she didn't try to find a place to hide. She wanted to for just a second—for less than a second—but she wasn't that child anymore.

She was a Hawk. A Ground Hawk.

Her feet were burning and numb. It would have made running hard. It didn't make much difference to fighting, yet. She caught the snap of a jaw with the flick of a knife; were it not for momentum—the feral's—it would have been easier. She'd expected the weight, but the speed was startling, and reflex took rein, kicking thought out of the driver's seat.

She brought her left arm up and in, thrusting the second dagger toward the feral's momentarily exposed throat. She felt fur, and heat, saw eyes that reflected light. The feral leaped back, bleeding.

The one attacking Severn didn't have that chance. He rammed his arm *into* the open jaw and cut through half its neck. The growl died into a gurgle, and Severn was in motion, forward motion.

Kaylin's first feral turned to snap at him as he moved past, and she brought both daggers down through the base of its spine, crossing them over in a neat, brutal movement. More blood. Less fur. A glint of exposed bone. She kicked the feral over, pulling the blades free in time—just—to fend off the third.

The halls were narrow.

The feral was loud. Louder than she remembered, and she remembered ferals. The smell of them. The fear they caused. The desperation of night in the fief. *Elianne.*

Her old name.

And not her name. Her arm jerked as she tried to pull it back; the feral had a mouthful of silk in its jaw, and it wasn't letting go. This would, Kaylin realized, be because she was bleeding. The fabric was shiny; the blood ran down its length before it was absorbed. Ferals in a blood rage were just that little bit more stupid.

And given that the teeth weren't connected to the bleeding parts—yet—this was to her advantage.

She couldn't use the one arm, but she did have two, and the feral had taken hold of the right sleeve. Had she time, she would have cut it loose. Instead, she let the feral decide how far forward she was going; she stopped resisting its pull. She pitched forward, and the dagger traveled ahead of her. It lodged in the feral's eye, and she put the whole of her weight behind its travel.

Yanking the dagger free, she paused to look at the weapon. One of Severn's, longer than what she was used to by maybe an inch, and sharper than her tongue at its harshest.

She looked up; Severn was finished.

They were standing a yard from the Barrani lord, who surveyed them with eyes that were…gray. He did not touch his sword. He did not otherwise appear to notice them. But he stood in the hall.

Severn stepped past him, tense, moving against the wall. When he did not draw weapon or otherwise move, Kaylin traced the same path, with the same watchful wariness.

The Barrani Lord began to fade from sight.

Kaylin looked at her dress. The rips—and the blood—remained where they were. There was a gash from her elbow to her wrist, but it was shallow. She'd gotten worse in training exercises.

Severn frowned and looked at her. She shook her head. "I guess the testing begins in earnest," he told her quietly.

"The Quartermaster is going to kill me."

He laughed. It was a wild laugh. "He's going to have to stand in line."

"Here's hoping." Kaylin cursed, ran back, and picked up her shoes. Her feet were slightly blue. She put the shoes on, teetered, and forced herself to stand normally.

They began to move forward, down the hall.

She was almost ready to ride on Severn's shoulders, gathering more fingernail dirt, when something in the distance caught her eye. It lay across the floor, not moving. Severn's frown seemed etched across his face, but he stiffened, and held out an arm, blocking her.

She glanced at him. She still held his daggers. He still held his blade.

"Barrani?" she asked him.

He shook his head. "Not like the last one," he added. "No armor."

"No movement, either."

He nodded carefully, but that was the whole of his movement. He seemed to have internalized all action, all physical motion. His eyes were narrowed, and his hand—the hand that held the blade—was white as the bone beneath skin.

She lifted her head slowly.

"Severn," she said. Her voice was steady. But only barely. The light began to gather, as if it were, like Severn, contained unnaturally. It grew brighter; the halls grew brighter.

Although they hadn't moved, the light deprived them of the need: They could see. They could both see.

Kaylin swallowed and closed her eyes.

It didn't help.

How could it? Eyes closed in the dark of her room—any room—for far too long, she had seen what now lay upon that floor. It had defined her life for seven years.

And it had defined Severn's life, as well.

Murder did that.

She opened her eyes again, and began to walk forward. When she hit Severn's arm, she reached up and pushed it to the side. It gave slowly, as if it were a stiff gate. He did not say a word.

She couldn't run in the shoes; she didn't try. Had she, she would have probably run in the other direction. It's what she had done the first time she'd seen them dead.

Steffi and Jade. The children she'd half adopted in the streets of Nightshade, a world and a life away.

They were bodies. Blood was fresh, but it had half dried. She could see as a Hawk saw; they were dead. Arterial bleeding. They'd both taken neck wounds; short cuts, but deliberate. So much blood for such a small mark.

She hadn't taken the time to examine them.

She hadn't taken the time to do anything but flee. It was her shame, and it marked her. Maybe some very stupid part of her mind had thought that if she *did good*—whatever the Hells that meant—it would count. And to who, in the end? It wasn't as if she worshipped gods. She mostly liked gods, as they minded their own business; it was their followers who gave her the occasional problem.

What she hadn't done then, she could do now.

She knelt by Jade's side, Jade, the younger of the two.

Steffi had been like day, Jade like Dawn. None of them had been like night, not in the fiefs. Their eyes were open and unseeing; wide, blue and brown. They were *so young*.

She lost the Hawk's view as she stared. She thought the color of the light had shifted, darkening and changing until all she could see was red. And she'd thought that was a turn of phrase.

Her mouth was dry. Her throat was dry. Words piled up behind closed lips, clenched jaw, as if they were a battering ram. She wanted to kill Severn.

And Severn was waiting.

She rose. Her skirts brushed their wounded bodies like a green shroud. She turned to face him. She hadn't touched them. She would have had to put the daggers down to do it, and the first rule of the fiefs was *never* disarm yourself in the presence of an enemy.

But this enemy, this Severn, was different.

He didn't even try to speak. All color had seeped out of his face, like sand through the slender neck of an hourglass. His expression remained unchanged. It was stiff, contained, unnatural. He moved down the hall toward her, his blade slowly falling as his arms reached his sides.

He didn't let go of it. She saw that.

Before she could speak—and she should, she knew it—he had drawn closer. Close enough that she could end it easily; she could drive the blades home.

But he wouldn't have stopped her. She saw this clearly. He had fought her in the Hawklord's tower. He had fought her in the Foundling Halls, and outside, in the streets that surrounded them.

He was done with fighting. Everything about him said that.

She did not want to meet his eyes.

She did not want to look away.

Caught between these choices, she lost both. He walked past her—inches past her shaking hands, her exposed knives—and knelt against the icy floor.

And then he did what she hadn't done; he touched their faces. He closed their eyes. He bowed slowly, bending at the waist until his head was almost level to the floor…was, in fact, level with their faces.

But he didn't speak.

He simply knelt and waited.

And it came to her as she watched, shaking, that this wasn't an act of penance; it was a reenactment. He was doing, at twenty-five, what he had done at eighteen. He hadn't run after her. He had stayed.

Almost horrified, she shifted her stance, her skirts swaying. She watched him, torn between rage and pity. Time passed.

At last he unbent, and then he lifted them both, one in each arm. They were limp now, and heavy. Rigor mortis had not yet set in. She almost called his name, but she bit her tongue instead, for he began to carry them down the hall.

She followed, as if she were a ghost, unseen. And in some way, she was. Her life turned, here, on this moment—but so did Severn's. And it *should*, gods, it should. The girls had had no one in the world but Severn and Kaylin, and Severn had betrayed them utterly.

She had thought to lead them, in this place. But as always, it was Severn who led. He staggered once or twice with the weight of the girls. Their girls. He paused once, his back against the wall, crushing leaves she was certain he wasn't even aware of. But he did not let go of them.

Had it been night?

Strange that she couldn't remember. She followed. She wanted to carry one of them. She wanted to offer. But her tongue was frozen. She would have sheathed the daggers, but Severn wore the sheaths, and it was suddenly important that she not touch him or disturb him.

He walked. She followed.

Stairs opened beneath his feet, and he struggled down them. It made no sense that he could do this; he should have carried them one at a time. He should have thought—

She swallowed. She had never asked him how *he* felt. Because it hadn't mattered. And it shouldn't matter now; he'd *murdered* them. But her throat had that peculiar tightness that spoke of trapped water, and she could barely breathe for the tightness, because with breath would come tears.

By your choice, you shall be known.

This had been his choice. And she had judged him by it.

It came to Kaylin as she followed Severn that she couldn't see what he saw. She had seen the rune, and touched it, and it had vanished; he had seen nothing. Now she saw the halls, the stairs, the odd root-bindings that made the roof. But his odd movements, the way he slid to the side here or there, implied that he saw something different.

He teetered. He stopped again, leaning on walls. She could see his face over the slump of Steffi's shoulders, her hair tangled and matted with dried blood, and she had to bite her lip. His face—oh, his *face*. For a moment, she could read everything in its lines. She couldn't look away.

But he did, and when she could see him again, he was stiff resolve. More walking. The halls stretched on from the stairs into a different sort of light than the light that lit the walls above. Here, it was almost moonlight. The time for ferals. Death in the fiefs.

And Severn walked on.

Ferals, she thought, would smell blood. Ferals would come; they already had.

She had her daggers ready, and she listened and watched because Severn couldn't. Perhaps because fighting would be a relief, no ferals came to interrupt this funereal procession, this silence.

Finally, Severn came to a stop. He staggered, and his knees buckled. He hit the dirt awkwardly. And it was dirt; no cold, icy stone. But the ground was hard, she thought. She didn't touch it. Instead, she watched over the girls while Severn turned away.

When he turned back, he carried not a blade but a shovel. Where it had come from, she didn't know; that it was magic, she didn't doubt. But neither of these seemed to be strange to her. She watched, and bore witness, to his pain and his determination.

He began to dig. Hours passed, or so it felt. She had no like shovel to help him. Just daggers, and daggers wouldn't help. They wouldn't expand the earthen bed. They wouldn't deepen it, or make it long enough that it could hold, in the end, the two things precious enough to work for.

She hadn't buried her mother.

Her eyes were watering. She could have pretended it was something other than tears; would have told anyone who watched that some of the flying dirt had lodged in her eye. Tears were weakness. But to herself? No lies, here.

Just Severn and her girls.

He lifted Steffi first, and brushed the hair from her forehead. And then he *kissed* her forehead, all the while whispering something she could not hear. Prayer was useful then; she never wanted to hear it.

He laid Steffi down in the grave, and then turned to Jade, who had been so difficult in her own way. Hard to love, wary to trust, plain and often sullen. But he held her more tightly. He didn't kiss her forehead because she had never liked to be kissed or touched much.

He laid her, gently, beside Steffi, arranging them with care so that they would never have to be alone. And then he knelt again, as if he had no further strength, and he stayed by the edge of the grave for a long time.

Almost longer than Kaylin could bear.

She tried to take the shovel in her hands, but her hands passed through it. She tried again, and again, she was reminded that she was simply an observer here. She couldn't help in any way.

It's not for him, she told herself in something very like fury and yet very different. *It's for them.* But no one was listening.

Severn finally rose. There was blood on his hands and on his shoulders, on his chest, on his face; their blood. He didn't seem to be aware of it. He lifted the shovel, and she saw that his hands were blistered. And that he clearly didn't notice, or didn't care.

He began to shovel the dirt back over them, like a blanket. She looked at his hands, at the growing dirt that covered Steffi and Jade, at the pointed end of the shovel. At anything but his face.

And when he finished, he sat again, the point of the shovel buried in the hard earth, his hand upon its handle. He said nothing. What could he say?

But he rose at last, and turned back the way he'd come.

She was there.

His eyes rounded perceptibly.

By your choice, she thought.

He saw the daggers in her hands. He saw her expression. He simply waited. And from the ceiling that should have been sky, the tendril of one great root eased itself out of the mass and dropped to the ground, planting itself beside the bodies. Had it been nearer the grave, she would have chopped at it in fury. Even though she could see the words written across it like a bright banner.

Shapes shifted, runes becoming different runes, and then becoming letters, until they were in Elantran and Barrani, a jumbled mix of languages ill suited to each other.

What is your will, now? the words said.

She shook her head. "I don't know."

You know. And now you have seen what you did not see, and more. What is your choice?

She said nothing. Severn did not seem to notice the root, although he must have heard her answer the shifting lines that appeared across its width in a band.

"I think," she said quietly, "that he's suffered enough." Words she could never have imagined she would say seven years ago.

Severn frowned; it was the look that stole over his face when he was concentrating.

"You buried them," she said to him.

He nodded. Stiff and guarded now, his expression neutral.

"Where?"

He shrugged. "Does it matter?"

Her turn to nod.

"Why? They're still dead. I killed them."

"I want to go there." She hadn't, until she spoke. Or hadn't realized it. But she *did*. And only Severn could take her.

She lifted a hand and touched his face; the tips of her fingers traced the scar he'd taken in a feral fight when they had both been young. To her surprise, he flinched, and she let her hand drop away.

But the root had thickened, and the writing was now glowing a faint luminescent blue. Severn's frown made it clear that he was, at last, aware of where they actually were; the past receded. But it would never let him go. She understood that now.

She had a better chance of escaping.

Yes, the root said. *You do. You were the Chosen, and you failed.*

"I couldn't save them," she whispered.

That was not your duty.

She understood then, and she did drive a dagger into the words of the root. Light sparked as metal hit wood; it did not even scar the surface.

"They *were* my duty!" she said savagely. "I promised—"

Your duty, Chosen, was to preserve the balance and the power. You failed. And this one was standing in your shadow. He understood what you failed to understand.

He took the burden upon himself. He killed them. He was not Chosen; he had no power. He has endured what you should have endured because you did not have the strength to do what must be done.

But it should have been your hand.

"I was a child!"

Ignorance is not an excuse. It is a fact, like any other. You wished him dead because he could do what you could not.

Choose.

But she had already chosen. Severn was a Hawk, not a Wolf.

Choose.

She snarled in Leontine. Had she fangs and claws, she would have ripped the root from its mooring and *eaten* the damn thing, just to shut it up. It was a favored Leontine threat. But she had neither.

She looked up, met Severn's eyes; he wavered in the frame of her vision. She said, "I want to see them."

He said nothing.

Her voice thickened. "Severn—"

But he shook his head. "I chose," he said harshly. "I killed them. Not you, Kaylin. You could never have done it." He believed it. Why wouldn't he? He had known her better than anyone; it was true.

Oh, she had hated him. Hate froze in her, hard and cold; it lost all life in that moment. "You saved the world," she told him. And this time, she meant it. She wanted to weep.

"What kind of a world," was his bitter reply, "did I save, that could demand this?"

"Our kind," she answered. She touched his face slowly, and this time, he didn't stop her. Instead, he lowered his head into her hand. She'd dropped the dagger, but it hadn't made much sound; it was caught in the folds of her skirt. The other one joined it. She wrapped her arms around his neck and drew his head down, and she held him for a long, long time.

Hating, at last, not Severn, but Kaylin.

He is yours, the root said, the words writing themselves in a flurry of motion and metamorphosis. *Because he bears your burden. Understand what is offered. Understand that ignorance will not save you.*

And she said, "I'll take him. We had each other, once, and we only had each other." She paused and added, "The world is still worth saving." Barely. But barely would do.

Then climb, the words said. *You have passed through the first door.*

CHAPTER 14

"Easy for you to say," Kaylin murmured.

Severn drew back and looked at her. He could see her face. He gently unwound her arms, and took another step back. He could see her skirt. The latter made him wince. "The daggers," he said.

"I can clean them."

"You can't sew with them."

"There is that. Do you think it's obvious?"

"Two gaping slashes and some blood?"

She grimaced. Took a step back and hit the broad root. It was still there.

Severn frowned at it. "We're going to have a bit of trouble getting past that," he said at last.

"I'm not sure we're supposed to." She placed her hands around the great root, and got dirt under her fingernails. Again. The words hadn't changed any further, and they no longer glowed. "I think we're supposed to shinny up the damn thing."

"To where?"

She raised a brow. "Someplace that isn't here."

"I'll go first."

"The hell you will." She added after a moment, "I'm going to need a bit of a push."

He laughed. Bracing himself, he intertwined his hands, and she put a shoe in them. He lifted her, and she caught root, and then a series of roots. She began to push them aside, and they fell away as if they were only barely lodged in some unseen surface.

"Is there a hole?"

"Not much of one. But I think we can push ourselves through this mess, if that's any help."

He nodded, and she came down. When he stood again, she was sitting on his shoulders. She began to work, pushing small tendrils to one side or the other around the trunk of the large root; it seemed to travel straight up now, instead of across the roof.

She nodded an okay, which he couldn't see; she smacked herself on the side of the head, and told him that she was about to let go. Which, in this case, meant clamber up his shoulders, standing on them as she tried to find purchase along the single vertical root.

She managed to do this; dirt was all of her vision for a minute, and dirt was not her favorite thing to inhale. But the smell of it was clean and new, and she contented herself with that. She edged up, and up again, and then her face broke surface, as if the earth were a river that moved slowly and imperceptibly, carrying life with it.

She could see something that looked like moonlight—the red moon was full; the bright moon must be hidden by something in the distance. She could see something that looked like grass at the level of her eye, and having been on the end of a few losing fights, was both familiar and uncomfortable with the view. She reached out, grabbed a handful of said grass, and pulled it up in an attempt to drag herself forward. Which was stupid, because she was sitting between the V formed by the exterior roots of a tree. A really, really tall tree.

She grabbed the exposed roots instead, and felt a familiar—and unwelcome—tingle that traveled up her palms. Which, given the lack of a warning mark, was a tad annoying. She pulled herself up and let go as quickly as possible.

Severn was a bit slower to follow, but not by much. He had height, and he had always been better at climbing than she had; he could find purchase on almost vertical walls in cracks that she would have sworn wouldn't aid a mouse.

"Where are we?" he asked her.

It was a perfectly reasonable question, and because it was, she was also annoyed. Being reasonable when the world wasn't reasonable wasn't always a gift to the person on the receiving end.

But, being a Hawk, she let her eyes acclimatize themselves to the faint light. "I think we're in a garden. Well, with walls. And pointy things on the top of the walls."

"Heads on the spikes?"

"I can't see them that well."

He shrugged, brushing dirt from his tunic. The dirt that had lodged in his mail would have to wait.

"Garden," he said after another minute. "With flower beds."

The way he said the word made her stiffen. Or cringe. Severn was, like Kaylin, not a big fan of cultivated plants that couldn't also be eaten. This meant that he only noticed the wrong kind. As if to underscore this, he lifted a hand and pointed.

Around the great tree, in a careful circle that was bounded on either side by low rocks, were white plants with four petals; they were open, and their golden hearts were exposed. Even in the moonlight, Kaylin could identify those flowers. Lethe.

She groaned. "If they are Lethe flowers—"

"They are."

"No one's harvesting them. Not here." The dirt that clung to her dress was sort of embedded. She didn't even bother to try to remove it. Instead, she touched the trailing weight of Sanabalis's medallion. The dirt there was easier to brush aside. "I could maybe try burning them—"

"Don't even think it," he snapped.

"Lethe doesn't work on humans."

Severn said nothing for a moment. "It doesn't work predictably. But it has an effect."

"You want to destroy them."

He shrugged. But he walked toward the white ring that circled them, and he stopped, his feet inches away from stone. It was gray with blue veins, and the blue veins were glowing slightly. The circle was wide enough that jumping over it wasn't a real possibility.

He lifted a foot, and Kaylin's arms burned suddenly. "Don't!"

His foot stopped in midair. He withdrew it.

Something was nagging at her. Damn it, there was something she was missing. She looked at the flowers. A wind began to blow across their open faces, moving through them in a way that suggested water on a white, white ocean. And carried in the fold of that breeze, a scent, strong and cloying.

"I have a bad feeling about this," she told Severn.

Severn had already pulled back in silence. He had many shades of silence; this was grim.

"Don't you have to—eat it or something?" she said without much hope.

He shrugged. "In our world, yes. But this is demonstrably not the same world."

She was quiet for a moment. Then she took his hand in hers. "Would you forget, if you could?"

"Forget what?"

"Anything."

He looked at her.

She gave in quietly. "That you killed them."

"No."

And bit her lip.

"Would you?"

She wanted to say yes. She didn't. For seven years, the answer would have been no. But in the High Halls, the answer had shifted, and the ground she was standing on wasn't so firm. She stalled. "Why?"

"Because I did kill them. Forgetting it wouldn't change the fact."

"It might change you." *It might change us.*

"It might," he said quietly. His voice was at its lowest. "But it wouldn't bring them back. It wouldn't change anything that's happened."

"But it—"

"Kaylin. Elianne. Whoever you are. It's part of who I am. It's part of my understanding of who I am. I spent a long time learning to live with it. There are days—" He shook his head, discarding the words. She wanted to hear them, but she knew Severn; they were gone someplace she couldn't follow.

"I wouldn't choose to forget. Besides," he added, squeezing her hand, "you're a Hawk now. You'd figure it out sooner or later, and we'd have to go through it all over again." His smile was tight. "And I won't put myself through those early years again. Not even for you."

She understood then. "This is a test," she told him softly.

He nodded, as if he had understood it the moment he'd set eyes on the flowers.

"It's a stupid test."

"Maybe the Barrani would feel differently. They live forever, and their memories dim much more slowly than ours. Truth is not their strength…they play games, they live and breathe deceit. It's why they make good Hawks," he added. "They understand deceit in most of its forms."

"And me?"

"You're not Barrani." He paused. "The Barrani wouldn't consider the deaths a crime. It wouldn't be murder. They barely understand loyalty to kin."

"That's not true."

"It's not true of all of them," he conceded. "But I pity those for whom it isn't."

"Why?"

But he shook his head again. "Do you want to forget?"

She swallowed. "Sometimes."

"Do you think it would change anything?"

"It would change how I see you."

"And is that important?"

She almost laughed, but it would have been the wrong type of laughter. "Severn—you were the entire world to me. You were the only person I counted on. I trusted Steffi and Jade in a different way—they were children. My children," she added bitterly. "But I would never have asked them to save my life. I could never have asked them to fight for me. I could never have believed they could save me."

"From what?"

"From *anything*."

"Do you understand that I wouldn't have remained your entire world? Even had they lived?"

The moonlight was bright here. The sky was hazy, and it made a soft ring of light around the bright moon's face. She could see it now, see it clearly; it was almost full. The red moon *was* full. Two days.

She had two days to save the Barrani from something bitter and terrible that she didn't understand, and for this small space of time, *it didn't matter.*

"You were thirteen," he told her. "You were a child."

"I'm not a child now."

"No? But you think like one."

It should have annoyed her. Maybe later it would. Here, it didn't quite have the barbs it should have. "Because I can remember how much I believed in you?"

"No. Because you still *want* to. Because knowing the truth, you still want to. I'm what I am," he added.

"It's not what you *were*."

"No. But I changed then. I understood what I was willing to do. You understood it, too."

She nodded.

"There's no way back."

"There's no way forward."

"There is, Kaylin. You weren't a Hawk. I wasn't a Hawk. Or a Wolf. We were trapped in the fiefs. We're free now."

"We aren't free," she whispered.

"We're as free as we're ever going to be. We make the choices we make…we live with the consequences. There's no other way. Take away the memory, and the consequences teach us nothing. In the end, I learned that I *could* live with what I did.

"I don't know if you can. But that's a consequence, as well. And I knew it then. The alternative was worse."

She looked at the flowers, felt her throat tighten. The scent was stronger. "What if we don't have the choice?"

"We always have the choice. Isn't that the point of all this, in the end? Wasn't that the rune that you touched?"

She nodded. Reaching up, she clutched the medallion of Sanabalis, Dragon Lord. "Is burning them really bad?"

"It would be."

"How bad?"

He frowned. "This isn't rhetorical, is it?"

"Not really. And yes, I know what the word means. If you explain it, I'll stab you."

"With what?"

She grimaced. "I'll kick you."

"Better." His smile was less tight. "I'll risk it," he added quietly. "The scent is…bad."

Holding the medallion as if it was a talisman, she lifted it high.

"Is that necessary?"

"Probably not." She studied its face, felt the comfort of its familiar weight. "I learned something," she added.

"Is it going to kill us?"

"Maybe."

He shrugged.

And she spoke the word *fire*.

Fire came, like the breath of a Dragon. What it touched, it burned, and flame spread, contained by stone, in a circle of heat and orange light. She lost the moons to its glow, the dance of its many tongues, the language of its crackling. She didn't lose Severn; he still held her hand as he watched. They held their breath because it was practical.

They stopped when it wasn't.

Smoke, white smoke, rose above the flames like a curtain of dense fog. But the wind that had moved scent did not move the growing wreath; it reached up, and up again, an illusion that spoke of walls.

And as it billowed, Kaylin saw words in the shapes; fleeting words, broken by flame, and reshaping, over and again, the scream of the flowers, all subtlety lost.

She would remember this.

That was the point.

"Kaylin?"

She lifted a hand, looking at the smoke; Severn fell silent. Then, pulling him by the hand, she retreated, walking backward, limned in light.

"It's the tree," she said softly.

"What of it?"

"We have more climbing to do."

"The Lethe?"

"It's gone. Even if we wanted to, we couldn't change our minds now."

"Do you?"

She shook her head; her hair was in her eyes. Pushing it back, she smiled. Raw smile. Real smile. "Forward," she told him softly.

The tree was waiting for them.

But Kaylin was wrong.

She saw the trunk. Saw, engraved in it, a simple rune. Which she cursed roundly, in all of the languages at her disposal. She even wondered, briefly, if you *could* swear in the tongue of the Old Ones. What would it sound like?

Severn waited until she had finished. "What is it?"

"It's a damn door-ward," she snapped. "It's too bad the people who built this place are long dead."

He laughed. She kicked his ankle.

And then, before she could lose all nerve, she lifted the hand that Severn wasn't holding and placed it, palm flat, against the rune.

Light flared, brighter than fire, in the dark of evening sky. Kaylin's reaction was typical.

"Do you *ever* stop swearing?"

"Yes. But it's not generally considered a good sign."

He laughed again.

The trunk of the tree began to dissolve. It was a slow dissolution, the texture of bark shifting beneath her hand as if to cling, to leave an impression. Her fingers curled around it for just a moment, holding it in place. There was peace here. She wasn't quite ready to surrender it.

But that was her life: ready or not, it went, smoothing and stretching until it formed the surface of a door. It was, she noted, a wooden door, and its edges were still tree shaped, bark colored. As if the door were a cross section cut from the trunk of a huge, old tree.

There was no handle.

"You ready?" she asked Severn.

He nodded.

She gave the door a little shove, and it fell away.

Standing here, in the frame of something that was still mostly tree, she saw a room. It was a very large room, and it was lit by torches in wall sconces. Those sconces were green, like the eyes of a calm Barrani.

The floor, she couldn't see clearly, but the walls were dark; stained, she thought. Wood.

She tightened her grip on Severn, and when he winced, she offered a crooked smile. "I don't want to leave you behind," she told him by way of apology.

"Oh. I thought you were just trying to break my hand." But his smile was familiar. Wearier. Older. But at heart, familiar.

They stepped through the door, one after the other, like two links in a very short chain. Kaylin wasn't surprised when the door vanished at their back.

"Kaylin?"

"Hmm?"

"What did you see in the smoke?"

"Words," she told him quietly.

"I guessed that."

She shrugged. "I'm not sure, but I think the High Halls consider me a bit of a cheat."

He chuckled. "Oh?"

"I gave the decision to you," she said without smiling. Nothing much to smile about, really. "I let you make it."

He shrugged. "They were my memories."

"Not just yours."

"It's about choice," he reminded her, the smile gone from his lips.

"My choice."

"It *was* your choice, Kaylin." He frowned. She recognized it; it wasn't aimed at her.

Turning—because she had turned to look at him—she surveyed the room. Large? Yes. The floors felt wooden; she was in her shoes, and the soles were a bit thin. Part of her considered taking them off, but it was a small part.

There was a table in this room. It was long and dark; wood, but a heavy, dense wood. The top was perfectly flat. Two chairs faced each other across its width. It wasn't a dining table, or if it was, people were expected to eat with their hands off the top of the table itself. Oh, and bring their own food while they were at it.

"Are we supposed to sit?" Severn asked her.

"Not sure. It looks…"

"Like a war room."

She shook her head. "Not war." She lifted a hand. "There's a door."

He nodded. But he was drawn to the table. Where he went, she followed.

The chair moved almost quietly across the floor. Given that Severn was dragging it, it said something about the floor. Or the chair legs. "It's heavy."

"Doesn't look it."

He set the chair aside. "Look at the table, Kaylin."

She did. And frowned. There were no engravings here—which she half expected. But the lines of wood grain were...unusual. It took about half a second to realize why: They were crawling, as if trapped beneath the surface. Roiling. "Not liking this table much," she said grimly.

"Don't touch it."

"Wasn't going to." But she was. Her hand had moved without much thought behind it, and it rested an inch above the table's surface. There were words beneath her hand; even in its odd rush of movement, the wood grain retained their shape, tracing them over and over again in a frenzy that increased as her hand drew closer.

She recognized them, although she couldn't precisely read them. "I don't think there are any games left to play," she told the table. "Severn—I need both of my hands."

"No."

"Severn—" She hesitated. Straightened out. Her sleeves were draped across part of the table's surface, and they irritated her immensely. "Can you cut these damn things off?"

"The Quartermaster—"

"Is already going to pitch the biggest fit the Halls of Law has ever seen. How much worse can it get?" But she didn't see his expression; her eyes were drawn to the surface of the table. It looked shiny. It reflected nothing.

"Kaylin—"

"I gave you the choice," she said quietly. "Give it back."

He let go slowly, but he did let go.

And she put both of her hands on the surface of the table. They slid through.

Words began to crawl up her arms, like a legion of small insects. She could feel their march, as if she were parchment and they were a thousand expert quills. She promised herself, gritting her teeth, that she would never hate cockroaches again. She could step on those.

"Kaylin—what is it?"

"Power," she told him grimly.

"Magic?"

"No. Power." She shook herself; her hands could move freely beneath the surface, but she couldn't withdraw them. She only tried once. "This is a Barrani test," she added bitterly. "Power would have to play some part in it."

She felt her arms tingle; the tingling grew in intensity until it was pain. Pain, she could handle. Fire, she could barely handle, and that came next. But if this was a game of cosmic chicken, she wasn't ready to blink.

Kaylin didn't play chicken.

"It's not a Barrani test," Severn said, his voice in her ear a relief from the buzzing that was growing in volume.

She bit her lip; tasted blood. Thought after. Blood was a bad idea.

Very bad.

* * *

Blood was the liquid of the living. Blood was the water of life. Blood was the ink in which old words—ancient words—were writ.

She knew this, as her blood touched her tongue. It was a trickle; she'd bit her lip harder just jumping down the stairs. Admittedly, she'd had three armed thugs on her tail at the time. Here she had a quiet room and a table that wouldn't let go of her hands. She'd had no reason to bite. Except vanity; she really didn't like screaming.

Teela would have hit her.

Severn was silent. If he even understood what had happened, he made no sign, gave no word. But she felt him by her side, like a shadow.

The surface of the table was no longer shiny, it was shining. The light was pale, diffuse, and ringed with a halo of pale blue.

The words—and they were words—had crawled up her arms, settling against her skin, matching, curve for curve and line for line, the words that were already there. They didn't speak to her, but the buzzing was loud. They were seeking some answer from her skin, some kinship, something—an answer came to her slowly, like the straggling result of a difficult numbers question.

They wanted a vessel.

A living vessel.

Blood, and bone, and flesh.

She remembered Castle Nightshade. She remembered the Long Hall; the silent Barrani who moved at the scent of blood as it passed them, as if they were *almost* dead, but could be stirred by the memory of, the desire for, life.

This was different. The Barrani had been housed in their own flesh, gone pale and slack with the passage of time and their endless inactivity, their guardianship of the doors that opened only at the whim of the fieflord.

The words? They were unleashed, uncontained. Almost frenzied.

And she felt them huddle against her, seeking sustenance. Or entrance. But they did not speak, and this frustrated her, although she wasn't sure why: Words were *spoken*; they didn't have a voice of their own.

And yet...

They were more than words.

Just as some names were more than words. They weren't her names. Hers, she could speak; she could hear without compulsion; she could ignore. But the names of the Barrani? They were *more*. And the names of the Dragons.

Their names were forever.

Old names, she thought. Old words.

What stories had she heard? What legends had she grasped from her time in Nightshade? Half-remembered—which is the way, in the end, almost all things were in her life—she thought of stone casements, the small windows sculpted into statues that would one day wake, and see through them as if they were eyes. Tall and elegant, large and ferocious, the daydreams of ancient gods; they had been carved and molded by Lords of Law and Lords of Chaos. And they had been given words of power so that they might live. Words that had meaning in her life in only the most superficial of ways.

But those words *were* these words.

She understood it, and was silent; in the face of words such as these, what power did her own have?

She whispered a name. Human name. *Severn.*

And he was there; she felt his hands upon her shoulders, the steadying strength of his silence. Was this power? Not as the words understood it.

Not as the words could be understood.

But she wasn't clay. She wasn't nameless. She wasn't—

"No," she whispered softly.

"Kaylin?"

"I asked him," she told Severn.

"Asked who?"

Calarnenne. She did not speak the name; her lips formed it, but it formed base sound, no more. She did not *think* it, although thought was present. The name that came to her was primal, primitive, visceral—something deeper than thought. It was the true name of the Lord who ruled the fief that bore his name: Nightshade.

And she heard his voice over the buzz of these words, although she couldn't see him. *Kaylin.*

You told me—

What did I tell you?

Nothing, of course. Nothing of value. The scant force of air over the shape of tongue, teeth and lip said nothing at all. Noise. Buzzing.

The children, she told him, concentrating.

The silence was almost complete; he would have withdrawn had she not called him again, forcing his attention

to focus upon her. She felt his surprise, his hesitance, and
yes, his anger. But she wanted none of those things.

How are the Barrani children named?

A pause. A swell of resistance. And then, beneath that,
amusement and…pity. *Midwife,* he called her with mockery.
You are in the High Halls.

I'm in the damn High Halls, she snapped, clenching her
hands. Words slid through, crushed but not destroyed. *And
there are names here, waiting for life.*

You…see much.

And hear less. Answer the question.

Silence.

Please.

The Lord of the High Court has a daughter, he said at last,
*and she will be Consort. To her will come all who are born. They
sleep; they will not wake until she takes them along the paths
that are open only for her. She is appointed.*

Kaylin swallowed. She knew where the Consort would
bring those children. *But she's—*

*Yes. She will be wife to one of her brothers; the Lord of the
Green or the Lord of the West March. I told you, Kaylin, that
her role was ordained.*

They're not born alive?

*They are, but life is flimsy, fragile; it passes fleetingly. They
will not wake until they know the whole of who they will be;
they are not given their name; they are taken by it.*

And do they remember the taking?

Silence. Profound silence.

She didn't ask again. Instead, she watched the writing
swirl and shift. The light was intense. The pain was worse.

They want to name me, she told him.

And the silence changed in texture; it was dark here. The only warmth in the room—if you didn't count the burning along her arms—came from Severn's hands.

You cannot be given a name.

Why?

You are mortal.

She understood that. And told him so, but not in words. *I already have the words,* she began, looking at them; they glowed brightly enough that her sleeves couldn't hide them.

They are yours, but they are not you. *If this is the gift the High Halls offers, refuse it.*

But they—

Kaylin, did you offer the altar your blood?

Ummm. Would it make a difference?

The silence was one of astonishment. And not the good kind.

It was an accident, she began defensively.

But he was concentrating, and she fell silent. She could feel his presence grow as she waited. She couldn't see him. But he was drawing nearer, along the length of the only thing that bound them: his name.

The name he had surrendered to her.

You are not alone.

Severn's here.

Good. You shed blood.

Not on the table.

Again the silence. She was a bit tired of it. Her teeth, however, were clenched about as tightly as they could possibly be, and she didn't feel like swearing. Barrani didn't have truly useful curse words.

Why did you touch it?

I—it seemed like the right thing to do.

Given how often your right is wrong, I would suggest you ignore your instincts in future. If, he added darkly, *you have one.*

Silence returned, and in it, he observed her from a distance. Not, she realized, a safe distance; she could almost see where, in Castle Nightshade, he was standing, and she'd walked that floor before. It had almost devoured her.

You are almost safe, he said at last. *The words find no purchase in you.*

They're…on me.

Yes. I can see that.

I, um, my hands are kind of stuck. In two fists. She tried to pull them free, purely as a demonstration, and they did not come; they were anchored there, in a sea of Old words. Anchored by them.

He frowned. She didn't see it, and was grateful for the distance, but the feeling lingered anyway. *You will pay a price for this,* he told her softly. *You cannot now withdraw your hands unless you take what is offered.*

She had a little quibble with his use of the word *offered*, but then again, he *was* speaking in the essence of High Barrani.

What does the Consort do?

She chooses a name.

But that means she can read *them.*

No, Kaylin, it doesn't. These are not mortal words, to be read and picked over; they are the gift and price of the Old Ones. They are the force of our lives. And you have your hands *in them.*

Look, it's not like I can pollute the damn things. They're all the hell over me!

You have to choose, he said softly. *And the wisdom to make that choice wisely will not be yours for centuries yet.*

Dust doesn't make many choices.

He didn't seem to appreciate the humor.

She uncurled her hands; the fists had been tight, and shaking. She couldn't see them clearly for the words, but she could feel the pain in her palms.

Ummm.

And feel, as well, the raised curve of one of the fieflord's brows.

If I bleed at all in the table—*or the altar, whatever it is—is that worse?*

His answer was silent; it contained no words. Barrani, as she had noted earlier, wasn't an aid to swearing. But she wasn't dead. And the tingling was less painful. And the words moved more slowly. None of this was cause for comfort.

She ignored him then, and began to trace what had seemed like wood grain, searching it for meaning. Searching it for something that *might* have meaning. And it occurred to her, as she did, that the act itself was futile.

That almost all acts were, in the end.

She would die; nothing could prevent that. The march of these disembodied words would go on beyond her, as if she were inconsequential.

She understood two things then. That if this was not exactly a testing ground for the Barrani, it had *never* been designed for mortals. And that, mortal, she was here, in its heart; that she had been given a choice.

Choice…

Calarnenne.

Kaylin.

You dared the High Halls

I am Lord, yes.

And you succeeded.

Yes.

How many fail?

Numbers beyond your ability to count.

She nodded. *When you came to the tower, what did you see?*

Stairs, he said, but there was a caution in the words that flagged them. He did not lie to her; she didn't think it was possible. But he didn't tell her the whole of the truth, either.

Did you see a word?

Yes.

What was it?

His silence was the silence of resistance. And she held his name. But the temptation to use it was vanishingly small. If he held answers—and he did—he would not part with them willingly. Maybe it was a Barrani thing.

But Kaylin wasn't Barrani. *I saw a single rune,* she told him, offering the same vulnerability she asked of him, and first. *I asked Andellen what it meant. He could see it.*

He would; he was tested, and he passed.

He told me it was a symbol that meant choice. That's not what you saw, was it?

No, Kaylin.

So this is—

Yes. Do not surrender this information to another. It is safe to do so with me; you hold my name.

She nodded, but it was an absent nod; a gesture of habit or the type of acknowledgment that breezes above actual understanding.

Andellen saw—

He was your guide.

She would have spit had she been anywhere else. She didn't. Her hands were glowing, and they were the pale green of Barrani eyes—children's eyes. She'd never seen a Barrani baby; they were rare. But she *knew* it for fact. Both of her hands. She opened them both. Saw nail crescents—three each—that had bitten their way through her skin. She'd had worse paper cuts in her life, but not here. Context was—as her very irritated history master used to tell her—everything.

She closed her eyes slowly. She could still feel her hands, but without vision to guide them, she could no longer see the runic words. Sight wouldn't help her; it kept trying to make the shapes into something they weren't: language. And comprehensible.

She felt the tingling in her arms lessen; felt the frenetic crawl of desperate shapes slow. Her skin was hers; it was dry and hot, as if all moisture had been absorbed. Or as if she were fevered. She was certainly dizzy.

But she let those go; they weren't for her. Or of her. What she held in her hands, what passed over her open palms like the shallow current of a brook, might be. And she had to choose.

Not one, but two. She understood this because the symbol itself had responded to both of her hands; the single hand had done nothing.

What if I don't choose?

A choice will be made for you; not choosing is a choice.

No good, then. Eyes still closed, she felt shapes. And the shapes gained weight, and differing textures, as the dark minutes passed. Her right hand closed upon something round and hard; it was neither too hot nor too cool, but it was heavy. Almost too heavy to hold.

Yet it felt, as she struggled with the immensity of its weight, like something solid enough to build a palace on; a foundation, a thing of strength. It was *large*. She'd never tried to carry something that large before; certainly not in the palm of her hand.

Her hand was almost flat, her fingers shaking with the effort to sustain her grip. She pulled. And felt her left hand come free.

But her eyes were still closed. One hand. One word.

She concentrated on the other hand, the empty one. And felt it as that: empty. Something nicked her palm, something as sharp and clean as Severn's daggers had been. She almost opened her eyes. Keeping them closed required more effort than running after a Leontine suspect who didn't want to be questioned.

Still, she'd done that, time and again.

Sharp. Hard. Both of these things. But her fingers closed effortlessly over the shape, and she felt, to her surprise, something softer and more giving beneath those fingers, something that was warm and light, like mossbed or flower petal. Clenching her hand drove the edges of the whole thing farther into her palm, but she did it anyway. There was…life here. Something living. Something that was utterly unlike the vast shape she contained in her left hand. It almost seemed to sing.

She lifted her hand without thinking, and opened her eyes. And screamed.

CHAPTER 15

Her hand was dripping blood.

She'd seen more, even of her own. The blood itself wasn't the problem; it was the thing she held in her hand.

Severn's grip tightened. "Kaylin—"

She shook. Not her head, but her whole body, a convulsive movement that had nothing to do with voluntary choice.

"Your hand is bleeding." The words told her more clearly what she wouldn't have thought to ask: He couldn't see what she carried in her right hand. She could.

It was…a symbol. A rune. But it was throbbing faintly, and it was red as dragon anger; it was both hot and cold, the edges sharp, the curves above them like scintillating light. It was pain.

It was more than pain. Sorrow, here. But also joy. Peace and despair. It was birth and death, and everything in between; a small microcosm whose shape somehow implied the whole of a world. She moved her left hand automatically, but it was heavy with what it carried, and had she been able to look away, she would have seen that, too—and it would have been far, far too much to take in.

"Kaylin." Pause. "Elianne."

She could not look away. Her eyes seemed to lend shape and substance to the rune; to give it dimension that it hadn't possessed when it traveled the currents beneath the surface. It was waiting, she realized.

And she had no idea what it was waiting *for.*

Or rather, no idea she liked.

Two hands. One rune. A choice. But she'd made more than one damn choice on the path that led to this one. And she wanted to be around to make a lot more of them.

Severn's hands left her shoulder; the cold in the air could be felt as his absence. As the absence of all things that meant life to Kaylin. She wanted to cry out again, but the single scream was all she was afforded; her mouth would not open in anything that resembled speech.

She heard the tearing of cloth as if from a great distance and wondered dully if he'd finally given up and cut off the damn sleeves that were such a horrendous pain. If she *ever* daydreamed about finery again, she'd make a beeline for the bridge across the Ablayne and throw herself over it. It would be wet, it would hurt, and it would be far, far more practical.

He came back. He had never really left her. Even during the seven years after she'd fled the fief of Nightshade, he had never left; she'd just never felt his shadow, the comfort of his presence. Guilt had done that. Hers. His.

He caught her right wrist and she almost cried out a warning—but she was mute. She saw, however, that he held a strip of green silk in his hands. Mute satisfaction was better than none, and it was all she was going to get; he meant to bind the wound.

And the rune was in the way. She had thought the words attracted to blood, but this wasn't a great, fancy leech; it didn't absorb blood. It sat above it. She saw Kaylin in the rune, as if it had changed shape, had granted her a moment of familiarity. She saw, as well, Elianne, and heard the distant sound of Steffi's voice, felt the discomforting presence of Jade's silent suspicion. She felt Catti there, and saw her, red-haired and mutinous; saw Dock as well; saw a gleam of golden fur, and claws that were red with blood. Greater claws than that appeared next, appeared on top of the Leontine ones; she saw the jaws of a Dragon open so wide it could swallow the rune whole.

Without thinking, she pulled the rune up—and pulled her hand away from Severn before he could bind the wound he could see. She wasn't certain that the silk would pass through the rune; wasn't certain what would happen if the rune no longer touched her skin, her blood.

She heard screams of anger, of pain, of joy and of pure irritation; she felt the flight feathers of Clint's gray wings, and then, on those wings, the feel of the wind high above the city, near the southern stretch Clint called home.

She heard the Leontine vows she had been taught, and she almost said them; this was the closest she could come to speech. Some of it must have forced itself out because Severn touched her again.

But her eyes were wide and unblinking. She saw the fief of Nightshade. And the fief of Barren. She had spent six dark months there; she saw the deaths. The training. The other vows. Dark and sharp, the rune bit her hand again. A reminder.

Everything was here, in this shape, every little scrap of knowledge that memory couldn't contain so elegantly. Everything she *was*.

And she understood, in a way she had never understood, what a cage was: this. This word. And it had her name on it.

No. Worse than that, it *was* her name; she had chosen it, and it had taken her blood and her permission. It would become what she was, and she would bear it as scar and threat, as vulnerability and fear, for the rest of her life.

She had envied the Barrani. Anyone less beautiful than the Barrani always did—and that was pretty much *anyone*. She had envied them their forevers; had envied them their Hawks, their golden crests, which they could bear long past her dotage.

But she did not envy them now.

Choice. She closed her eyes again. There was *too much* of her life here, and she was living it all in brief flashes so intense they made her nauseated. The hate she had felt for herself, the contempt, the disgust, were brighter and clearer than they had been in—hours. Hours ago. When Severn had buried Steffi and Jade.

She lifted her right hand. What it held was now weightless, almost insubstantial. Closing her eyes because open eyes were infinitely worse, she brought the hand to her chest; the word was crushed against a part of her dress that she *hadn't* managed to rip, slash, bleed on or otherwise deface.

And she bled on it. And bled.

The sharp edge of the word cut her dress and her skin as if neither were of consequence. She understood that this was symbolic—but symbolic was something that involved long robes and funny hats, cheap wine and incense, stupid words repeated by people who were so accustomed to saying them they'd lost all meaning in the drone.

This was different; it was the *root* of symbol, the thing from which the branches grew, distinctly different from the power-less repetitions that might follow. Or even the powerful ones.

She accepted the choice. Accepted the irony in the Elantran translation. And she pressed the rune into her flesh, into her skin, into her heart. It was an act of suicide.

Or an act of birth.

The pain ebbed slowly as she drew her bloody hand back. She heard Severn swear. Words.

First words.

And she heard, blended with his syllables, the rush of his welcome worry, his obvious fear, another sound like the crash of thunder momentarily given sentience and voice.

Ellariayn.

Her name. Her *true* name.

By your choice you shall be known, she thought bitterly. And now, by her choice, she would be, and in a way that no mortal should *ever* be known.

Severn's hands touched her cheeks; they were wet. His eyes were dark, the same shade they had always been. His hands were gentle as he brushed the tears away.

"You've cut yourself," he told her softly, as if she had gone mad, or had come so close there was no other way to speak to her.

She nodded. Felt the weight of the word take root inside her, where no others had gained purchase. Or permission. And the words that were crawling up and down what had already been written on her arms stilled; they faded until she could no longer feel them.

Looking at Severn, she reached out to grab his hand; hers was ice. And smeared with blood. But he didn't seem to notice.

And her left hand? Weighted and heavy, she looked at it: It was empty. Whatever she felt, whatever she had pulled from the miasma, it was gone.

And it was not gone.

"Elianne," Severn whispered, stroking her face, calling her back.

It had once been her name. Kaylin had once been her name. She felt them as words—Elantran words—shorn of life or power. No, not power. There was power there: When Severn called, she looked up.

"Severn," she whispered. "What do you know of Barrani names? True names?"

He shook his head, drawing her close; she went into the hollow of chest and arm, and found shelter there. But not truth. She wanted to tell him. She'd never been good with secrets, and she was terrible with lies.

But the instinct that shut her mouth was older and stronger than either, and she said nothing at all.

Minutes passed, or hours; Severn was stroking the dirty mess of her hair; he was whispering something that made no sense, in the most quiet of his voices. She wanted the peace of the moment, and took it, High Halls be damned. She had seen too much, and this was the way she accepted it: in his arms. In that safety.

If safety was illusion, comfort was not.

"It's over," he told her. That's what he'd been saying. "It's over, Elianne. It's over."

She let him say it again and again until she half believed it. The wanting was stronger than the ability to have, but hadn't Severn himself said as much? She held on to it anyway.

And then, looking up from his chest, pulling herself a little way from the harbor of his arms, she looked at the only door in the room. "It *is* over," she told him quietly. "For now."

As it happened, she was woefully optimistic.

Severn led her to the door, and she followed him, learning to walk again. Halfway there, he bent and removed her shoes. He didn't offer to carry her, and she wouldn't ask. What he carried instead, he did without physical effort, but it was more important. Well, except for the shoes.

They reached the door together, and to Kaylin's relief, it wasn't warded. It was a simple door, an elegant door, and engraved across the planks of its surface was a tall tree. Severn caught the door's handle—because it had to have one, missing the ward—and pulled it open.

Sunlight seen through the height of forest leaves fell at an angle through the open door, and the sound of soft music and softer voices drifted toward them.

So, too, did a breeze, and it carried the scent of food.

Kaylin's stomach did a sharp turn and grumble, which would normally embarrass her. She was beyond embarrassment.

Mostly.

But when she stepped through the open door, her hair mired in root-dirt, her nails a mix of blood and earth, her one whole sleeve resting above the slash made by dropped dagger, her torn sleeve exposed and ragged, she stopped. Beneath her feet was familiar stonework, and she could feel it all against the soles of bare feet; it was sun-warm and hard, but not so hard that she couldn't walk it with ease.

She looked around with a growing sense of dread.

And found herself in the center of the circle of the Lord of the High Court, somewhere about three feet to the left of his seat.

There should have been noise.

Or shouting.

There should have been surprise, or at least consternation. Guards should have drawn swords. Barrani should have sneered or looked down their noses or *said something.* Anything. At all.

But as Severn joined her, standing by her side in such a way that his shadow covered her, she realized that they were *all* watching the Lord of the High Court. Every single one of them. Kaylin had often been in crowded, large rooms; she'd carried words that caused surprise or shock. She'd watched that surprise spread, like the ripples around a stone dropped in still water, but even when it didn't, it never shut *everyone* up; there was always a child, a buffoon or a man too deep in his cups to notice the Hawks were there.

This attention was therefore entirely unnatural, and it made her nervous. The fact that she was underdressed in the extreme didn't seem to have caught anyone's attention. And it *should* have. It should have been either a joke or an insult.

She looked at Severn. He did not touch her with anything but his eyes; those eyes were slightly narrowed. A silent reminder that she wasn't among friends. As if she needed it.

And maybe she did. She felt disoriented. The High Circle looked strange to her eyes, as if the luminous and magical light that mimed the sun had increased both in brilliance and the multiplicity of its colors; as if it fell on one thing more heavily than the object just beside it. She wanted to talk to Severn. She wanted to ask him if he saw what she saw.

To ask him *anything*, really. To hear the sound of his voice. Because she knew that sound; knew all of the variants of it. Knew its weight, its seriousness and its mockery. He offered her silence instead, and his silences had never been so comfortable or predictable.

The Lord of the High Court rose from his seat beneath the bowers of the central tree. He trailed odd light, and his expression was not so sharp as it had been; it was as if he stood in mist, or was of it. Kaylin wanted to slap herself; she felt like she'd been drinking a shade too much.

Well, where a shade meant several hours' worth.

He turned to Kaylin, and to Severn, and he studied them in silence for what seemed far too long. He did not speak.

The woman by his side, the silent slender woman, came to stand beside him, facing Severn. She touched her Lord's arm, and he looked to her; their eyes met. They were an odd shade, an almost unfamiliar color. Pale blue. But then again, her hair was pale and fine, as unlike Barrani hair as human hair would seem.

It was the Consort who spoke first. "Lord Kaylin," she said quietly, and then, "Lord Severn." And she inclined her head. "The Lord and Lady of the High Court greet you and bid you welcome to the Circle. Take your place."

She was speaking in High Barrani. She might as well have spoken in Dragon, for all the sense she made. Except that she *did* make sense. Dim sense. Political sense.

Kaylin had failed politics at least once, but the failure there—the profound inability to recall the right dates or names—had been theoretical; confined to scratches on board or paper, and the weary disapproval of a Master of the Halls of Law.

Here, it was worse. But here, she was willing to try a hell of a lot harder. She bowed to the Lord of the High Court, and then bowed, more deeply, to his Consort. At this, a whisper did rise among the Barrani, but it was like the sound of wind in leaves; she couldn't pinpoint its source.

"You have been tested by the High Halls," the Consort told her almost gently. "And you have returned to us." Her words were formal, and they should have been stiff—but they weren't. There was an odd warmth in her expression, something that spoke of kinship and secrets. Then again, *everything* about the Barrani spoke of secrets. Especially on the rare occasions they claimed not to have any.

She straightened, feeling every inch of dirt that had been ground permanently into her dress. That, the blood on her hand, the blood on her chest, and the ragged half sleeve, finally hit home, and she almost winced, looking down at herself.

But the Consort said, "The Barrani have that effect on humans. Were you to arrive at *this* tree wearing nothing but scars, you would still be worthy of honor. That you have arrived at all is a story that will be told long after you have gone the way of mortals." Her smile was not unfriendly. Which was shocking in and of itself.

As if those words were a signal, the Barrani were suddenly free of their strange paralysis. The first to approach Kaylin was the Lord of the West March. And by his side, Andellen and Samaran. She almost forgot to breathe, seeing them here, in the High Court; the Lord of the High Court had been very, very specific about their duties. And the value of their lives.

But if his word was law—and it was, here; there was no other—he seemed neither surprised nor ill pleased; he offered no expression at all.

Andellen bowed to her.

"You said you'd wait by the arch," she hissed. She couldn't help herself. Her brows, she was certain, had disappeared into the unruly mess of her dirty hair.

His expression was grave, but his eyes were brown. Entirely brown. They almost looked human.

"Lord Kaylin," he replied. If she expected an excuse or an explanation, it wasn't going to come from him. It occurred to her that Samaran had no place at all in the High

Court. It must have occurred to Samaran as well; his eyes were blue. But he showed no fear and no hesitation as he offered his respect—and possibly his envy—to Kaylin and Severn.

The Lord of the West March offered her a bow as deep, but he held it longer. When he rose, he smiled, and his eyes, green, were ringed with the same brown that had changed Andellen's eyes. "There is only one place to wait," he told her quietly, "when the trial has been undertaken. And it is here, in the heart of the High Circle, at the feet of the Lord of the High Court."

"I—"

"You were granted your freedom of the High Halls," he said gravely, "by the Lord of the High Court himself. And the laws that bind the test are older than he. He will not visit judgment upon your guards."

"But—" She looked into the crowd. Saw Teela. Saw, beside Teela, Lord Evarrim. She expected Lord Evarrim to argue; saw by the cast of his features that he had no argument to give. His expression was neither cold nor warm, and he was just distant enough that she couldn't see the color of his eyes.

Or shouldn't have been able to. But they were blue.

Teela's were a blue-green, a pale blue, and flecked with gold.

"If you were not to be offered the opportunity," the Lord of the West March told her, "to undergo the rite, you would never have found the tower. We do not speak of these things to outsiders," he added, "but you are no longer an outsider.

"And the High Halls are yours to wander now, at the pleasure of the Lord of the High Court."

She didn't understand.

She looked at Andellen because he seemed to, but he offered her nothing to hold on to. As if this, too, were a test. Then again, he was a Barrani; it could just be malice. But his eyes were brown. Approval.

"You have missed the meal," the Lord of the West March told her quietly, "but food will be brought."

"I—"

"Food will be brought," he repeated, with just a little more force.

She smiled brightly, and saw Teela wince.

What she really wanted was a bath, a change of clothes, a bed and about a week's sleep. But she was going to have to settle for food.

Before the food came music. It started everywhere, as if it were part of the light, but it coalesced, at last, into instruments held by two Barrani; they were draped in a pale sky-blue, and their hair was braided and fell almost to the stones of the circle. They looked like twins. It had been a long time since Barrani had looked like twins to Kaylin's eyes, and she wondered, then, if they really were.

But their music was pleasant, even soothing, and they added no words to mar it; the strings of their small harps seemed to speak of peace, and only peace; of repose, of the small joys that came at the end of a successful journey.

Barrani songs were usually high tragedy or dark lay; she expected that they would get around to those sooner or later, and profoundly hoped for a later that didn't include her.

But as she sat—beside the throne itself—she felt her stomach's familiar grumble, and winced. Food, when it came, came in the hands of other Barrani—tall and proud and dressed like Lords or Ladies. They carried thin platters and fine goblets; they carried slender-necked bottles, and fruit—peaches, berries, brown furry things that she hoped weren't actually alive. They set these on the ground around her; there was no table, and there were no implements of destruction.

Which is pretty much how she felt about the seventy knives, forks, spoons and other things that she had failed to learn the correct use for back in school.

They expected her to eat with her hands. It was a relief. Probably the only one she was going to feel.

The Lord of the High Court watched her, and she realized that relief was bound to break sooner or later; she wasn't accustomed to being the object of theater.

Which this was, more or less.

Severn had bound her hand. The blood had seeped through the binding, blending with green until it was just a dark stain. She saw it every time she moved her right hand, and she would have eaten with her left hand, but she wasn't left-handed. Besides which, her left hand was numb and heavy; it responded slowly when she tried to use it.

Teela approached her as she sat, Severn by her side. He ate more than she did, and with more comfort—but then again, even dirty, the Hawk that glittered between strains of dirt was still the Hawk: it was a source of pride. Not so what remained of the dress.

"Lord Kaylin," Teela said, kneeling to join her.

Kaylin started to say *don't you start, too,* but Severn touched the back of her hand in warning. The same warning that he had often given in the fiefs, when noise might mean discovery, and discovery might mean death.

"Lord Teela," Kaylin began. "Lord Anteela."

Teela raised a dark brow. But she smiled. She did not, however, touch bread, cheese or fruit. "Lord Severn," she said, inclining her head.

"Lord Anteela." He swallowed before he spoke. Kaylin hadn't. Gods, she hated Court. And uncomfortable silence seemed to be part of Court.

"It is unusual that the test of the Halls is faced by two," Teela told them quietly. "And it is that fact, more than your mortality, that will be spoken of for centuries."

"Why?"

"Not one of the Barrani Lords has ever faced the tower with another by his—or her—side."

Kaylin shrugged.

"It is not the lack of willingness on the part of the Barrani," Teela added with just the hint of Hawk's frown. "But on the part of the High Halls itself. You know something of the Barrani, but you do not fully understand the ties that bind us, one to the other. It has been tried before," she said quietly, "and it has never succeeded.

"How did you manage this?"

Kaylin frowned, and looked at Severn.

Severn—damn him—shrugged.

"He wasn't willing to leave me," Kaylin replied. "He followed. He usually does what he wants. I can't imagine a building would stop him. *I* can't."

Teela shook her head. But she lifted a hand and she placed it above Kaylin's wounded palm. Before Kaylin could speak, she touched the hand, gripping it firmly.

When she withdrew, her eyes were…almost golden. She said nothing, but she said it loudly; her shoulders were rigid. "Kaylin," she whispered, and then, in Elantran, added, "what have you *done*?"

Kaylin shook her head. But the contact told her something that she had never clearly felt before: Teela had a *name*. Oh, she'd *known* it; she'd learned that much from Nightshade. But knowing it intellectually, and feeling it as if it were a force, were not the same. And would never be the same again.

Kaylin didn't answer. And Teela, after her momentary outburst, didn't seem to expect an answer. Or, in fact, want one. She withdrew her hand and put it back in her lap, and her smile seemed natural and unfeigned.

But the surprise she'd shown was uncharacteristic enough that it drew attention. And red robes—unwelcome, even here—bore down upon Kaylin as Lord Evarrim of the Arcanum approached.

He knelt, as Teela did; not in supplication, but in mimicry of companionship. It was pretty poor mimicry; he might have been a Leontine for just that moment.

He was not pleased. That much, she could see in the lines of his face, although they hadn't changed much. His eyes were a dark blue, his skin pale. His forehead, however, was weighed down by circlet and ruby.

"Lord Kaylin," he said. "Lord Severn." To Severn, he inclined his head, the bastard. Kaylin put the bread that had been an inch away from her mouth down.

"Lord Evarrim." She hoped he could see bread crumbs.

"Your companion appears unscathed," he said genially. Or would have, if she could have closed her eyes and pretended she was listening to someone else talk. The words themselves sounded friendly. Which was enough of a warning.

"I'm clumsier," she offered cheerfully. "Bread?"

"I have eaten," he replied coolly, staring at the broken loaf as if it were a cockroach. "I am curious, Lord Kaylin. What did you see when the tower opened to you?"

"A lot of stairs," she replied, with a pasted-on smile that she was aware was entirely unconvincing.

"And nothing else?"

"Oh, a lot of other things. Brass railings, walls. Stone. Stuff."

His frown—and he did frown—was pronounced. She might have gained the title of Lord, but she hadn't gained much ground on the battlefield of Evarrim. She was mortal, in his eyes. She found it oddly comforting.

"Nothing else of interest?"

She shrugged. "Of interest to an Arcanist? I doubt it. You've seen the tower," she added.

"I have. Many centuries before you were born."

"Well, it probably hasn't changed much."

His smile took her by surprise; it was momentary and genuine. "So," he said. "You are not entirely foolish."

"Not entirely, no."

"Very well. Guard your secrets. It will be important that you learn to do so now—because now, you have secrets worth guarding." He started to rise, and she turned back to the food.

He grabbed her hand. Grasped it, as Teela had done, but without warning and without friendship.

And she felt the force of his name in the touch as if it were fire, or worse; as if it could scorch the skin and flesh from her hand and leave nothing but seared bone beneath it.

He felt it, too. He drew back slowly, but he let go quickly. And his eyes were blue that went on forever, deepening. "So," he said again. And rose.

She waited while he tendered his respects to the Lord of the High Court, making a note of how he did it. Apparently, when rising in the presence of said Lord, obeisance was required. She could learn this. She had to.

But what interested her was not his brief obeisance; it was the look the Consort gave her. It passed through the Lord and the supplicant, and it was meant for Kaylin, and Kaylin alone. There was weariness in it, and the burden of inestimable years.

The burden, Kaylin realized, of being mother to an entire race for far, far too long.

Kaylin loved the midwives. She loved what they did. They charged money for it—but Kaylin expected to be paid for performing her duties as a Hawk, and pay didn't lessen her pride in those duties. Midwives had leeway; they charged when they could. Where money was absent, they went anyway, and they brought life into the world. They saved life, in the bringing.

And in the Consort, to her lasting surprise, she saw a mother—and also a midwife. But a midwife who had worked alone, with no companion and no apprentice, with no Kaylin to call when things were at their grimmest and death at its closest. A woman who was responsible for breathing life into the sleepers—but worse, and she saw this clearly, too—responsible for the shape of who they would become.

In some sense, she defined the whole of their lives. Not the fact of it, as mortal midwives did everywhere, but the *whole* of it. It was a staggering responsibility.

She whispered a word. *Leoswuld.*

And the Consort smiled. It was both sad and grim, and the edges of the expression were hard.

It was not just the Lord of the High Court who would pass on the gift of his life, she thought. The Lady would, as well.

And then she frowned. Saw more.

She rose, brushing crumbs off her ruined skirts, and she offered a perfect bow to the Lord of the High Court. But it was the Consort she approached.

"Come," the Consort said quietly. "There is a fountain beyond the tree…it is mine. No one will approach us there who does not wish to face my wrath."

Kaylin nodded. She cast a backward glance at Severn, and Severn read her expression. He nodded once and returned to his food. To the conversation between he and Teela, which was broken by silences, the way streams are by large rocks.

The fountain was so simple, so unadorned, that it looked out of place in the garden. It boasted no fine statue, no alabaster arms, no pillars, no funny fish. It was a burble of water in a stone basin that was wide enough at the lip to accommodate sitting. The Consort sat, and she indicated, by the simple dip of her head, that Kaylin should join her.

Kaylin said, "You know their names."

And the Consort raised a pale brow. "Is it mortal, to speak so bluntly and without recourse to grace and idle pleasantry?"

"I can't speak for anyone else," Kaylin replied. "But we feel time differently. Or I do, at any rate," she added, thinking of the teachers in the Halls of Law who could drone on for hours without pause for anything but breath. And sometimes she wondered, given the color they often turned in her presence, if they bothered with that.

"Then be mortal," the Consort replied. "For time, here, is drawing at last to an end. For me," she added quietly. "The *leoswuld* is coming, and I am bound to it."

Kaylin frowned, trying to decide, in the space of that expression, how blunt she *could* be. It didn't take her long, but she *was* Kaylin. "If I had to guess," she said, trying to speak with tact or what passed for tact, "I'd say you aren't bound to it, you're driving it."

The Consort's silence was oddly textured, and music seemed to play in its shallows. It was a strange music, something that was just within range of hearing, but contrived to escape its reach.

"It is not a horse or a carriage, to be so driven," she said at last. "But Kaylin—I think you've seen the source."

Kaylin could have lied. Or tried, at any rate. She could have bluffed; she was slightly better at that. She could have played the confusion card, which was kin to the stupid-me-what-was-I-thinking card, and which occasionally got her out of difficult situations.

She didn't. She nodded.

"Then you understand," the Consort said quietly.

"But I don't."

"Can you have truly seen—and touched—the source of life, and come away unchanged?" Her eyes were green and bright, but they were also slightly narrowed. She did not suspect Kaylin of lying; she was trying, in her way, to bridge the gap that race imposed. It was a big damn gap, and there were no obvious bridges.

"No," Kaylin said quietly. "Not unchanged."

The Consort nodded. "You chose a name," she said.

Kaylin nodded. And then she frowned. "How do you know—"

"I can see that you bear one," the Consort replied. And then, in a slightly different tone, "Or two." And she met Kaylin's gaze and held it. Expecting answers.

Kaylin lifted her left hand. It was numb, and it tingled; it hadn't stopped. She could flex her fingers but movement was difficult. She could not, however, see the word she had lifted from the river of words; she could see the lines of her hand, the mound of her palm, the strange geography of her flesh.

And knew, then, that she was looking for something else—after all, who thought of their own damn hand as *geography?*

"I kind of had to take two," she said, as if confessing a crime. "I—" She winced. "I couldn't leave unless I did."

"But your companion bears no such…change."

"No."

"Why is that?"

"He didn't need to."

The Consort frowned.

"We don't like change all that much," Kaylin said. "I would have thought Barrani—who change so little—would like it even less."

"There are some changes we contemplate. But if we abhorred all change, there would be no *leoswuld*. You understand my burden," she added quietly.

And Kaylin swallowed and nodded. "But only part. I don't think I could do what you do for the rest of my life—and my life is pretty damn short."

The Consort said nothing.

"You do know their names."

"I know some part of them," she replied. "Just as a mortal mother knows some part of their children. It is not the holding of a name," she added quietly, "but it is not entirely unlike. When I was younger—" She looked away, at the rippling surface of water. As if the sight of it offered strength.

As if speech required it. And maybe speech did.

"Few of our kind are born. We are not like mortals. We exist between the cracks of history, part of one age and part of the other, but not wholly one or the other.

"When I was younger, I did not see as clearly, and I did not have the strength to choose as wisely." She waited.

Kaylin wasn't certain for what. "Can you read the words?"

"I can read them in the same fashion that you did," was the reply, which wasn't much of one.

"I didn't."

"Then perhaps I can read them more clearly. I will not ask what you did. Each Consort must find her own way."

"Not a Consort, here," Kaylin said quickly.

"No. Perhaps not. But the Barrani who pass through the tower do not find the source. Only the Consort is led there."

"You had to take the test?"

"Oh yes, Kaylin. And pass it."

"But there was—"

"There was only one daughter to the High Lord of that time. Yes. But *leoswuld* is the gift that we pass to our kin. And what I pass to my daughter is part of the path that will guide her to the Source. From there, she must return on her own, as all Barrani do, who face the High Halls."

"And if she fails?"

The silence was terrible; even the water seemed to freeze.

"Never mind."

"No, I will answer. If she fails, another must stand in her place, *without* the gift I have given. And if she is not strong enough, if she is not determined, we must wait until one comes who is, and the children that are born must die, in truth, for without the *word*, we have no life. It has happened before," she added.

"But—"

"Yes?"

"But this waiting—I don't understand. You can't wait for the birth of another—" Kaylin froze.

"No. It is not upon a new generation that we will rely. The women will come. They will come at need, one after the other, and they will try the Tower."

"Your daughter?"

"She is my youngest. I think she has the strength." She paused, and then said, "The Lord of the Green is my oldest, and he was born when I was very young. His birth was a gift, or so I thought it at the time. And I went to the source, carrying him, and I chose for him a name that seemed auspicious." Again she was silent, but this time the water moved. The wind moved. She was beautiful in a way that didn't make Kaylin feel dirty or ungainly. A lie.

Kaylin had to clear her throat. "The Lord of the Green—"

The Consort touched Kaylin's hand.

The lights that dotted this tranquil, sparse place brightened until they were white; Kaylin blinked against the sudden brightness. She could see the Consort clearly—and only the Consort; even the fountain had vanished.

I ask you not to interfere.

I don't understand.

I know. I know, child. But I chose his name, and I have come to understand what that choosing entails. It is bitter to me, but life has grown bitter to me. I ask you again—because I cannot command it, and because the Lord of the High Court cannot— do not interfere.

But he's—his name—

I know. It was a mother's voice. A mother's pain. *I know what you are. I see it. You are a Hawk, and it defines you. You fly and you hunt. Fly, little Hawk, and hunt. But do not interfere.*

Kaylin almost promised. She even tried, because she thought—for just a moment—that the promise would offer peace to this strange and beautiful woman.

But her lips—if she was moving them at all—wouldn't open. She couldn't say the damn words.

And she recalled something Nightshade had said. *You cannot lie to me.* Not like this.

It wasn't meant to be a lie. It was meant to be the truth. But it was riven from her.

The Consort's smile was a bitter one, but there was no anger in it; just the guttering of something that might have been hope.

I'll try, Kaylin said. It was all she could force herself *to* say.

And the Consort lifted a hand and touched the mark upon Kaylin's cheek. She whispered something that sounded like a name. Like Nightshade's *name.* But there was no anger or hatred in the whisper. Just pity and pain.

She let go, and the world returned. "Go now, and speak with my son. My younger son," she added with a grim smile. "He is waiting, and he presses upon me. He will not disgrace himself by interrupting us, but he is impatient."

CHAPTER 16

The Lord of the West March was, indeed, waiting. And he was waiting along the path that led to the fountain. He hadn't stepped over the invisible line that clearly stated Cross This and Die, but he must have been lingering awfully close, given the color of the Consort's eyes.

On the other hand, given the resignation in her expression—and it was open enough that Kaylin found it obvious, where so little Barrani expression was—it wasn't the first time he'd done it. She wondered, then, what he'd been like as a child. And how much he'd changed. She had a suspicion if she asked his mother, the answer at the moment would be "Not at all," and decided against it.

"*Kyuthe,*" the Lord of the West March said, choosing the intimate form over the formal one. His bow, however, made up for the lack of the title Kaylin didn't want anyway. "Your companion was weary, and has returned to my wing with your guards. I promised them that I would personally see you there in safety."

She imagined that he had, and that the weight of that promise would have broken the backs of lesser mortals. It didn't seem to bother him.

"I will leave you, Kaylin," the Consort said, also choosing to forgo the title. "For I fear my son has much he wishes to discuss, and *any* who pass the test are often weary." It was a warning to the Lord of the West March, and he accepted it with grace.

Then again, he would probably have accepted a dagger with grace. He stepped aside to allow his mother free passage, and when she had gone, he met Kaylin's eyes. His were green again. Approval, it appeared, didn't last long.

"It seems," he said, looking down the path at his mother's back, "that you have impressed the Lady of the High Court."

"I'm not sure *impressed* is the right word."

"You are not familiar with the Consort," was the wry reply. "It is the correct word. She is seldom impressed enough that she seeks private audience with one newly come to the Court."

"I'm not exactly—"

"As Lord," he added quietly.

"Oh." She let the word hang there, and found other ones to add to it. "Andellen—"

"Yes. I had words with the Lord of the High Court. He was prepared to execute your guards for breaking his law. But the circumstances were such that older law had precedence—should he choose to grant it—and he so chose. He was interested in the outcome, and little interests him now."

"He didn't expect to see me."

The Lord of the West March frowned. "I would not say that, *kyuthe*. I would almost say the inverse. He *did* expect to see you, and he decided that it would go ill if your guards were disposed of. It is seldom that he deigns to show mercy, and when he does, it is never without cause. Or price. Come. I will lead you to the West Wing. Lord Evarrim is not pleased with the outcome, but not even he was bold enough to argue against it. You are of the High Court now, whether you wish it or no."

"What does that grant me?"

"Freedom of the High Halls."

"I already *had* that."

The unfettered smile was beautiful; it was a gift. It made her feel awkward. "You did. But now you may walk those halls without escort."

"I have to have the escort, by your father's word."

"The escort is now decorative," the Lord of the West March replied. "I understand what I did not understand when you first arrived with Lord Andellen."

This time, she understood that the title granted was *not* a title granted by many. "What's that?"

"He was your anchor, in the High Halls. Samaran could not be what Andellen could, should the need arise. Now, Kaylin, there is no such need."

But that wasn't the whole of it. She didn't say as much.

"I will not ask you what you saw. Lord Evarrim was bold, and assumed much ignorance on your part."

She nodded.

"But I will ask you, instead, how you knew not to answer."

She saw the edge in the Lord of the West March. "Can we walk?" She countered. "I'm stiff, and if I don't start moving soon, I won't be able to."

"Ah. Very well." He lifted his hands, and hanging by the straps were her shoes. She grimaced; she didn't remember when she'd taken them off. But she accepted them and put them on—it was that or let him carry them, and even she wasn't that stupid. They began to walk in the gardens, and birdsong replaced bardsong; the screeching and the squawking was almost a comfort. Looking up, she saw passing flashes of color. It was said that Hawks had no sense of color; she wondered.

They left the garden by a door that Kaylin didn't remember seeing. It had the advantage of *not* passing by the throne or the rest of the High Court. It led instead to halls that felt—rather than looked—vaguely familiar.

She looked up at him, and caught him studying her expression. "It is," he said, "the way to the wing I claim."

She nodded.

"And you are aware of it now."

Nodded again.

"You have exceeded my expectations here. You have confounded the expectations of many. Do you understand that you have made yourself a threat?"

She frowned.

"I thought not. You do much without thinking of consequences."

"I kind of like living," she said sourly. "And it was do or die."

"True enough. But you were tolerated in spite of the mark

you bear because you were mortal. What you have made of yourself now, not even the Lord of the High Court can say."

"And his younger son?"

The Lord of the West March smiled; it was a cold smile. "I see the hand of Nightshade in this. He has always had a long reach."

"He didn't—"

"No. He did not tell you what to do. He couldn't. And if I do not claim any expertise in the ways of mortals, even I am aware that you would be difficult to direct. Lord Andellen was here. And I believe he approves. But you are now a danger."

"I'm still mortal."

"Are you, Kaylin?" He paused. Stone girded them on either side, featureless except for the Barrani runes that bounded it by floor and curved ceiling. "No mortal has passed that test."

She shrugged, uneasy. "No mortal has taken it before."

"It is held as common knowledge that those without power *cannot* pass it. And you have. Therefore you are not without power as we understand it—and you are Nightshade's. You bear his mark." He was waiting for her to say something. She had no idea what.

"Severn passed it."

The Lord of the West March raised a brow. His nod was a concession. "We do not fully understand how, or why, he was allowed to accompany you. We understand—from the little that Lord Andellen was willing to say—that it was meant to be *your* test."

"Why?"

"You saw the rune," he replied. "And your companion did not."

Fair enough. She lifted a hand and touched the wall, appreciating the texture of smooth, cold stone; it dampened the pain in her left arm. "Do you think Lord Nightshade intended for me to go to the tower?"

"That is my belief, yes."

"Why?"

His smile was thin. "You are his," he replied. His smile deepened as her expression soured. "There is another concern," he told her as she lowered her arm. "You are a Lord of the High Court by rite of passage, but you have not undertaken any oaths of fealty to the Lord of the High Court."

She said quietly, "I've sworn the only oath of fealty I can."

"To the Lord of Hawks?"

She nodded.

"The Lord of Hawks has no purchase within the High Halls, and no control of what passes within them. Not even the Emperor himself would be so bold, or so unwise. An oath sworn here is of this place. Or could be."

"But I'm not," she replied. "And I don't intend to stay here. I'm not Barrani."

"As you say. But you will remain two days at least, unless you wish to surrender your title—and possibly your life."

That, as usual, caught her attention, not that it had been wandering much. "Say that last part again."

"The High Court will gather in strength to witness *leoswuld* and the passing of the Lord. It is a Barrani rite, and there are few who have witnessed more than one such gifting." He paused and added, "Lord Evarrim is one."

"He doesn't want me there."

"Perceptive." It was a dismissive set of syllables, given in exactly the tone she might have used had one of the foundlings dumped a bucket of water over their own head and then said, "I'm wet."

She said, "I don't understand the Arcanum's role in this."

"The Arcanum? Inasmuch as it exists within the High Halls—and Lord Evarrim is not the only Barrani Lord to work within the Arcanist league—it wants nothing."

She frowned.

"He is Barrani first, Arcanist second. What power he derives from his association with the Arcanum is used to further his goals as Lord. No more and no less. They do not use *him*."

She was silent for a long moment. "But the Arcanum is somehow involved."

He glanced at her, and away. She could not see the color of his eyes. "Why do you say that, Kaylin?"

"There was a backlash in the Arcanum."

"And that could not have been caused by their actions throughout the rest of the city? It *is* the Festival season, and I believe the streets of Elantra are heavily populated."

She frowned. "No."

"No?"

"No, as in you know what the Arcanum was doing."

"Do I?"

"Yes."

"And how are you so certain of this?"

Because you're not looking at me, she thought. And because you're asking the wrong damn questions. She stopped walking, and after a step or two, he paused, as well. "Do the games here ever end?"

"Almost never, Kaylin."

"You want something from me," she told him quietly, "and I don't play games. Tell me what you know."

"I know very little. And it is not our custom to speak of certainty when so little exists."

"It's your custom to lie. I think it's a recreational pastime."

He was quiet. "You bear Lord Nightshade's mark," he said at last, his voice neutral. "And for that reason, Kaylin, no one will answer your questions."

"Not even you?"

"Not even I." He began to walk again; he had not turned to face her. She followed. Thinking. The backlash had occurred four hours *before* the Lord of the West March had risen.

The Lord of the West March himself had said that his brother, the Lord of the Green, was responsible for his coma, and having touched him—having barely touched him—Kaylin couldn't bring herself to doubt him.

So what had happened four hours earlier?

What had—

"Lord of the West March."

He stopped again, and again, she had a great view of his back. Of his Court robes, his perfect shoulders, his utterly straight spine, his long, dark hair.

"When exactly did you say you encountered the Lord of the Green? When did he try to—take your name?"

"I didn't."

Four hours, she thought.

Five minutes after the second noon hour. She allowed him to lead her to the West Wing, although she no longer had any intention of sleeping.

Severn was waiting for her in the room with the multi-hued glass walls. Where waiting, in this case, meant he was once again standing so close to them it should have been impossible to focus. He heard her enter the room but took a few minutes to react.

Those few minutes were occupied by Andellen and Samaran; they bowed in a truly annoying way as she entered. The Lord of the West March failed to notice, and they tendered him their respects in a similar fashion.

Kaylin looked down at her dress.

"I don't suppose," she began.

But the Lord of the West March nodded to the bed; laid out upon it was a whole lot of silk that looked vaguely as if it had been touched by seamstresses once or twice in its existence. It was a paler green than the remnants of the dress she now wore.

"Bath?" she asked.

He nodded again. "If you wish an attendant, I will summon one. If you would rather trust your guards—"

"I can bathe myself," she said curtly. And then thought the better of it. "Do you know where Teela—Lord Anteela—is?"

"If that is your quaint way of asking me to summon her, I will do so." His eyes were green, and the corner of his mouth moved up in something that resembled a smile. One offered at her expense.

* * *

Kaylin wasn't certain whether a bath was a tub—like the one she didn't own—or a lake with a small waterfall; the latter, in these halls, seemed more natural.

But if it were the latter, it was contained in what was a *huge* room—almost larger than the Aerie in the Halls of Law—with almost no floor. Unless you thought you could walk on water, and Kaylin's arrogance, while noted by many, had not yet reached that height.

The Lord of the West March left her at the door, indicating towels—yards of cloth, really—before he took his leave.

She looked at them, and looked longingly at the water. The truth—which she'd momentarily forgotten—was that she couldn't *exactly* bathe herself because she couldn't get out of the dress. And asking Severn to unbutton her before she traipsed down the open corridors hadn't occurred to her. Even if it had, she wouldn't have asked.

She took off her shoes and put her toes in the water; it was warm. Hot, really. But clear and still, regardless. If there had been fish here, she would have given up and lived with the dirt. Whole winters in her childhood had been spent without much in the way of cleanliness; the water was either cold or ice, and warmth was in short supply.

But Teela entered the room, and changed its character. What had seemed peaceful and solitary shrunk at the force of her presence. She wasn't exactly angry; she wasn't exactly happy. In this inexact state, she was most often to be found in a tavern, fleecing the drunks before she became one.

The lack of gaming tables and a bar made themselves instantly felt. But the look she turned on Kaylin was one of familiar exasperation. "Look, Kaylin," she said in sharp Elantran, "I'm *not* a servant here."

"I know. You're a Lord of the High Court."

"Which part of Lord means 'helps another Lord bathe'?"

"You don't have to help me bathe." Kaylin turned her back almost helplessly. "You just have to cut me out of this thing. I can do the rest myself."

Teela snorted. "The Lord of the West March is an idiot," she muttered under her breath as the buttons began to open beneath her slender fingers. "I don't suppose he thought to tell you that anyone else would be insulted for—oh—ever?"

"Not really. Maybe it escaped his attention."

Teela snorted again. But she undid the rest of the buttons quickly; Kaylin had the distinct feeling Teela was biting back disgust.

As she eased her shoulders and arms free of the dress, she gained enough freedom that she could turn around. Disgust didn't quite do Teela's expression justice. But more than disgust was folded into the familiar frown: This was how Teela worried. She looked up from the dress—she was still holding a small part of it between carefully pinched fingers—and studied Kaylin.

Undressed, the marks on her arms were exposed. "Do they look different?" Kaylin asked, trying to sound casual.

Teela stared at them for a moment, her brows bending as she concentrated. Barrani had good memories; they weren't Records, but they were the next best thing. If you didn't happen to have a Dragon with you. "No," she said at last. "They're the same."

"Not darker?"

"I think you're paler."

"Oh." Kaylin stepped free of the skirts, and gave the dress a halfhearted kick; the silk was soft against her wet, and bare, feet. "Can we get rid of it?"

"I'd suggest burning, myself. But not," she added, "in this room. Start a fire here—if you could—and you'd have half the Hall in an uproar."

"Why?"

"This is the Water Room," Teela replied. "Or hadn't you noticed?"

Everything Kaylin knew about sarcasm, she'd learned from the Hawks, and Teela foremost among them. She bowed to her better, and bit back a reply.

Teela rolled her eyes and tossed her head to one side; black followed in a perfect sheen, reflecting some of the light at the heart of the pool. "I could use a bath," the Barrani Hawk said. She still spoke Elantran. "I'll join you, if you don't mind. That way, when you decide to fall asleep and drown, I can pull you out before anyone notices." It was her way of offering comfort.

Kaylin, almost born a beggar, did what came naturally: She took what was offered. She removed the rest of her undergarments, peeling them from her skin; she was sweaty and sticky. These, on the other hand, she'd keep, mend and wash. She'd paid for them, after all.

She slid into the water and found, to her surprise, that it was deep. She was up to her neck before her feet hit bottom, and she drifted, slightly buoyant, in the heat.

"Come to the edge," Teela told her. Being Barrani, and being competent, she had undressed in about as much time as it had taken Kaylin to remove a few scraps of cloth, and her dress was the finer of the two.

Kaylin swam to the edge, until she could almost touch Teela.

"There are ledges here. Sit."

She sat slowly; the water still rose to her neck, but she had more control of where she was drifting, and held the edge of what seemed a seat in her hands.

"Soap?"

Teela shook her head. "You won't need it here. Just…sit. And shut up," she added as an afterthought.

"Shut up about what?"

"Everything."

Kaylin was quiet for as long as she was capable of being quiet. Actually, given the comfort of the water's current, it was longer than she'd intended. When she turned her head to look at Teela, Teela's eyes were closed. She almost seemed to be sleeping.

"Teela—"

"Which part of shut up didn't you understand?"

"I just have a couple of questions—"

"You *always* have a couple of questions. And then a couple more. And then another dozen."

It was more or less true. "Don't you?"

"No."

"I mean, we're in the High Halls—"

"I had noticed that, Kaylin."

"I mean, I'm in the High Halls. Doesn't that strike you as worthy of questions?"

"Not ones that should have answers, no."

"Is it the mark?"

"Is what the mark?"

"You don't want to answer questions here because I bear Nightshade's mark."

Teela reached out almost languidly, and Kaylin ended up with a faceful of water. She sputtered, and Teela waited until she'd finished. "Don't," she said in a voice that could have been Marcus's, "insult me."

"I just wondered," Kaylin began in a much quieter voice.

"The Hells you did. The reason I don't want to answer your questions—aside from the one I just gave—is that you don't understand the High Court, and you have a big mouth."

"But if I don't understand, won't I just make more mistakes?"

"I don't think that's possible," Teela replied. But she shifted, lowering herself into the water. "But it might be," she said, grudging every word.

"You don't think Nightshade can control me through the mark."

"No. I thought he might be able to until you fought in the fiefs." She didn't mention the black Dragon whose plan had almost destroyed an empire, but then again, almost no one did. "Even then, it was a distinct possibility. But now? No, Kaylin. I'm not afraid of that."

"Then—"

Teela, continuing her Leontine impression, growled softly. And said something that even Marcus seldom said. "You're here because of me," she told the younger Hawk. "And it was made very, very clear that you were to come back in more or less the same condition you left in.

"By Marcus. He wasn't joking."

"He doesn't, usually."

"He was deadly serious."

That was bad. "I'm not hurt," she offered.

Teela slammed her hand against the tiles that surrounded the pool. The sound echoed. "I cannot for the life of me figure out how it is that Marcus hasn't eaten you yet. *Kitling*," she added, using the Leontine word.

"I need to know something."

"All right, all right. I'm listening. I'm not happy, I'm looking forward to either being rended limb from limb or dropped off the height of the Hawklord's tower by the Hawklord himself—did I mention he also indicated you were to be watched?—but I *am* listening."

"When was the Lord of the West March discovered?"

Teela's expression didn't change at all. But the growling stopped. "Almost four hours before I brought you to my chambers."

"They *were* yours."

"Yes."

"You found him?"

"Kaylin—"

"I think it's important," Kaylin said, her voice low, her eyes unwavering.

"You've got the look of the Hawk about your face," Teela said with just a glint of brown in her eyes to lend warmth to the words. "And you're on a hunt. What have you seen, Kaylin?"

"I don't know yet. I don't understand all the pieces. I'd bet money—even mine—that I haven't *seen* them all." She waited.

"I discovered him, yes."

"You were following him."

"Yes, if you must know. I was following him."

"Why?"

"I can't answer that."

"Okay. So you had orders to follow him."

Teela didn't deny this. In some ways, this type of conversation reminded Kaylin of youth in the fiefs; Twenty Questions, a game played at night or when the rains were harsh and there was nowhere else to go. Severn had nicknamed her bulldog when she played because she resolutely refused to count the questions she asked. On the other hand, when she'd first started, she *couldn't* count them.

"And you can't tell me who gave those orders."

"They weren't orders."

"A suggestion in the High Court can be an order." Kaylin stopped. More thoughtfully, she added, "But not from someone less powerful or less senior than you."

Teela's nothing was like a nod. Except for the actual movement.

"The Lord of the West March told me about *leoswuld*," Kaylin said quietly.

"It is your right to know. You are a Lord of the Court."

"He told me before."

Teela said nothing.

"But I don't think what he said was entirely accurate."

"He *is* a Barrani Lord, Kaylin, and accuracy is always a matter of context."

"Okay. Context. The context there was a bit unnerving. Let's leave that for now. You found him."

"Yes."

"And the Lord of the Green?"

Teela tensed, her eyes shading to blue. That was almost enough of an answer, but Kaylin had to keep going. Had to. "Did you find the Lord of the Green?"

"Kaylin—"

"I've *seen* him, Teela," she said, voice lower and more urgent. "I've *touched* him." She paused, and then added, "I think Lord Evarrim was present when you found them. Or he was already there."

Teela said nothing, but it was the wrong type of nothing.

"Lord Evarrim tried to contain the Lord of the Green. That's what I think happened."

"Do you?"

"It caused a backlash in the Arcanum. Whatever power Evarrim called upon, it *wasn't enough*. But the funny thing about it? Backlashes like that only happen when the spell is *already* in place. Or so I've been told. Correct me when I'm wrong, hmm?"

"I should just drown you."

"Marcus would kill you."

"I don't have to leave the High Halls."

Kaylin frowned; she didn't feel entirely safe, but she didn't feel threatened. "Why did you leave them, anyway?" She got another faceful of water in reply.

"You're not an Arcanist, that I know of," she continued.

"No."

"And Lord Evarrim could only have known to place a spell of power *in advance,* if one of two things were true."

"And those?"

"Either he understood the difficulty the Lord of the Green was having," Kaylin said, choosing her words with deliberate care, "or the Lord of the West March summoned him. I don't like Evarrim…he doesn't much like me."

"Like is irrelevant."

"Not to me. Human, remember?"

Teela snorted. "I keep trying to forget, but you make it damn hard."

Kaylin laughed. It was short, but felt good. The ebb of the water, the warmth of it, was eating away at whole months' worth of tension. She *wanted* one of these. Of course, her whole apartment would fit in the corner if it were twice its size, but the idea was still appealing.

"I don't like Evarrim. I think I wanted to believe he was somehow responsible for—for the Lord of the Green."

"Why?" There was honest curiosity in the question. At times, Teela could be too Barrani.

"Because he's too fond of his own power, and maybe there was some chance he could increase it here."

"Not now, Kaylin. During any other Festival—but the High Festival? *Leoswuld?* There isn't a Barrani alive—not even the outcaste—who would play death games *now.*"

Kaylin nodded. "So I had to give up on that theory. And given how often Barrani are actually *truthful,* it was damn hard. This is what I think happened. Lord Evarrim somehow managed to contain the Lord of the Green for long enough. Long enough to somehow save him, or stop him, or something. Long enough to save the Lord of the West March. But not—"

Teela lifted a hand; water didn't so much drip down her skin as slide.

"You must have helped," Kaylin said quietly.

Teela let her hand fall back. Her eyes were blue. Kaylin was flying in the right patch of sky, but there were some things that even a Hawk couldn't take down on its own.

"I'm not a mage," Teela said with care.

"No. But neither am I, and I'm wearing a medallion that says otherwise."

"Kaylin."

She nodded.

"Do you understand the purpose of the test?"

"Not really. It's a game. A gauntlet."

But Teela shook her head. "It's far, far more than that. To the Barrani. I don't know what you saw. I don't know what you faced. We do not speak of it."

"I can."

"You were wise enough not to speak with Evarrim."

"That's different. I wouldn't tell him the name of Mrs. Evan's dog."

Teela chuckled. But it didn't last. And her eyes didn't lose the shade of blue that always meant danger.

"It is a test of life," Teela told her quietly. "For the Barrani. It is a test of *name*."

"I don't understand."

"I didn't think you would. Mortals don't have names. And I would bet every cent I'm owed that you didn't either, before you passed the test." Her face was completely still, her expression neutral. She leaned back, and managed to make languor look stiff and unnatural. "If the High Halls can, it takes our name from us. If it can't, we retain our lives. No more and no less than that."

"That's not what it tried—"

"The High Halls were built by the Old Ones. They had no understanding of a life that existed outside of their abilities, their words, their magic. They could not have dreamed you. They could not have prepared for you. Whatever you faced was an echo of the old test, no more. It was a test of true life."

"I passed."

"Yes. You passed, and in a way that the Old Ones would understand. You kept your name. Except you didn't have one." She waited.

"I—I chose."

"Yes, Kaylin."

"But Severn—"

"As I said, no one understands Severn's role in this. I don't. I would have bet that he would be devoured by the Halls—he wasn't. I would have said that he would bear what you now bear, but he doesn't. I touched him. It's not there. He's a part of you in a way that no Barrani—not even the fieflord—could possibly understand. Maybe this is human." She shrugged, and water eddied out from her, returning to lap against her skin.

"This isn't about Severn. It's about the Lord of the West March. He wants me to save his brother," Kaylin said quietly.

"I know." Teela closed her eyes. "It is not always the case that brothers are close. It is almost never the case when so much power is involved. But there is a bond between them that the desire for power cannot break. Ballads have been written about them," she added quietly.

"He took the test, didn't he?"

"The Lord of the West March?"

"The Lord of the Green."

"He did."

"And he passed?"

"He returned," Teela said quietly.

"That's not much of an answer."

"No, it isn't. We speak now of things that cannot be spoken of. I was young. I was born the year the Lord of the West March was born," she added quietly. "We are cousins, but distant kin. And I saw the affection between them—all did. It was tested, it was bound to be tested. But it held. It always has.

"He is not playing a game with you. He wants you to save his brother."

"Do you think that's possible?"

Teela didn't answer.

"Do you think the Lord of the Green *passed* his test?"

"He returned."

"That's not a damn answer!" She struggled to lower her voice. Frustration was its own volume. "Teela—if you had failed, what would have happened?"

"I would have lost my name. It would have remained in the High Halls."

"And you?"

"I'm Barrani. Without a name, I'm nothing."

"Was there ever any negotiation? Did you see—" She tried to finish the sentence, and failed; her tongue was suddenly stuck to the roof of her mouth.

"Negotiation?" Teela asked softly.

Kaylin nodded.

"Let me tell you some of our legend. Since we're not in a classroom, pay attention."

"Yes, Teela."

"The High Halls weren't built by Barrani, but the Barrani mastered them in a fashion, long before there were Empires. Long before the Dragons chose to master themselves. Have you never wondered why the fiefs exist at all?"

"All the time."

"And you know some of it now. You've seen Castle Nightshade, and it is not at the *heart* of the fiefs but at the edge. We believe that such places were built as watchtowers, in a fashion. There are older places still, and darker, but what the darkness builds is not…like the Castle, or the High Halls, and it exists mostly in the fiefs. We cannot destroy it by any means we now possess. We can guard against it, and this, we have done. But the darkness doesn't have structure or form in the way that the High Halls can."

Kaylin nodded.

"It's our belief that in the absence of the Old Ones, some ancient magic still lingers, and it's alive in a sense that only the Old Ones truly understand. Such places as the High Halls were meant to stand against that magic, to defend order or life as *we* know it. But to defend, we had to control, and to control, we had to accept." She paused. "And so we are tested, if we wish to take our place here.

"Those that fail do not return. The Lord of the Green returned."

But Kaylin felt the water's warmth at a distance as she

heard the words. A great distance; there was a cold in her that was sharp and cutting, like cruelty, but without the intent.

"This was long ago?" Kaylin whispered.

"As I said, I was young. Too young to witness his return. But he was Lord before either I or his brother."

"If the High Halls held his name, what would that mean?"

"He'd be dead. And he isn't."

She shook her head. Thinking. "Did they—did the Old Ones—build *here* for a reason?"

Teela's eyes were an odd shade; blue and green and brown.

"Did you never wonder why Elantra was built upon this spot? Did you never wonder why the Dragons did not choose a place with less history?"

"No. Um, I failed history."

"This wasn't discussed in history."

"Then how would I know?"

Teela laughed. "I wondered, as a child. I asked once. The Lord of the High Court answered. The magic that we can bring to bear must be centered here, where the greatest danger lies. If we live in distance and ignorance, we may well lose the world if it wakes."

"And it's waking," Kaylin whispered, looking at her arms.

Teela said nothing.

"And you think that the High Halls are here because—"

The Barrani Hawk tilted her head to one side, looking for a moment like a wet cat. "I know it. If you ask me how, I'll drown you. I swear it."

"He was born to be the Lord of the High Court."

"Yes."

"Which means he was born to be the Lord of the High Halls."

"Yes."

"And the testing the Lord of the High Halls faces—"

"Yes, Kaylin," Teela said quietly. "Do not name our fear. Do not give it voice. There are shadows here, and they are strong."

"Stronger," Kaylin whispered.

"The *leoswuld* strengthens us," Teela replied. "But it weakens us, as well. The weakness lasts only as long as the rite."

"And if it lasted forever?"

Teela said nothing.

"I'll just wash my hair now."

"Good idea."

CHAPTER 17

The Barrani had obviously never had to dally with the seamstress guild, which was probably a damn good thing—for the guild. The dress that had been laid out for Kaylin was not only graceful and elegant but also practical in ways the dress requisitioned by the soon-to-be-berserk Quartermaster could never have been. It was long, yes, and fine, and its sleeves ran the full length of her arms—or she wouldn't have worn it.

Severn made a comment, and she frowned. "What?"

"I asked you what you would have done instead."

"I'd have made *you* wear it and I'd have worn your damn armor."

She was *comfortable* in this dress. First, it had very few buttons, which meant, with some effort, she could put the damn thing on by herself. Second, she could bend and touch her toes without being crushed by the seams, boning and the shape of the cloth. Third, she could kick a man's face without ripping the hem of the skirt. Or skirts. They fell as if they were one piece, but they seemed to be layered and split to allow for something as practical as running. She could probably do splits in this dress. Not that she was about to try where anyone could see her. She had little enough dignity as it was.

She wished she'd thought of asking for the dress *before* she'd asked Andellen for a tour of the Halls.

"Okay. You're wearing a dress," Severn said. He'd actually taken the time to get something like sleep. That, and he'd shaved his face. Or had it shaved. Either way, he looked awake and alert.

She could tell, by the slight compression of his lips, that she probably looked like crap. Or what was left of crap after it had been kicked around and stepped on lots.

"I'll sleep," she told him. "Just—I have a couple of things I thought I'd check first—"

"You can do that in your dreams."

"Severn—"

He folded his arms across his chest and looked down at her.

"I'm really not as tired as you look—I mean, as you think I look—"

His smile almost defined the word *smug.* "Before you continue to wedge your foot into your mouth—while it's still moving—Teela did mention that she had to fish your face out of the water when you fell asleep washing your hair."

"I wasn't sleeping—I was washing my face!"

"While choking a lot. She was fairly impressed."

"I bet."

"Your money."

"My money."

He laughed. "Kaylin, you can't hunt forever. You need to sleep, even if it's only for a few hours. Now is a good time."

She really wanted to argue more. Partly because it came naturally, and partly because in some perverse way she enjoyed it. But she was *yawning,* or rather, doing the world's worst job of stifling a yawn.

She did need the sleep. But she wasn't home.

You slept at the Castle, she told herself with some heated contempt.

But the Castle was different.

"Kaylin?"

"I don't want to sleep here," she finally told him.

"It's better than underwater." He looked at the guards. "Wait outside," he told them. "Watch the doors."

They both looked at him for a moment, but Samaran looked at Andellen before he nodded. Andellen took orders from Severn as if he'd spent a life perfecting the art.

Kaylin was too tired to work out why.

"They'll wake you if anything happens."

"And you?"

"I'll stay," he told her quietly. "I had some sleep. I'll watch."

"You'll watch?"

He nodded. "I'll watch over you."

Seven years dissolved as the words reached her. She managed to wobble her way over to the very large bed; it bounced a little—or she did, she couldn't be certain which.

She listened for the sound of ferals, in a room filled with colored light, half a city away. She listened for the wind. And she listened for the sound of Severn's breathing; it was distant.

She lifted her head, trying to focus on his face.

He was there. He saw her expression. His was an odd thing, half-broken, unadorned by sarcasm or neutrality or irony. He waited for her to speak.

She lifted a hand, instead.

And he came to her, quietly, his steps absorbed by the floor, by fading consciousness. He sat beside her awkwardly, but he sat. The sound of his breathing was close enough now that she could rest.

The Lord of the West March faced the Lord of the Green. They looked like twins, to her eye, but she was sleeping, and knew it. Which should have been more disturbing than it actually was. There was an unreality here that was much, much stronger than the lack of cohesion she had faced in the High Halls.

They greeted each other politely, raising their hands. As if in ritual. Or in public. As she watched them, she examined their clothing; they wore, of all things, armor—chain, something flexible and shimmering. No helms, but that was typical of the Barrani; they wouldn't want to hide their faces or encumber their vision.

They wore capes, though; one was brown and one was green. By this, she could tell them apart. As she studied them, as they stood facing each other, she could tell other things about them. The Lord of the West March was worried. It was an odd shade of blue that expressed that worry; it was lined with a green that was deep and dark, and she thought—gazing at him—that his eyes would always hold some depth of green when he regarded his brother.

The Lord of the Green, however—his eyes were almost black. And black was not a color she had ever seen Barrani eyes take. She wondered what it meant.

And he turned, at that moment, to stare at her.

"Do you not know?" he asked. There was no scorn in the question, but it was not neutral; it was weighted with pain, and a twisted longing.

She shook her head. Mute.

He walked away from his brother, and she saw the Lord of the West March flinch but hold his ground.

The Lord of the Green raised a hand, but he did not try to touch her; she could see, in fact, that he was struggling to do the opposite; to keep his hand from its natural trajectory.

"I understand what I am now," he told her.

I don't. But she didn't say the words. She couldn't.

He pointed at her arms. She looked down. They were bare. The rest of her wasn't; she was dressed in Barrani silks that fell from her shoulders, and only her shoulders, as if they were anchors. The skirts were long enough to hide the other marks, but those, too, were present.

She lifted her arms. The words were moving across her skin, losing and taking form as they traveled. She shook her head.

He said, "I was ambitious."

She nodded at this simple statement of fact. From a Barrani, it was the equivalent, in Kaylin's mind, of saying "I'm breathing."

"And I was firstborn. I went to the tower."

She met his gaze; it was black, but she could see some small trace of color in the darkness, and she found it comforting.

"My brother went with me," he added.

"To the test?"

"No. That, the High Halls would not allow, nor would I. But that was his desire."

"What word?" she whispered softly.

"Do you not know? Can you not guess?"

She shook her head.

And he traced a rune in the air between them; his finger, glowing, trailed blue light.

She saw it clearly, and took a step forward; he took a step back, maintaining the small distance between them. "That was—it was—the same. As mine."

"Yes."

"But—" Speech, it seemed, had returned to her.

"Yes. The same."

"Did you see what I saw?"

"No, Kaylin. You will never be Lord of the High Halls." He grimaced. "And neither will I. It is a truth that the Lord of the West March will not accept." He paused, and then he whispered another word. *Lirienne.*

His brother's name.

She didn't know how to pretend she hadn't heard it. Nor did he seem surprised that she could.

"Do you know what rune he saw?" the Lord of the Green

asked her, and turned, then, to look at his brother, standing in isolation.

"No."

He lifted a hand again, and again he traced a symbol in the air. This one, however, although it looked familiar to her eyes, was not. She frowned.

"It means *duty*," the Lord of the Green told her quietly.

She nodded. It made sense. Probably because she was dreaming; in dreams, all things had their own logic.

"He told you?" she asked softly.

"He told me."

It didn't surprise her. "He passed," she said quietly.

"He passed as if there was no test, and no testing," the Lord of the Green replied. There was pride in the voice. It wasn't mirrored in the eyes, but the blackness of the eyes were almost impenetrable. Color had so little purchase there, she didn't expect more.

"He passed and he came to us in the High Court." He paused, and added, "In our history, his was the shortest of the tests offered by the High Halls. It was almost as if…as if they had already made their decision."

"Yours wasn't so easy."

"I do not say his test was easy, I merely say that he bested it without doubt."

She said quietly, "And you didn't."

Black, black eyes.

"But you returned."

"I returned." He looked again at the Lord of the West March. "He understands his duty," he said quietly, and again, with pain and hesitation, "and he *will not* do it."

"You—" She stopped talking. She almost stopped breathing. "You can't expect him to *kill you.*"

"He is the Lord of the West March. He faced his ordeal, and he accepted it."

"He had no choice *but* to accept it! He had to take the test—"

"Kaylin," the Lord of the Green said. "Elianne."

She nodded.

"You faced the test of *duty* yourself. You failed."

And felt a sudden surge of wild anger take her, hemming her words in. Honing them. But when they were sharp enough to cut, she found that she could no longer speak. Speech, it seemed, was at the whim of the damn Lord of the damn Green.

"He did not understand, when he returned, that his test was yet to come."

"And you did?"

"Then? I was envious, Elianne. I was envious and afraid. My brother is in all ways a better man than I. He had duty...I had choice."

"But *what the Hells choice did you make?*" The words came out in a jumble of syllables that seemed to go on without break.

He looked at her, his black eyes unblinking. "I should never have returned," he whispered. "I should have died there."

It wasn't much of an answer.

"And," he added softly, "I would have. Laws were broken on the day I went into the tower. They are not your laws, little Hawk. They are not your negotiations. They have no guardians, they appoint none." He hesitated. "My brother must not fail," he said at last, and turned and began to walk away. "Because I still do not have the strength to do what must be done. I live.

"And while I live, we face a death that you can neither comprehend—nor allow." He did not turn back to her. "You faced the test my brother now faces, and you failed it, and you were saved the consequences of your failure by another.

"If my brother fails, in the end, remember your own life with kindness."

And she remembered Steffi and Jade, and woke screaming.

Severn knew the scream, and held her anyway. She saw his face upon waking, and she struggled a moment before reality asserted itself. Then she stilled.

The Barrani guards had opened the door, but they had not entered; they stood in the frame a moment, as if assessing the situation. They couldn't see Severn's face, but hers told them enough. They closed the door, and remained on the other side of it.

She said indistinctly, "I hate the Barrani."

He tightened his grip for a moment, and then let her go. "What have they done this time? And keeping in mind that anything that happens in your dreams isn't a subject for the Law."

"It's the *leoswuld*," she told him.

He said nothing.

"And their law. Which isn't our law. Or really, law at all." She sat up.

"Kaylin."

And looked at him. "You never told me what the Lord of the High Court said to you after I left."

"No. I didn't."

"What did he say?"

"I didn't tell you for a reason," he replied stiffly.

"He knew."

"Knew what?"

"About you. About the—about our past."

Severn said nothing. She reached up and touched his face, and he almost shied away. But he was Severn; he didn't. "He told you—"

"Kaylin, leave it. Please."

She nodded. "How long did I sleep?"

"A few hours."

"I don't feel much better." She slid off the bed. Looked at the shoes that lay on the floor. She wondered if she could get Barrani shoes to match the dress. Probably. But not now, and she wanted them now.

"Where are you going?" he asked her softly.

"Back," she said grimly, "to the tower."

His face went still. "I'll go with you."

She hesitated, but it wasn't much of a hesitation. "The ceremony—it's tomorrow, isn't it?"

He nodded. "Where are we going?"

"Oh," she said breezily, "almost anywhere."

He muttered something about Leontines and acting.

"I heard that."

They got up and left the room.

Andellen and Samaran parted like gates as they left the room. Andellen actually bowed.

"Do you listen to every damn word I say?" she asked him.

His face was a study in neutrality. Armored neutrality. But his eyes were an odd shade of green.

She marched along the halls, failing to notice the striking elements of singular beauty that could be found in it—if someone actually cared. At the moment, Kaylin didn't.

"What do you seek?" Andellen asked her after they'd been walking for five minutes in a grim silence.

Without looking at him, she said, "The heart of the High Halls."

"I would have said you found it."

"Funny, so would I."

He stopped walking, which she barely noticed. Severn did, however, and caught her arm. She turned, not even bothering to hide her growing irritation. Because it was a lot like agitation. So much so, that she wasn't sure she could separate them.

"There is a risk in this, Lord," Andellen said quietly.

She stared at him. For a long time. And then she asked him a question. "Where do the ferals come from?"

He frowned.

Severn frowned, too.

"The fiefs," Andellen said eventually.

She turned to Severn. "So, what we faced weren't ferals?"

"They were ferals."

"They weren't real?"

Severn's frown deepened in that I-don't-like-where-this-is-going way. "They were real," he said at last. But he said it as if it were dragged out of him.

"You don't want to go, stay in the room," she told Andellen and Samaran curtly. And in Elantran. "But I have to go."

"Why?"

"Because I had a dream, okay?"

"Kaylin—"

"And I want to see how *much* of a dream it was."

"The Lord of the High Court—"

Kaylin told Andellen what the Lord of the High Court could do. Given it was anatomically possible, Andellen shut up.

For five seconds. "You had best hope that whoever's listening doesn't speak Elantran, Lord Kaylin."

"At this point? I don't give a rat's ass."

He looked oddly nonplussed. And she realized that he was trying to take the comment literally. She snorted. For smart, immortal people, they could be awfully dense.

She stomped off, and everyone followed. They even followed quickly. Had she been wearing her boots, they wouldn't have had much choice.

The tower arch opened up before them out of nowhere.

And it looked different. The keystone was still there, but the rest of the arch beneath it seemed to have been rebuilt; it was wider, thicker, and a lot more craggy.

But it was the *same* arch. Kaylin knew it the moment she laid eyes on it. She glanced at Andellen. He said nothing.

Beyond them, beyond the arch, was an unfamiliar set of stairs, and it offered only one passage: down. There were no brass rails to gird it either; a clumsy person would get down much more quickly than they probably wanted.

And Kaylin, looking at those stairs, had a very strong feeling that jumping was not a viable option, unless the goal was suicide. She glanced at the wall the stairs ran up against; it had the look of sheared stone, rather than worked stone, as if this had been taken, whole, from a cliff face. Or was part of one.

There was a rune there, as she had expected. In fact, there were several. None of them were the one she now thought of as hers. She looked at Andellen again. Caught his stiff profile.

"This isn't a test," she told him quietly.

"It is, Kaylin. It is not the test of Lordship, however."

"What do they say?"

He shook his head. "I recognize only one of the thirteen."

"And that one?"

"Death."

"Great." She lifted one arm, and shoved the sleeve up to her elbow; it went with ease. "That's…this one, right?"

Andellen looked at her arm. "No."

And she deflated. "No, why?"

"The shape is right. The center portion is slightly wrong. Here," he added. "And here." He paused, and then offered her the faintest of smiles. "I cannot read the old tongue."

"But you recognized—"

"Yes. But this," he said, his hand above her arm without touching skin, "is older still. The Dragons could tell you some of what it said—but I have grave doubts that they would allow you to retain the arm."

She'd heard it before. And wished that the Dragon who had said it—Lord Tiamaris—were beside her. Wearing the Hawk.

He wasn't. "Will you risk a second time what you risked a first?"

Lord Andellen nodded.

"Samaran?"

"It is not my test," he began. And then he straightened out. "Nor, I think, is it yours. The High Halls will decide. If we *can* pass through the arch with you, we will."

"Good enough." And she turned and walked through the arch, while the keystone flickered above her. They followed.

One difference, one immediate difference, was that the arch didn't vanish at their backs. Kaylin considered this a sign, but wasn't certain whether or not it was good or bad. "The light here sucks," she said to no one in particular.

Severn glanced at Andellen, who raised a brow. "Light is seldom a difficulty for the Barrani," he finally conceded when Severn failed to look away. The Barrani Lord lifted a hand, and light began to trail from it, as if it were mist. Or liquid.

Kaylin cursed.

"It is not magic," Andellen told her. "It is part of the High Halls."

"I can't do it."

"In a century, it will come naturally."

She wanted to kick him but refrained. Instead, with the comfort of light—even this odd, amorphous light—she began to make her way down the stairs. The darkness that waited beneath her feet was eaten away by the light, but only slowly; her progress was difficult. She didn't, however, remove her shoes. She didn't want to touch the stone steps themselves; they seemed to shine in a way that implied light without actually giving any.

Severn was unwinding his chain.

Andellen, when she looked up to see him, had already drawn his sword, as had Samaran. She, like a human noble, didn't actually *have* a weapon, and looked up at Severn, who indicated his dagger sheaths. He must be nervous; he wasn't willing to let go of the chain to get them himself.

She pulled them free, and continued to walk, hoping she didn't trip and impale herself. On the whole, though, there were probably worse things.

Like, say, that distant sound of growling.

The expression "hair stood on end" did not do Kaylin's justice; the skin on the back of her neck seemed to ripple, and not in a good way. As if it were Leontine fur.

"It's not ferals," Severn said. One look at his face made it clear that this wasn't meant as comfort.

"Severn?" Two more steps passed beneath her before she turned, her back against the wall. "I told you about the Old Ones, right? And the beginning of life? The Barrani and the Dragons? That they were made of stone, and lifeless, until they were given their names?"

He nodded slowly.

"Why did they only make two?"

"Two races?"

She nodded.

His expression shifted.

And Andellen said quietly, "They didn't."

The heart of the High Halls was a dark, dark place. It wasn't precisely a dungeon; it wasn't, however, enough like anything else that Kaylin bothered to find a word for it. The steps did not, as she had feared, descend forever; they walked for some time, but reached the end. The growls had grown in volume, but they weren't near enough yet.

And because they weren't, Kaylin now agreed with Severn's assessment. Not ferals.

They stood in a stone corridor that looked more like a tunnel. Evidence that it wasn't natural existed; there were runes on the walls at odd intervals, although some had been cracked or damaged. And there were no rats.

The hall's ceiling, such as it was, looked like it had been gouged out of rock by large hands, it was that uneven. In places, it went high enough that it couldn't be seen by the light Andellen offered; in places, it was low enough that it skirted Barrani hair. The ground was also uneven, but not as much; someone intended people to walk here.

Where people was a very broad description.

The growls were closer now. Which meant they were heading in the right direction. Or the wrong one, given that there *was* only one; there were no branches, no other halls, nothing at all in the rock itself.

She thought she would be happy to see a door.

Until she did.

Even Andellen took a step back as they approached it. Because it was made of ebony, or seemed to be, and it absorbed every damn bit of light that wasn't the single rune on it. She cursed in a loud, loud voice that echoed in the cavernous ceiling above.

Andellen caught the bits that weren't swearing and shook his head. "It isn't a door-ward," he said calmly.

She stopped midstream, her hand half raised. "What is it?"

"A warning."

And she realized then where she'd seen this type of black before. The portcullis in Castle Nightshade. This occasioned less swearing and more actual worry. But she looked at the door, and said softly, "He came here."

They all looked at her, as if waiting for more.

"The Lord of the Green. He came here. So we have to go, too." And sucking in air as if she might not get more of it, she walked into the door, just beneath the glowing rune.

CHAPTER 18

She expected to be dizzy and disoriented. She expected the world to change. She expected to be spit out someplace different.

But the passage through *this* door was entirely unlike the passage through the portcullis, because it looked like it wasn't going to end. She was trapped in darkness; mired by it; it clung to her in ways that nothing *should* be able to cling. She felt it almost on the inside of her skin, and had she been able to, she would have taken her skin off just to be rid of it.

She hoped that she wasn't trying. She could see very little, and feel very little. She could hear growling, which didn't help much. This *wasn't* a place. She couldn't step forward—or back, which at this point seemed preferable. She wasn't really aware that she was moving at all, or even that she could; she couldn't feel her feet. Couldn't tell if she was shouting, either, because she couldn't feel her lips.

She could feel her arms and her thighs. She could feel them as if they were furrowed, living stone; could feel the shape of words engraved there that she still didn't understand, and usually did her best not to think about.

But she thought about them now because they were almost her only sensation in this place, and sensation reminded her that she *was* somewhere. That she was, in fact, alive.

And as she did she heard words that sounded entirely unlike language. Not chanting, although she couldn't say why, because it seemed to be carried by a multitude of voices. She felt cadence in those voices, but she couldn't make out syllables; they spoke, and spoke, and spoke.

As they did, she became aware of physical sensation, a deepening of the odd tingling in her limbs. It moved, darting back and forth. As if—

As if she was being read. Literally read.

And judged. She had endured judgment in her life; had come to expect it. Some of it angered her because it came entirely out of profound ignorance. Some of it shamed her because it didn't. But none of it stood so far beyond her that she couldn't react.

The last word, the last word she *heard*. And *felt*. It resonated not across her limbs, but within her, as if it had been struck, as if she were a bell. It had a noise, and a shape, a sharpness and a sweetness, that she had experienced before—but it had been outside of her then.

Her name. The name she had chosen.

She held on to it ferociously. It took no thought, no deliberation, no active decision; it was far more primal than that. It was like fear, except that it defined fear. She felt vulnerable in ways that she had never felt vulnerable. As if this word could be riven from her, and everything she knew, thought or felt could be sucked out of it, leaving her with *nothing*.

She spoke it to herself, again and again, as if repetition made it more familiar. Or as if it made it *hers*.

But if this was what Nightshade had felt, if this was what the Lord of the West March had felt, she wondered how they could have given her what they had: how they could surrender their names to her keeping. And decided that Barrani acting lessons? She wanted them.

Easy to think of those things. Easy to think of Marcus, and his Leontine ability to be utterly himself. He wouldn't need a name, and even if he had one, it wouldn't make a difference; he couldn't be anything other than Marcus.

Easy, as well, to think of the Hawklord, his wings spread, his feet upon the ground. To think of his name, which wasn't a name, and to feel it profoundly as if it had the same meaning.

She was *Kaylin*. She was *Elianne*. They had been her identity long before she'd taken the word that was supposed to define her and give her life, and she suddenly found that the syllables of her name—her two names—replaced the ones that she had taken. She spoke these, or felt them, not as magical things, but as something more profound. Herself.

Her true self.

If she didn't understand the whole of that self, if that self changed—and it might, given it had once—it didn't matter. What she was *now*, at this minute, was in those two words.

The darkness parted.

She wasn't spit out; she didn't get dizzy; she wasn't disoriented; she felt it open, and then saw it open, as if it were a great curtain in which she'd been entangled.

And she saw, as it opened, that Severn, Andellen, and Samaran were standing beside her; they were ashen. The light from Andellen's hand had banked.

"I will not follow you here again," he told her gravely. His breath fell like mist from his mouth, although it wasn't cold here.

"I won't ask it." She meant it.

Samaran said nothing.

Severn shook his head once, as if to clear it, and looked up; his hands were on his chain, and his knuckles were white. But she knew that if she had to come here again, he would follow. And she knew, as well, that she would let him.

She turned from them, and looked into darkness.

"Andellen?"

"I do not know if light will come here."

"Try?"

He nodded, gathering himself as Severn had done. His sword was in his hand. She could see that, and wondered how.

But in his other hand, light did come. It hovered above the hand, rather than trailing away, as if the hand itself were a torch.

"Still not a mage?" she asked him softly.

He raised a brow but said nothing further.

They were standing in a cavern. Or half a cavern. It was bisected in the middle by something that looked like a dark gap. One that went down a long way. There was, however, a bridge. If, by bridge, one meant an outcropping of slender rock that had no guardrail, and looked like it might collapse if enough weight passed over it.

She nodded. They began to walk toward the bridge, and out of the chasm, mist rose in response, growling and snarling with familiar hunger. Voices, she thought, contained there. The mist had form and some substance; as they approached, it seemed to solidify. But it remained dark and ghostly.

Dark and ghostly feral packs. Not pack. Not just one. She started to count, and gave up at fifty. She wondered how far Severn had got, if he tried at all; the visual cue was enough. If these were real—if they *became* real, counting wasn't going to be a problem. There were more than enough to mean death; the particulars didn't matter to corpses.

"The answer to your question, Kaylin," Andellen said softly. He moved, but gave the impression of being transfixed. "About where ferals come from. Remember this—not all questions are meant to be asked. You may receive the answer."

"You have these in the Castle?" she asked casually.

"Not...these," he replied. She wondered if he was even aware that he had. She filed it away for future use because she desperately wanted there to be a future.

The cavern seemed to stretch out forever on either side— and the chasm followed it. Stone here was dark, and almost red in tint.

"This is why the High Halls were built," she told them all. Mostly because she was talking to herself. She approached the chasm, and saw that it was much wider than it had first looked. She stopped at the edge of the mists, and felt the ice of jaws snapping at her feet, her arms. They passed through her, and her dagger passed through them. Détente. Of a sort.

She continued to walk toward the bridge. "This is what they contain, or keep contained. This is why the Barrani rule here." Her brain raced ahead, and her mouth kept pace, but only barely.

"This is why they *have* to rule here. This is why the Emperor tolerates their Court in Elantra. Because if they don't rule, if they don't command the High Halls—"

And out of the chasm, mist rose, touching the midsection of the bridge. It roiled there, curling in on itself, and she could see distinct shapes and forms pass in that mass of movement; a hint of face, of fang, of claw; an arm, several arms, eyes that were too large and far too numerous.

But they fell way, all these extraneous bits, and what remained was like a giant, a thing of mist, something that might be human or Barrani writ large. They watched it take form, and the form grew distinct, although Kaylin could still see through it.

But the distinct form was no longer possibly human; it was Barrani. Tall, dark, elegant—the heart of arrogance, of all their arrogance, combined. It was anchored to the bridge they were approaching, which made approaching it seem a lot less wise.

Kaylin, not known for her wisdom, stopped walking anyway. She recognized the man. Even though the mists were dark, and the cast of his features was ebon.

The Lord of the Green.

* * *

Andellen froze then. Samaran took a step back. Severn held his ground. They were noticed, but the gaze that swept past them didn't stop until it reached Kaylin.

"Yes," it said then. "The High Halls contain them."

"You," she said automatically.

He raised a brow the color of his skin. "I am not contained," he said softly. He gestured, throwing both hands wide.

And the growling and snapping right beside them grew suddenly very real. Severn was already in motion; Andellen and Samaran were right behind him, even though Barrani were in theory faster. Kaylin's daggers were up.

She kicked the feral closest to her, and it staggered back, across the lip of the chasm. The mists swallowed it. Severn's ferals—both of them—fell headless; his chain in motion spread blood across his comrades. Andellen and Samaran were not in danger, but they followed Kaylin's example; they used the cliff's edge, and sent the ferals back into the darkness.

The darkness grew dense.

And other shapes loomed above those of the ferals.

Andellen said a single word. Kaylin had never heard it before. She didn't want to know what it meant but knew anyway; he recognized at least one of those shapes.

"Can we fight it?" she shouted.

His expression made the answer clear.

She turned to the Barrani upon the bridge. To the Lord of the Green.

"You're not Barrani," she said calmly.

"And you are not Barrani, but you are here. Why? Why have you come at the behest of these creatures who care so little for your kind? They have hunted and destroyed you in number, and they have done far, far worse in their history. I have seen it all. Would you care to witness?"

"Not really," she told him. "I believe you."

"Believe, then, that the Lords of these Halls have been tricked. They are not the masters here—they are the victims. They have been devoured, who dared to come here. They have been absorbed. They have been born, and lived their pathetic centuries, and have led themselves to us like sheep to slaughter, and we have taken them *all*."

"Not all," she told the Barrani.

"Some cleave to the Halls," he said with a cold shrug. "Some choose a life of *service*. It is a form of slavery, is it not?" He turned, then, to Andellen. "I have tasted your name," he said quietly, taunting. "I have felt your passage.

"And you have escaped once, who come again. To me. What was your reward for your service? What was your reward for your vigilance? Your *name*. Your servitude."

He seemed to realize that he was blathering, and drew himself up. And up. Kaylin was annoyed.

But his voice was lower and sweeter when he spoke again; it was almost paternal. She hated it.

"We were never meant to be your chains. We have been. But there is freedom from servitude, and freedom for your people, if you have but the courage to grasp it. Do you not believe that you are slaves?"

Andellen did not reply.

"Then let me show you."

The chasm rumbled.

"Let me show you what you have failed to see."

And rising from the mists, again, rising and writhing as if in torment, came not monsters, not ferals, not creatures with faces too bizarre to *be* faces. Barrani rose. And if the ferals had been beyond her ability to count, the Barrani here were ten times their number. A hundred times. A city was here, and a city of far greater significance than the one above. She had never, ever seen so many Barrani gathered in one place.

And these—ah—these—

Andellen was bracing himself. She could see it, although nothing about his stance seemed to change. Samaran, on the other hand, had fallen to his knees, his eyes round and so dark a blue they were almost—almost—black. Without thinking, she put a hand on his shoulder and pressed it down firmly.

He said, "My father." And lifting a hand, he pointed. "My father." In Barrani. In broken Barrani.

And one of the many thousands of Barrani turned at the single word, and he made his way through the crowd, mist dissolving and re-forming where it made contact with other mist. He walked until he stood within the ranks of the ferals that suddenly seemed so sparse.

"Samaran," he said.

Kaylin flinched. And held on. But she didn't accuse the darkness of lies. Not here. Not in the face of what she could suddenly see so clearly.

Samaran was mute.

"I came to the tower," his father continued. "When you

were of age, I came. For you," he added. "You were not the son of a Lord of the High Court. And you could not be part of the Court otherwise."

"Father—"

"And here, I lost my way, and my name, and my life. And I have waited these centuries for a time when I might find it again."

They cried out in number at his last words, this host of Barrani, these dead.

She had thought the undying were bad. This was so much worse; she *felt* their pain. She knew them as real. She could almost call out names, they were that clear to her.

"And you have come at a time when we might almost be free," he whispered. "Will you wait for me? Will you deny me?"

Kaylin put her other hand on Samaran's other shoulder, and stood behind him. He had not faced the tower, and now she knew why. But the fact that he *hadn't* was infinitely more significant now.

She'd led him here. She'd led him here without thinking, without worrying, without counting the possible cost. And she had *known* that she would face, in the end, the darkness that the High Halls had been created as fortress against.

But she hadn't known what it contained.

And telling herself that? It didn't make her feel a whole lot better. Because ignorance was not an excuse.

"Andellen." She whispered the word.

It carried anyway, and he turned to look at her, as if for once he could find some sustenance from the merely mortal.

"You recognize them."

"I do," he said with bitter wonder. "They are—were—my

people. Some of them were my kin. Some were my enemies. They are one now." And then he shrugged, and the tightness about his mouth relaxed. "They are dead."

She stared at him; could feel her jaw go slack and her eyes round and her brows stretch up to her hairline.

"They're *dead*?" she shouted, half shaking poor Samaran. *"Look at them!"*

"I can see them," he told her calmly.

"They're *not* dead—they're trapped!"

"They are dead," he replied softly. "The price of their freedom is too high." And he turned away.

Samaran let out a noise that Kaylin had never heard from a Barrani before; she'd heard it from other humans. Other mortals. But in Samaran, it was wrong. "Andellen—"

He joined her instantly, just as Samaran rose and attempted to throw off her hands. He was taller than she was, and he dragged her up with him as he unfolded.

Andellen hit him, hard, with the butt of his sword.

Samaran folded slightly.

"Do *not* let them beguile you," he snarled. Gone was neutrality; gone the icy distance that was the usual Barrani expression of anger.

Beguile? Kaylin wanted to shout. *They're not trying to beguile him—they're trying to—*

And she stopped.

Because it was true. They weren't trying. They were the sum of centuries spent here, in this horrible place; this was hell. And the hell was written plainly on their faces, at the core of their identities; it was their fate.

Unless someone could lead them out.

Oh, the desire was strong and terrible. But the uneasy sense that what followed would be the ferals and the other creatures was sharper.

She looked at the Lord of the Green. The only one of them—the only one—that seemed out of place. And she spoke to him, her voice shaking in fury. "You aren't Barrani," she snapped. "You're trapped here, but you aren't Barrani."

"I am almost as you see me," he said with a smile. And he lifted his gaze. "And the time is coming when I will be more." The smile shifted; his expression grew remote. Or bored.

She knew then.

"Andellen, grab Samaran. It's time to leave."

Severn, silent, watched the creature that was not quite the Lord of the Green.

"You, unfortunately, are an unexpected interference." He dropped his hands in a plunge.

And a creature stepped out of the chasm, gleaming—as the door had gleamed—ebon. Nothing about him spoke of mist; he was substantial, as the ferals had been. If "he" was even the right pronoun.

"Andellen, what is it?"

Andellen, sword in hand, said wearily, "One of the first-born."

"Firstborn what?"

"The Lords of Law were not the only Lords to attempt to create life. But the Lords of Chaos were less certain, and their creations, less biddable."

"This one seems—"

"Run, Kaylin." He lifted his sword. "Run quickly." And he turned and shoved Samaran into her arms. The creature drifted toward them. It had eyes. It had too many eyes. They weren't really facing forward, or rather, they were facing in every damn direction. It had limbs, of a sort, and claws that were as long as bent swords, and it defined the color black.

It almost reminded her of a Dragon. But a hideously distorted and warped dragon, without the wings.

She would have run, but her knees locked. Some animal part of her mind told her that if she stood very, very still she could escape its notice. She wasn't significant, and she wasn't a threat. But she raised her pathetic daggers anyway, and she stood her ground. The knees not bending was a larger part of that than she wanted to admit.

It came and passed over the ferals, crushing the few who were too stupid to move out of its way. The fact that they weren't actually solid made the feat more impressive. The Barrani ghosts—it was the only way she could think of them and still be sane—fell silent, watching. They bore no weapons, no armor; they had only their voices, and those were silenced.

Severn's blade was in motion; the chain caught the light Andellen hadn't doused. The fact that it was no longer cupped in his palm didn't seem to make a difference; it was bright now.

But Severn's blade clattered against the claws of the creature; if it seemed to amble, it was damn fast. Too fast. He drew it back just before the creature severed the chain links.

Andellen raised his sword, and let out a cry that filled the cavern.

Hell was a very dark place.

But there was fire in hell. A blaze that singed hair and curled cloth; that melted the damn *rock*. It erupted around the creature in a glow so bright Kaylin lost sight of the rest of the cavern for a minute.

Sight and sound were not, however, the same.

She heard the fire, heard the roar of fury, and *felt* something snap around the flame, binding it in a tightening circle. The creature's anger was greater than the strength of the containment; greater than the voice of the fire.

But fire—she'd called fire before.

And here, in the heart of the High Halls, the word was on her tongue and in her mouth as the thought coalesced. She grabbed the medallion that hung around her neck, dropping one of Severn's daggers to do so.

And she spoke the word slowly, forcing each syllable to be distinct, to have an edge.

Fire, her fire, joined the flames. It was not as bright, but where it *burned,* the creature writhed and screamed. It fought her fire as the odd circle around it grew bright, and brighter still.

Andellen backed away, and Severn did the same. They reached her side. She let the last syllable fall from her lips.

"You have power," a voice she recognized said softly. "And the wisdom of an unnamed babe."

And turning, she saw Lord Evarrim of the Arcanum, and another man, whose face was obscured by the hood of a long cloak. Evarrim was dressed in red, even here, but she saw that the circlet at his brow was now missing a ruby. His eyes were blue, dark blue, but they didn't miss much. He saw what she'd noticed.

And turned to the man by his side.

The man lifted his hands and drew the hood from his face,

and she met the blue gaze of the Lord of the High Court. "You are safe here," he said rigidly, "now." But his words and his tone of voice were tight.

She looked at the containing circle.

"Yes," he said curtly. "It will hold." His gaze fell to the figure upon the bridge. There was no love in it, but there was recognition—and not the type a man gave his son, even if that son was estranged.

"Go back," he said softly.

The man on the bridge smiled. "I cannot yet go forward," he said. "But I have your son's name."

"Yes. You have. But he has it, as well. And you do not have *mine*."

"I do not, but soon I will not need it."

"I will not pass the gift to my son."

"Then you will kill him...there is no other way."

"There is one," the Lord of the High Court replied wearily. "Go back." And he gestured, and the bridge *moved,* dislodging the mist.

Lord Evarrim looked at Kaylin with something that bridged the distance between contempt and respect. "It is time to leave this place," he told her.

She hated to be agreeable, but considered the options even less appealing, and nodded. They retreated from the cavern.

This time, there was no door to bar their way. The Lord of the High Court led, and where he led, the path was clean and flat. The natural arch in which the door had nested was there, unchanged; there just wasn't anything within it.

He left the chambers, and she followed. He traversed the

tunnels, stopping at each rune, as if to read it, or to take strength from it. At length, he led them back to the stairs. All of this passed in silence. Kaylin was aware that she was walking beside Evarrim, but she felt no threat from him; he was barely walking. Oh, he didn't stumble or falter. He didn't so much as lean on the wall for support. But the edge of his expression was dulled. He had eyes for two things. The Lord of the High Court and the floor.

The climb up the stairs was less threatening than the climb into the unknown had been. The growls were still at their back—but worse than that, the wailing of the damned. She could hear them clearly now. She wondered if she would ever be free of their voices in these Halls.

They came, at last, to the top of the stairs, and Lord Evarrim passed the Lord of the High Court, who had turned in the arch. He looked at Kaylin.

"You," he said, "will accompany me."

She nodded.

"Your guards will go to the Lord of the West March. They will not leave his side until I summon them."

She nodded again.

He looked at Severn, and hesitated. "Your *kyuthe,* however, I will allow."

She started to say that Severn wasn't *kyuthe,* and paused. What was the point? She nodded again. He turned and swept out of the arch, almost carrying them in his invisible wake.

He did not go to the High Court Circle. Kaylin didn't expect him to. She didn't expect him to go anywhere, exactly, and was surprised when he led them into what seemed an ordinary hall. Well, for the High Halls. It was bordered top and bottom with Barrani writing, and it had mirrors and small alcoves in which things grew, but there were no weapons, no sign of older, unsanded stone; these were Halls built by the Barrani, and not by the Old Ones.

Doors flew open as he approached them, even though they had wards, which in theory needed to exact their ounce of pain. She followed quickly. The one or two Barrani she thought she glimpsed out of the corner of her eye vanished, like faint stars, when she turned her full attention on them; the whole of the building might have been deserted.

The Lord of the High Court led them to one small door at the end of a hall; this he opened the normal way.

It led into a room that was very like Kaylin's guest room at first view, except without a bed. There was no throne here; there was no desk, no shelves; it was almost empty, and the one thing in it that drew the eye was—yes—colored glass.

But this glass was different.

Like a mosaic, it depicted the host of the lost Barrani: garbed now in black, shorn of weapon and armor and dignity. She stared at it in horror, and a slowly building realization. Her hand stretched out, almost of its own accord, and she touched one of the faces depicted in the glass.

"It is a…reminder," the Lord of the High Court said heavily. "To one who rules these Halls."

Without turning from the window, she said, "That was his test, wasn't it?"

"Yes."

"To stand there. To see them. To speak with them."

"Yes."

"To leave them."

This third question went unanswered.

"That was the test he failed."

And from the corner of the room, unseen until the moment she lifted voice, the Consort replied, "Yes."

Kaylin, unmoved by the Lord of the High Court, did not fail to look to the Consort, to the woman who sat in her pale robes with her midnight eyes. "I told you," she said softly, "not to interfere."

Kaylin met her gaze. "You went," she said. It wasn't a question. "He failed. You knew. And you went to him."

The Lord of the High Court began to speak, but his Consort lifted a hand. It was not an imperious gesture, and it was not—quite—a plea. Yet he fell silent, his hands behind his back. He looked…old. Inasmuch as someone with eternal youth could.

"That is not the way the tower works," she began.

"But it *is*," Kaylin said sharply. "For you. For the Consort. It *is*. You can walk it freely. You *have to be able* to walk it freely. You said as much. I wasn't paying enough attention."

"You walked it yourself just now," the Consort replied, her voice calm and remote.

"No. I didn't. I walked the path that was there. I walked the path that exists. Anyone could walk that path. The path of the tower test is different. Where he went, no one could follow—no one but you."

"You have a Hawk's eye," the Consort replied, her voice shading into grim.

"You know all their names."

"I have some knowledge of their names," the Consort conceded. "But I do not hold them."

"You hold at least one."

Silence extended, growing an edge. Severn was no longer looking at the window. And he had not returned his weapon to its resting place across his hips, although she could see that the chain had indeed been severed.

"Yes," the Lord of the High Court said. "She holds at least one, and she has held it these centuries. She has held it against the darkness."

"She's losing."

"She has already lost," was the grim reply. "Long before she touched again what she had given."

And the Consort, her voice cool and regal, continued. "You have seen the truth of the High Halls. And you understand it. You will not claim that it is illusion or test. You know what waits those who have failed."

Kaylin nodded.

"I could not let my son join them."

"And so," the Lord of the High Court said, "she, too, failed."

"And you couldn't kill him," Kaylin said quietly. "Not without exposing the crime."

"Oh, I could have," was the castelord's grim reply. "Not upon his return. Not then. But later."

"You didn't."

"No."

"Why?"

"Because," the Consort replied, a small crack in her perfect composure opening slightly, "he belongs to the darkness. It is only by living that he is kept from it."

"He tried to kill himself."

"No. He understands what he faces. He tried to divest himself of his name, to become undying."

"And now?"

"My second son went to face the test of the tower, and what he found there was our answer. It is a bitter answer," she added. "But my power over the words is fading. I can reach the source," she added, "but only at great cost, and the return is difficult."

"But if he has no name, his name is there—"

"Yes. My oldest, understanding, tried to do his duty. But it would not have worked."

"You can't give him the *leoswuld*."

"No. But I think that was the intent," the Consort said bitterly. "I was young, and foolish. I believe that my son was to be the vessel, that I was *allowed* to leave with him, allowed to believe that I had the control necessary."

"But now he's not."

The Lord of the High Court exchanged a glance with his Consort. "No," he said at last. "The Lord of the West March will kill him, and the Lord of the Green will go, at last, to the reward of those who fail."

"He won't kill his brother."

"He has his duty, and he understands it fully now. He will kill his brother, or he will doom us."

"He can refuse the *leoswuld*."

"And that will doom us as well," the Lord of the High Court said. "You understand much. Too much. He can refuse what I offer. But if he refuses, there will be no new Consort, and his mother cannot continue. It is understood that there will be war among our kin in the outlying lands, even as our hold upon the High Halls diminishes. It is not understood how quickly that hold will diminish, nor is the price clearly written.

"We will perish as a people."

"It seems," Kaylin said with bitter pity, "that you already are." And she looked again to the window. "Has the Lord of the West March seen what lies at the heart of the High Halls?"

"He has."

"Then he won't do it."

"He will."

But she knew the truth. She had his name, after all, and it spoke to her in the silence, lending strength to certainty. She said to the Consort, "What name did you choose for your oldest son?"

"A bitter name," was the reply. "But I was young. And I had hope for the future that I no longer have."

"What shape did it have?"

There was a silence so sharp it could have cut. "What do you mean?"

"What did it *feel* like when you touched it?"

"Like my son."

"Like what you wanted for your son?"

"At the time, they were the same."

Kaylin nodded. Trying to think like a Barrani mother. Failing utterly. "I will speak with the Lord of the West March," she said at length, "as his *kyuthe*."

CHAPTER 19

"Kaylin," Severn said quietly when they were quit of the room with its terrible mosaic and the burden of its legacy.

She nodded. "Don't say it."

"You take a greater risk than perhaps you understand—"

"I've worked beside Barrani for all of my adult life," she told him bitterly. "I understand well enough. I know *too much*. He might as well have pronounced a death sentence then and there. But he won't, I might be of use." She paused, and then turned to Severn. "Think of what he's lived with every day of his life since he…passed his test. Think of what he *knows* every time someone attempts it. Do you think I don't understand how little his gratitude might mean in the end? And knowing it, I'll still do everything I can to *be* of use."

"I'd guessed that," Severn replied with just the hint of a smile.

"Do you know why?"

He shrugged.

"Because——" And she stopped. *Because I don't want the Lord of the West March to suffer what you suffered. I don't want that.* And she saw him clearly as he shoveled dirt away from—and toward—a grave. "Because I'm me."

"Then you—"

"I have to speak with the Lord of the West March." She looked around her, at the halls they now walked. "Because I'm sure the Lord of the High Court will know if I don't."

They walked for some time in the silence of footfall and distant chimes, the hours sounding. The notes were hollow and mournful to Kaylin's ear. They marked the passing of more than time. Her left arm ached. "I couldn't be the Lord of this Court," she said softly. "If I had been offered the same test as the Lord of the Green, I would have failed utterly." She already had. "I can't judge him. I can't judge his mother. His father passed the same test," she added. "So he can."

She turned then, and caught Severn's arm in both of her hands. "And *you* can," she said quietly. "You can judge the Lord of the West March."

Severn shook his head. "It's not the same test," he told her almost gently. "If I had been given the choice of killing *you,* or letting the city burn—that would have been the same. And I would have failed. Let it go, Kaylin. Let it go, Elianne." He paused, and then said, "If you had paid attention in class—and I'm going to assume you never took philosophy—you would have heard an old adage. It's an important one, if you work in the Halls of Law…something to live by."

"What?"

"We're judged by our successes," he said, brushing the hair from her eyes. "We all expect that. But we are *also* judged by our failures, noble or ignoble. Success and failure are two edges of the same blade, two sides of the same coin. To fear the one is to forever deny the possibility of the other." And he kissed her forehead.

She closed her eyes.

"I'm willing to fail here," he told her. "And you must be willing to fail, as well. There's no single road to success."

"Thank you." She pulled away slowly and straightened her shoulders. "I remember a different adage."

"Oh?"

"A successful man—or woman—has friends beyond number. A failure? Almost none." She caught his hand and held it.

His smile was lopsided. "In our case, that will probably be because there won't be many people left." He began to walk again, holding her hand.

The Lord of the West March was, oddly enough, waiting for them before they reached the wing of the High Halls he claimed for his personal use. He met them in an atrium, coming from around a dense thicket of oddly shaped leaves; they were green with purple hearts, and as long as Kaylin's arm. His eyes were blue.

She offered him a courtly bow. It wasn't as graceful as a Barrani bow should have been, but she wasn't expected to tender that—and she meant to give him what she could. Not more, but certainly not less.

He accepted her bow with a grave nod. *"Kyuthe,"* he said

quietly. "I have been waiting for you." He nodded to Severn in turn, acknowledging his presence.

I bet you have, she thought. But she said, instead, "We returned to the tower."

"I know. I spoke briefly with Lord Evarrim." There was warning in those words.

"Lord Evarrim was…helpful. We had almost lost the way," she added.

His smile was an odd thing. It was devoid of humor but not of warmth. "Don't speak like a Barrani," he told her gently. "It doesn't suit you."

She shrugged. "I like the dress."

"It is clothing, no more—it does not define you."

"No. But it's a hell of a lot more comfortable than what did." She took a deep breath and switched to Elantran. "We talked to your father," she said. The blunt words felt almost foreign in her mouth because in the end, there were some things she *didn't* want to speak about.

A brief flash of something like insight came to her then. She wondered if, in living for centuries, one accumulated *so much* one didn't want to speak about, Barrani was the only natural tongue in which not to speak.

He nodded. Turned his attention to the leaves that were thick and almost unbending.

"And your mother," she added.

"My mother was present?"

She bit her lip.

"And have you now been sent to speak to me of duty?"

"More or less."

"Consider the words said," he told her, an edge in his

voice, his eyes darkening. "And *do not* say them. I will for-give you much, for the gift of my life. But not all."

"Okay. I'll just consider the whole lecture given. I can sympathize. I never listened to lectures much, either. And I failed a lot of classes."

He raised a dark brow, and beneath it, the color of his eyes shifted, turning from sapphire to something pale enough to be cheap emerald. "Absent lectures, *kyuthe,* what is left to say?"

"Leoswuld," she replied quietly.

"That, I think, is part of the lecture."

"Sort of. But it's practical, and I was better with practical things." She realized that she was still holding on to Severn's hand, and quietly disentangled their fingers. "We have a day. The bright moon isn't full."

"The bright moon is not full," he agreed.

She looked at him, pinning him down with her eyes, which were brown and unchanging. "Did you know," she told him evenly, "that the rune I saw when I first entered the tower was the same rune the Lord of the Green saw?"

She didn't need to do much pinning; he became utterly still. And given how little he'd been moving before, that said something. His eyes flickered, green darkening there; it did not—quite—give way to blue.

"And how would you know that?" he asked her softly.

"He told me."

"He...told you."

"Well, more or less. I was dreaming," she added self-con-sciously. "But it was a dream of the High Halls." She paused, and then added, "He told me what yours was too."

His brows rose. And fell. "If this is a game—"

She said, "Oh, he's Barrani. It probably is."

"What did he say?"

"Duty."

"And his? Yours?"

"Choice."

He was silent; it was the silence of frantic thought. Of, Kaylin realized bitterly, hope. Because hope *was* bitter here. And it was all he had.

"This is not information the Lord of the High Court chose to impart?"

"No. Well, okay, yes, but I already knew it."

He hesitated, and she cringed. He wanted to believe her, and because he wanted to, he didn't trust the desire. She drew a deep breath and squared her shoulders, feeling the difference between the understatement of Barrani movement and the overstatement of hers.

Lirienne.

His eyes widened and darkened. But only for a moment. He understood what she was doing, and even smiled.

Kyuthe.

I cannot lie to you here.

No. Is it true? Did you speak with my brother?

Only in dream, she said, hating herself for a moment because in dream, there *was* doubt. *Not in life.*

Tell me of this dream.

She did.

And he wore a cloak?

Green, she said softly. *But his eyes were almost entirely black. He wants you to kill him,* she added. *But I don't.*

You would be perhaps the only one, he told her bitterly.

Not the only one. I think your father would have already killed me if not for the Consort. She hadn't thought it until she spoke the words, but they were true.

And what hope do you offer us?

I don't know, she said, almost helpless. But she lifted her left arm. *But when I left the Tower, I didn't take one name. I took two.*

His frown was more felt than seen. *Two?*

She nodded. *I had to. I couldn't leave with just one.*

I don't understand.

Well, if you don't, and you're the High Lord's son, don't expect me to.

His eyes were…golden. And she understood then that gold was the color of shock or surprise. But it dimmed quickly. *I think I understand,* he told her grimly. *And I even thank you. But that is not our way. You have seen what waits,* he added bitterly. *Do you not understand that our names are what we are? No new name will save him. If it could even be done, it would change the nature of his life.*

She deflated by several inches. "Isn't that better than dying?"

"By our measure, *kyuthe,* it *is* dying."

"How do you know? Has it ever been done before?"

He was quiet for a moment, slipping away from the force of his name, and the speech of silence. "Do you believe that mortals have souls, Kaylin?"

She shrugged. "I don't know. I imagine I'll find out one day."

"Ah. Pretend, for a moment, that you do."

"Okay."

"If your soul flees your body, you are dead. But if another replaces it, are you any less dead? The body may—or may not—live. But what you were—it's gone."

"How do you know?"

"I don't. I merely surmise."

She let her arm drop. "I want to see the Lord of the Green."

He shook his head.

"I don't actually need your permission."

And the Lord of the West March turned to Severn, who had remained silent throughout. "Is she *always* this difficult?"

"He's going to die anyway," Kaylin told him. "Isn't it time to try something different?"

"Not," the Lord of the West March replied grimly, "if it will kill him."

He didn't trust her, but there was no reason he should. He led her back to her room, and as he entered the wing, four of his men joined him in silence. They, unlike the Lord of the West March, favored her face with a fixed blank expression; the mark of Nightshade drew and repelled. They wouldn't trust her, and they certainly wouldn't listen to her.

She wanted to scream. For just one insane minute, she wanted to use the Lord of the West March's name to *force* him to listen.

It passed, but only with a lot of effort, and with the distinct help of less suicidal impulses. She could speak his name; she *could not* contain him by its use. And if she could, she was no better than the darkness that lay at the heart of the High Halls, waiting to devour the weak.

Andellen and Samaran were shut into her room with her. Andellen was silent until the door was closed. He approached it with care, inspected it with more, and then gestured almost dismissively. Had she not known the Barrani, she would have assumed the wave of his hands to be theatrical. She did know them; she didn't have that comfort.

"You are prisoner here," he told her quietly. "What have you done to offend the Lord of the West March?"

"I asked to speak with his brother."

"After what we saw?"

"Yes."

His eyes narrowed. "Why?"

"Because I had some hope that something I took from the tower during my damn test would be *helpful*," she said, spitting fury.

Andellen looked at her for a moment, and then said, "You spend too much time in the company of Leontines. It is not a habit I would encourage."

She laughed out loud, and he raised a dark brow. Obviously, the comment was not meant as humor. But how he spoke the words, and how she received them, were a matter of choice.

Choice. Her smile eased off her face. "Why can't they wait?" she asked him.

He could have pretended ignorance but chose instead to answer. "The Consort has all but lost the path," he told her quietly. "In one more year—which should have no significance to those of our kind—she will not be able to find it. And if she cannot, she cannot pass that knowledge on."

"The Lord of the Green won't be present for *leoswuld* "

"I can't see how he could."

"But everyone else will be."

He nodded. "Not one such as I," he added in a softer voice.

"You're commanded to be my escort—"

"Not to *leoswuld*," he told her firmly. "As you will find, if you attempt to press this. You, of course, will be expected, as will Lord Severn."

"Andellen—"

"I understand your urgency, Kaylin. It is not our way to speak quickly or bluntly, but believe that I *am* making the effort." His frown was thoughtful. And damn slow. "The Lord of the West March *will* be present. Were I the High Lord, I would condemn my eldest son for his absence from the rite, and I would do so publicly. His condition is not widely known."

"He will offer the gift to his second son."

"But the Lord of the West March will refuse."

"Will he?"

"Yes!"

"Kaylin, you understand much about the High Court that even I did not. You led us to the heart of the darkness," he added. "Not even I have seen it before, who lived here for centuries. But in this, your certainty is misplaced. I believe that the Lord of the West March *intends* to refuse what his father will undoubtedly offer.

"But his father *will* offer it. The daughter will accept the mother's gift. But the mother's gift is tied to the source, not the High Halls. And if the father makes the offer, the High Halls will be—for one moment—without its ruler.

"Without its guardian."

She froze. "But the darkness—"

"Yes. It will rise. It is almost uncontained now."

"You think this will be a game of chicken."

He raised a brow. "I fail to see what fowl has to do with *leoswuld*. You will, no doubt, enlighten me."

"A game. It's a stupid game. You can play it with knives or almost anything. You can play it on the edge of rooftops. You can play it near the wagons by the market. It means—it's just—whoever blinks first. Whoever surrenders first, loses."

"Ah. And you think that the High Lord will place us all in jeopardy in order to force his son's hand?"

"No—you think that. The Lord of the High Court can't be certain that the Lord of the West March will take the gift. But if he doesn't—"

"Yes. We will almost certainly perish."

"Can anyone else take what's offered?"

"Anyone else can try," he replied. "But Kaylin, there is no guarantee of success. Although in that circumstance, war is less likely. Even the Barrani value their lives. Perhaps, given how much is lost with the life, they value them *more*. The Lord of the High Court is canny. He is also desperate." He looked at Kaylin. "You are certain the Lord of the West March will refuse?"

She said, instead, "You know I hold his—"

He lifted a hand. "A simple yes will suffice."

"Then yes, damn it." She looked at the doors. "We can't get out of here?"

"Not without killing the guards," he replied. "And that would be unlikely to earn you the freedom you seek."

"Then what will?"

"Time," he told her. "How long can you wait?"

"I can't wait. We don't have time."

There was something too close to pity in his expression. "You will wait," he told her quietly. "Because the *only* time you will have any chance of success will be on the way to the rite itself. At that point, all Barrani Lords will be required to leave their quarters, and their plots, behind. They will attend at the command of the Lord of the High Court."

Kaylin frowned. "The Lord of the High Court gave me free run of the High Halls."

"Yes. And were you to be able to reach him, he would most assuredly enforce that grant. Welcome," he added with just the hint of a cruel smile, "to the High Court."

She cursed. A lot.

Two hours later, she gave up and retreated to her bed. It was like a besieged island in the sea of her unfortunate temper, and if her temper was childish, she really didn't give a damn. It's not like anyone could see it.

Sleep came eventually. She really needed it.

She heard Andellen's voice; it was pitched not to carry. So, for that matter, was Severn's. She was irritated, but not enough to get up and shout at them. Her voice was a little on the hoarse side for that, and besides, she'd already done it, and it hadn't had much of an effect.

Her arm ached. Her head ached. Her eyes ached.

How long had it been since she'd really slept?

How long could she afford to sleep?

She closed her eyes, and tried to relax her jaw muscles; she kept grinding her teeth.

They woke her from the edge of nightmare when food was delivered. It came in the hands of guards, and they left it with care and silence. Her stomach was growling, but she wasn't hungry. Or rather, the thought of food made her distinctly queasy.

Severn looked at her.

She shook her head. She looked at the windows. "Was I out long?"

"Long enough," he replied. "I wasn't with you when you…saw the Lord of the Green."

"Uh, no. I think I'd remember that."

He batted the side of her head. "Can you find him again?"

She nodded. "I think."

"Can you find him at a run?"

"I don't know. If you mean, can I find him while I'm being chased by Barrani who are a hell of a lot faster, then probably not."

"They'll be a bit distracted."

She frowned. And woke up. "I don't want anyone to risk their lives—"

"From what's been said, there's no way around that," Severn replied calmly. "All we can do is choose when and how, and if we wait, we won't even get that choice." He paused, and then added, "I trust you."

Which was another burden.

He watched her face for a moment. "You're not certain," he said. It was almost a question.

"No." She held out a clenched fist. "I'm not. He could be right. He probably is. I've helped to birth a lot of babies—but I've always done that the normal way, and most of those babies weren't a hundred times older than I am."

He hesitated. "And the risk?"

"What risk?" She swallowed.

"Kaylin, you could have died the first time."

She threw Andellen a dagger-sharp glare. Andellen failed to notice. "So you can choose the when and how but I can't?"

"No. You can. I just wanted to know."

"When, then?"

"In an hour. Maybe an hour and a half." He paused and added, "I can't see the moon, but apparently, this close, Andellen can."

She swallowed air. Food was beyond her ability to cope with. "All right." She paused. "When I first came here with Teela, we were almost killed by a door."

Severn nodded.

"Who laid that trap?"

Andellen shrugged. "Anteela has her enemies at Court. It is part of why she left."

"Good."

"Why?"

"Because it was powerful, it was magical, and we can't afford more enemies."

They waited.

* * *

The chimes started first. They were distant and high, clear as free birds' song. They were also sustained; once they started, they didn't stop. A single note was joined by another, and then another, and then another. All were harmonious.

Andellen rose. "It is time, Kaylin. Lord Severn."

Severn rose, as well. "On my signal," he told her quietly.

She nodded. She took her shoes off. Outrunning Barrani was impossible. On the other hand, outrunning an *ant,* in these shoes, was impossible. She left them in the corner.

She wore the ring given her by the Lord of the West March; she wore the medallion given her by Lord Sanabalis. She wore the dress of the Barrani, but her hair was unbound. She pulled it back from her face in a knot, and then cursed at the absence of sticks. "I really hate it here," she told no one in particular.

"It looks better down," Severn said.

She glared.

The doors opened.

Guards stood there. She counted four. They wore different armor, and they did not bear obvious weapons. They wore headbands with different runes written in their center.

"It is time," one of them said gravely.

They left the room. But Severn indicated, by the slight motion of one hand, that she was to go first. She obeyed, trying to find calm, as if it were a place or an object she could hold.

She almost found it, too.

But over the beauty of the chimes, she heard the familiar sound of baying.

She turned to look at Severn. He had stiffened. All of the Barrani had. "Ferals," she said grimly.

"We can hope," Severn replied.

It was a pretty piss-poor day when you hoped to see ferals.

The guards were holding the hilts of their swords; they did not draw them. She wondered if they were Lords in their own right. Decided they must be when they politely indicated that Samaran and Andellen were to remain behind, in the room.

"They follow the outcaste," one guard said when Kaylin began to argue. "They are no longer part of the High Court."

"I bear his damn mark, and *I'm* going."

"Yes," he replied. If a word could be a slap in the face, this was it. But he clearly had his orders.

Severn's breathing changed, but only slightly. It was enough to tell Kaylin that he'd expected Andellen to be beside him for at least the journey between these rooms and the High Court Circle.

He walked when the guards moved; he was thinking.

She walked beside him, hoping he was better at thinking than she was. The sound of howling unnerved her because she *knew* what would follow if it was, at last, unleashed.

They passed through two halls contained by the crisp formation of Barrani guards—two in the front and two in the back. She knew where the halls would eventually lead, and knew, further, that once there, she would be allowed no escape. Well, not of any kind she actually wanted.

But when the guards stopped, she bumped into them. It was awkward, more than awkward. They pretended not to notice, but the disdain in the pretense was loud. It was not, however, long.

Standing before them, in a pale white dress, was a Barrani woman. She was tall and slender, as all Barrani were, and she was paler than the bright moon. Her eyes were green, but dark and hard; she seemed like ice personified.

They bowed to her.

Severn followed their lead; Kaylin just stared. Her jaw was still attached to the rest of her face, but not by much. The woman was beautiful. Beautiful and haunted.

"Lady," one of the guards said as he rose. "You are without escort?"

"I need little in the High Halls," was her reply. "And apparently, two mortals require more."

"The Lord of the West March ordered—"

She lifted a hand. "The chimes have started," she said gravely. "Do not speak of my brother's orders, or we will stand until the song ends."

Her brother. Kaylin was looking at the third child of the Lord of the High Court. She should have known; her hair was as pale, and as long, as her mother's.

"I will speak," she added quietly, "with my brother's *kyuthe*."

They were still for a moment.

"And if you will not yourselves be late to the High Circle, you will not gainsay me. She *is* a Lord here. And she was granted the freedom of the High Halls."

Kaylin had never heard the word *freedom* used in that fashion before. And profoundly hoped never to hear it again.

"Lady," the guard began again. She stepped toward him and he fell silent.

"I will not harm her," the cold Barrani woman said. "She is *kyuthe* to my kin. *Go.*"

They exchanged a brief glance, and even the barrier of race couldn't obscure its meaning. The Dragon in front of you was more of a threat than the Dragon at a distance.

They went; they took Severn with them. Kaylin was almost glad to see them go. Because Severn hadn't been forced to start a fight in the High Halls.

"I am called The Lady," the Barrani woman said quietly when they had retreated.

"Not of anything?"

"Of the Barrani," she replied. Her eyes were green now, and she hesitated before smiling. It transformed the whole of her face. She looked, at that moment, like the Lord of the West March. "The Consort sent me," she added. "And I fear we must go in haste. If my absence is noted, my brother will follow, and he will *not* be pleased."

Kaylin nodded, and they hurried—there was no other word for it—down the hall. The Barrani was taller than Kaylin, and her stride was longer. Kaylin had to abandon all dignity just to keep up. Loss of dignity, she could handle. But she wanted to talk, and that was more difficult.

She heard growling in the distance, and almost froze; The Lady of the Barrani grabbed her hand and yanked her off her feet. "Yes," she said. "It is almost upon us."

They made their way, at last, to a familiar door.

The Lady lifted a palm and all but put it *through* the planks. Apparently, she had the same fondness for door-wards that Kaylin did—and a lot more muscle to back it up.

The door did not buckle or snap, and it didn't fly off its hinges, but it did swing open with a great deal more speed than it had the first time. Kaylin stepped into the torchlit gloom of a familiar room.

The door closed behind them. The chimes were lost. The growling, unfortunately, was not, and without the sweet music to drown it out, it sounded obscenely close.

"Why?" Kaylin asked as the woman made her way across the rune-etched floor.

The woman turned to look at her. Turned away. But she answered. "I love my brothers," she said quietly. "Both of them. And they will both be destroyed. I have waited," she added bitterly, "and I have worked. But I am not Consort, and the tower is not open to me."

"I'm not, either."

"No. But I know what you did, Kaylin. The Consort told me. And she told me as well of her hope. It is a fool's hope," she added bitterly. "And we have proven ourselves, to the last, fools.

"But I am not the Lord of the West March. I am not what he will be, or what he has been. I am to be mother to my people, and I will *not* see them die without even the faint hope you offer."

"Did he tell you—"

"No."

"Then how—"

"Do not ask. It is best that way. My father fears your knowledge."

"Will I kill the Lord of the Green?"

"He is almost dead," was the stark answer. Shorn of cold and ice, it held only pain. "I will take the risk."

She touched the lip of the seal, and Kaylin stepped forward to join her, watching as the runes lit up. She had seen this before, and had seen, as well, the waters—the thick, turgid waters—peel back like layers of something almost solid.

This time, she looked at the liquid.

"What *is* this?" she asked.

The Lady did not answer.

And rising from the heart of this circle, bounded on all sides by words too old to be read, rose the Lord of the Green for a second time.

CHAPTER 20

Kaylin turned almost instinctively and gave The Lady—she really hated the Barrani love of titles—a very unladylike shove. It wasn't expected—by either of them—and The Lady staggered back a couple of steps. She didn't lose her footing. She did, however, lose her place on the periphery of the circle.

Kaylin hoped that she didn't hit back.

She met the gaze of the Lord of the Green; it was black. If there was color in it, as there had only barely been in dream, she couldn't see it. She blamed the torchlight out of desperation. But the torches that lined the circle in eight even intervals were bright enough.

He was pale, and he was not lovely in the same way either of his younger siblings were. He couldn't be, here. He did not attempt to step toward her. She almost took a step toward him, but thought the better of it before her bare foot connected with what could charitably be called slime.

"My brother is not with you," he said. His voice sounded normal to the ear. It sounded—and almost tasted—of ash to the part of Kaylin that listened in other ways. The healer, she thought.

"I dreamed about you," she told him.

And he did something strange and terrifying: He smiled. There was genuine humor in the expression. And it shouldn't have been there. "In my youth," he told her, "many mortals did."

She had the sense, then, that he was trying to ease her. Or distract her. Either would be a kindness, and the Barrani weren't famed for their generosity. Or rather, they were, but not by its presence.

And yet, this one—this one had been marred, marked, and damned by his. She knew that now. She had seen what he had faced, and in his failure, she saw her own. Proud failure. What it said about him—to Kaylin—was not what it said to the Lord of the High Court. It spoke to her in ways that almost nothing in any other Barrani legends had ever done.

She said, clearly, and in Barrani, "I chose to come here."

He looked at her from the center of the circle. "My mother," he told her softly, in *Elantran,* "was never very strong. She was a girl, and a foolish girl. You would have liked her, in her youth."

"I like her now."

"It is a fault," he replied. "In a Lord of the High Court. She wanted for her children what she herself had not seen among her brothers. And she chose. And now we are here, all of us. It would have been better had she been like my father."

Death in his voice. And the flicker of life, clinging to the edges. She recognized them both now.

"I can't judge her."

"No. You are too human. You cannot even judge me." He lifted a hand. To her.

She swallowed. She heard the sister move, and felt a presence by her side—but a step back.

Lifting her left arm as if it weighed as much as she did, she reached out, shaking, and touched the hand the Lord of the Green had extended.

And in the darkness, she felt both ice and fire, and she heard the voice of the darkness *speak*. She couldn't understand the words, and was glad.

The Lady by her side said nothing.

The Lord of the Green closed his hand over hers; he raised the other hand, and caught Kaylin's left wrist. Where he touched her skin, it burned; where he touched the marks upon the skin, they flared, blue and bright.

But this time she didn't see the whole of her life pass before her. She wasn't forced to relive it. She wasn't tossed into those currents. She felt, instead, the great, great weight of a word, a living thing, a rounded curve that was almost flat in the palm. Not her name.

And she remembered it, remembered lifting it, as if she were straining against the stream and the current of Barrani life.

She looked at his eyes. They were black, and open wide. And she looked into them, seeing shadows, seeing the chasm, hearing the whispering voices of the damned. Their accusations. Their pleas.

Lost, all. But not *this* man. Not yet.

He took the word from her. She felt it leave, felt his hands pass above and through it, seeking purchase. It was larger in all ways than he was, and as her marks glowed blue, they illuminated what she had chosen to touch. She hadn't seen it. Couldn't see it. Not then.

But now, it was vast, taller than she was, one long, obsidian curve that seemed to stretch from one end of this huge, rough cavern to the other. And she saw it clearly not as a word but as a single curve, a single mark.

She knew then that she had been right: She had carried this for him. But it *wasn't* a word. It wasn't a *name*. She might have wept had she time or strength; she had neither. To hold the weight of this one, long stroke demanded everything she had.

She whispered something. She couldn't say later what it was, or rather, what the words were; the meaning was clear. Desperation did that.

Give me your name.

It wasn't a command. It couldn't be.

But the darkness heard it, and there was laughter in the distance far more disturbing, in the end, than the sounds of the creature Andellen had called firstborn. She was late. She was *too* late. The baying of the ferals grew loud.

And blending, at last, with that baying, the sounds of horns. The war cry of the Barrani. The Lady stood by her side for just a fraction of a second longer, and then she cried out and turned, running toward the door.

Kaylin was held, transfixed. Had she wanted to run, had she wanted to *join* the fight—and she had no doubt that The

Lady had gone to do just that—she wouldn't have been able to do so.

Because, just as she needed the name of the Lord of the West March in order to return from the odd world she'd entered to heal him, she *needed* the name of the Lord of the Green. She wasn't caught in the heart of arboreal forest; the room was *real*. But the trap was the same; the cost of failure was higher.

Noble failure. Proud failure.

And she wasn't going to settle for it until she had no other choice.

She said again, *Give me your name.*

And the darkness told her that the Lord of the Green no longer *had* it.

His face was twisted with hunger and pain and—yes—humiliation. He fought; she could sense the Other in him. It was the source of the voice. But the darkness was lying, and she knew it. Prayed—which, given her stance on gods in general, was stupid, but entirely human—that the Lord of the Green would know it just as clearly.

He struggled.

And she reached out with her right hand and slapped his face. It was harsh, yes, but it was *real*. There was no ghost voice in it, no Barrani damn words, nothing that wasn't Kaylin. She wanted his attention.

She got it. But in order to slap her back, he had to let go of her hand. And she realized that he couldn't. They were anchored together by both of his hands and her left one. And beyond them, the time of *leoswuld* had begun. Or ended.

That didn't bear thinking about.

But she had his attention, and she could almost see glints of blue in those eyes, like tiny fractures in ebony. It could have been the midnight blue of rage or terror. She guessed rage. "You *have* your name! It's yours. It's *still* yours. Yes, you can be controlled by it. Yes, you can be forced to do what you *do not choose* to do—but it's *your* name. And damn you to your own hell, I need it!"

But he hadn't the power to speak it; she saw that clearly. Healer's vision saw the weakness in the body through the tips of her fingers. She started to curse because she couldn't think of anything else to say—and then she stopped because she saw that he was, in fact, doing something. Not speaking—if names ever came that way. He couldn't do that.

But…he was the Lord of the Green, and she knew that he would not allow himself to be bested by a mortal girl who was barely an adult.

Between them, in the air above her hands, and beneath the great weight of the single, huge stroke she had borne this far, delicate curves began to form. She knew what they were. She had seen something similar before, in Castle Nightshade, when Lord Nightshade had given her, in the end, his name, the truth of himself.

To speak it? No.

But to *think* it, to write it in this fashion—if it were real and not an elemental part of their joining—this much he could struggle to do. It came slowly, curve and dot, curve and dot, line and line. It was a complex word, in a way that Nightshade's hadn't been.

She couldn't *read* it as she had read Nightshade's, and for a moment, she foundered; she let fear take hold. Heard the voice of the darkness as a physical force, demanding that the Lord of the Green release her. Kill her. Devour her.

But he couldn't.

The marks on her arms were now so bright they almost dwarfed his own rune. Their glow rose in the air in the shape of words, each dense and perfect, each complete in and of itself.

His was *not*.

Understanding robbed her knees of strength, and had the Lord of the Green not had a literal death grip on her hand, she would have fallen.

The Barrani had a mother; they had no midwives. They had no concept of midwives, and why should they?

But *this* birthing—ah, this one had been difficult; it had gone wrong. She understood, looking at the name as he finished it and his strength seemed to ebb, that she had come, in the end, not as Hawk, and not as Healer, but as midwife. What the Consort had failed to understand—as mother—Kaylin could now see, as midwife. The Consort had grasped, not the *whole* of the thing but only part; the part she *could* grasp; the part she could carry. She had been young then. Too young. She had chosen what she could carry.

And Kaylin had finally come to help her. To carry the *rest*. She brought the large, last stroke up, although her hand was bound, and with it, came his. She brought it to rest to the left of the symbol that lay between them, incomplete. She was aware that the symbol, incomplete, had *meaning*. How could it not? Had it not, the Lord of the Green would never have awakened.

But it was not the whole of the meaning the source had

intended for him. And she brought the hard curve of the last stroke to complete it, to transform it, to make it *more,* and not less, than it had been.

The stroke touched the lines that composed the rest of his name, and when it did, it began to resonate, to shake, to transform both itself and the rest. She could *hear* it, then, keening, and she tried not to listen as it spoke the whole of *his* name.

And he cried out with it, cried out what it said. She could feel this, as well. He swallowed what he had offered at the edge of his ability to defy the darkness, and with it, the last stroke.

Some midwives considered newborn cries to be a sign of health. They didn't differentiate between cries and screams because in an infant there wasn't much difference.

She didn't have that comfort. He was *screaming* in a voice that shook the High Halls themselves. That broke stone. That shattered stonework and drove shards into the underside of Kaylin's bare feet. She bled again, but he held her up, shaking now with the force of this new name, this *whole* name.

When silence came, she opened her eyes. She hadn't been aware that they were closed. He stood in the circle, and he held her up by her arm. She dangled, watching in dim fascination as the runes that rimmed the circle began to go out.

And she heard a distant roar of rage, and it, too, shook the Halls and shattered stone. It wasn't a conversation she wanted to be part of, but she'd made a choice, and she'd live with it. She hoped.

He stepped out of the circle, still holding her. In the gloom of the room, she couldn't see the color of his eyes, and she desperately wanted to know what they were. Anything but black, she prayed. Anything but that.

But he *wasn't* undying; the taint of the effort to end his existence in that particular fashion was gone from him.

He strode across the fissures in the floor, still holding her. When he reached the door, it flew wide, and this time, it splintered. The halls on the other side of the arch were like a different country, and he stepped across the boundary. Only then did he set her down. She gave a little yelp of pain, and followed it by a one-footed dance as she tried to dislodge stone shards.

He gestured, and they flew, carrying her blood with them.

He was, and was not, the man she had seen in her dream. But his eyes—his eyes were blue. Warrior blue, she thought. Or hoped.

"The *leoswuld,*" he told her. He wore light, or so it seemed, and she remembered that he had worn light the first time she had seen him. Light transformed, shrinking and dwindling until he wore armor, and a cloak that was forest-green. Familiar. He drew his hood up, and also drew his sword. In fact, to her surprise, he drew two.

He handed the second to Kaylin. "It is not your chosen weapon," he told her, "but you are not yet a master of the weapon that is, and I am not…yet…whole enough to contain you if you falter."

She didn't understand what he meant. And then, as he looked at her exposed arms, she *did*. She pulled the sleeves down in a hurry, wondering when it was that she'd yanked them up. If she had.

"It has started," he told her grimly, "and now, we face opposition. If we do not arrive in the High Court Circle soon, all of your effort will count for nothing. There will be none to accept the gift, and none to take the keys of power from the Lord of the High Court, for I fear you were right—my brother will not take them."

As he spoke, she saw them: black shadows racing down the halls behind a set of fangs. Ferals.

The fangs of the Lord of the Green weren't really, but his smile was a hunter's smile, and if he had any fear of ferals *at all*, madness drove it from him.

She wanted to hide behind him, but she knew ferals; it wouldn't do her any good at all.

Lirienne! she called.

And the ferals leaped.

She couldn't see the blade move. She knew it had because bits and pieces of feral flew free. They didn't have time to roar in pain; they just died. She hadn't wanted to hide, but she didn't want to step up. The hall wasn't wide, and the sweep of his damn sword *was*.

He didn't seem to need help, though. He was the Lord of the Green. And these were his rats.

He moved forward, cutting them down. If they wounded him at all, she couldn't see it; the ferals bled red, and that red covered his armor, darkened his cloak, adding color to his face.

And to hers.

She heard horns in the distance and wondered how many ferals had been unleashed. Prayed it was only ferals.

Kaylin. The Lord of the West March spoke, his voice clear above the horns and snarls of ferals.

The Lord of the Green is coming, she told him desperately.

Heard his silence. *But it's going to take a bit of time. How much do we have?*

Tell him...to hurry.

She looked at the Lord of the Green. *Uh, no.*

Kaylin—

I'm not telling him to do anything. I'm right here. You're somewhere safe.

She heard his wild laughter inside of her mind, and knew that *safe* was not quite the right word.

She looked down the hall; the ferals were thick there. She should have felt rage; she didn't. Just...fear. The Lord of the Green was right—she didn't have control of her power. Couldn't just turn it on and off. She saw the darkness, and in it, some part of herself.

She could *not* afford to call her power here. If it came, she wasn't certain what it would be, or do.

But she had one other choice. And she lifted the medallion of Lord Sanabalis, and blessing Dragons in general, she spoke the word of fire.

The hall erupted in a flame that shot out from the medallion like the breath of a dragon. It devoured the ferals, leaving a wet ash in their wake.

The Lord of the Green looked at her in some surprise, and then, looking at what she held in her hands, he laughed. "Come," he told her, racing ahead. "You've bought time, but they will fill the Halls soon."

Where he ran, the High Halls seemed to shorten in length, as if the building itself was attempting to aid them in their passage. She stretched her legs, keeping up, but only barely. His sword should have weighed her down, but it was light for its length, lighter than Severn's daggers had been. She wondered what it was made of.

She lost any sense of geography; she lost the ability to keep track of where she had been. It didn't matter. If she could remain in the wake of the Lord of the Green, she didn't need to know. But it was hard to keep up.

She saw black mist cross the floor, and she would have skidded to a stop. She was barefoot and bleeding, and she knew better than to offer her blood to what lingered, attempting to take form.

But he swept her off her feet, knowing—and approving of—her fear, and she let him, although it would slow them down.

It should slow them down.

But he seemed to take strength from the motion, from the necessity, from the passage of time. She allowed herself to cling to him while he ran. The mists parted or squelched unpleasantly beneath his mailed boots. He did not set her down, and she wondered if there would be *any* safe place he could do so. She hated shoes more than she could say; she couldn't even begin to think of the words with which she could express the loathing. Which, given she wasn't wearing any, should have been a surprise.

And then, she could swear the wall *parted,* and they looked into a forest of green and brown and gold, with sun-mired shadows and the paths of stone that lay, like works of art, for the wary foot. Rising above the forest, she saw the bowers of the tree—*first tree*—that formed the throne of the Lord of the High Court, that bowered his Consort.

And saw, as well, patches of flame, and black smoke, in the distance.

He set her down then, and ran, and she ran after him. He disturbed nothing, and she stubbed her toes, tearing slender stems from their thin moorings, and crushing open blossoms beneath her feet. His cloak didn't tangle in anything, and her skirts—well. The less said, the better, because pausing to swear meant losing him.

She was losing him anyway.

Fires appeared to the left in the heart of the forest that she had thought of as garden until this moment. He stopped, hesitated, and then threw an arm wide, and the fires banked. She didn't stop to watch them die; she took the moment to catch up.

But she was aware that she had done what she could. Now she was decoration, no more. The blackness that she had thought smoke when the wall had first parted was *not* smoke; she had seen it before.

He followed the path, and it led him, at last, to the High Circle. He entered it. Kaylin paused at a circumference made, not of words in stone, but of trees, and she looked upon a battle that might have been the source of legend.

She saw swords flashing, and armor glinting, and blood—blood everywhere—saw feral corpses, and the corpses of things that were larger than angry bulls. She saw Barrani Lords—and their Ladies—in number, and some of these had fallen, and would not rise again.

Still, she hesitated as the green-cloaked form of the man she had pulled from the edge of the abyss waded into the fighting.

They saw him, the men and women who mounted their last defense, and a cry rose at his passage. They parted, and she knew that she had one chance—this one—to follow. She had a sword, and no armor, but she could read his name as if it were part of her, as if she still carried it.

She could read it, but she could not pronounce it, not even on the quiet inside of her mind, where Nightshade's name and the name of the Lord of the West March were so carefully held.

She leaped across the corpse of a feral, carried by the fight, and made her way to the throne itself.

And there, at last, she saw the bloodied man who was—who had been—the Lord of the High Court. He was shining, not like fire, but like light, pale and gold, and his sword was twin to the sword his eldest son carried. His side had been pierced by horn or claw, although the creature that had caused the damage was nowhere to be seen, and he fought grimly.

But he did not fight alone.

By his side, to the right and left, stood The Lady and the Lord of the West March. They, too, were wounded, and The Lady would bear a scar across her brow, but they were un-bowed and undeterred.

They fought, in the end, one man. One man who seemed to be made of obsidian, and who looked very like the Lord of the Green in face and form. He lacked only color—and life—and the latter, he took. But what he took did not sus-tain him.

The Lord of the Green stopped there, and then he lifted his sword to center, and held it a moment. "Go back!" he shouted.

And the creature turned. Kaylin could see that swords had wounded him, could see those wounds closing, as if they were insubstantial. He did not bleed, this shadow being, and he did not die. How could he? You had to be alive to die.

As one person, the three looked up at the sound of the voice of the Lord of the Green. Sister, brother, father.

"Go back," the Lord of the Green said to his shadow twin. "The High Halls are barred against you. The abyss is your home, and your only home. *Go back.*"

"I have your name," the darkness said.

The Lord of the Green *laughed.* All around Kaylin—and admittedly, that wasn't far—silence fell. His laughter was wild and low, like the sound of horns. It was not defiance, and not delight, but some mingling of the two.

"You could not contain my name," the Lord of the Green said, raising his sword. "Not the whole of it. And what you hold, you cannot use against me. You are welcome to try." He drove his sword down and forward, and shadows swallowed the blade. The savage thrust brought the Lord of the Green to the heart of the darkness, and they stood, joined by sword, for a moment.

And the Lord of the High Court stepped forward and thrust like blade into the back of the creature.

The darkness began to twist. Not to fade as Kaylin had hoped, and not to melt, but to lose the form it had taken; to lose the shape of the arms, the fine length of face and jaw, the height of cheekbones and the fall of ebon hair. In their place grew other things, ancient things, glimpsed only in the chasm below the High Halls.

As it struggled to take form—any form—the Lord of the High Court reached forward and touched his oldest son. The light that limned him grew in brightness until Kaylin could hardly bear to look at him. She could not, however, look away, and settled on being blind as her only option.

But his smile, the blindness couldn't dim, didn't hide; she saw it clearly. He whispered a word, a long word, and Kaylin could hear its edges. Understood it as a name, and more than a name. It was a duty and a burden almost beyond bearing.

Certainly beyond her ability to bear.

The Lord of the Green accepted it, and with it came the light, moving between them, and erasing, in its strange passage, the scion of the old, dead gods. It settled about the Lord of the Green like a mantle, and she could see in its texture—for it had texture somehow—the rocks, smooth and worn, old and new, red, black and pale alabaster, marbled, glittering and dull, that were the body of the High Halls. The armor of the world.

The shadow dissipated, but it did not spread. It seemed to sink into the stones as if it were liquid. Its only passage was down.

Wiping her eyes, Kaylin looked at the father and the son, and then, beyond them, to the brother and the sister who now waited. The Lord of the West March moved first, although he was slower. The Lady, lighter and faster, pushed past him, nearly shoving him over in her haste to reach her brother. She threw her arms around him in a way that Kaylin had *never* seen a Barrani of any gender or rank do, and her pale hair blended with his cloak and the sheltering fall of black.

Someone touched Kaylin's shoulder, and she jumped, spinning on heel.

Severn was bleeding from the lip and the side, but his smile was grim. "You made it," he said.

She shrugged, smiling weakly. "As usual, just in time for the cleanup." She reached up and touched his face; it was bruised. "You're bleeding."

He shrugged. "I'm standing."

Her smile dimmed. Because she knew what he meant: So many others weren't.

The rite of *leoswuld* was a combination of the practical and the ritual. No one, gazing upon the Lord of the Green, could doubt that the first part had been achieved. Kaylin, gazing upon the rest of the High Court Circle, could believe that the second would be.

There was a grim anger in the Court, and a grim satisfaction. There was a keen, sharp quality to Barrani faces that made them seem almost young. Not, of course, that they ever looked anything else. In ones and twos, they began to tend to their fallen, to lift those that could be lifted, and to move those that would never rise again.

Kaylin started to help—it was what she was good at, after all—but the Lord of the West March stopped her. She met his eyes; they were green now, and flecked with…gold. "*Kyuthe,*" he said quietly. She could see evidence of the battle across his armor, his tunic, and his skin, but none of it remained in his expression.

She grimaced. "I'm sorry," she began.

But he lifted a finger to her moving lips. "I was wrong," he said gravely.

"It has to happen once."

At that, he smiled. It was an odd smile. He turned to look at his brother and their father, and then turned back. "He...is the Lord of the Green," he told her quietly. "But he is changed. What did you do?"

"I carried his name," she told him softly. And then, in an even lower voice, "The *rest* of his name."

The Lord of the West March frowned. "I don't understand," he confessed. It was not the normal tone of voice she associated with those words and a Barrani. Usually, there was more frustration, more anger, and a touch of Leontine cursing for emphasis.

As if she could hear the thought, Teela joined them quietly. Her eyes were green now, but she looked...tired. "The Consort is waiting for you, Kaylin," she said, no trace of Leontine anger in her. There was gravity. More.

Kaylin froze. "She's not—"

"She was injured in the battle, yes. But she is not—yet—beyond us. We work now to save her."

"Can I—"

"I don't know."

Kaylin swallowed and nodded. She looked at the Lord of the West March. His expression was once again pure Barrani. But he nodded and let her go.

The Consort was seated as Kaylin approached her fountain. She was not alone; her daughter sat beside her, an arm around her shoulders. But they both looked to Kaylin as she approached. Not even in these circumstances had Teela dared to follow.

The Consort smiled at Kaylin, her eyes a pale green.

The Lady's eyes were darker, and Kaylin thought she'd been crying. She failed to notice, and for once her acting wasn't brought into question. But she bowed to both of them and held the bow until the Consort bid her rise.

"Lord Kaylin," she said, her voice quiet. "You have—"

Kaylin lifted both hands, as if in plea.

"You went to the source," the Consort said, choosing different words in deference to Kaylin's gesture.

Kaylin nodded, almost mute. "I went to the source," she added. And was surprised to *hear* the word. She repeated it almost to herself.

"Here, it is possible for you to speak of it," the Consort told her, as if aware of what caused the momentary surprise. "I have seen it, and it is my daughter's legacy. It is not so bitter a legacy as that left my oldest son. What did you do there, Kaylin?"

"I took the rest of his name," Kaylin whispered.

The Consort closed her eyes.

"I'm—sometimes I'm called a midwife." Kaylin was forced to use the Elantran word; she had no idea what the Barrani word for midwife was.

It wasn't a word that was familiar to the Consort.

"I come when there's difficulty in the birthing," she said quietly. "When the child's life is threatened, or the mother's. Or both."

"Then you came to us, as needed." The Consort opened

her eyes. "You will help me rise," she added. "You will aid me. My daughter will accompany us."

The Lady's arm shifted.

"I can try to heal—"

But the Consort shook her head. "Not yet, Kaylin. If there is a time, it is not yet. I no longer hold my son's name," she added softly.

"You hold the part of it that matters," Kaylin replied. And meant it.

"I hold only the part that failed," was the bitter reply. And yet there was some pride in it.

Kaylin shook her head. "He made a choice," she said. "And his brother, a choice, as well. Duty can mean many things. What you couldn't do then was done, in the end."

"By a mortal."

She shook her head again. "By time, maybe. The darkness is rising, here and in the fiefs. The magic is growing. I don't understand Barrani names, I don't know if I ever will, but I understand this now—he *is* to be Lord of the High Halls when the High Halls face their harshest test. He was to be that, even then, and you knew it. Or the High Halls did. I don't know how the source works. I don't know—" She smiled weakly as she put an arm around the Consort's waist. The three women began to walk.

"He needed a name that would sustain the High Halls. *I* couldn't have carried the whole of it. I don't think that *any* one person could have. You carried what you could. I carried less. What I carried couldn't have given him life. Sometimes we need each other."

"It is not our way," was the quiet reply.

"No. It's not. It's not really been my way either. But…there's a sense to it. If you hadn't broken the law—" And here she stiffened, aware of the daughter's regard. "If you hadn't held on to his name and brought him back to the High Court, there would now be *no one* with his name. No one with a name that could contain the darkness and hold the Halls against it at *this* time.

"I know what the Lord of the High Court wanted from the Lord of the West March. But Consort, if this is a comfort to you—*no one* could have taken the gift. Not now. The Lord of the West March would have failed, had he tried. His name is not the equal of his brother's."

"And you know this because you have seen both names." It wasn't a question. It wasn't a threat. Kaylin still hesitated.

"You have seen the source," the Consort replied, serene, blood trailing the corner of her lips. "And I? I have seen my son, whole, and in possession of the High Halls. I have seen the chasm denied him. It is more than I thought I would live to see, but it is all that I hoped for. I am not the Lord of the High Court." She led, sagging between them, her steps bereft of grace. They followed, bearing her weight.

"And he will have his brother, where my husband had none." Her lips were thin as she spoke the last words.

"But I thought—"

"We had a brother, yes. He was killed."

"By the Lord of the High Court."

"By the desire for power, yes. In the end, it is usually that desire that takes us all. But not always."

"If he wanted the High Halls, he mustn't have known—"

"No. He didn't."

They continued to walk. After a while, Kaylin noticed that the ground beneath their feet was just that: ground. No artisan had labored here. The path existed, but it was a wild thing, and made by footsteps. There were even weeds here, and the birds that flew above were neither brightly colored nor loud.

"Where are we going?"

But she needn't have asked; the forest crept away on either side and left them, at last, in front of a cliff face. In it, there was a cave. Not a door.

"This isn't the tower—"

"The tower has many entrances," the Consort whispered. "But none of them are barred to one who has seen the source."

They made their way to the entrance of the cave.

The ground here was flat stone, weathered by season, and not by the work of hands. The Consort stepped upon it, and her eyes closed.

Kaylin understood then that she had one more duty.

CHAPTER 21

Kaylin stepped upon the stone, and it began to glow, as it had not done for the Consort. She didn't speak to the Consort; she didn't speak of the journey. If she had wondered why she had been summoned, she had her answer. She wanted to tell the Consort that she *didn't* know the way, but she bit back the words; it would have been the same as telling a terrified father that she had no idea how to save his wife: Even if it were true, it wasn't welcome. There was no point in saying it.

But the light from the stone spread out, into the cave entrance, and a path could be seen, tracing its way into the darkness of a stone mouth. Kaylin, taking more of the Consort's weight on her shoulders—which, given the difference in their heights, was awkward—took the lead quietly. She looked to the Consort for guidance, but it was an empty look, offered now for the comfort not of the mother but of the daughter.

They made their way down the path, their steps echoing

against rough walls. Tunnel walls. "This is old," Kaylin whispered.

"As old as the chasm," the Consort replied.

But not so cold as that, and not without light.

They walked together. The Consort's eyes closed again, and Kaylin felt a sharp stab of panic. But the weight across her shoulders didn't change.

The walking didn't, either; the path was still glowing, and she followed it without thought.

"Won't we be missed?" she asked at one point.

"Missed?"

"By the High Court."

The Lady laughed. It was an uneasy laugh, but not without genuine amusement. "They won't expect to see us yet," she told Kaylin. "There are two parts to *leoswuld*. And they've other things to worry about for once."

"I thought you had to do this—"

"Alone. And I do," The Lady replied. "But in the end, the Consort leads until I face my test."

"What test?"

But The Lady shook her head. "No one can say."

The path led forward, and then down. Kaylin followed it until the moment it began its descent, and stopped, nearly stumbling.

Down was a long way, to her eyes.

And at the bottom of down was the *rest* of the light. It was as vast, in its way, as the chasm had been. But where there had been shadow and darkness that moved like a slender river, twisting its way between stone gaps, there was…light. It moved, rippling, like a lake.

And in it, at this distance, Kaylin could see moving shapes, small, black lines that twisted around one another, forming patterns and breaking them almost before she could discern their shapes.

"This one doesn't speak, does it?" she asked.

The Consort opened her eyes and gave Kaylin an odd look. "Speak?"

"Like the darkness did."

"It speaks," was the whispered answer. "Did you not hear its voice?"

"Um, not really."

"Did you not come to the lake?"

"Uh, no."

She had the attention of The Lady, as well. They were both staring at her, as if she were a particularly fascinating and intelligent growth that was alien in every conceivable way.

Fair enough.

"What *did* you see?" the Consort asked.

"A table."

"A table."

"A big table, if that helps."

The two Barrani exchanged a glance. "Why?" the Consort asked.

"I don't know. Maybe because…it's words, and I tend to write at tables."

"Not desks?"

"Not so much." She thought of explaining her school experience. Decided it wouldn't make sense to them. "Most of the real writing I've done is usually at a big table. With maps on it."

"Oh."

The two Barrani woman gazed out into the lake. And then the older woman took her daughter's hand. "Are you ready?" she asked softly.

Her daughter nodded without hesitation.

"Wait—" Kaylin began, when it became clear what they were going to do. "You can't—"

The Consort looked at Kaylin. "I am *weary*, Kaylin. I am dying. I know what you did for my son," she added softly, "but it would be no kindness to me." She gazed out bitterly across that moving sea and added, "I have been the Consort for many years. I have brought our young to the source, and I have awakened them. I have chosen their names, and *every time* I have done this, I have tried to choose names that will hold against the testing.

"But I have failed so many of my people. You have seen the cost of that in the darkness below. Those whom I gave life are *all* my children, and I hear them. I know what they suffer. I will *always* know it," she added. "You bring hope to my sons and my daughter. You have sustained me on my journey here.

"But I have earned the right to return my name to the source."

"But—"

"Perhaps, in time, I will be born again, from these waters," she added. "But may it be a long time in coming, if it ever does."

Kaylin looked at The Lady, and found no help there. She wanted to shout *she's your mother!* But she had no voice for it.

Because she could *barely* live with the knowledge of Steffi and Jade; had she had to endure their suffering and pain for eternity, she would have gone mad. Death would have been a blessing.

And it was a blessing she couldn't withhold.

"A midwife," the Consort told Kaylin, using the Elantran word as her daughter once again put a sustaining arm around her shoulders, "must be a title of great honor among your kind."

She should have said something about how often that honor had caused her pay to be docked, but it would have been wrong. She saw the two through mist; her eyes were watering. She willed herself not to cry because she'd come all this way to bear witness, and damn it, she was going to.

And then, The Lady and the Consort, the daughter and the mother, stepped over the edge of the path, falling straight and stiff into the luminous, moving source. There should have been a splash; there should have been a sound.

But there wasn't. There was a single ripple, a movement of lines and curves and dots, before the source closed over them both.

Kyuthe.

The voice was familiar. She frowned and turned; there was no one else there.

I am in the High Circle, the Lord of the West March told her, his voice almost gentle. *We await you, now. You must return to us.*

But The Lady—

She, too, must return on her own. You faced your test. You were allowed to face it. Allow her the same choice, and the same risk of failure.

Kaylin nodded. Watched for a few minutes longer, and then, turning, she made her way back along the path. Without the Consort as a burden, the path was short and easily navigated, and she came out into the same forest she'd left. She followed the footpaths through the wild trees, and these led to the Consort's fountain.

The path continued beyond it.

And at its end—or beginning—the Lord of the West March was waiting. His eyes were bright and green.

"I'm sorry," she began as she reached him. "Your mother—"

But he lifted a hand to her lips and shook his head, looking down on her as if, for a moment, she were a child, and only a child. "Come, *kyuthe*," he said quietly. "You have a place of honor by the side of the Lord of the High Court."

He offered her his arm, and she stared at it for a minute. Then she remembered her manners, or rather, the manners she was supposed to have learned. She took his arm, walking barefoot beside him, dwarfed in height.

"How could you speak to me?" she asked as they walked.

"You are my *kyuthe*," he told her quietly.

"But—"

"You have been at the Heart of my forest," he said softly. "And some part of you remains there, still. I will never remove it," he added. "It is a reminder. And a gift. And when you are long dead, it will still be both." He reached up and brushed her cheek, his fingers tracing Nightshade's mark. It did not burn, as it had when Lord Evarrim had tried to touch it in the merchants' guild.

"Tell the outcaste," he said quietly, "that if this was some part of his game, it has still served us." He paused, "And tell him, also, that you will remain a Lord of the High Court until your death."

"But what if I—"

"You have a name," he told her quietly, "but it is not the name that grants you that right. Lord Nightshade held his, and still does. You owe us no fealty and no obedience while you walk with the wings of the Hawks. You owe us no subservience while you walk within the High Halls." He let his hand fall away from her cheek. "It is possible that my brother could remove the mark you bear."

She was silent. "And if he can't?"

"He will fail…that is all."

"I thought it would kill me."

"If any other man made the attempt, or if he made it in any other place, it would. But here, there is a chance."

He held her gaze, his eyes still green. Very green. "But if you do not choose to take that risk, if you choose to bear that mark, you will still be welcome at Court."

She nodded. And they entered the High Circle.

He led her to the throne, and to the man upon it—and she saw that the man was the Lord of the Green. He nodded gravely to her, although he did not rise. "Lord Kaylin," he said. "Attend me."

She came to stand by his side, in the shadow of his brother. Saw that the other Lords were now gathered, even Evarrim. Teela was in the distance, but Kaylin recognized her anyway; the Barrani Hawk nodded.

"Lord Severn," the Lord of the Green—no, the Lord of the High Court—said, "attend me."

And Severn, still bloody, bowed deeply and joined Kaylin and the Lord of the West March.

"Now," the Lord of the High Court said quietly, before Kaylin could ask—and she was going to—"we wait."

"Wait?"

"For the Consort," he replied. His eyes were green; there was no blue in them.

Kaylin nodded. She wanted to bite her nails. She wanted to talk to Severn. She wanted to fill the silence because when it came right down to it, the silence was getting on her nerves. She had never been good at waiting.

Time passed. The light didn't change, but Kaylin's legs were stiff from running and her feet were sore. She wondered if they were still bleeding. She looked at Severn, and thought he probably did just fine as a dress officer; he was as straight and tall as the rest of the Barrani.

Lirienne.

Kaylin.

When will we have waited for long enough?

When she arrives.

But what if she—

When she arrives, kyuthe. There was a warning in the words.

They waited. She couldn't see the moon, but it was there, above this false sunlight, this eternal day. She wondered what the streets were like; the Festival had been opened, the festivities—if you could call most of the activities that drunkards engaged in festive—were well under way. She wondered how many drunk-and-disorderly charges were being filed. Wondered how many brawls had broken out, and how the Swords had handled it. Wondered, as well, if the desperation for money had resulted in murders. It usually did. That was Hawk work.

This was harder.

She waited.

And then she heard it; the movement of something like bark against bark, the turning of a key in a lock—which, given that there wasn't a lock, should have been a clue—and she turned just a second before anyone else did.

The Lady—ah, damn it, the *Consort,* came out of the side of the great tree, just as Kaylin had done. She should have been wet, but she wasn't; she should have looked tired, but she didn't. Her clothing wasn't dirty, and it wasn't torn, and it certainly wasn't smeared by blood. Her hair wasn't tangled or matted.

But she wore white, and a small circlet gleamed platinum across her forehead—just over the wound that Kaylin had seen earlier.

The Lord of the Green—the High Court, idiot—turned, and rose, and met his sister. They joined hands, the Consort smiling in a way that Kaylin had never seen the mother do. Her eyes were a dark shade of green, some blue at their depths.

"Lord," she said, nodding.

"Consort," he replied. And he led her to the other side of the throne. He did not resume his seat, however. Instead, he lifted his voice. "The gifts have been given," he said in a voice that was not a shout but that carried anyway. "And the Consort has returned."

The Lord of the West March fell to one knee and bowed

his head. Severn did the same. Kaylin started to follow suit, but the Lord of the High Court caught her hand and lifted her, an echo of their earlier flight. She was made to stand, but given everything, she wasn't that much taller than the men who were kneeling. Which was, oh, everyone else in the clearing except for the Consort.

"There will be music," he told her quietly. "And song. Each song is part of the legacy of the High Halls. I fear you would stand a week if you listened to them all, and I excuse you if this is not your desire."

She swallowed. "Severn, too?"

"Lord Severn, as well, for I believe he has finished his…observations." As he said this, his gaze passed over Teela's bowed head. "And I believe that he will find nothing out of order, as the Officers of the Law are wont to say. It is odd that he had cause to arrive at all, for I have had no word of Lethe. He carried the flower as evidence, or he would not have been allowed to remain in the High Court. But such is the High Festival, and many things cannot be explained, even by those who have experienced them."

She understood the warning he offered. And she understood that he would kill her if she spoke. It should have angered her or frightened her. But it brought her a strange sense of comfort instead—because the man who could hold these Halls had to be made of stone and steel.

And he was, now, but she knew that it wasn't *all* he was. His mother had wanted something different for him than she herself had had. In the brother who loved him and the sister who would be the mother of their race for some time, she had provided him with that.

He lowered his head slightly. "If you desire it, I will take from you the mark you bear."

Kaylin reached up to touch her cheek, and realized, as she did, that she was cupping it almost defensively. She hadn't wanted it. She had hated what it meant, or what she thought it meant.

But she might not have left the source at all were it not for the voice of Nightshade and his distant words.

She smiled wanly. "Ignorance," she told him softly, "is not an excuse. Even mine. Especially mine."

"Then what will you have?" he asked her quietly.

She met his gaze, took a deep breath, and said, "A day of clemency."

"I have granted you clemency, although you do not require it."

"Not for me."

"Ah. Your *kyuthe?*"

"I don't think your brother—"

"I meant Lord Severn."

"Oh. No." She exhaled. "Lord Andellen," she said quietly.

His eyes shaded blue. "You ask much."

"For a day. For *this* day. Give him the High Court. Give him the High Festival and the rituals that will follow."

"It is longer than a day," he said gravely. But he did not look entirely displeased. Then again, he didn't look thrilled, either. He turned to the Lord of the West March and said, "See that it is done."

And the Lord of the West March bowed.

"You will eat with us," he told her.

She winced.

"It is the only part of the ritual which you must attend, and I would be honored by it." He paused, and then added, "You won the right to be called a Lord of the High Court when you returned from the tower. But you took the test for reasons that I cannot comprehend, and having finished, having survived it, you did more.

"Why?"

She wanted to lie. But his gaze was pressing and cutting at the same time, and she couldn't retreat into the safety of silence, because it wasn't there.

"Because," she said quietly, "I have my own dead to answer to. And I saw them here, in you. I saw Severn—my *kyuthe*—in your father. I saw myself in your brother. He honors you above all others, even himself."

"He is foolish that way."

"You—" She had no way to speak of *love*. Not to the Barrani. Oh, there was a Barrani word for it, but it was one of those words that was sung or written. She had never heard it spoken aloud without heavy sarcasm. Not between Barrani. They guarded all their weaknesses. So she couldn't tell him that the love his brother had for him defined his brother, in her eyes, couldn't tell him how much she wanted to preserve life because of that love.

She said instead, "Because not all weakness has to be weakness. Weakness, strength, power, failure—they're just words, and *we* can define what the words mean if we have the will or the courage."

"You can rewrite a life?" he asked, his smile heavy with irony. He looked at her mark for a long time. There was no suspicion in his gaze, or if there was, it was not for her.

"No one can do that," she answered softly, aware of what he meant but unwilling to descend into his levity. "But we can give it a different meaning." She paused, and then in frustration said, "Because I'm *mortal,* and sometimes we need each other. We aren't perfect, and we aren't always smart, but we're what we have.

"Sometimes," she added, looking at Severn, who stood a little ways off, "it's enough."

And Lord Andellen arrived at the side of the Lord of the West March. He looked wary, but in a cautious way. He knelt before the Lord of the High Court.

"Lord Andellen," the Lord of the High Court said in a voice very different than the one he had exposed—and that was the word for it—to Kaylin.

Andellen lifted his head, and only his head; he did not rise.

"You are welcome, should you choose to accept it, to the hospitality of the High Court. And while Kaylin Neya lives her span of years, and in her name, you will be welcome in the High Halls."

There was gold in Andellen's eyes. Just…gold.

This was so much more than she could have asked for. And he didn't ask Andellen about his allegiance to Lord Nightshade; he didn't ask him to revoke whatever vows bound them. He could have done either. She knew that his father *would* have. But this High Lord was a different man.

She would have hugged the Lord of the High Court had he been anyone else, even the Hawklord. Instead, she turned away and quickly rubbed her palms over her eyes.

They were bright and shiny when she turned back.

And her stomach grumbled.

There was a very awkward silence that bracketed the unfortunate noise, and then the High Lord laughed. So, too, did the Lord of the West March, and even the Consort's smile was one of joy and indulgence.

Severn, on the other hand, snickered, and she could hit *him*. So she did.

In the morning—and it was morning, although there hadn't really been enough night for Kaylin to appreciate it more than she usually did—she packed up what was left of the dress the Quartermaster had been so apoplectic about. The Lord of the West March was waiting for her, as was Severn; the former had taken leave of the gathering in order to escort her out of the High Halls.

Seeing the dread with which she rolled up the dress, he offered to have it burned. She considered this with care.

"You don't have to leave," he told her quietly, although Severn was listening.

Given just how angry the Quartermaster was likely to be, the option had its attractions. But so did the real world, and geography that didn't change, and tests that didn't have such a catastrophic cost for failure.

She looked up at the Lord of the West March.

And he smiled. "It was a simple offer," he said, "and no offense is taken by your refusal. This place—you are now of it, but it will never be yours. You seek a type of flight that the High Court cannot provide you.

"Tender my regards to Lord Sanabalis," he added quietly.

She nodded. Samaran was waiting; Andellen had not left

the High Circle. She had no doubt he would, eventually. But she didn't want him to leave yet.

She glanced at Severn, who nodded genially. There wasn't much left to say. And besides—she had the Lord of the West March's name, and she could talk to him anytime she wanted.

So she walked by his side until they reached the statues that stood at the front of the entrance, and when he reached their shadow, he bowed formally. "Hunt," he said softly, "and kill when you must."

She nodded again, as if it made sense.

And then the carriage rolled up, along the stones, and after ascertaining that the driver *wasn't* Teela, she let Severn open the door and help her in. She'd kept the Barrani dress because changing into what was left of the old one had about as much appeal as wearing something that hadn't been washed in so long it stood up by itself.

The drive to the Halls of Law was peaceful, and involved no screaming pedestrians, which was a distinct improvement. Even the jarring movement of the wheels added a sense of reality and familiarity to the experience, and she treasured it.

When she left the carriage, she left it at the front doors, and not the courtyard, and entered between two rather grumpy Swords. Festival had passed, all right; one had a black eye. And a scowl.

She guessed he'd had as much sleep in the last three days as she'd had, and tried not to smile too brightly.

Inside, the Aerie was waiting, and if it was not the utter perfection, in architectural terms, of the High Halls, it was still perfect; the Aerians were flying maneuvers above her head, and she almost tipped over backward, watching them. Severn caught her before she fell. She'd put the shoes on, but still hated them. Those, she was damn well going to burn, Quartermaster or no.

But she moved past the Aerians somehow—Severn pulling probably had a lot to do with it—and made her way to the office that was ruled by a Leontine. By a besieged Leontine with—yes—a fortress of paperwork behind which to hide. If a wind didn't blow it all over.

He knew she was coming; his sense of smell was just as impressive as his hearing. He was up and around the desk before she'd set foot in the office proper, beating Caitlin, who had to rely on her eyes to notice that Kaylin had returned.

Marcus growled and sniffed the air.

"It's the dress," she offered.

"It's formal enough," Marcus replied.

She didn't like the last two words in combination. "Formal enough for what?"

"A meeting," he said, "with a mage of the Imperial Order."

She groaned. "Can't you tell him I'm dead?"

"I could try," Marcus replied, touching her shoulders as if to ascertain that she was actually there. "But—"

"But it is considered less than wise to lie to a Dragon Lord."

She turned; Lord Sanabalis was standing ten feet behind her. "Private," he said. "I am glad to see that your visit to the Barrani High Court has not altered you beyond recognition. I would like to speak with you," he added, and pointed to the West Room.

* * *

The bastard made *her* open the door. And then walked in first. Not really a good start, given that Dragon hearing and Leontine swearing weren't a good combination. He lifted a gray brow as he took a seat.

She saw a damn candle in the center of the table.

After everything she'd been through—well. If he wanted to play games, fine. She started to speak, and he lifted a hand.

"First," he told her quietly, "I would appreciate the return of my medallion. I see you managed to retain it. Given the rest of your records—and the Quartermaster's rather harsh evaluation—I consider myself blessed." He held out a hand.

She removed the heavy gold links and placed them, with the medallion on top, in the curve of his palm. He closed his fingers and smiled. It was a teacher's smile. Which was to say, unpleasant and slightly smug.

"Now," he told her, "the candle."

But she wasn't an idiot. She was tired, and her body ached, and she was about to be a corpse if the Quartermaster had his way, but she wasn't stupid. Her brows rose. And fell.

"The fire—"

"Ah. Yes." He offered her the lazy smile of a cat. Or a very, very large lizard who was sitting on a warm rock in the sun.

"It was *yours*."

He shrugged. "It was not, as you so emphatically put it, mine. It was, however, augmented." He shook his head. "Students are often lazy," he told her, "and prone to believe in their own brilliance unless corrected by a firm hand."

While she did her best imitation of a fish, he studied her

face. His eyes were gold, but he lidded them. "I believe that I was incorrect."

"That has to be a first," she said sourly.

"The High Halls have left you changed. But not," he added, feigning disappointment, "in a way that is of use. You *will* be able to light the candle, Kaylin. You know the word. But saying it without my power to guide the shape will be vastly harder, and what you achieve will be less…reliable."

"I am aware that you called the fire," he added. "Three times."

She nodded.

"Given that you are still alive, and no formal war has been declared, I am going to assume that you did so at need, and in a way that did not displease the Lord of the High Court." His eyes changed shape and shade; they were orange now. "There is a new Lord of the High Court?"

Her brows rose again. And lowered. She did her very best not to swear. Which, given she was in the Halls of Law, wasn't enough to stop her.

"You know," she finally said.

And his expression was, for a moment, a Dragon's expression; it wasn't a comfort. "I was here, at the founding of the Empire," Sanabalis replied, and his voice was a Dragon's voice, loud and rumbling. "And I know why the city of Elantra was founded in this place.

"But the High Halls still stand, and that is all that is required." He paused. "Of the Barrani. You, however, have other work ahead of you."

"But I want to—"

"Learn magic."

"Seen enough of that to last a few, oh, decades."

He looked pointedly at the candle, and she wilted. "*Kyuthe* to the Lord of the West March," the Dragon said, "and friend to the Lord of the High Court. You've done well, Kaylin Neya. If faith and risk were bound together in you, you have begun to unwind the strands.

"You might be the last pupil I take," he added, his voice softening until it sounded almost human. "And if this is the case, you must be a memorable one. Students are in part our legacy."

"Tell that to my teachers."

He chuckled. "I have. They were not pleased with the observation." He lifted his medallion and set it around his neck before folding his hands on the tabletop.

EPILOGUE

The Lord of Castle Nightshade sat upon a throne in the Long Hall of Statues. Silence and stillness were gathered here, as if they were scarce and rare, and therefore to be hoarded. Where statues stood, movement, however instantly captured, suggested life; none of the statues were of the Barrani. Nor, of course, the Dragons. What remained, mortal all, would pass—was passing—into age and decay, with time.

But one Barrani Lord was present, and he waited upon one knee, his head bent, before the throne upon which Lord Nightshade sat, casting no shadow.

"Lord Andellen," Lord Nightshade said, "rise."

Andellen unfolded slowly.

"The Lord of the High Court?"

"He is well."

"And the ceremony?"

"It was completed."

Nightshade nodded gravely. "I heard the horns," he said at last, looking toward—and beyond—the Ablayne, where the High Halls stood behind the statue of the first High Lord and his Consort. That a wall stood between them— several, in fact—counted for less than nothing; he knew where the High Halls lay.

Andellen nodded. If there was any desire or regret in the room, it was—as much as it could be—hidden. "I was not present when they were sounded."

"No." The Lord of Castle Nightshade rose from the throne's stone confines. "Who now sits beneath the first tree?"

The silence was hesitation; Lord Andellen showed none. But after a long pause, he said, "The man who was once Lord of the Green."

Nightshade closed his eyes a moment. "And the Lord of the West March?"

"He will return to the West March," was the quiet reply. "And he will bear word."

"What did she do, Andellen?" High Barrani shaded into Barrani. Inasmuch as two such complicated men could be, they were friends.

"Kaylin Neya? She proved herself worthy," was the quiet reply.

"Of the High Court?"

"No, Lord Nightshade. That was never in doubt."

"Then?"

"Of you."

Nightshade smiled; it was a weary smile. "That," he said softly, "was never in doubt to me. But she is changed, I fear."

"She must be. I confess, however, that I saw little sign of it."

Lord Nightshade began to walk toward the doors, and Lord Andellen fell in beside him; they sounded like one man by the fall of their step.

"She found the tower, as you predicted she would."

"And passed its test."

"And passed. If I had doubts, I have none now."

"Less than none…you are guarded, Andellen."

"Lord." Acknowledgment; no argument. No lie.

"Did she see what lies at the heart of the Halls?"

Footsteps lost their perfect synchronicity. Andellen regained composure, but slowly for a man of his power. "Yes," he said at last.

"You were with her."

"Yes."

"Good. And what will she take from it?"

"I…do not know, Lord Nightshade." A pause. But it was not followed by question; nor would it be. "She has power, and even the will to use it—but the will is entirely mortal."

"And to what use, in the end, did she put the power of which you speak?" The fieflord smiled. There was no amusement in it, and no warmth. "Guard your secrets, Lord Andellen. You are capable of such caution. Kaylin Neya is not.

"Or was not, when she left. When the time comes, she will speak of what she saw. I heard the voice of the Lord of the West March," he added softly, "when he offered her the chance to be free of my mark. No," he added, although Andellen had not asked, "I was not with her. She did not call me. But he touched the mark, and he spoke through it—I heard his challenge clearly.

"Yet she bears the mark, still." The smile that had briefly moved his lips was gone; his eyes were a pale shade of blue-green. "She is unwise, to the end, and in time, she will come to me."

"And when that time comes, will she be *Erenne?*"

Lord Nightshade said nothing for a moment. When he spoke at last, he did not choose to answer the question. "Tell me," he said instead, "of Severn."

Severn left his home when the light of the sun was shading toward evening; the sky was still blue, but in an hour, its edges would be crimson. Three days after the close of the Festival season, the day was still long. Long enough to encompass hours of beat duty, and the beginnings of three different investigations into the murders that the passing of the season often left in its wake.

Kaylin watched him from a safe distance—across the street, in fact. She was wearing the Hawk, and her old boots. Her pants were new. She had chosen to braid her hair, for lack of anything she could stick through a top knot, and she looked slightly younger than she was, and vastly older than she felt.

He started down the street, toward the tavern in which he so often ate—they saved him a table—but he stopped before he passed her.

Her smile was cautious as she approached him; his frown was more pronounced. "What," he asked her succinctly, "are you doing here?"

"Minding my own business," she replied.

"You have business that brings you here?"

She shrugged. "Maybe. I thought I could, you know, walk with you for a bit."

"On patrol?"

She shrugged. "I'm off duty."

"And the mage?"

"Still not annoyed. Pretty damn annoying, though."

"Law of conservation," Severn told her.

"I don't know that one—can it be broken?"

"If it can, it'll be by you." He ran a hand through his hair. "Kaylin—"

She put a hand on his arm.

"You've been waiting here every day for three days. What are you waiting *for*?"

She met his eyes and bit her lip. "You," she said at last. She thought he would shake his arm free of her, and he almost did, but he stilled at the last moment, and met her gaze. His narrowed. "What are you carrying?" He looked pointedly at the bulging satchel by her side.

"Just stuff."

"Why?"

She shook her head. "Where are you going?"

"The Spotted Pig."

"Liar. You ate there half an hour ago."

He raised a brow. "And you know this how?"

"I asked. After you left."

"You're getting better at following."

"You didn't know?"

His turn to shrug. It was a gesture that bounced between them, a deflection they were both expert at.

"You watched me for seven years," she told him quietly. "You can live with me and a couple of days."

"I was quieter."

"You always were."

"Kaylin—"

"I want to go with you," she told him quietly.

His expression suggested about a hundred replies, and she guessed most of them weren't considered polite in *any* company. But none of them made their way past his lips, which were closed in a pinched frown.

"It was my choice," he told her at last. Some of the rawness slipped into the words.

"I know. Let me make one, too." She was not above pleading with him. But pleas in the fiefs had often been silent. And Severn? He'd never been good at saying no to her. She wasn't that child, but she had been. Nothing would change that now.

And if Severn had changed, he was not unlike the first tree; he had grown from roots that were planted in the same fief as Kaylin's. He turned away from her, but he said nothing, and she still had his sleeve in her grasp.

He began to walk—as she had known he would—toward the bridge across the Ablayne. She didn't so much follow as cling. She wanted to talk. About anything. About work, because it was safe. About the High Halls, because in its way, that was almost safe, as well.

But she couldn't quite force the words past her lips; idle chatter seemed wrong here. The day seemed wrong, as well. She had lived in the upper city for seven years, and night had slowly shifted in meaning. It was the time for sleeping— and the occasional emergency call from the midwives guild.

Yet she felt, as she stepped across the first plank of the bridge, that it should have been night. That the streets should have carried the threat of ferals, that they should have been empty. It was not yet close enough to evening that they were; people filled them.

Curious people. But curiosity in the fiefs had a different tone. They were watched, but they weren't approached. The Hawks emblazoned across their surcoats glittered, caught light, hinting at flight. At hunting. At a freedom that was beyond the men and women who labored here.

She wanted to ask him where they were going. But she knew him well enough to know that she wouldn't get an answer. She gazed out at the streets instead, walking with the ease of long practice as if she owned them. As if the Laws of the Dragon Emperor meant something, even here.

And they did—but only to Kaylin. Severn had made it clear that Wolf or Hawk, he was still Severn. She didn't deny him that truth; she had survived because of it.

The streets narrowed. The buildings grew older and far less stately; repair was a thing that was done haphazardly and without the proper materials. Doors sagged in frames that were weathered and old. Windows—shuttered or open—gaped above them like open mouths. There was glass in the fiefs, but it was rare. And it wasn't found here.

She remembered this street. There was a tavern here, and the four corners were just a few blocks away. She wondered if he would go there, and followed in silence, holding his sleeve as if it were a talisman that just happened to come attached to the rest of him.

"Severn?"

He shook his head. They passed the four corners, and the attention they garnered slowed them a moment; one or two of the older people almost seemed to recognize them. But if they did, the armor and weapons they carried were a moving wall, a sign that said keep away. In the fiefs, such signs were generally obeyed. Arms were the force of law most respected here.

But he kept walking, past those corners, and past buildings damaged enough by time that no one lived in them anymore. Not even the desperate orphans that Kaylin and Severn had been. "You're going—you're going to the watchtower."

He nodded.

"We found Catti there."

And nodded again.

So much stiffness in that gesture.

"But how did you—"

He lifted a hand, and she fell silent. So many secrets, she thought. They had never *had* secrets worth keeping, when they had lived here. Not from each other. Not more than once.

Once? It was enough.

Her fingers were frozen, although it wasn't cold. She could think of the past, walking in the present, and it didn't enrage her. It numbed her instead. But numbness and fear were not the same. The High Halls had tested her. But they had tested Severn, as well.

He came to the gates, to the black, pocked metal of a fence. They opened inward, creaking as they did, and she saw the hole in the rounded wall of the watchtower. She wondered what it had been used for, when it had first been built. It was not like the Castle, not like the High Halls. Round, it went up several storeys, and ended in a roof that probably couldn't even keep sunlight out. She was sure birds nested there.

But not Hawks.

She slowed as they passed through the gate, and slowed again as they walked the flat ground. Weeds grew here, although the lack of rain had turned them a golden brown that fire would consume in an instant.

No fire she could call.

"Here?" she asked him, hating his stiffness. Hating her own.

He nodded. "It was the only place," he added softly, speaking from a place that she could almost reach, if she had the courage.

Courage was a funny thing. Like gods, it came and went at its own pleasure, and at the moment, it had deserted her so entirely she could hardly remember its presence.

The only place, he had said, and it was true. The fiefs themselves were often crowded, and very little grew here. The watchtower was surrounded by a small field of weeds, tended by seasons, and no other hand.

And yet, he led her through them. They were higher than her waist in some places, and no lower than her knees, and they bent when she stepped on them, folded when she pushed them aside.

He came at last to a place beyond the wall, nearest the eastern part of the fence. And in the weeds, he knelt, searching a moment. It wasn't a leisurely search, although it wasn't a desperate one; he expected to find something here.

And she saw it before his hands touched it: a stone. A

large stone, uncut and uncarved. It bore no names, no symbols, and no traces of human craftsmanship. It was just…a rock. A large, bare rock.

He closed his eyes, and knelt in front of it, and she almost left him then, because she could see his face clearly in the daylight. *This* is why she had desired night and night's shadow, even a night that contained ferals.

Because ferals weren't the threat they had once been, and this—this absolute surrender—was worse.

She had let go of his sleeve when he had begun his search in the weeds, and she didn't dare to take it back. Instead, after a moment of silence, she twisted her satchel around so that it fell into her lap when she knelt.

Her hands were shaking as she undid its metal buckles.

He said, without looking at her, "What are you doing?"

But she didn't answer him; not in so many words. She had brought with her, after some careful thought, and a bit of angry haggling in the market—and at this time of year there was no other type of haggling—a few things.

He watched her as she removed them.

One was a simple doll, a thing of cloth, with wool hair and button eyes, and a small pink bud of a mouth. The other? A small wooden flute.

"Kaylin—"

"I know I can't bury them," she told him without looking at his face. "I know we can't dig them up. I can't give them these things. They can't touch them."

"They're dead," he said almost harshly.

She nodded. "But I'm not. We're not," she added, still staring at the stone. She placed these odd gifts in front of it. The weeds would spring back soon, and they would be hidden from sight. Just as the grave now was.

"I wasn't here," she added softly and bitterly. "I *should have been* here, and I wasn't."

He said nothing. There was nothing he could say. But after a moment, with just a snort of something that might be disgust, he rearranged them, doll and flute, placing the one in the padded, mittenlike hands of the other. "Steffi wanted a doll. For Jade," she added quietly. "And she wanted a flute for herself. This isn't much of either."

"Kaylin—"

"But I promised them. When we had money. We never had money," she added. As if he didn't know. "I should have been here."

"You said that."

"I should have helped you. I can't believe you carried them *both*—"

"I couldn't leave one behind," he whispered. "I couldn't choose just one of them."

"They were already dead."

"Yes."

She closed her eyes. The wind—and it was scant—made the dry stalks of weeds rustle as if they were leaves, and for a moment, she could almost feel the forest floor beneath her hands. She had planted some part of herself in that forest—but the better part of herself? It had been buried here, by Severn, while his hands blistered and bled. And it had been cold here. Cold then. The ground much harder than the ground she'd broken.

"Not even to save the world," she whispered, bringing her hands to her face, to her mouth, to muffle the words.

She felt his arms enfold her then. She felt his chest against her back, his chin above her head. Felt his silence, like the space between heartbeats. "I keep wondering," she continued, because she had to untangle the knot in her throat, "if someone could do for me what I did for the Lord of the Green. If they could give me the strength that I needed to bear it all."

"Elianne."

"And I know they can't. Because I'm not Barrani. I'm not the High Lord. If there really are gods, Severn, I owe them. I'm never going to have to be the High Lord."

He held her as he had not held her for years, and the years were dwindling, in this wild, untended graveyard of two. Her eyes were dry. She told herself her eyes were dry. Lying? She wasn't good at it. Not, at least, to others.

"There's no going back," she continued. Harder to speak now. But just as necessary. She whispered two names. Steffi. Jade. She listened for their answer. And was relieved not to hear it, for the Barrani castelord would *always* hear the dead. And would understand how close he had come to truly freeing them.

And he would regret it. She *knew* he would regret it.

How could she not know it? She knew his name. She would never say it. Wasn't even certain she *could* say it all. But she would know, and he would know.

This was the price that love demanded of those with power. Or duty. And Severn had paid it. She could tell, by the way his arms were locked, that he would always pay it; that it would never dim.

How had he lived with it, alone? She couldn't. She could not be here without Severn.

The third name she whispered was his. She knew he heard it because his arms tightened, as if he could somehow contain her, or protect her. But she had not come here, in the end, for protection.

She had come here for peace.

She leaned back into the hollow of his collarbone; felt, instead, the links of armor beneath her neck. "You can't protect me from myself," she told him quietly.

He said nothing for a moment; the moment passed. "According to Marcus, no one can." There was a bitter warmth in the words. "On the other hand, according to Marcus, if he hasn't strangled you yet, he still retains the rights."

She laughed, but it hurt. Everything hurt. She twisted around, dropping the empty satchel. It was awkward because Severn didn't let go.

"Not for you," he whispered. "Not because of you. Can you remember that?"

She nodded. "I can't believe it, though."

"Try."

She wrapped her arms around him. "I'm sorry," she whispered.

"You have nothing to be—"

"I have seven years," she told him. "You came here for seven years, without me. You came here *that night*. And if it weren't for the test of the tower, I would never have seen it. I couldn't think about it. I was that selfish."

"You loved them."

"Yes. I *loved* them. But Severn—so did you."

"Not enough," he whispered.

She wanted to argue; she couldn't. "What does enough

mean? I'm alive," she added. Meeting his gaze, although it was hard. "I *hated* that I was alive. I—" And closed her eyes. "I hate—that…I want to *be* alive."

He held her.

"But I don't—I can't—hate you. I don't know how."

"You can remember," he whispered into the mess of her hair. "If you need to, you can remember."

She pushed herself away, kept him at arm's length, even though her arms were shaking. "I would have forgotten instead," she said bitterly, and because it was true. "And I would have been happy to forget.

"And you were right—it would have been wrong. I want to move forward," she added quietly. "But I don't know how. I just don't know how to go back."

"They didn't blame you."

"It doesn't matter. I do now. I did, for the Barrani castelord, what I couldn't do for myself. I did, for the Lord of the West March, what I never even thought to do for you. Why didn't you tell me?"

"Kaylin, Elianne, whoever you are—"

But she knew the answer. She pulled away from him, and this time he let her go; go to the stone and the doll and the flute; go to the silence of her dead. And it *was* silent, and blessed silence, and she knew it for that because she had seen Samaran's father in the darkness of the High Halls, and she had heard his plea, had heard the burden he had laid upon his son.

"We won, didn't we?" she asked him, both of her hands against the hard surface of this faceless rock, that seemed the perfect marker for what lay beneath it.

"Elianne—"

"That's not my name."

"Kaylin, then."

She shook her head quietly, and turned, and saw him through tears. "Don't come here again," she said softly.

"I can't promise that."

"Don't come here without me."

He nodded, and he caught her cheeks in his hands, and held her face. His eyes were brown; just brown. His face was white enough that his scars were almost invisible.

And when she had had enough of his eyes, when the sky was a little too pink, she whispered, at last, another name. Her lips moved over the syllables, but they made no sound at all. She reached up and caught his hands and pressed them into her skin, aware of each knuckle.

Aware, as his eyes widened, that he had heard her clearly, that in some part of his mind and memory, the name she had chosen for herself—the third name, with its cutting edge and its softness—now lay.

But she felt no fear at all as she exposed it, and none at all when he spoke, his lips motionless, the syllables that would define her.

Ellariayn.

Severn.

This is…your name.

Yes.

But you—

You can't lie to me here. And I don't think I can lie to you. Ask me. Ask me whatever you have to.

He was silent.

Call me, she whispered. *And I'll hear you. Wherever I am, I'll hear you. Whatever I'm doing, I'll hear you. I'll answer.*

But he was still Severn; if she'd changed, he hadn't. He asked her nothing. Instead, he gathered her in his arms, and this time she went, and the coming of night—and it was coming—could not move her from this spot, this rock, this grave or these offerings.

These were hers. For now, they were hers.

And maybe he had changed, because night was descending in the streets of the fief, and he did not warn her, did not tell her to move, did not speak of practicalities or waiting death.

He spoke her name instead. All of her names.

And when his lips stopped moving, she reached up and touched them with the tips of her fingers, her healer's hands moving like moths near the heart of flame.

* * * * *

But Nightshade's plans have yet to end.
Don't miss the next installment of Kaylin's adventure!

Nobody said juggling a career and
a relationship would be easy...

bring it on

On sale July 2006.

Valere's life as a retriever used to be simple, but now that she
and Sergei are in a relationship, things are getting much more
complicated. What's more, the city Valere loves is now at grave
risk. There's only one thing left for Valere to do—bring it on....